美國留學會話

申請學校・校園英文・實用資訊

Conversational
English for
Overseas Study

美國留學會話──申請學校、校園英文、實用資訊
Conversational English for Overseas Study

CONTENTS

目次

音檔使用說明──006
EZ TALK｜編輯台──007
N NEWS ROUNDUP｜綜合新聞──008

PART 1
FEATURE TOPICS

1

專題特輯──010

● 近五年來去各國留學人數
● 沒錢也能出國留學 學海計畫幫你圓夢
● 英語系國家留學必考的語言檢定與入學考試──托福名師‧布曦
● 我是如何從社區大學成功轉到柏克萊大學──知名駐美 YouTuber‧Lisa
● 不是名校出身，也能申請到英美名校獎學金──英語教育碩士 Ping 老師
● 職場面面觀：一趟以色列留學之旅給了我人生的方向
　──Ani Ann 創辦人‧陳俞安

Stay Where I Am

Study Abroad

PART 2
ESSENTIAL ENGLISH FOR OVERSEAS STUDY
完勝國外大學 必備英語

第一章｜CHAPTER 1
申請學校 Applying to Schools

CHOOSING THE RIGHT SCHOOL

第一話 **決定適合的學校**——026

談論大學

● **好用句**：詢問學校問題、學校問題回覆
● **實用資訊**：美國各種大學與研究所的差異、我的 GPA 可以申請什麼學校、GPA 計算法、college 和 university 的不同、英文成績未達學校標準，該怎麼辦？、大學先修課程（**AP course**）、培養菁英課程（**American Honors**）

TUITION

第二話 **學費**——030

學費還真貴

● **好用句**：詢問學校學費問題、詢問機構獎助學金問題
● **實用資訊**：美國各區與各大城市的學費差異、赴美念書較省錢的方法、國際學生可以申請美國當地的學費補助嗎？國際學生可以向學校申請獎學金嗎？獎學金申請步驟

OTHER FEES

第三話 **其他費用**——034

住在校內宿舍或校外、學校餐飲計畫

● **好用句**：詢問學校住宿問題、詢問校外租屋費用問題、表達費用高
● **實用資訊**：美國住宿費用比較表、其他生活費和交通費比一比、其他隱藏費用

RÉSUMÉ

第四話 **履歷**——038

範本1則、寫作重點教學

● **主題說明**：Résumé 是什麼？和 CV 有什麼不同？

ACTIVITIES

第五話 **課外活動**——041

範本2則、回答重點教學

● **主題說明**：審查官究竟想看出什麼？

SHORT QUESTIONS

第六話 **簡短問題**——044

範本3則、回答重點教學

● **主題說明**：特色說明

LONGER ESSAYS

第七話 **長篇文章**——046

範本2則、寫作重點教學

● **主題說明**：撰寫須知

RECOMMENDATION LETTER

第八話 **推薦信**——051

範本1則、寫作重點教學

● **主題說明**：挑選推薦人重點

STATEMENT OF PURPOSE

第九話 **讀書計畫**——054

範本1則、寫作重點教學

● **主題說明**：什麼是讀書計畫

LETTER OF ACCEPTANCE

第十話 **學校錄取通知**——058

● **圖解**：錄取通知、有條件錄取信
● **主題說明**：收到錄取通知後，要做什麼？
● **實用資訊**：學期制與學季制、什麼是 conditional admission（有條件錄取）？ TOEFL iBT

COLLEGE ACCEPTANCE —THANK YOU LETTER

第十一話 **回覆錄取通知的感謝信**——062

範本1則

● **主題說明**：收到錄取通知信後該做什麼？

REJECTION LETTER

第十二話 **拒絕入學信**——064

範本1則

● **圖解**：拒絕錄取信
● **主題說明**：回覆錄取通知寫作重點
● **實用資訊**：收到拒絕信，你可以怎麼做？

第二章｜CHAPTER 2
開課前準備 Preparing for Your Studies

APPLYING FOR A U.S. STUDENT VISA

第一話 **申請美國學生簽證**——068

F-1 學生簽證面試

● **好用句**：資料處理和指紋掃描、申請學生簽證面試聽與說、形容自己的學校
● **實用資訊**：學生簽證種類、申請流程、簽證面談程序、答題技巧

APPLYING FOR CAMPUS HOUSING

第二話 **申請宿舍**——072

● **圖解**：室友偏好表
● **好用句**：詢問宿舍相關問題
● **閱讀測驗**：宿舍名單
● **實用資訊**：房屋配備、挑選室友

STUDENT HEALTH INSURANCE PLAN

第三話 **學生健保計畫**——076

● **好用句**：健保問題聽與說
● **閱讀測驗**：學生健保保單
● **實用資訊**：國際學生健保、學校健保包含項目、學生健保的建議

AIR TRAVEL FOR OVERSEAS STUDENTS

第四話 **留學生美國出入境**——080

入境、過海關

● 圖解：海關申報單
● 好用句：入境問題聽與説
● 實用資訊：入境文件、獲得學生簽證就一定能入境美國？入境必備知識、其他可能問題與建議回答方式

BACHELOR AND MASTER'S DEGREE GRADUATION REQUIREMENTS

第五話 **學士和研究生畢業需求**——084

● 圖解：畢業需求、主修選課需求
● 好用句：各種「科系」與「學位」的説法
● 實用資訊：我想了解更多各校系所資訊，該上哪裡找？畢業需求通常包括哪些？怎麼知道畢業需求為何？ department 和 program 有什麼不同？碩士該選哪一種課程？ concentration 是什麼？

REGISTRATION: ADDING AND DROPPING COURSES

第六話 **註冊：加退選課程**——088

● 圖解：課程敘述、課程介紹
● 好用句：詢問註冊問題、詢問加退選問題
● 實用資訊：如何選課？關於課程、課程有分很多種（lecture、seminar、lab），差別在哪裡？選課技巧、如何了解更多課程相關資訊

ORIENTATION AND INTRODUCTIONS

第七話 **迎新、自我介紹**——092

詢問問題、聊聊主修

● 好用句：新人自我介紹、迎新活動、形容自己的個性
● 閱讀測驗：迎新海報
● 聽力測驗：校園迎新導覽
● 實用資訊：關於校園迎新

CAMPUS AND THE COMMUNITY

第八話 **校園和校區**——096

詢問方向

● 好用句：詢問位置聽和説
● 閱讀測驗：請根據以下學校地圖，回答下列問題
● 實用資訊：校園內的秘密

OPENING AN ACCOUNT AND USING MONEY

第九話 **開帳戶和使用金錢**——100

開帳戶、提款、匯款、信用卡付款

● 圖解：提款單、信用卡
● 實用資訊：一定要認識的銀行英文
● 好用句：付款及退換貨

APARTMENT RENTAL

第十話 **海外租屋**——104

找房子、屋況與設施、租金

● 好用句：尋找租屋處、看看租屋
● 閱讀測驗：租屋廣告
● 實用資訊：學生租屋資訊、租屋廣告常見縮寫、學生在校外租屋要特別注意的事

MEAL PLANS

第十一話 **餐點方案**——108

詢問餐點方案建議、討論餐廳餐點方案

● 好用句：餐點方案聽與説、詢問餐點方案建議、討論與詢問餐點方案
● 閱讀測驗：學生的餐點方案
● 實用資訊：大多數學校的餐點方案、餐點方案選擇建議

HOMESTAY FAMILY

第十二話 **寄宿家庭**——112

首次見面、參觀房間、溝通狀況、回應邀約

● 好用句：詢問問題
● 聽力測驗：寄宿家庭生活常規説明
● 實用資訊：如何挑選優良的寄宿家庭 homestay、住在寄宿家庭的注意事項

HOUSING SAFETY

第十三話 **居住安全**——116

投訴噪音、大雪通報、住宅入室竊盜、要求護送、通報可疑人物、偷竊

● 好用句：通報案件、安全相關問題聽與説
● 實用資訊：校外安全建議、校內安全建議

GETTING TO KNOW YOUR ROOMMATES

第十四話 **和室友混熟**——120

入住派對邀請、閒話家常、訂立守則

● 好用句：和室友溝通、委婉溝通説法
● 閱讀測驗：生活公約
● 實用資訊：生活公約建議包含事項、國外室友相處重點

TIPS ON SAVING MONEY

第十五話 **省錢妙招**——124

超市省錢作戰、買二手課本、買折扣衣服、學生優惠、汽車保險折扣

● 好用句：詢問折扣
● 閱讀測驗：搬家拍賣廣告
● 實用資訊：學生相關的優惠、其他非學生相關優惠

STUDENT ID

第十六話 **學生證**——128

申請學生證、學生證遺失、進出宿舍、接駁車免費搭乘、租借腳踏車

● 好用句：學生證相關聽與説
● 實用資訊：學生證可以做什麼？學生證還可以怎麼説

SERVICES FOR INTERNATIONAL STUDENTS

第十七話 **對國際學生的服務**——132

國際學生服務處、學術輔導員、諮詢處、國際學生輔導計畫

● 好用句：聽不太懂對方的話、想家
● 實用資訊：國際學生服務處提供的服務、國際學生可使用的資源、國際學生該如何適應新環境

第三章 | CHAPTER 3

上課囉！Going to Class

COURSE SYLLABUS

第一話 **課程大綱**——138

● 圖解英文：教學大綱
● 聽力測驗：教授課程介紹
● 實用資訊：TA（助教）、第一堂課要注意聽的事

GETTING TO KNOW YOUR CLASSMATES

第二話 **認識同學**——142

詢問講課內容、借筆記、和同學閒聊、加熱人到社群媒體上、出去吃點東西

● 好用句：認識同學聽和説
● 實用資訊：為什麼多認識些同學很重要？我要如何認識同學？

DISCUSSING CLASSES AND PROFESSORS

第三話 **討論課程與教授**——146

談論課程、談論教授、詢問建議

● 好用句：討論課程、討論教授
● 實用資訊：選課後，不喜歡的課可以退選嗎？學校行政和教職人員怎麼説、如何知道教授評價、教授對成績的影響有多大、成績分佈曲線

SPEAKING UP AND ASKING QUESTIONS IN CLASS

第四話 在課堂上發言、提問──150

回答問題、發言、提問

- 好用句：在課堂發言、提問
- 聽力測驗：教授給分標準
- 實用資訊：發言的重要性、發言的小技巧、發言禮節

COMPUTERS, INTERNET AND PRINTING

第五話 電腦資源、網路、影印──154

連線、尋找電腦、手機充電站、詢問軟體

- 好用句：校園網路、電腦資源
- 實用資訊：學校網路、學生論壇、校園科技

USING LIBRARY RESOURCES

第六話 使用圖書館資源──158

在借還書處、搜尋方法

- 好用句：詢問借書與館藏
- 閱讀測驗：借閱規則
- 聽力測驗：圖書館員導覽
- 實用資訊：圖書館使用規則、圖書館趣事、如何有效使用圖書館資源、何時會需要使用圖書館資源

WRITING AND ACADEMIC ASSISTANCE

第七話 寫作與課業協助──162

在寫作諮詢服務處、回答助教問題、詢問助教問題

- 好用句：形容自己的寫作問題
- 聽力測驗：實驗室安全守則
- 實用資訊：寫作協助、為何有 TA 制度、TA 的職責

PARTICIPATING IN GROUP PROJECTS

第八話 參與小組專題研究──166

加入小組、約討論時間、討論主題、工作分配

- 好用句：提出見解、表達不同想法
- 實用資訊：如何尋找組員、如何參與討論、若遇到組員意見分歧時，該怎麼做、可以表達不同意見嗎？

TALKING TO PROFESSORS

第九話 和教授談──170

自我介紹、詢問講課相關問題、尋求建議、要求提供推薦函、研究論文

- 好用句：討論論文
- 實用資訊：如何讓教授對你有個好印象、如何有效率的寫研究論文、同儕審查（peer-reviewed）、MLA 論文格式

PART 3 EXTRACURRICULAR ACTIVITIES

課外活動

3

CAMPUS RECREATION FACILITIES

第一話 校園娛樂設施──176

一般詢問、運動課程費用、健身中心設施、球場預約

- 好用句：詢問校園娛樂設施聽與說
- 閱讀測驗：游泳池時間表與門票方案
- 實用資訊：校園娛樂設施、使用校園娛樂設施的好處

JOINING CLUBS AND ORGANIZATIONS

第二話 參與社團和組織──180

挑選社團、談論社團、加入專業協會、成為社團幹部

- 好用句：社團資訊聽與說
- 閱讀測驗：社團敘述
- 實用資訊：兄弟會、姐妹會、參與社團的好處

CHATTING WITH FRIENDS

第三話 和朋友聊天──184

在學業和社交生活間尋找平衡、增進英文能力、當地活動、時間管理、邀約上教堂、談論台灣

- 好用句：介紹台灣、介紹美國
- 實用資訊：可和同學聊些什麼、請避免聊到這些話題

INTERNSHIP VS. CO-OP

第四話 實習和在校生實習──188

國際學生實習、實習第一天

- 好用句：身為實習生，你要做這 8 件事、實習生要會說
- 實用資訊：co-op 和 internship 的相同差異處比較、每所學校、每個 program，都提供 co-op 或是 internship 嗎？如何找 co-op 或是 internship？什麼是 H-1B 簽證、找實習機會的建議

INTRAMURAL AND CLUB SPORTS

第五話 校內和社團體育活動──192

袋棍球社團隊招募新血、羽球社團隊、參與運動的原因、球衣

- 好用句：討論體育活動、看美式球賽
- 實用資訊：參與國外大學運動活動，很重要嗎？Intramural Sports, Club Sports, Collegiate Sports 有什麼不同、看美式足球賽、美國大學運動文化

DATING

第六話 約會──196

打招呼、搭訕、要電話號碼、邀約約會、感情狀態

- 好用句：追求對象、表達想法
- 實用資訊：如何描述某人的感情狀態、大學生談戀愛注意事項、和美國男女溝通

GETTING A JOB ON-CAMPUS

第七話 申請校內工作──200

助教職務、談論兼職工作、提交履歷、後續追蹤、面試預約

- 好用句：詢問校內工作、校內工作答覆
- 實用資訊：何時可以申請校內打工、國際學生可以從事的校內工作、如何得知校內工作資訊、國際學生校內打工、社會安全號碼（Social Security Number）、美國聯邦獎助學金的一部分（work study）

CAMPUS ACTIVITIES

第八話 校園活動──204

校友返校日、英語學習坊、校友講座

- 好用句：詢問校園活動、介紹校園活動
- 閱讀測驗：活動公告
- 實用資訊：校友返校日、車尾派對、學校活動有哪些

FINDIING A JOB

第九話 就業──208

校園招聘、和招聘人員談、建立聯繫、製造好印象

- 好用句：了解業界、了解職缺
- 實用資訊：工作簽證、招聘活動、常用的找工作網站

閱讀測驗和圖解英文翻譯──212

音檔
使用說明

STEP ①

立即註冊

👤 帳號　限3-21碼小寫英文數字

✉ 信箱

🔒 密碼　限8-24碼小寫英文數字

　　　再次輸入密碼

完成

─── 或 ───

社群帳號註冊

f 使用Facebook註冊

Google 使用Goole註冊

掃描書中 QRCode

STEP ②

EZ Course
聆聽最新英日韓

👤 帳號　請輸入電子郵件

🔒 密碼　請輸入密碼

登入

快速註冊 | 忘記密碼

─── 或 ───

f 使用Facebook登入

Google 使用Goole登入

快速註冊或登入 EZCourse

STEP ③

請回答以下問題完成訂閱

一、請問本書第65頁，紅色框線中的英文＿＿＿＿是什麼？

答案　請注意大小寫

回答問題按送出

答案就在書中（需注意空格與大小寫）。

STEP ④

二、請問本書第33頁，紅色框線中的英文＿＿＿＿是什麼？

答案　請注意大小寫

送出

完成訂閱

該書右側會顯示「已訂閱」，
表示已成功訂閱，
即可點選播放本書音檔。

STEP ⑤

點選個人檔案

查看「我的訂閱紀錄」
會顯示已訂閱本書，
點選封面可到本書線上聆聽。

EZ TALK 編輯台

本期刊物在最後製作時期，恰巧碰上近期全球海外人士最嚴峻的時刻—新冠病毒來襲，許多留學生在安全考量下暫時回台。如果你的留學計畫也因疫情而產暫時生變，那何不在出國前做好準備，讓你屆時在當地留學遊學，能夠更快進入狀況。

又或者你已經出國念書一段時間，卻還沒有效利用學校資源：沒去過國際學生辦公室，沒有使用過寫作諮詢（writing tutorial），甚至還不知道學校有學術輔導員（academic advisor），又或是無法順利溝通表達：要向同學自我介紹總是卡卡，小組討論時，想表達反對意見，卻不知該怎麼説。如果花了高額的學費，這兩年到四年卻是辛苦吃力，沒有留下好友名單與快樂回憶，未免也太可惜。畢竟懂文化、會開口説、看得懂，學習才能事半功倍，有了適應順利的孩子，爸媽在台灣也才能放心！

這次《美國留學會話》做了改版，首先新版開本變小，更好攜帶，閱讀手感也更輕鬆。再來，增加「News Roundup 綜合新聞」，讓你用英文讀時事。另外「Feature Topics 專欄特輯」特別針對欲出國留學者最想知道的問題，邀請相關人士，以報導或採訪方式撰寫，像是高額學費能否克服、英文檢定考試成績不到該如何申請學校等問題。讓讀者在對主題有更深入認識後，再來探究相關英文。

英文部分分為寫作教學和對話教學，寫作教學涵蓋各種申請學校資料撰寫範本與寫作重點教學，對話教學的情境包含：開課前準備、課堂相關、課後活動，除了受歡迎的「Useful Pattern 實用句型」和「Common Phrases 好用句「，直接列出各種狀況會用到的萬用句，如：各種「科系」與「學位」的説法（I want to pursue a ___ in ___ .）、形容自己的個性（People say I'm a/an ___ person.），臨時遇到狀況，就可以隨看隨用。除了「説」的需求以外，看懂各類圖表或是聽懂狀況也是留學生的一大難題，如：主修選課需求、租屋廣告、寄宿家庭生活常規説明，因此書中也收錄各類「圖解英文」、「閱讀測驗」、「聽力測驗」，幫你輕鬆理解看不懂或聽不懂的校園英文。

最後一定要提的特色是這次的編輯群，包含：美籍柏克萊大學畢業老師撰寫英文內容，長駐美國加州、總是分享美國留學大小事 WaWa TV 的 YouTuber Lisa 撰寫實用資訊，以及曾經在加拿大留學的主編我本人規劃主題，所以書中所有文化解説皆為當地最新資訊，所有當時曾經有過的卡關處、痛點與不確定之處，也都編寫成「實用資訊」，幫助讀者能夠順利跨過語言與文化障礙，快速融入當地學生，並享受學校生活。

EZ TALK
主編

Amy

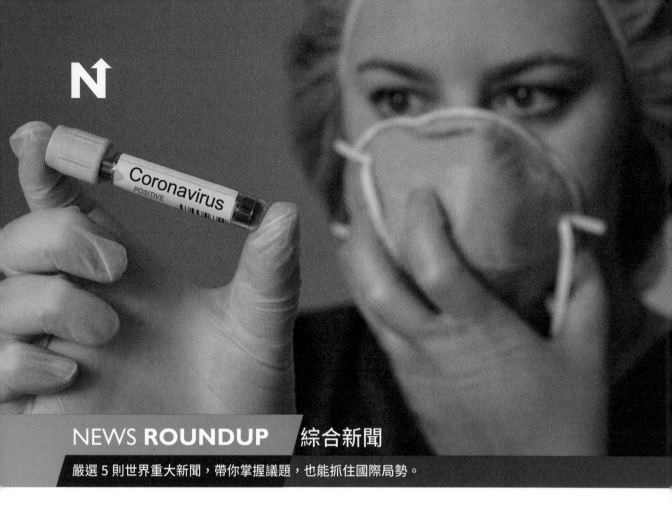

1

Prince Charles Tests Positive for Coronavirus
王儲查爾斯王子確診感染新冠肺炎

Royal officials confirmed on Wednesday that Prince Charles, **heir** to the British throne, has tested positive for **COVID-19**. According to the prince's Clarence House office, the 71-year-old is showing mild symptoms of the new coronavirus and is **self-isolatin**g at a royal estate in Scotland. His wife, Camilla, 72, has tested negative.

Parasite First Foreign Language Film to Win Best Picture Oscar
《寄生上流》為首部贏得奧斯卡最佳影片的外語片

2

South Korean **satire** *Parasite* captured the Best Picture award at the 2020 Oscars on Sunday, making history as the first foreign-language film to win Hollywood's top honor. Bong Joon-ho was also crowned best director for the film, another first. Parasite took home Oscars for best original screenplay and best international picture as well.

U.K. May Walk Away from Post-Brexit Talks
英國可能退出後脫歐談判

3

The U.K. has warned the EU it may leave trade talks in June unless an outline of a deal is agreed on. **Cabinet** minister Michael Gove told MPs the U.K. wanted to reach a comprehensive free trade agreement within 10 months. The government would not, however, accept any **alignment** with EU laws. "We will not trade away our **sovereignty**," said Gove.

4

Kobe Bryant Dies in Helicopter Crash
柯比死於直升機失事

Retired NBA legend Kobe Bryant and his 13-year-old daughter Gianna died Sunday morning in a fatal California **helicopter** crash. Seven others were also killed, including the pilot. There were no survivors in the crash, which occurred around 10 a.m. in the Los Angeles suburb of Calabasas, says the L.A. County Sheriff's Department.

Locust Swarms Invade East Africa
蝗蟲群入侵東非

5

The worst **locust infestation** in 70 years has hit East Africa, threatening economies in a region that depends heavily on agriculture. Locust swarms have begun to impact South Sudan, Uganda and Tanzania, having already destroyed crops in Ethiopia, Kenya and Somalia. According to the U.N., a one-square-kilometer swarm can devour as much food as 35,000 people in a single day.

新聞單字

heir [ɛr] (n.) 繼承人／ **COVID-19** [ˋkovidˏnaɪnˋtin] (n.) 新型冠狀病毒，冠狀病毒為 **coronavirus** [kəˋronəvaɪrəs] (n. ／
self-isolate [ˏselfˋaɪsəˏlet] (v.) 自我隔離／ **satire** [ˋsæˏtaɪr] (n.) 諷刺作品／
parasite [ˋpærəsaɪt] (n.) 靠他人維生者，寄生蟲／ **Brexit** [ˋbrɛksɪt] (n.) 脫歐／ **cabinet** [ˋkæbənɪt] (n.) 內閣／
alignment [əˋlaɪnmənt] (n.) 結盟，符合／ **sovereignty** [ˋsɑvrənti] (n.) 主權，統治權／
helicopter [ˋhɛlɪˏkɑptə] (n.) 直升機／ **locust** [ˋlokəst] (n.) 蝗蟲／ **infestation** [ˏɪnfɛsˋteʃən] (n.) 侵擾／
swarm [swɔrm] (n.) 一大群（昆蟲）／ **devour** [dɪˋvaʊr] (n.) 狼吞虎嚥地吃，吃光

PART 1

專題特輯

Feature Topics

常見的留學六大疑問：

Six common study abroad questions

Q1

我該去哪裡留學？

這五年來台灣去各國留學的人數，做成圖表，讓你參考。

● 請參考：《近五年來去各國留學的人數》

A

Q2

出國留學費用太高了，有花少少錢也可以留學的方法嗎？

教育部有所謂的「學海計畫」，也就是公費留學，由政府和學校共同資助，讓優秀的在校生得以順利出國增廣見聞。

● 請參考：《教育部學海計畫，用最少的預算出國留學》

A

Q3

去美國念書，我該考哪些檢定考試呢？

要考語言檢定考試和入學考試，語言檢定考試包括：TOEFL（托福）、IELTS（雅思）或 PTE Academic（培生），入學考試包括：SAT 和 ACT（大學）與 GRE 和 GMAT（研究生）有詳盡深入的介紹。

● 請參考：《英語系國家留學必考的語言檢定與入學考試》

A

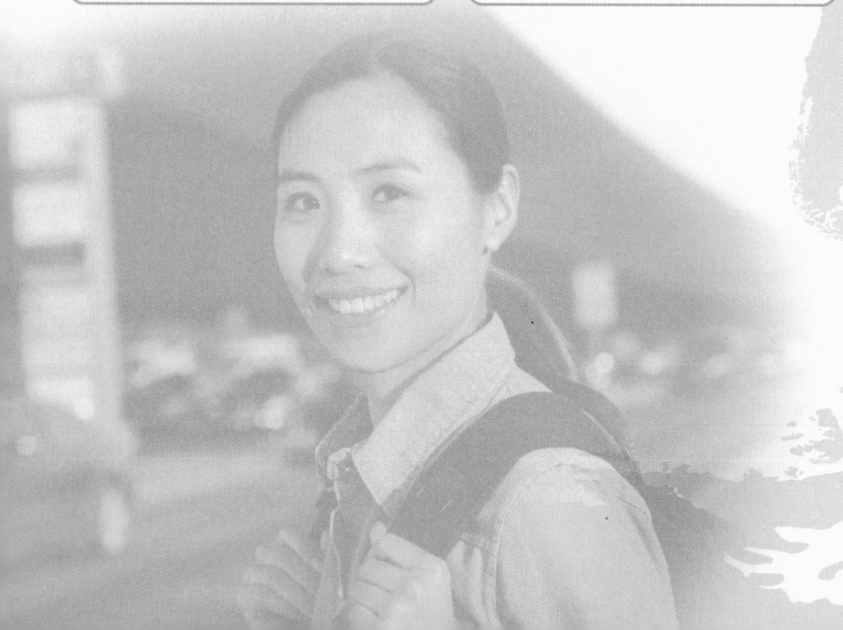

關於留學，你是否已決定了未來的方向，
費用問題是否已經解決了呢？
如果對於這些問題，還沒有什麼想法，
不妨來看看以下幾篇報導，看看曾走過這條路的名人，他們怎麼說，
也許能幫你釐出方向。

Q4

我的托福成績就是考不到，但我真的很想出國念書，可以嗎？

可以考慮先進美國社區大學，美國社區大學學費低、申請門檻也低。若於社區大學二年內成績優秀，二年後轉入名校也是有機會的。

───────────

●請參考：《托福成績不到，一樣能上柏克萊》

A

Q5

我目前就讀的大學並不算是知名大學，這樣也有可能申請到獎學金嗎？

Ping 老師告訴你，要提早申請，成績要顧好，備審資料要凸顯出自己的優勢，你還是有機會的！

───────────

●請參考：《不是名校出身，也能申請到名校獎學金》

A

Q6

我去念的科目是我自己喜歡，但不確定是否是我未來的路，那還要花錢去念嗎？好猶豫喔。

You never know. 你愛的東西也許會在你的留學過程中茁壯，長成大樹，賦予你未來工作的具體樣貌。

───────────

●請參考：《一趟以色列留學之旅，給了我人生的方向》

A

你究竟為什麼要出國留學？

hy do you want to study abroad?

近五年來去各國留學人數

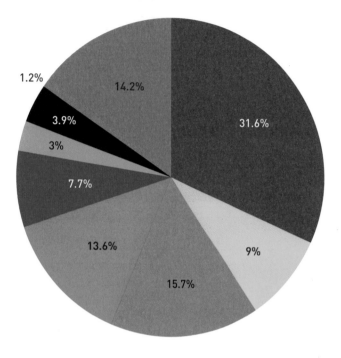

2018 留學各國人數

UNITED STATES 美國	13,000
UNITED KINGDOM 英國	3,686
AUSTRALIA 澳洲	6,454
JAPAN 日本	5,589
CANADA 加拿大	3,170
FRANCE 法國	1,250
GERMANY 德國	1,620
NEW ZEALAND 紐西蘭	480
OTHER 其他國家	5,841

總計

41,090

從 2014 年來到 2019 年，出國留學的人數逐年上升，
其中又以去美國留學的人數最多，
雖然呈緩步減少，但就各語系來說，還是以去英語系國家佔最大宗。
現在就讓我們來看一下各國留學人數，以及這五年來人數的變化。

● 近五年來**出國留學**的總人數

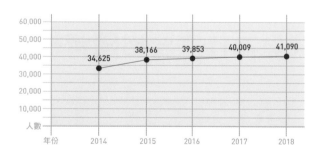

●近五年來留學**美國**的總人數　　**UNITED STATES**

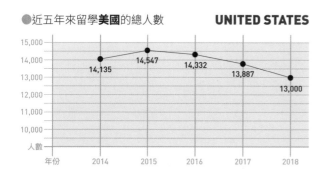

●近五年來留學**加拿大**總人數　　**CANADA**

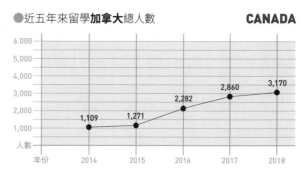

●近五年來留學**英國**的總人數　　UNITED KINGDOM

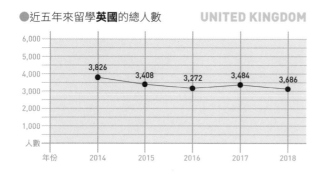

●近五年來留學**法國**總人數　　FRANCE

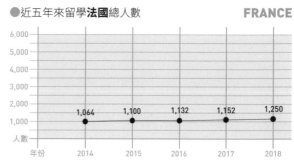

●近五年來留學**澳洲**的總人數　　AUSTRALIA

●近五年來留學**德國**總人數　　**GERMANY**

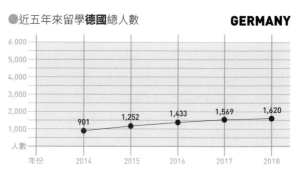

●近五年來留學**日本**的總人數　　**JAPAN**

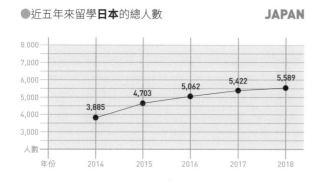

●近五年來留學**紐西蘭**總人數　　NEW ZEALAND

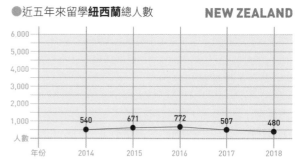

沒錢也能出國留學
學海計畫幫你圓夢

邱鈺玲——文

出國留學是大多數人都有的夢想，但留學衍生的高額費用，就足以讓美夢幻滅。然而，現在已經有越來越多補助計畫、貸款或獎學金供學子申請，像是教育部最著名的「學海計畫」，由政府和學校共同資助，讓優秀的在校生得以順利出國增廣見聞，不必因經濟狀況限制自己的夢想。

本篇我們將詳盡介紹何謂學海計畫，以及其他獎助學金，讓你一圓出國增廣見聞的夢想！

什麼是學海計畫？

過往若要出國留學，除了公費留學、申請獎學金或貸款以外，鮮少有其他減緩經濟壓力的選擇，但上述補助方式，申請資格也十分侷限，多半都是要攻讀研究所、博士、博士後等學位才有機會，大專院校學生若想出國留學、實習，往往只能靠家裡資助，或努力打工存錢。

為了增進學子視野，教育部在 2007 年（民國 96 年）起開辦「學海計畫」，讓大專院校的在學生，能藉由補助的方法，赴國外大專院校修讀學分，或至國外企業機構進行職場實習，提升國際視野與職場競爭力。計畫開辦後，每年從不到 1,500 人參與，到目前每年已有 5,000 多人參加，至今此計畫總共已經幫助超過 3 萬 6 千名學生出國。

讀完大一上學期就可申請

學海計畫依身分、目的和國家的不同，一共分為四個獎助類型，分別是「學海飛颺」、「學海惜珠」、「學海築夢」，和 2017 年（民國 106 年）才新增的「新南向學海築夢」。

此計畫是專為具中華民國國籍、設有臺灣戶籍、非軍警校院的公私立大專校院的在學學生設立的獎助計畫，只要修讀完大一上學期的課程，並檢附計畫所需之資料，即有機會獲得補助。

然而，除了軍警校院以外，並非全台大專校院都有參與，而若欲前往大陸、港澳等地的學校或企業修讀或實習，也不在計畫補助範圍內。

因此如果有意願申請，最好先到「教育部國內大專院校－選送學生出國研修或國外專業實習補助系統」網站詳閱各校簡章辦法，也務必要參與校內舉辦的講座，以了解學校行政程序和時程，免得因為錯估作業時間，喪失寶貴機會。

海外修習、實習皆有機會享補助

和以往的留學補助不同的是，學海計畫不僅提供出國修讀學分的同學補助，海外實習也有機會享有，而計畫下四種補助類型又各有一些區別：

專為出國修讀學分的類型為「學海飛颺」和「學海惜珠」，兩者的差異為申請的身分和獎助的額度，「飛颺」是為成績優異的一般生設立的項目，獎助額度雖有表定金額範圍－新台幣 5 萬元以上 30 萬元以下，不過實際金額仍需視

該年度教育部預算、各校的配合款、學校的行政績效、前年度計畫成果表現，以及該年度申請人數而定，每年每人的補助金額不一定相同。

「惜珠」則專為勵學優秀生，也就是早期指稱的清寒優秀生所創立的項目，補助額度會根據學生所提供的資料背景、留學國別城市和航空公司票價而定。但無論是「飛颺」還是「惜珠」，都可申請一學期或一學年，補助項目都得包含一張來回經濟艙機票、國外學費和生活費。

而「築夢」系列，則是專為出國實習的學子所設計，再依據地區之別，分為「學海築夢」和「新南向學海築夢」，後者是因應新南向政策所新增的項目，主要補助前往新南向

國家進行實習的大專院校學生，雖然開辦僅 2 年，但迴響熱烈，每年都有超過千人參加。

「築夢」系列除了目的與「飛颺」、「惜珠」不同之外，申請人數也不一樣。「飛颺」與「惜珠」可個人單獨申請，「築夢」系列則需超過 3 名以上學生共組研究計畫，並由計畫主持人－通常是系上的教授、助教提交申請計畫案，才會進行審查。

此外，補助期限也有相異之處，修讀學分類型的補助項目，期限最短為一學期；企業實習類型的補助項目，最少則不得低於 30 天。建議申請前最好仔細閱讀計畫相關內容。

教育部學海計畫

	出國修讀學分		海外實習	
	學海飛颺	**學海惜珠**	**學海築夢**	**新南向學海築夢**
補助期限	1 學期（季）或 1 學年	1 學期（季）或 1 學年	扣除來回交通途程，不得少於 30 天。	扣除來回交通途程，不得少於 30 天。赴印尼實習者不得少於 25 天。
每次可申請人數	個人	個人	計畫團隊需包含 3 名以上學生，可遴選他校學生參與計畫。	
申請條件	●具中華民國國籍 ●在台灣設有戶籍 ●於薦送學校就讀一學期以上在學學生（不包括國內及境外在職專班生） ●應通過薦送學校規定之專業及語言能力條件 ●同一申請人，同一教育階段，限補助一次 ●當不同計畫名額及經費有剩餘時，學校可遴送學生至不同類型計畫		●具中華民國國籍 ●在台灣設有戶籍 ●於薦送學校就讀一學期以上在學學生（不包括國內及境外在職專班生） ●應通過薦送學校規定之專業及語言能力條件 ●同一申請人，同一教育階段，限補助一次 ●當不同計畫名額及經費有剩餘時，學校可遴送學生至不同類型計畫	
申請檢附資料 ※ 每校規定檢附資料略有不同，詳情請以各校公告為準。	●申請表 ●個人簡歷 ●成績單 ●語言能力證明 ●赴國外研修計畫書	●申請表 ●個人簡歷 ●成績單 ●語言能力證明 ●赴國外研修計畫書 ●**中低收入相關補助證明及戶口名簿影本**	●申請表計畫主持人規劃（國外實習計畫） ●國外實習機構同意書或合作契約書影本 ●學校聲明書（遴選他校生，需附他校同意書）	
預定補助額度 ※ 實際補助名額，需依當年度經費預算調整。	●每人新台幣 5 萬元以上至 30 萬元以下。 ●**每人實際獲補助額度由學校自訂**，但須包含一張國際來回經濟艙機票、國外學費及生活費。	每人實際獲補助額度**由學校評估學生資料而訂**，但須包含一張國際來回經濟艙機票、國外學費及生活費。	●實際補助金額**由學校自訂**。 ●補助至少包含一張國際來回經濟艙機票（一次為限），以及生活費。 ●計畫主持人或共同主持人之補助以一人為限，生活費最多為 14 日內，並以計畫期程結束前為限。	●實際補助金額**由教育部定**。 ●補助至少包含一張國際來回經濟艙機票（一次為限），以及生活費。 ●計畫主持人或共同主持人之補助以一人為限，生活費最多為 14 日內，並以計畫期程結束前為限。
補助名額	共 1300 名		1200 名	1000 名

還有哪些出國留學的獎助管道？

假設不符合學海計畫的申請資格，或申請失利，仍然有其他方式獲得出國留學的補助，可依照自己的身分跟條件尋找適合的獎助管道。教育部創設的「Taiwan GPS 海外人才經驗分享及國際連結計畫」網站中，就不定期為全台學子整理海外獎學金資訊，還開放了「全球獎學金地圖」供大家查找。

而台北市政府教育局也推出了非常划算的「希望專案－

青年留學免息貸款」，只要在台北市設籍一年以下，年齡在 20 歲以上未滿 45 歲之青年都可申請。對於無法參加學海計畫、公費留學考試，但仍想出國進修攻讀碩博士的朋友來說，是非常好的選擇。

最後，就算上述管道都無法申請，也能向臺灣銀行、台北富邦銀行、上海銀行或中國信託銀行等機構，申請銀行自辦的出國留學貸款，雖然較為昂貴，但只要能一圓夢想，也算值得。

英語系國家
留學必考的語言檢定
與入學考試

布曦——文

如果你打算要去英語系國家讀書，那麼 TOEFL（托福）、IELTS（雅思）或 PTE Academic（培生）很可能是你須要準備的考試。

上述考試皆為申請去英語系國家留學的語言檢定考試，用來評估申請者英文能力之標準。其中 TOEFL 或 IELTS 為大多數考生的選擇，舉凡美國、英國、紐澳、加拿大等國的機構幾乎都接受，兩者的差異在於 IELTS 多用於申請英國機構，TOEFL 主要用於美國。但事實上，近年 TOEFL 已廣泛被英國各機構認可。而 PTE Academic 是英國近年才推出的學術英文考試，一樣適用於英語系國家機構的申請，只是在亞洲地區，多數同學對它並不熟悉，其考試資源、考場相對也較少。

考試內容的部分，TOEFL 大多為學術文章，文章內容用字遣詞都偏學術校園為主，例如天文學、地質學、歷史與藝術。IELTS 也會有學術內容，但相對上包含更多生活上的用字。PTE Academic 考試的題型眾多，著重考生聽力、口說與單字量，對學生能力的要求不亞於 TOEFL 或 IELTS，甚至更高。若以「世界名校」當作申請目標，托福一般需要 100 分以上、雅思 7 分以上，培生 68 分以上。有些美國學校接受曾有在英語系國家就讀三到四年的經驗來滿足學校認可你英文水平的條件。詳細規則仍需視不同學校而定。

美國入學考試

SAT 和 ACT 為美國大學入學考試，為高中生進入美國大學的標準考試。SAT 考試重點為閱讀詞彙及推理能力，適合喜愛英語文學、詞彙量大的學生。ACT 則著重考生的數學邏輯能力，適合詞彙量較少、熱愛科學、理工類題目的學生。從歷年美國長春藤名校等代表性的大學來看，提交 SAT 分數的學生比例仍大於 ACT，但目前每年參加 ACT 考試的考生數量正直線上升。目前，若是申請美國大學，有些美國學校接受 SAT evident-based reading（循證閱讀，即依據文章中的證據選出正確選項）成績來豁免托福成績。詳細規則仍需視不同學校而定。

GRE (Graduate Record Exam) 為美國研究生入學考試，作為研究生錄取的標準之一。GMAT (Graduate Management Admission Test) 為申請研究所「商學院」考生能力的考試。總體來說，商學院一般偏好 GMAT，但也可接受 GRE。其細節還是要看各學校各科來決定。GRE 成績除了可以被當成錄取的參考標準，還能做為院校獎學金、助學金發放的標準。最後，GRE 考試著重考生詞彙量和邏輯思維，GMAT 著重金融經濟內容、數學、數據解題能力。若學校同時可接受 GRE 或 GMAT，考生可依自身優勢抉擇。若以申請獎學金來看，成績落於 SAT 1550、ACT 34、GRE 330、GMAT 740 以上會較容易申請到學校獎學金。

●美國前總統歐巴馬也是從社區大學申請轉入名校的例子。

托福改制重點

2019 年八月 ETS 公布托福改制，許多考生對於改制非常擔心。但其實托福考題難易度並沒有改變，ETS 聲明在不影響考試可信度之下，只是將題數減少而已。整體考試時間縮短為三小時。對考生來說，是一項人性化的改革。也讓托福考試和其他留學考試比起來更有競爭力。托福改制後，托福聽力部分減少一篇長篇（6 題）。托福口說部分減少二個題型，這兩個題型原先主要是要求考生「發表自己意見」，這兩題型被刪除，意味著考生要更注重自己聽力理解與改寫的能力。托福閱讀部分由每篇 13~14 題，減少為固定每篇只考 10 題。托福寫作的部分沒有改變。相較於其他留學考試，托福擁有龐大的考古題可供練習，能有效熟悉並預測考試內容與答題技巧，是許多考生選擇托福為語言留學檢定的原因之一。

2019 年 TOEFL 托福改制第二個亮點為，考生可合併兩年內各科最好的成績，整合出一張 superscores（超級成績單）。這項改制，讓一些多次參加考試，卻因某一單科無法破百的同學，增加了破百的可能性。然而，超級成績單的制度，並非每間學校都認可，還是要視各別學校而定。

最後，美國 ETS 更於 2019 年 10 月 26 號公布，托福成績由原先的 10 天公布，縮短為六天左右公布。官方的成績報告，也會在考試日期後，大約 9 天時間發送到學校。而托福考試的「報考間隔時間」也做了改變。由原先的 12 天後才能報下一場托福考試，縮短為三天後即可報名下一場。也就是說，考生於報名時，可以「直接報名連續兩個週末的考試」。此舉加快了學生提高、達成成績的速度。

考生仍需注意下列狀況，若是你參加了這週末的考試，感覺發揮不好，依 ETS 新制，考生可以一出考場就直接報名下週末的考試。但考生若是考試前 3~7 天報名（不含測驗日），需要額外支付 40 美元的延遲報名附加費。

社區大學：躋身名校的另一個管道

若本身程度不夠，目前仍無法順利考過語言檢定與入學考試，但急於出國的考生，可以考慮美國社區大學。美國社區大學又稱為二年制公立大學。它不但可以培訓專業職業技能，也提供了考試失利但仍渴望就讀名校的學生。美國前任總統歐巴馬即曾經就讀加州西方學院兩年，兩年後轉入哥倫比亞大學，獲得文學學士學位。相較於美國大學，美國社區大學學費低、申請門檻也低。若申請者自律能力好，於社區大學二年內成績優秀，二年後轉入名校也是有機會的。一般來說，美國各州大學對各州社區大學都有優先錄取的政策。因此如果想去唸賓州州立大學，先去賓州社區大學讀二年，再轉賓州州立大學讀大三大四，也是個進入名校就讀的方法。

Teacher

布曦老師簡歷 | 美國長春藤名校賓夕法尼亞大學（university of Pennsylvania）英語教學碩士，目前專職教授 TOEFL、SAT 等留學考試課程，托福聽力課程已超過 1000 位同學熱情推薦，獨創托福《區塊破題式聽力》教學，世界第一華頓商學院商用英文教學會員，美國非營利性語言機構英語會話文法講師，曾受邀至各大學高中演講。

我是如何
從社區大學
成功轉到
柏克萊大學

潘亭軒——採訪

Lisa 是一名 YouTuber，目前有 1.5 萬訂閱者。她時常在自己的頻道上發布美國留學與生活相關影片，目前定居加州，畢業於美國加州柏克萊大學音樂系，現為音樂老師。許多人都對美國名校充滿好奇與憧憬，也對於去柏克萊讀音樂系有莫名的幻想。今天就請 Lisa 來和讀者分享一下她轉學的經過，以及在柏克萊念書的苦與樂等，讓讀者一窺名校真面目，也讓有志留學者，可以仿效她的經驗，進而成功轉入名校。

Q Lisa 好，請問你是幾歲的時候到美國，當初怎麼會想要去美國念書？

A 我是 19 歲高中畢業後到美國的。因為國高中都是在中國讀國際學校，所以早已規劃高中畢業後出國。

Q 妳當初好像是先念社區大學，再轉到柏克萊大學的，可以和我們分享這個經驗嗎？當初是已經確定想進柏克萊，再選擇念合作的社區大學嗎？

A 高中畢業的我，學校成績太差，加上我托福也考的很差，所以申請不到任何學校。後來從學校師長口中了解到了，社區大學是通往大學的另一條道路，不僅小班授課，而且學費不貴，這也算是再給自己一次機會。我一開始並沒有想過能讀到柏克萊大學，因為從小成績就一直不太好，都是及格邊緣而已。到社區大學後因為能自己選課、選老師，而我大部分選的課都是自己有興趣的課程，所

以我努力拼了 2 年半，把成績拉高，順利的被柏克萊大學錄取。

Q 學校裡有哪些地方讓你印象深刻？求學時是否有哪些有趣的事？

A 柏克萊大學有個有趣的課程，叫 DeCal，這是一種由學生帶領的課程。DeCal 包含的課程有很多，例如，烹飪、跳舞、攝影等，甚至還有台語課。我在柏克萊兩年，拿過一個叫 Cal Star Yoga 的課程，這是個幫助行動不方便的人做瑜伽按摩的課程，在課堂上我們需要依照學生老師以及顧問老師的指示去幫助他們拉筋按摩。我覺得這是一門很有意思的課程，因為不僅可以幫助人，還可以透過跟他們的聊天來了解他們，另外還可以學到很多對身體有幫助的知識，讓我放假回台灣時可以幫我奶奶按摩。雖然我在柏克萊兩年，但我發現 DeCal 時已經是

大四了，雖然沒時間體驗當老師，但如果有機會的話，我還蠻想試試看的。（※ **想看到更多 DeCal 介紹→ https://www.ocf. berkeley.edu/~archery/index.php/decal-2/**）我們學校還有個有趣的習俗。我們期末考試前會有一個禮拜的複習週，在那週學校圖書館會開 24 小時。聽說那時會有人不定時、不定圖書館（柏克萊有 37 個圖書館）的集體裸奔，雖然我沒有看過，那個活動很神秘，沒有人知道什麼時候在哪裡，期末要到的時候就會有人開始問有沒有人知道裸奔的時間地點。

Q 在柏克萊大學念書時是否有覺得困難的事？

A 到柏克萊大學後，可以明顯的感覺到身邊的人都是瘋子，從大一就開始在柏克萊的同學，幾乎人人雙主修或至少有一個主修、一個副修。這讓我曾經想過是否也要在去找個副修，不過最後發現我的能力與時間上不允許。

Q 所謂的「名校」和其他等級的大學，在教學或是找工作上，會有什麼差別嗎？

A 柏克萊大學是屬於研究型大學，顧名思義就是專門做研究與帶領研究生的學校。「名校」之所以會是「名校」，不是因為教學特別好，而是因為他們的研究出名、為社會做出貢獻、有諾貝爾得主。研究型大學的教授比較重視研究所，他們對大學生一般都是比較屬於放牛吃草型的，不過一些不需要做研究的科系的教授還是很認真負責，重視大學生跟教育的。

Q 我想大部分的鄉民都還蠻好奇你為什麼會念音樂系，在美國念音樂可以找那些工作呢？

A 我讀音樂系是因為媽媽是鋼琴老師，而我從小就開始學音樂，對音樂有濃厚的興趣。在美國念音樂系可以選擇像我一樣當老師，也可以當演奏家、作曲家、音樂製作人（助理），另外矽谷是科技城市，如果你有電腦相關背景，也可以做電腦相關的音樂工作，例如，遊戲音樂、開放音樂 APP 等。

Q 柏克萊音樂系學什麼？

A 柏克萊音樂系基本上什麼都可以學，我們有學樂理、音樂訓練、音樂歷史、音樂鑑賞、音樂表演，另外每個樂器也都有私人的老師指導。學校的音樂表演有很多種類，除了交響樂團、合唱團等樂團外，還有一些比較特別的樂團，像我上過印尼傳統樂器的 gamelan 樂團跟非洲鼓樂團，我們每個學期都有 1~2 次的表演。

Q 你的 YouTube 頻道幫助了許多想去美國念書的人，請問 Lisa 當初是什麼契機，想要拍影片介紹美國求學的大小事呢？

A 當時申請到柏克萊大學後，開始有很多長輩問我相關問題，於是我就開始做了一系列影片讓他們可以查看。沒想到越做越有興趣，也有越來越多人問我很多問我很多問題，這些問題都是我靈感的來源。而且看到有很多人因為我的關係得到幫助我也覺得很開心。

Q 每支影片的下面，都會看到許多讀者的回覆，這是不是也是你的成就感來源？

A 觀眾們的留言是我繼續做下去的動力，畢竟有人看我才會想繼續做嘛！大家的問題也是我靈感的來源，我常常把大家問我的問題做成影片來幫助更多有一樣問題的人。

Q 最後你會給想去美國讀書的人什麼樣的建議呢？

A 如果你有能力、有財力的話，能一次申請到好的四年制大學那當然是最好，這樣就不用花時間再去準備轉學。如果沒能力或財力的話，最好的方法就是先讀社區大學再轉入四年制大學。大家可以依照學校升學率跟自己想讀的科系去選擇社區大學，並不是所有學校都適合所有人，因為有些學校可能會沒有你要的科系。建議大家可以先上網調查一下，如果可以的話，到學校去走走，看看學校氛圍與周圍環境也是不錯的選擇。

YouTuber

Lisa 簡歷｜美國加州柏克萊大學音樂系畢，目前定居加州，是音樂老師兼 Youtuber。平常在教課之外，喜歡拍影片紀錄生活、分享美國文化及提供美國大學各項事務幫助想到美國讀大學的莘莘學子。

● YouTube 頻道── **WaWa TV**

不是名校出身，也能申請到英美名校獎學金

Ping 老師──文

　　因目標和工作興趣明確，加上有英語教育研究所的常春藤名校只有兩間，所以我申請了三所學校，分別是美國哥倫比亞大學 (Columbia University)、美國賓州大學 (University of Pennsylvania)、英國倫敦大學學院教育研究院 (UCL Institute of Education)，三間學校我都有申請上，其中幾間也有給我獎學金，以下分享我申請國外名校準備的經驗，希望能幫助未來想出國念書的學生，或想讓孩子出國念書的父母。

　　一般準備留學申請，會需半年至一年，但因當時我遇到些人生低潮，在最後一刻才下定決心要出國念書，所以當時我只有三個月準備期，並同時還在工作，故更需有效率準備留學申請，時間軸順序會是關鍵，建議先考 GRE、TOEFL 或 IELTS，再寫履歷。寫好履歷，才能請教授寫推薦函，再寫讀書計畫。若可能，還是建議大家留給自己至少半年到一年的準備期，才不會像我得在極大壓力，不眠不休，和一步都不能出錯的情況下完成申請。

　　我大學時不是念台灣名校，而是一般大學，但經由我自身與朋友的經歷，即使不是名校出身，要申請上常春藤名校，又希望拿到獎學金，仍是絕對有可能的，但有幾點一定要注意。

　　第一點是，若要申請獎學金，申請時間一定要提早，一般申請獎學金的申請截止日期會比一般申請截止日早許多，所以決定出國唸書時，建議首先第一步是要查各目標學校的獎學金申請截止日期，以及要求的文件和門檻，然後整理成一個 excel 檔案，才可以清楚掌握各校申請要求，以利自己時程安排，以免錯過申請獎學金的截止日，我申請哥大和賓大時，在填申請表格時，學校就有問是否想申請獎學金，我有勾選該選項，但每個學校與學生的情況不同，所以這情況不一定適用，請自己務必要詢問想申請的大學再做評估。

　　第二點，既然想要申請上常春藤名校，又希望拿到獎學金，那就要有一定的決心和準備，因是要跟世界各地菁英競爭少數的名額。雖然不是不可能，但以下幾點都必須盡可能做到最好。

（一）在校成績（GPA）：很重要，一定要顧好和注意。

　　GPA（Grade Point Average）是指學科成績平均績點，越高即表示在校學術表現越好。GPA 滿分是 4.0，對於申請名校和拿獎金需要多少 GPA，眾說紛紜，但當時我問了我申

請上名校的朋友們，基本上大家最低 GPA 也有 3.7 左右。

我個人認為 GPA 比托福成績更為重要，因 **GPA 是學生長期的學術表現**，故英美大學非常重視這項指標，很幸運的是，這點我大一就知道，所以在校成績顧得還不錯，也提高了我申請上國外名校的機會。

（二）履歷（résumé）：非常重要。

履歷要豐富，即在大學或碩班期間，**就要儘早準備**，可以讓自己多參與些活動，無論是學術上、生活上、服務性質都好，呈現自己是個多元的人才，而非單一面向人才，更能提高自己申請上名校和拿到獎學金的機會。我本身在求學期間，除認真念書外，社團活動也滿活躍的，系、所上活動也都滿積極參與，無論是競賽性質或服務性質，如：籌備研討會，所上活動義工等，雖不敢說是哪些活動，幫我申請學校加到分，但從我履歷中可看出，我是個多元，且樂於團隊合作的人。

（三）推薦函（cover letter）：非常重要，是申請名校和拿獎學金的關鍵之一。

不一定要找自己系所上最有名的教授，**建議找真正認識你的教授幫你寫**，推薦函的內容才會精彩而不平淡，推薦函的內容精彩與否，會依據在校期間，你是否讓教授認識你，畢竟一個系或所上學生很多。讓教授認識的方式有：課堂上學業表現突出、是否積極發言或參與討論、是否曾與教授約時間做討論，或和教授做專題研究等。

（四）讀書計畫（statement of purpose）：非常重要，是申請名校和拿獎學金的關鍵之一。

讀書計畫建議不要只講自己成績多好，或有多少豐功偉業，首先因履歷都已包含這些內容，不需再重複講，再者會申請常春藤名校的人多為世界各地菁英，大家都非常非常優秀，如果只強調自己成績多優秀，反而突顯不出個人特色。反之，建議在寫讀書計畫前，先做好以下幾件事：

1. 分析自己的優勢或強項，從最突出到一般的優勢特點依序排出。

2. 瀏覽想申請系所的網頁，研究其特色，建議同時可以了解一下該系所教授的研究興趣和專長，研讀他們的研究論文，然後寫信去請教他們研究相關的問題，國外教授很欣賞這種學生，如果你的目標是拿獎學金，這點會讓你非常加分。

3. 將第一點「自己的特色表」與第二點「系所特色和教授研究領域」做比對，思考如何將這兩點做結合，好突顯自己

的長處外，也符合學校找人才的需求，然後建議以寫故事的方式來撰寫讀書計畫，其實這也是檢視和探索自己的好機會，仔細想想究竟為什麼要出國念書，千萬不要為想出國，或為唸名校，或因還未找到職涯方向，而出國念書。若可能，建議在出國念書前，**先找到自己的熱情，讓自己的國外求學經歷**，成為幫助你達到你的熱情或目標的助力，如果能朝這方向寫讀書計畫，內容會相對精彩與吸引人。

（五）TOEFL（托福）、IELTS（雅思）、GRE 成績：一般重要。

基本上名校都清楚規定這些考試的門檻，盡最大努力準備後，達到該門檻即可，畢竟時間有限，應把多的時間放在準備以上更重要的四點，但有些科系很重視 GRE 或 GMAT，也就需要盡可能去準備。

另外，不建議以抱佛腳的心態去準備這些考試，要出國念書和生活，英文能力即需要一定的標準，故建議**要以提升英語實力的心態去準備，而不是只為了考高分**。雖考了高分，但若遇到外國人，口語上溝通仍有障礙、聽不懂上課內容，或無法參與課堂討論，其實是會被國外教授看不起的。如果平時都有在累積自己的英語實力，IELTS 考好其實不難，因我決定較晚，所以只有不到一個月的時間可以準備，但我的聽力、口說還是考了 8 分，主要還是靠平時英語力的累積。

最後，出國念書，雖然很辛苦，但是我人生中最棒的投資和經歷之一，建議若想留學，先思考自己的興趣和想留學的初衷，甚至不用一畢業就急著出國，先工作一陣子，累積自己的經驗外，去更了解自己，更能找到合適自己的系所，我自己和朋友也是工作一陣子才出國念書，這些經歷也能提升我們申請上國外名校，和拿到獎學金的機會。

Teacher

Ping 老師簡歷 | 國立陽明大學腦科學碩士，美國哥倫比亞大學（Columbia University）英語教育碩士，美國哥倫比亞大學教育學院優秀畢業生代表及傑出英語教案設計大獎得主，並考取美國紐約州立英文教師證照。現任國立陽明大學兼任講師和英語教育培訓講師，因熱愛英語教學，在國內外長期投入教師培訓工作，期許透過好的教育，讓孩子愛上英語學習。

一趟以色列
留學之旅給了我
人生的方向

專訪 Ani Ann 創辦人——陳俞安

事過境遷近 4 年，陳俞安至今仍說不明白當時深受以色列吸引的具體原因，只說那時是跟團旅行，並未獨自深入或接觸當地人文，然而縱使初來乍到，卻感覺像回家。

以色列異於東西方的獨特人文風情，讓陳俞安一見鍾情，返台後這股情思不僅沒有消退，反而激起了她的鬥志，想方設法找到「回家」的途徑。

天龍女孩，在以色列找到家的感覺

當時陳俞安還是北藝大劇場設計系大四的學生，系上老師聽聞她去以色列的心得後，便告知她學校與一間以色列學校有締結姊妹校之約，可以試著申請教育部學海飛颺計畫，取得交換學生的機會。

於是大四下學期，她在畢業製作與準備備審資料和作品集的雙面夾殺之下，順利通過學海飛颺計畫審查，於 2017 年前往以色列歷史最悠久、最著名的貝札雷藝術與設計學院影像動畫系留學。

右圖：第二學期素描課期末作業自畫像，呈現平時看不到的狀態。

無畏希伯來文冷門 積極自學盼成優勢

在申請學海計畫之前，為了想更了解以色列，陳俞安開始著手自學希伯來文。一開始她和大多數人一樣，不知道其實有許多以色列人在台灣學習中文，所以只透過報名網路語言課程學習，一段時間後，她覺得光只有上課無法創造一個良好的語言環境，所以她下載了語言交換 APP「Hello Talk」，藉此認識了數十位在台以色列人，為自己創造練習語言的環境。

「我真的蠻鼓勵大家下載 APP 學新語言，除了有練習對象，還可以順便複習英文。」她說，雖然大多數時間都還是用英文跟以色列網友交流，但至少能了解他們的文化。

許多人學語言都是為了替自己的職涯加分，基於此，陳俞安的友人常對她的決定有所耳語，認為她學希伯來文無益於未來發展。儘管這樣的閒言閒語不少，她也沒打消念頭，反而轉念告訴自己，即便希伯來文非主流，用處不多，但也

正因為物以稀為貴，反能成為她的特色跟優勢。

陳俞安說，希伯來文的難度與德文不相上下，學習資源很少，因此學習門檻頗高，但還好有以色列朋友的熱情與鼓勵，還有她對其文化的強烈好奇，才讓這些困難顯得微不足道。

我在以色列交到的朋友

虎刺巴精神，翻轉內向個性

質疑她決定的人，不只身邊的朋友，家人也認為她「太過瘋狂」才會選擇前往以色列。「他們對於以色列的印象就是戰亂，非常不懂我為什麼要去這麼危險的地方。」陳俞安說，自己實際在當地生活一年後才發現，並沒有想像中那麼危險。

「雖然我也有遇過飛彈警報，鄰居還親切從容地帶我去防空室，但那真的是很難得的情況，一般來說加薩走廊附近比較嚴重。耶路撒冷、特拉維夫這些大城市其實很少見。」她說明自己的經驗。去以色列後，她開始在 Facebook 上記錄自己在以色列的生活，破除人們的錯誤印象，也讓家人安心。

安息日的耶路撒冷街頭，猶太教徒步行前往猶太會堂祈禱

採訪侃侃而談的陳俞安說，若不是去了一趟以色列，她無法想像此時的自己，說話的聲量能這麼大聲。過去內向、不愛給人添麻煩的她，在以色列同學的說服下，憑著（Chutzpah）竟主動爭取延長留學期限，扭轉原本看似無望的局勢。虎刺巴精神是一種帶有反叛意味、鼓勵爭取權利、獨立思考的無畏精神，也是以色列獨有的特色，促使猶太人顛沛流離 2000 年後得以建國，也是他們創新精神的基礎。

這次經驗像開啟了她的開關，讓她變得更加勇敢，不再輕言放棄，也間接成為創業的催化劑。

創業成為「以台橋梁」促進文化交流

因為以色列鼓勵創新的環境，以致陳俞安周遭有許多以色列同儕退伍後就自己創業，身為恐懼失敗的台灣人，她曾問其中一名友人為何以色列年輕人如此踴躍創業，該名友人毫不猶豫地回答：「以色列人連國家都建立了，還怕建立事業嗎？」

短短一句話像一劑強心針打在陳俞安身上，因此在經歷部落客、演講和策展之後，她更加確信自己要透過創立個人品牌實踐想法。2019 年 7 月，「Ani Ann」誕生了，以希伯來文命名，意為「我是 Ann」。她希望透過服飾、帽子等生活常見小物，為以色列人和外國人之間搭起溝通的橋樑。

曾有一位美國客人因為穿戴 Ani Ann 走在路上，意外引起美國猶太人好奇，還因此成為朋友。這個故事激勵她開發出更多商品，也和以色列藝術家合作設計 T 恤，其中也包含台灣特色的小物，期許能藉此推廣台灣文化。未來她希望能在以色列拓展通路，也夢想著在台北開設實體店面。

一個過去沒有離開過台北的女孩，因為一趟旅程，對以色列人愛護自己歷史與傳統的程度印象深刻，所以開始試著像當初她初次造訪以色列那般，用純粹的觀光客視角，重新認識家鄉，還有自己。

她更深刻體悟很多事該計較的並非是否會無功而返，而是無憾無悔。

Designer

陳俞安 Ann 個人簡歷｜圖文部落客、策展人。台北藝術大學劇場設計系畢業，2017 年前往以色列耶路撒冷貝札雷藝術設計學院留學一年。曾於 2019 年策畫台灣第一個妥拉藝術文化展「妥拉－生命之道 淵遠流長」。現為文創品牌「Ani Ann」創辦人。

STEP 2
搜尋理想的學校

搜尋各校特色、要求的學業成績，挑選幾間與自己的預算、能力和需求符合的學校，並把學校要求記錄下來。

STEP 1
獲取好成績並保持下去

你一定知道該怎麼做！

STEP 3
準備邏輯能力考試

大多數的美國大學，都會要求申請者提供 SAT 或是 ACT 成績。申請研究所商學院者，會需要提供 GMAT 成績，其他科系者，需要提供 GRE 成績。

STEP 4
準備語言能力考試

一般來說，申請美國大學與研究所，皆要提供 TOEFL 成績。若要申請英國、澳洲、紐西蘭的大學與研究所，則需要提供 IELTS 分數。

準備時間
從入學起開始持續努力

準備時間
從入學兩年前即可開始

準備時間
從入學時間兩年前即須開始

準備時間
從入學時間一年半前

App

申請學校準備時間建議
Schedule for Applying to Schools

申請美國學校的程序多且繁雜，
稍一個不小心就可能錯過重要時間點，
這裡先以申請學校的各個關卡，配合申請與準備時間，
讓你能夠輕鬆通過申請學校各項流程！

8 STEP

錄取／拒絕入學通知

收到學校通知後，不論決定是否會去學校報到，基於禮貌，皆須通知學校。若不幸都被拒絕，則需考慮補申請其他學校，例如社區大學，或等半年～一年再出發。

6 STEP

推薦信

美國大學通常要求申請者提供 1～2 封推薦信，研究所則要求提供 3 封推薦信，仔細選擇和你較熟悉的推薦人，一般來說最好提供二個月的時間撰寫。

7 STEP

在線上申請

線上申請時，學校幾乎都會要求申請人填寫學經歷、回答問題、撰寫短文等，別忘了存檔，可供持續檢視和更改。

5 STEP

讀書計畫
（只有申請研究所者須提供）

讀書計畫的目的是，要讓審查員看出你未來在學業上的力，並告訴他們你是最適合的申請者。

通知時間

提早申請者，將於 1 月中～2 月中收到通知，需決定學校並回覆。2 月中～3 月：一般錄取者申請結果揭曉。

申請時間

大學部：前年 10～11 月，最晚該年 1 月中。研究所：12 月～1 月中。

準備時間

從入學時間一年前

準備時間

9 月底 10 月初即可請老師撰寫

第一章：**申請學校**

Lying to Schools

LESSON 1
Choosing the Right School
第一話：決定適合的學校

🎵 **001** | 好用句

🎵 **002** | 單字

Vocabulary Bank

1. **application** [ˌæpləˋkeʃən] (n.) 申請 (書)，**applicant** [ˋæplɪkənt] 為「申請人」
   Have you sent in your college applications yet?

2. **financial** [faɪˋnænʃəl] (a.) 金融的，財務的，名詞為 **finance** [ˋfaɪˌnæns] (n.) 金融，財務，財政
   There's a rumor that the company is having financial difficulties.

3. **valid** [ˋvælɪd] (a.) (法律上) 有效的，合法的，名詞為 **validity** [vəˋlɪdətɪ] 有效性，正確性
   It's illegal to drive without a valid driver's license.

4. **minimum** [ˋmɪnəməm] (a.) 最低限度的，最小量的
   The minimum purchase to qualify for the rebate is $100.

5. **visa** [ˋvizə] (n.) 簽證
   They won't let you on board an international flight without a visa.

6. **purchase** [ˋpɝtʃəs] (v./n.) 購買；購買，購買之物
   The couple purchased their first home after they got married.

7. **insurance** [ɪnˋʃʊrəns] (n.) 保險
   Auto insurance for young drivers is quite expensive.

8. **freshman** [ˋfrɛʃmən] (n./a.) (高中、大學) 一年級生 (的)
   I hear Anthony is dating a freshman.

美國各種大學與研究所的差異

	University - 大學		Liberal Arts College - 學院	Community College - 社區大學
	公立大學	私立大學		
GPA	大學最低標準：2.5 研究所最低標準：3.0 (不同排名之學校 GPA 要求不同)			無 GPA 要求 (有高中畢業 / 高中同等學歷即可)
托福成績	80-100 左右 (不同排名之學校分數要求不同)			61 分
SAT(大學)	美國 TOP 100 學校：1200-1600			—
GRE/ GMAT(研究所)	GRE：150-170 GMAT：640-750 (不同學校不同科系不同標準)			—
上課人數	100-200 人 (不同課程人數不同)			10-30 人
費用	(大) $25,000-$47,000/ 年 (研) $20,000 - $40,000/ 年	(大) $30,000-$55,000/ 年 (研) $40,000-$60,000	$17,000-$25,000/ 年	$8,000-$15,000/ 年
課程難易度	★★★★★	★★★★★	★★★★	★★

我的 GPA 可以申請什麼學校

GPA 3.7 以上：可申請到美國 TOP50 學校。除了 GPA 之外，較好的托福、SAT 成績和豐富的課外活動背景 (義工、獎項、比賽、社團等) 也是學校錄取必看的資料。但相較於申請大學，申請研究所時課外活動沒有那麼重要。

GPA 3.0-3.7：可申請到美國 TOP50-100 學校。若想申請 TOP 50 左右學校，建議多做一些有意義的課外活動來彌補 GPA 上的不足。若某方面特別優秀，甚至如果得過獎，那麼申請到 TOP 30 學校也不是不可能。申請研究所者，GPA 最低需達 3.0。

GPA 3.0 以下：可申請到 TOP100 左右學校。若某方面特別優秀，例如，鋼琴比賽全國冠軍、國際象棋全國冠軍等，也是有機會申請到 TOP 50 以上學校的。建議如果 GPA 較低，又沒有優秀背景的學生，可先讀社區大學，努力補足 GPA 後再去申請插四年制大學大三。

Common Phrases | 詢問學校問題，你要會寫 / 說

1. Does your school accept the Common [1]**Application**?

貴校接受通用申請嗎？

2. Can international students apply for [2]**financial** aid/scholarships?

國際學生可以申請學費補助 / 獎學金嗎？

3. Are international students required to take the *SAT or *ACT?

國際學生是否必須考學術水準測驗考試或美國大學入學考試？

4. How long is a *TOEFL/*IELTS score [3]**valid**?

托福 / 雅思成績的有效期限有多長？

5. Does your school have a [4]**minimum** *GRE/*GMAT score?

貴校是否有研究生入學考試成績的最低標準？

6. Can international students work on campus?

國際學生是否能在校園打工？

7. What should I do to get a student (F-1) [5]**visa**?

我要如何取得學生（F-1）簽證？

8. Do I need to [6]**purchase** health [7]**insurance**?

我是否需要購買健康保險？

Common Phrases | 學校問題回覆，你要看 / 聽得懂

1. We accept the Common Application for [8]**freshman** [9]**admission** only.

我們只接受新生入學的通用申請。

2. Yes. Financial aid/scholarship information is available on our International Student Resources web page.

是的。國際學生資源網站上可找到學費補助 / 獎學金的資料。

3. SAT and ACT scores aren't required, but they may increase your chance of admission.

不需要 SAT 和 ACT 成績，但可能增加錄取機會。

4. TOEFL/IELTS scores are valid for two years.

托福 / 雅思成績的有效期限是兩年。

5. The GRE is only required for Masters programs, and there is no minimum score.

GRE 只適用於申請碩士班，而且沒有最低成績標準。

6. After you [10]**submit** your financial [11]**documents**, we'll send you the I-20 Form and visa application instructions.

在提交財力證明後，我們會將 I-20 表格和簽證申請說明寄給你。

7. Yes, all international students are required to have health insurance.

是的，所有國際學生都必須購買健康保險。

---

9. **admission** [əd`mɪʃən] (n.) 入學，進入許可，當動詞為 **admit** [əd`mɪt] 允許進入

Betsy gained admission to one of Taiwan's top universities.

10. **submit** [səb`mɪt] (v.) 呈送，提交，投稿，名詞為 **submission** [səb`mɪʃən] 提交，呈遞

All applications must be submitted by September 30.

11. **document** [`dɑkjəmənt] (n.) 文件

What documents are required to apply for a student visa?

補充字彙

* **SAT** [ˌɛs.e`ti] (n.) 全名為 **Standard Assessment Test**，即「美國學術水準測驗考試」，美國大學入學考試的一種

* **ACT** [`e.si.ti] (n.) 全名為 **American College Testing**，即「美國大學入學測驗」，一般做為美國各大學申請入學的參考條件之一

* **TOEFL** [`tofəl] (n.) 全名為 **Test of English as a Foreign Language**，又稱為托福考試，大多數的美國大學或研究所要求外國學生在申請時提出

* **IELTS** [`aɪlts] (n.) 全名為 **International English Language Testing System**，又稱為雅思考試，大多數英國、澳洲等大學或研究所要求外國學生在申請時提出

* **GRE** [`dʒi.ɑr.i] (n.) 全名為 **Graduate Record Examinations**，又稱為美國研究生入學考試

* **GMAT** [`dʒi.mæt] (n.) 全名為 **Graduate Management Admission Test**，又稱為研究生管理科入學考試，是測試商學院申請學生能力的考試

CHAPTER 1

申請學校

Applying to Schools

🎵 003 | 對話

🎵 004 | 單字

Vocabulary Bank

1. **probably** [ˋprɑ.bə.blɪ] (adv.)
   大概，很可能
   I think that candidate will probably win the election.

2. **economics** [ˌɛkəˋnɑmɪks] (n.) 經濟 (學)，經濟狀況
   William wants to pursue a major in economics.

3. **relative** [ˋrɛlətɪv] (n.) 親屬
   How often do you get together with your relatives?

4. **selective** [səˋlɛktɪv] (a.)
   選擇性的，挑剔的
   Harvard has a highly selective admissions process.

5. **backup** [ˋbæk͵ʌp] (a.) 備用的，
   backup plan 即「備案」
   It's wise to always have a backup plan.

Talking colleges
談論大學

(Joseph, a Taiwanese high-school student, is talking to his American friend Lisa)

Joseph With my GPA, do you think I can get accepted to a good college in the U.S.?

Lisa Let's see. You have a 3.6 GPA, which is pretty good. You could [1]**probably** get into a top 100 school, and maybe a top 50 school if your SAT or ACT score is high enough.

Joseph I got a 1330 the first time I took the SAT. I just retook it, but I haven't got the results yet.

Lisa Good. Your score should be higher the second time. Do you have any idea what major you'd like to pursue?

Joseph Yes. I'm really interested in [2]**economics**. I'm also hoping to study in California, because I have a lot of [3]**relatives** there.

Lisa Well, the schools in the UC system all have good economics programs. The minimum GPA is 3.4, but most students have much higher grades, so you'll have to get a high SAT score. And I see you're taking two AP courses, which could also raise your GPA.

Joseph How about USC? Isn't it easier to get into?

Lisa That used to be true, but it's much more [4]**selective** these days. If you want a [5]**backup** plan, you can also apply to some Cal State schools. Cal Poly and San Diego State both have good economics programs.

Joseph So Cal State schools are easier to get into?

Lisa Yes. You should have no problem getting into one.

約瑟夫	以我的平均成績來看，你覺得我能被美國的好大學錄取嗎？
麗莎	來看看，你的平均成績是 3.6，還不錯。你應該可以進前一百大學校，你的 SAT 或 ACT 成績夠高的話，或許能進前五十大。
約瑟夫	我第一次考 SAT 時的成績是 1330 分，我剛重考了，但還沒收到成績單。
麗莎	很好，你第二次的成績應該會更高。你對主修有什麼想法嗎？
約瑟夫	有，我對經濟學很有興趣。我也希望能到加州念書，因為我在那裡有很多親戚。
麗莎	加州大學系統各分校的經濟學課程都很棒。最低 GPA 要求是 3.4 分，但大部分學生的成績更高，所以你的 SAT 成績必須高些。我看到你在修兩堂大學先修課程，這應該也能提高你的 GPA。
約瑟夫	南加州大學怎麼樣呢？那不是比較容易錄取嗎？
麗莎	以前確實是，但他們最近更會擇優錄取。你若想要有備用計畫，也可以申請一些加州州立大學。加州州立理工大學和聖地牙哥州大都有不錯的經濟學課程。
約瑟夫	所以加州州立大學會比較容易錄取嗎？
麗莎	沒錯，你想進任何一所分校應該都沒問題。

college 和 university 的不同

這兩個字翻譯成中文都是「大學」，但在美國，大家一般說到「大學」都會說 college。college 除了有大學的意思之外，還有學院的意思，一般來說，是比較小型的學校，其中包含二年制的社區大學 (community college)，授予副學士的學位 (associate degree)，還有一般的四年制大學，授予學士學位 (bachelor's degree)，只有少部分的學校提供碩士學位 (master's degree)。

而 university 則是由多個不同的 college 和研究所所組成的學校，且有提供碩士以上的學位，不只著重教學，也要從事研究計畫。除此之外，四年制 college 與研究性大學的不同點在於，它常被稱為文理大學 (liberal arts college)，這種學校注重通識教育及全人能力，多數學生必須住宿，以便參與學校各項活動，發展人際關係。學校不以培養學生的單一學科專業、技職能力為考量，不會特別教授職場相關的實用課程。

培養菁英課程 (American Honors) 是什麼？

American Honors 是社區大學裡面的一種項目，主要是培養優秀人才的課程。它跟普通社區大學裡提供的學科項目是一樣的，不過他們的學費比起一般社區大學的學費來的要高，原因是他們擁有最優秀的師資，課程也比一般課程來得靈活、有挑戰性，其主要目的是為了培養學生能夠更靈活地思考、解決一些問題。且由於 American Honors 的課程難度較高，所以比起其他學生，更容易被學校錄取。

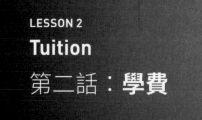

LESSON 2

Tuition

第二話：學費

Vocabulary Bank

1. **tuition** [tuˋɪʃən] (n.) **學費**
   Students held a protest against the tuition increase.

2. **attendance** [əˋtɛndəns] (n.)
   出席，上課，就讀
   The costs of college attendance rise every year.

3. **installment** [ɪnˋstɔlmənt] (n.) **分期付款**
   We're paying for our car in monthly installments.

4. **payment** [ˋpemənt] (n.)
   付款，支付款項
   Payment is due on the first of every month.

5. **deadline** [ˋdɛd͵laɪn] (n.)
   最後期限，截止日期
   Be sure not to miss the application deadline.

6. **eligible** [ˋɛlɪdʒəbəl] (a.)
   合乎資格的
   With your grades, you should be eligible for a scholarship.

7. **assistance** [əˋsɪstəns] (n.)
   幫助，協助
   If I can be of any assistance, just let me know.

8. **loan** [lon] (n./v.) **貸款，借款**
   It's hard to get a loan when you have bad credit.

美國各區與各大城市的學費差異

　　美國大學學費最大的決定因素是大學的性質，一般來說公立學校學費會低於私立學校，公立學校學費在 1-2 萬美金之間，私立學校平均在 2.5 萬 -4.5 萬美金之間。

　　而美國大學學費大致可分為幾個級別：

	第一級大學	第二級大學	第三級大學	第四級大學
學費範圍	4 萬美金以上	2.2 萬 -2.5 萬美金	1.5 萬 -1.9 萬美金	1 萬美金以下

赴美念書較省錢的方法

　　前面的單元有提到台灣有提供公費留學考試、公費留學獎學金、教育部學海計畫補助等，若你的成績優異（GPA 3.7 以上），可以考慮於入學時，同時申請獎學金。另外也可先就讀和你想進入的大學合作有轉學合作協定的社區大學，先拿共同科目（general education）。剩下的科目可上以下網站 https://assist.org/，挑選你現在的學校，以及想上的學校，就會顯示出現在社區大學的課，等同於大學的哪些課程。

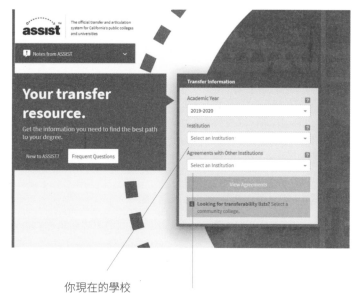

你現在的學校

你想就讀的學校

Common Phrases | 詢問學校學費問題，你要會寫／說

1. What are the [1]**tuition** rates for international students? 　國際學生的學費是多少？

2. What is the total cost of [2]**attendance**? 　就讀的總花費是多少？

3. Can I pay my tuition in [3]**installments**? 　學費可以分期付款嗎？

4. What are the [4]**payment** [5]**deadlines** for tuition and fees? 　學雜費的最後繳交期限是何時？

5. Can I request a ***deferral** for tuition and fees? 　我可以要求延後繳交學雜費嗎？

6. What forms of payment are accepted? 　學校接受哪些付款方式？

Common Phrases | 詢問機構獎助學金問題，你要會寫／說

1. Are international students [6]**eligible** for ***work-study**? 　國際學生有資格參加工讀計畫嗎？

2. Can international students apply for scholarships/***fellowships**? 　國際學生可申請獎學金和研究生獎學金嗎？

3. Does your school provide [7]**assistance** in finding financial aid? 　貴校會協助學生尋求學費補助嗎？

4. Will applying for financial aid affect my chance of admission? 　申請學費補助會影響我的錄取機會嗎？

5. Are there [8]**loans** available for international students? 　有適合國際學生的貸款嗎？

6. Can I apply for financial aid after I've been admitted? 　我被錄取後可申請學費補助嗎？

補充字彙

* **deferral** [dɪˋfɝrəl] (n.) 延遲，延後

* **work-study** [ˋwɝk.stʌdi] (n./a.) 工讀；半工半讀的

* **fellowship** [ˋfɛlo.ʃɪp] (n.) （給研究生等的）獎學金

國際學生可以申請美國當地的學費補助嗎？

美國聯邦政府對於美國公民與持有綠卡者可提供學費補助 (financial aid)，又稱為 FAFSA，不過學生需要自行申請，補助分為三種，包括助學金 (grant) 不須歸還、學生貸款 (student loan) 要歸還，以及 work-study 在校內打工。但很可惜的是，國際學生通常無法申請上面的學費補助，只能於在校一年後，申請在校打工。不過別灰心，各個機構也有推出不同的獎學金，請見 TaiwanGPS 全球獎學金地圖，http://bit.ly/2BGgSFh，上面提供各公私立機構提供的獎學金。

英文成績未達學校標準，該怎麼辦？

你可以先上語言學校，期間邊考 TOEFL，考到以後就可以申請大學，或直接就讀社區大學。有些社區大學有附設語言學校，只要通過校內英文語言考試，即可免托福上此社區大學。許多社區大學和四年制大學有達成轉學合作協定（Transfer Admission Guarantee，又稱為 TAG），意味著學生畢業後如果想繼續深造進修，可轉學分進入四年制大學繼續後兩年的大學課程，從而確保社區大學的學分可以在四年制學位中抵掉。

♫ 007 | 對話

♫ 008 | 單字

Vocabulary Bank

1. **figure out** (phr.) 想辦法，搞懂
   Did you figure out how to use
   the new printer?

2. **sophomore** [ˋsɑf.mor] (n.)
   (高中、大學) 二年級生 (的)
   Our daughter is a sophomore
   in high school.

補充字彙

* **in-state** [ˋɪn.stet] (a.) 本州的

* **out-of-state** [ˋautəv.stet](a.)
  州外的

* **pay one's way** (phr.) 自行支
  付費用

Tuition isn't cheap
學費可真貴

(Casey, a high-school student, is talking on the phone to her cousin, Raymond in the U.S.)

Raymond	Hey, I hear you're going to apply to study in the U.S. after you finish high school.
Casey	Yeah, but it's gonna be expensive. You pay less because you have a U.S. passport, right?
Raymond	Actually, most schools charge the same tuition for foreign students.
Casey	But didn't you say your tuition at UT was around 10,000 dollars? My classmate's older sister goes there, and she says she pays over 30,000.
Raymond	Well, that's the difference between *in-state and *out-of-state tuition. Someone from another state would also pay the higher tuition.
Casey	Oh. It's still a lot of money though. My parents are trying to [1]figure out how to pay for it.
Raymond	At least your parents are going to pay for your education. I've paid most of my tuition by working part-time.
Casey	I'd like to help *pay my way too, but I can't work legally until my [2]sophomore year—and I can only get a job on campus.

雷蒙	嘿，聽說你高中畢業後要申請到美國念書。
凱西	對，但學費一定很貴。你有美國護照，所以學費會比較低，對吧？
雷蒙	其實大部分學校對外國學生收取的學費都一樣。
凱西	但你在德州大學的學費不是大約一萬元嗎？我同學的姊姊也去那裡念，她說她的學費超過三萬元。
雷蒙	這是因為德州本地學生和外地學生的學費不一樣。來自外州的學生也要付較高的學費。
凱西	噢，但還是很貴。我父母正在想辦法怎麼付這筆學費。
雷蒙	至少你的父母要替你付學費。我要打工付我大部分的學費。
凱西	我也要幫忙自己付學費，但我要等到大二才能合法工作，而且我只能在校園裡找工作。

國際學生可以向學校申請獎學金嗎？

　　一般來說公立學校提供給國際學生的獎學金項目比私立學校來的少。國際學生可以向想進去的學校申請獎學金，但要先評估一下自己的能力，若有持續穩定的學業表現（3.45 以上），課外活動也多，也能撰寫出很厲害的 statement of purpose，其實可以申請，反之，不要申請獲得入學許可的機會較高。

　　入學獎學金分為學術成就獎學金 (merit-based scholarship) 和自身需求獎學金 (need-based scholarship)，自身需求獎學金又分為 (need-blind) 這類學校不會去看學生是否有申請獎學金來做為是否接受入學申請，通常為資金雄厚的學校，以及 need-aware 這類學校會以申請人是否申請獎學金作為錄取參考。不過關於各校的獎學金或補助標準，請上各校網站的 Admission（入學許可）頁面確認最準確。

01 與想申請之學校聯絡

索取獎學金申請相關資料

02 準備申請資料

申請表、財力證明、TOEFL 等必要考試成績、推薦信、學校成績單、簡歷、讀書機會、學歷證明等

03 繼續與學校保持聯絡

有些學校申請人較多，如資料不完整，學校可能不會通知補充資料，所以學生最好主動詢問校方資料是否有送達、是否有齊全、是否有需要補充哪些文件、審理進度等

04 等待獎學金審理結果及錄取通知

校方得出結果後會以書函形式通知你，並告之你金額多少等信息。學生應慎重考慮後盡快回覆學校是否接受獎學金及錄取通知。

LESSON 3
Other Fees
第三話：其他費用

🎵 009｜好用句

🎵 010｜單字

Vocabulary Bank

1. **dorm** [dɔrm] (n.) **宿舍，為 dormitory** [ˈdɔrmɪˌtori] 的簡稱

   Would you rather live in the dorms or rent an apartment?

2. **housing** [ˈhauzɪŋ] (n.) **住宅，住宿**

   The villagers were moved to temporary housing after the typhoon.

3. **residence** [ˈrɛzɪdəns] (n.) **住宅，官邸，residence hall** 為「**學生宿舍**」

   Which residence hall do you live in?

4. **listing** [ˈlɪstɪŋ] (n.) **列表（的一項），一覽表**

   That website has good restaurant listings.

5. **rental** [ˈrɛntəl] (n./a.) **租賃，出租，租賃的房屋**

   How expensive are rentals in this neighborhood?

6. **transportation** [ˌtrænspɚˈteʃən] (n.) **運輸，交通工具**

   Using public transportation is cheaper than owning a car.

7. **search engine** (phr.) **搜尋引擎**

   DuckDuckGo is my favorite search engine.

美國住宿費用比較表

	on-campus housing 學校宿舍	off-campus housing/sublet 校外租屋 / 分租	homestay 寄宿家庭
價位	約 $3000-$7500（9個月）	約 $3600-$7200/ 年	$500-$900/ 月
適合族群	剛入學新生	想提供自理能力、希望擁有獨立空間的學生	想學習語言的學生
優缺點	優點：學校提供伙食、宿舍提供休閒活動交流區、離學校近、寒暑假不住無須付房租。缺點：無獨立空間、寒暑假需依照學校規定時間離開 / 搬離宿舍。	優點：能擁有獨立空間、較自由、多人分租較便宜。缺點：大部分不提供基本家具（床、沙發、桌子等）、寒暑假不住也需付房租。	優點：快速提高英文能力、盡快融入當地生活、負責三餐。缺點：需尊重主人隱私及生活習慣、沒那麼自由。
備註		屋況、地理位置、不同房型及入住人數會影響房租價位。建議可與多人分租 (sublet) 較便宜。	

其他交通費比一比

● 學生交通費平均 $100-$200/ 月，有些學校有與當地公車公司配合則免費。

● 交通費波動性較大，因除了一些大城市外，其他城市是沒有地鐵的，公車也不一定方便，所以大部分人會買車。如買車，保險和油也是一筆不小的開銷。

Common Phrases | 詢問學校住宿問題，你要會寫／說

1. Would it be cheaper to stay in a [1]**dorm** or live ***off-campus**? 　住在校內宿舍還是住在校外比較便宜？

2. Do I need to pay a deposit to reserve a dorm room? 　預定宿舍需要付押金嗎？

3. Can the [2]**housing** fee be paid in installments? 　住宿費可以分期付款嗎？

4. Do most students live ***on-campus** their first year? 　請問是否大多數的新生第一年都住校？

5. Is it possible to stay in the [3]**residence hall** during summer break? 　暑假時可以待在學校宿舍嗎？

6. Do you have photos of the different room types available? 　有不同宿舍房間格局的照片可以參考嗎？

7. Are the residence halls quiet/safe? Are there security officers? 　請問學校內宿舍是否安全／安靜，晚上是否會有巡邏人員查看？

Common Phrases | 詢問校外租屋費用問題，你要會寫／說

1. Is it easy to find a room/apartment off-campus? 　在校外尋找雅房／公寓容易嗎？

2. Does your housing office provide [4]**listings** for off-campus [5]**rentals**? 　學生住宿中心是否會提供校外租房資訊？

3. Are there any resources for finding shared rentals? 　是否會提供尋找合租的資源？

4. Which neighborhoods are easiest to reach by public [6]**transportation**? 　哪些社區搭大眾運輸最方便？

5. Is it safe to live off-campus? Which neighborhoods are safest? 　住在校外安全嗎？哪些社區最安全？

6. Is there a [7]**search engine** where I can look for houses within my budget/based on my [8]**criteria**? 　有什麼搜尋引擎可以根據我的預算／條件尋找住房？

---

8. **criteria** [kraɪ`tɪrɪə] (n.) （判斷的）標準、準則、尺度，為 **criterion** [kraɪ`tɪrɪən] 的複數

   Every applicant who meets our criteria will be considered for the position.

補充字彙

* **off-campus** [`ɑf.kæmpəs] (a.) 在校外

* **on-campus** [`ɑn.kæmpəs] (a.) 在校內

其他生活費比一比

特大城市
代表城市：紐約、舊金山、洛杉磯、波士頓、華盛頓、芝加哥
生活費：$1000-$2000/月

大城市
代表城市：匹茲堡、西雅圖、拉達斯、亞特蘭大、奧斯汀、底特律
生活費：$800-$1000/月

南部、中西部、東南部
代表地區：德州、威斯康星州、依利諾州、密西根州、猶他州、科羅拉多州、喬治亞州、維吉尼亞州、北卡羅來納州
生活費：$600-$800/月

其他地區
代表地區：俄克拉荷馬州、密蘇里州、路易斯安納州、南卡羅來納州
生活費：$450-$600/月

CHAPTER 1

申請學校

Applying to Schools

🎵 011 | 對話＋好用句

🎵 012 | 單字

Vocabulary Bank

1. **pro** [pro] (n.) 優點，優勢
   What are the pros of owning a car?

2. **con** [kɑn] (n.) 缺點，不利條件
   We need to look at the pros and cons of each choice.

3. **hassle** [ˋhæsəl] (n.) 麻煩，困難
   Driving in bad weather is such a hassle.

4. **definitely** [ˋdɛfənɪtli] (adv.) 一定地，絕對地
   I'm definitely going to the concert.

5. **pricey** [ˋpraɪsɪ] (a.) 昂貴的
   The restaurant's a little pricey, but the food is delicious.

6. **overpriced** [ˌovɚˋpraɪst] (a.) 價錢過高的
   Everything in that boutique is overpriced.

7. **all-you-can-eat** (a.) 吃到飽的
   I stuffed myself at the all-you-can-eat buffet.

補充字彙

* **astronomical** [ˌæstrəˋnɑmɪkəl] (口) 非常昂貴的

---

① Living on- or off-campus
住在校內宿舍或校外

(Samuel, a college student, is asking Victoria in the U.S., for some advice.)

Samuel　I'm having trouble deciding whether to live on- or off-campus when I go to the U.S. for grad school. Any advice?

Victoria　Well, both have their ¹⁾**pros** and ²⁾**cons**. If you live off-campus, you have more choices and freedom, but finding a good apartment can be a ³⁾**hassle**.

Samuel　How about living in a grad dorm?

Victoria　Well, I **learned the hard way**. During my first year of grad school, I rented an apartment because I wanted the freedom.

Samuel　And you regretted your decision?

Victoria　⁴⁾**Definitely**. It wasn't cheap, and I had to waste a lot of time on transportation.

Samuel　So did you move to a grad dorm in your second year?

Victoria　Yes, and I loved it. It was close to classes and the library, so I had a lot more time to study.

薩米爾　我要到美國念研究所，但我很難決定要住在校內宿舍或校外，妳有什麼建議嗎？

維多莉亞　嗯，各有利弊。若是住在校外，你有更多選擇和自由，但想找到好公寓是件麻煩事。

薩米爾　那住在研究所宿舍呢？

維多莉亞　我吃了些苦頭才學到。我念研究所第一年時，我在校外租公寓，因為我想要自由。

薩米爾　妳後悔這個決定了嗎？

維多莉亞　確實。租金不便宜，而且我浪費了許多時間在交通上。

薩米爾　所以妳第二年搬進研究所宿舍了嗎？

維多莉亞　對，而且我很滿意。宿舍距離教室和圖書館都很近，所以我有更多時間念書。

1. Housing prices in in San Francisco are ***astronomical**!
   舊金山的房價太高。

2. Renting an apartment will **cost an arm and a leg**.
   租公寓費用很貴。

3. Bus fares are steep compared to Taiwan.
   公車票價和台灣比起來偏高。

4. Meals at restaurants around here are pretty 5)**pricey**.
   這裡附近餐廳的餐點很貴。

5. The meal plan at the dorm seems 6)**overpriced**.
   宿舍的餐點方案看起來偏貴。

School meal plans
學校餐飲計畫

(Amelia, a prospective college student, is asking her American friend, Jacob, for some tips.)

Amelia　Aside from tuition and housing, what was your biggest expense in grad school?

Jacob　I'd have to say meals. I was on the meal plan, and it cost over $2,000 dollars a semester.

Amelia　Was that for three meals a day?

Jacob　Well, I was on the full plan, which includes unlimited meals. They also had cheaper plans that include a certain number of meals a week.

Amelia　Is the food any good?

Jacob　It's a lot better than the cafeteria food we had in grade school, but it can get boring after a while.

Amelia　Are the meals 7)**all-you-can-eat**?

Jacob　Yes, so it's easy to gain weight. You really have to watch what you eat—especially the desserts!

艾米莉亞　除了學費和住宿，你在研究所最大的開銷是什麼？

雅各　應該是伙食費。我加入餐飲計畫，一學期花費超過兩千美元。

艾米莉亞　包含一天三餐嗎？

雅各　我加入的是全餐計畫，餐數沒有限制。他們也有比較便宜的計畫，一星期有固定的餐數。

艾米莉亞　伙食好嗎？

雅各　比我們在小學食堂的伙食還好，但吃了一陣子後就膩了。

艾米莉亞　那裡的飯菜都是任你吃到飽的嗎？

雅各　對，所以很容易發胖。你真的要酌量吃，尤其是甜點！

---

learn (sth.) the hard way
從錯誤和不好的經驗中學習，讓自己了解情況或發展技巧

A: I told Sam to apply to more than one school, but he didn't listen.
我告訴過山姆一次多申請幾所大學，但他就是不聽。

B: That's not very smart. I guess he'll have to **learn the hard way**.
那實在不是很明智，我想他只好從錯誤中學習了。

cost an arm and a leg
非常昂貴

A: Did you have to take out a student loan?
你有申請學生貸款嗎？

B: Yeah. Tuition **costs an arm and a leg** these days.
有啊，現在學費超貴的。

其他隱藏費用

● **消費稅** (sales tax/consumption tax)：在美國，商品的標價都不是你最後付錢的價格，而是還要再加上額外的消費稅。

● **小費** (tip)：在美國需要付小費的場合很多。例如，按摩、剪頭髮、餐廳、飯店等，基本上被「服務超過 5 分鐘」的職業大部分都是需要付小費的。以這種邏輯來判斷的話，速食店、餐廳外帶、超市結帳這種的都是不需要給小費的。

● **醫療費**：雖然學校有強制就保的醫療保險，不過大部分並不能涵蓋所有就診的費用。

● **額外租房費**：美國租屋有時需要經過信用背景調查，所以有些房東會收取申請費來做信用調查。此外，由於新國際學生並無信用紀錄，所以一般房東會向你收取高額的押金來保障自己。

LESSON 4
Résumé
第四話：履歴

🎵 013 | 單字

Vocabulary Bank

1. **résumé** [ˋrɛzʊˌme] (n.)
   履歷，簡歷
   An internship will look good on your résumé.

2. **objective** [əbˋdʒɛktɪv] (n.)
   目的，目標
   My objective this semester is to improve my grades.

3. **accounting** [əˋkaʊntɪŋ] (n.)
   會計
   Carol wants to study accounting in college and become an accountant.

4. **analysis** [əˋnæləsɪs] (n.)
   分析
   This problem requires further analysis.

5. **administration** [ədˌmɪnəˋstreʃən] (n.)
   行政、管理（人員），business administration 即「企業管理」
   Kevin has a degree in business administration.

6. **major** [ˋmedʒɚ] (n./v.)
   主修科目；以⋯為主修
   William wants to pursue a major in economics.

7. **minor** [ˋmaɪnɚ] (n./v.)
   輔修科目；以⋯為輔修
   I majored in chemistry with a minor in biology.

履歷範本

Chang, Wen-hao

5F, No. 53, Sec. 2, Jinshan S. Rd.,
Taipei City 10603 Taiwan

changwenhao@yahoo.com.tw
Phone: +886-2-2466-9743

[2)]**OBJECTIVE**

[A1] To complete a Master's degree in [3)]**accounting** and [A2] pursue a career in financial management or financial [4)]**analysis** at a major international firm in Taiwan

EDUCATION

[B1] **National Taiwan University (NTU)**, Taipei, Taiwan — Sep. 2014 – June 2018
Bachelor of Business [5)]**Administration**
● [6)]**Major**: Accounting, [7)]**Minor**: Finance; GPA: 3.6

PROFESSIONAL HISTORY

[B2] **GigaMedia Limited**, Taipei, Taiwan — June 2018 – present
Accounting Assistant
● [8)]**Reconcile** account [9)]**balances**: accounts ***receivable**, accounts ***payable**, cash accounts
● Prepare monthly projected ***cash flow** and ***income statements**
● Receive and organize sales ***invoices** and official receipts
● Prepare company and ensure [10)]**prompt** payment of employee benefits

[11)]**EXTRACURRICULAR ACTIVITIES**

[12)]**Undergraduate Student Association, Dept. of Accounting, NTU** — Sep. 2017 – June 2018
[C1] [13)]*Chairperson*
● Planned and [14)]**coordinated** large-scale student activities
● Led meetings and managed communications with other student associations

[15)]**Affiliated Senior High School of National Taiwan Normal University**, Taipei, Taiwan

Tutor — Sep. 2015 – Jun 2016
● [C2] Tutored [16)]**disadvantaged** students in math and Chinese

HONORS & AWARDS

[17)]**Presidential** Award (3 times) in Department of Accounting, NTU — 2016 - 2018
Membership in the Phi Tau Phi Scholastic Honor Society — 2017

SKILLS

[C3] [18)]**Fluent** in Mandarin and Taiwanese, good command of spoken and written English
[19)]**Proficient** in MS Excel, MS PowerPoint, QuickBooks

（人物為虛構）

英文版本

Résumé 是什麼？和 CV 有什麼不同？

一般來說 résumé 是履歷表，CV（又稱 Curriculum Vitae）和 résumé 差不多，只是 CV 上會有更多學術能力證明（academic credentials）、研究工作（research work）、學術論文（academic papers）等。

一般來說，履歷的長度為一頁，要讓人在一頁中看完你的個人資歷。許多學校為線上申請，不過還是會有些學校要求紙本。在請推薦人幫忙寫推薦信時，多半會一併提供 résumé 或 CV，讓推薦人更認識你，才能寫出最有力的推薦。

寫作重點

A. 請先表明你的申請目的，若已經決定了主修也可寫上，還可包括自己未來工作上的目標。

例如：

—— A1 To complete a Master's degree in accounting →主修

—— A2 pursue a career in financial management or financial analysis at a major international firm in Taiwan →未來的工作目標

B. 一般來說，都會先放最高學歷（education），剩下的項目，就看你要申請的是大學還是研究所，若是研究所，且已經有工作經驗，可以把就業經驗（professional history）放在最前面，然後再列出剩下的其他活動。

例如：

—— B1 **National Taiwan University (NTU)**, Taipei, Taiwan, Bachelor of Business Administration →此申請者，目前為止的最高學歷為大學學士

—— B2 **GigaMedia Limited** →曾在 GigaMedia 的工作和所申請科系最為相關，同時也是最近期的工作，所以列出

C. 其他項目，包括：課外活動（extracurricular activities）、得過的獎項（Honors and Awards）、社區服務（Community Service）、其他培訓（Additional Training）等。

例如：

—— 列出的細項中，最好大部分的項目和你申請的科系相關，當然成績好是一定有幫助的。沒有直接相關，也可以有間接的關係，如：當過數學家教 C2 就表示數學能力頗受肯定，對申請會計系有幫助，另外申請者還展現出優秀的領導 C1 與語文 C3 能力，更是加分！

8. **reconcile** [ˈrɛkənˌsaɪl] (v.) 使一致，對帳

   Who's in charge of reconciling accounts?

9. **balance** [ˈbæləns] (n.)（帳戶）餘額，結餘，權衡，斟酌

   The balance in my bank account is getting low.

10. **prompt** [prɑmpt] (a.) 及時的，準時的

    Employees should be prompt in dealing with complaints.

11. **extracurricular** [ˌɛkstrəkəˈrɪkjələ] (a.) 課外的，課餘的，curricular [kəˈrɪkjələ] 為「課程的」

    I don't have time for extracurricular activities this semester.

12. **undergraduate** [ˌʌndəˈgrædʒuɪt] (n./a.) 大學生（的），graduate [ˈgrædʒuɪt] 即「研究生」

    All undergraduates are required to take at least one science course.

13. **chairperson** [ˈtʃɛrˌpɜsən] (n.) 主席

    The chairperson called a meeting of the committee.

14. **coordinate** [koˈɔrdəˌnet] (v.) 協調

    The work will go faster if we coordinate our efforts.

15. **affiliated** [əˈfɪliˌetɪd] (a.) 相關附屬的

    I plan to study medicine at the university's affiliated medical school.

16. **disadvantaged** [ˌdɪsədˈvæntɪdʒd] (a.) 處於劣勢的，處於不利地位的

    Many disadvantaged children drop out of school.

17. **presidential** [ˌprɛzɪˈdɛnʃəl] (a.) 總統的

    Did you vote in the last presidential election?

014 | 單字

Vocabulary Bank

18. **fluent** [ˋfluənt] (a.) (語言) 流利的

It takes years to become fluent in a foreign language.

19. **proficient** [prəˋfɪʃənt] (a.) 熟練的，精通的

Only proficient swimmers are allowed in the pool.

補充字彙

* **receivable** [rɪˋsivəbəl] (a.) 可接受的，應收的

* **payable** [ˋpeəbəl] (a.) 應付的，到期的

* **cash flow** (phr.) 現金流量

* **income statement** (phr.) 損益表

* **invoice** [ˋɪnvɔɪs] (n.) 發貨單，請款單

張文豪 　　　　　　　　　10603 台灣台北市
changwenhao@yahoo.com.tw 　金山南路二段 53 號 5 樓
電話：886-2-2466-9743

目標
完成會計碩士學位並在台灣的大型外商公司
從事金融管理或是金融分析的工作

教育

台灣大學 台灣台北市　　　　　　　2014 年 9 月 – 2018 年 6 月
企業管理學士
主修：會計，副修：金融；GPA: 3.6

工作經歷

核心超媒體 台灣台北市　　　　　　　　2018 年 6 月至今
會計助理

●定期對帳：應收帳款、應付帳款、現金帳目
●製作每月預計現金流量表和損益表
●收到和整理請款單和正式收據
●計算員工薪酬並確保準時發放員工福利款項

課外活動

臺灣大學會計系學生會　　　　　2017 年 9 月 –2018 年 6 月
主席
●策劃和協調大型學生活動
●主持會議，與其他學生會協調溝通

國立台灣師範大學附屬高級中學，台灣台北

家教　　　　　　　　　　　　2015 年 9 月 –2016 年 6 月
●輔導弱勢學生的數學和中文

榮譽與獎項

臺灣大學會計系總統獎（三次）　　　　2016 年 – 2018 年
斐陶斐榮譽學會會員　　　　　　　　　　　　2017 年

技能

國台語流利，英語說寫精通
精通微軟試算表、微軟投影片簡報軟體、
會計軟體 QuickBooks

（人物為虛構）

中文版本

Activities
第五話：課外活動

審查官究竟想看出什麼？

　　大學一般喜歡看到學生表現出他們在某些領域中的天賦或熱情，如果可以達到某種成就，例如比賽得獎之類的，那當然是最好，但並不是每個學生都可以找到自己的才能並發揮出來。這類的學生，學校想看到的是他們嘗試多種不同領域的活動，並為找到自己的興趣而努力。

　　每間學校著重的地方不一定相同。所以請先調查學校的特性與偏好，可以從學校網站觀察，以及和學長姊聊聊。

回答範本 1

Q: Briefly [1]**elaborate** on one of your extracurricular activities or work or **family responsibilities**. (50-150 words)* *

問題：請說明你從事的一項課外活動、工作或是家庭責任。（50-150 字內）

Because I always did well on [2]**essays**, in my junior year I decided to join the school paper. **B1** I soon found, however, that I didn't like writing articles about school affairs. And I wasn't very good at it either. But something about the [3]**chaos** of the newspaper office was exciting, so I [4]**stayed on**. **B2** I began assisting with whatever was needed, and discovered that I enjoyed helping the editor coordinate the schedules of the writers, photographer, designer and printer. In my senior year, **C1** I was given the title of [5]**production** manager. In that role, I did my best to help everybody work together to meet deadlines. We didn't always succeed, but I loved the challenge of making all the parts work together like a *well-oiled* machine. The office became a little less [3]**chaotic**, but the excitement was still there. This is when I began thinking about pursuing a management-related career.

由於我的作文一直成績不錯，在大三時我決定加入學校校刊社。然而我隨後發現，我並不喜歡撰寫學校大小事，而且我也並不擅長。但報社內的混亂卻非常刺激，所以我也繼續留在那裡。我開始協助處理需要協助的事務，發現我喜歡幫助編輯協調作者、攝影師、美編和印刷的進度。大四時，我的職稱為製作經理，我需要盡力幫每個人合作以在截稿前出書。我們並不是每次都能做到，但我熱愛讓每個部分合作無間的挑戰，就像上了油的機器。辦公室變得比較有條理，但仍舊刺激，這時我開始考慮也許自己應該從事管理職。

回答範本

---

015 | 單字

Vocabulary Bank

1. **elaborate (on)** [ɪˈlæbəˌret] (v.) 詳細說明，闡述
   Would you care to elaborate on that statement?

2. **essay** [ˈɛse] (n.) 短文，論文
   Mike got an A on his English essay.

3. **chaos** [ˈke.ɑs] (n.) 混亂，雜亂，**chaotic** [keˈɑtɪk] (a.) 即「混亂的，凌亂的」
   The country was in chaos after the war.

4. **stay on** (phr.) 繼續待下去，留下來
   After graduating, she stayed on at the college, working as a lecturer.

5. **production** [prəˈdʌkʃən] (n.) 製作，生產
   World coffee production is down this year.

6. **bass (guitar)** [bes] (n.) 貝斯吉他，低音提琴
   The band's lead singer also plays bass.

7. **ambitious** [æmˈbɪʃ.əs] (a.) 野心勃勃的，志向遠大的
   The company announced an ambitious growth plan.

8. **promotion** [prəˈmoʃən] (n.) 宣傳，促銷，推銷
   How much is our budget for advertising and promotion?

 016 | 單字

9. **venue** [ˋvɛnju] (n.) **表演、運動比賽、會議等活動的場地**
Staples Center is the largest indoor entertainment venue in L.A.

10. **bulletin** [ˋbʊlətɪn] (n.) **公報，公告，bulletin board 即「佈告欄」**
The company publishes a weekly bulletin for employees.

11. **thrilled** [θrɪld] (a.) **極愉快的**
Becky was thrilled that so many people came to the party.

補充字彙

* **well-oiled** [͵welˋɔɪld] (a.) 運作順暢的

* **PA system** (n.) 有線廣播系統，為 public address system 的縮寫

* **word-of-mouth** [͵wɝdəv ˋmaʊθ] (a.) 口耳相傳

課外活動包含哪些？

告訴你申請的大學你曾經參加過的校外活動，可以幫它們更了解你的個人生活。這些活動的範例可能包括：藝術或音樂 (arts or music)、社團 (clubs)、社區參與 (community engagement)、家庭責任 (family responsibilities)、嗜好 (hobbies)、運動 (sports)、工作或義工 (work or volunteering)，以及其他對你有意義的經驗。

family responsibility 指的是什麼？

指的像是由於父母都在工作，所以照顧年幼的弟妹。這也可以用來解釋申請者花在從事課外活動比較少的原因。

回答範本 2

I started playing [6]**bass** in high school, and joined jazz club when I got better. I figured we would give a few performances on campus, but this was an [7]**ambitious** group. We decided to start giving off-campus performances, and everybody was given a task. I didn't know much about ***PA systems** or poster design, so I was in charge of [8]**promotion**. I created a Facebook fan page and placed our posters all over campus. **C2** But the crowd at our first performance was even smaller than the tiny [9]**venue**. **B3** So I worked with our designer to make better posters and flyers, and placed them at record stores, cafes and music clubs. I also designed online ads and posted them on music-related forums and the [10]**bulletin** boards of other high schools and colleges. **C2** I was [11]**thrilled** when crowds started getting bigger, but I like to think that ***word-of-mouth** played a role too!

我在高中的時候開始彈貝斯，當我越彈越好時，我加入了爵士樂社。我以為我們可能偶爾做校內演出，但社團的野心卻不僅止於此，我們決定開始做校外演出，且每個人都分配到任務。我對廣播系統或是海報設計不太了解，所以我負責宣傳。我架設了臉書粉絲專頁，並把我們的海報貼在學校各處。但來看我們首場演出的觀眾比小型劇場內可容納的人數還要少，所以我和美編一起設計更好的海報和傳單，並把它們放在唱片行、咖啡店和音樂展演場地，我也設計了網路廣告並把它們貼在音樂相關論壇以及其他高中和大學的電子公佈欄。當參與的觀眾越來越多時，我超級高興的，但我覺得口耳相傳可能也是因素之一！

回答範本

寫作重點

A. 不要廢話,盡量精簡,寫重點。

B. 寫經驗時,請寫自己從中學習到了什麼。

例如:

—— B1 I soon found, however, that I didn't like writing articles about school affairs. And I wasn't very good at it either.

→發現自己不喜歡、不擅長也是種學習與自我認知。

—— B2 I began assisting with whatever was needed, and ... photographer, designer and printer.

→路不轉,人轉。找到自己能做的事,何嘗不是種學習呢!

—— B3 So I worked with our designer to make better posters and flyers, and ... other high schools and colleges.

→找到需要改善的地方,並能夠調整方向,就算是學習!

C. 寫能夠表現出個人正面特質的經驗。

例如:

—— C1 I was given the title of production manager.

→從失敗中學習成長,表現出了自己愈挫愈勇與解決問題的能力。

—— C2 But the crowd at our first performance was even smaller than the tiny venue.... I was thrilled when crowds started getting bigger.

→具體的表達出自己遇到挫折後,因為自己的努力,而做的改變。

CHAPTER

申請學校

Applying to Schools

1

LESSON 6

Short Questions

第六話：簡短問題

017 | 單字

Vocabulary Bank

1. **mainland** [ˈmenˌlænd] (n.)
   大陸，本地
   Michael moved from Hawaii to the mainland United States.

2. **counselor** [ˈkaʊnsələ] (n.)
   輔導員，指導老師，諮商師
   The school counselor can help you explore different career options.

3. **recommendation**
   [ˌrɛkəmɛnˈdeʃən] (n.) **推薦**
   I'm looking for a USB drive under 30 dollars—do you have any recommendations?

4. **witness** [ˈwɪtnɪs] (v.) **目擊，證明**
   Dozens of people witnessed the accident.

5. **mechanic** [məˈkænɪk] (n.)
   技師，機械師
   The mechanic checked under the hood for loose connections.

6. **spark** [spɑrk] (v./n.) **點燃，激起；火花**
   It is believed that the forest fire was sparked by lightning.

7. **engineering** [ˌɛndʒəˈnɪrɪŋ]
   (n.) **工程，工程學**
   The position requires a degree in electrical engineering.

簡短問題

　　一般有字數限制，審查官想通過這些問題更了解你的想法，看看你跟學校理念是否適合，你獨特的人格特質，未來能否幫學校加分。

Q: What is the most significant challenge that society faces today? (50 word limit)*

問題：現今社會面臨的最重大挑戰是什麼？（50 字以內）

回答範本

In my view, **A1** the *proliferation of fake news is the most significant challenge facing the world today. In my country, for example, **B** as the Taiwan presidential election approaches, fake news stories from both [1] **mainland** China and within Taiwan are making it harder for voters to make informed decisions.

我認為，假新聞氾濫是現今世界面臨的最重大挑戰。例如在我國，隨著台灣總統大選即將來臨，來自中國大陸和台灣本地的假新聞使選民更難做出明智的決定。

回答範本

Q: How did you spend your last two summers? (50 word limit)*

問題：過去兩個暑假你是怎麼度過的？（50 字以內）

回答範本

回答範本：

A2 In 2017, I worked as a [2] **counselor** for a summer program that brings overseas Chinese college students (mostly from North America) to Taiwan to learn about Chinese language and culture. On the [3] **recommendation** of one of these students, in 2018 I attended a summer English program at UC Berkeley.

2017 年時，我在一項暑期營隊中擔任輔導員，該營隊由海外華人大學生（大部分來自北美）參加，到台灣學習中文和當地文化。在其中一位學生的推薦下，我在 2018 年參加加州大學柏克萊分校的暑期英語課程。

回答範本

Q: What historical moment or event do you wish you could have
"witnessed? (50 word limit)*

問題：你希望能親眼目睹哪個歷史時刻或事件？（50 字以內）

補充字彙

* **proliferation** [prə͵lɪfə`reʃən]
  (n.) 增殖，擴散

* **millennium** [mɪ`lɛnɪəm](n.)
  一千年（複數為 **millennia**
  [mɪ`lenɪɑ]）

* **feat** [fit] (n.) 功績，英勇事蹟

▍回答範本：

回答範本：

I wish I could have witnessed the Wright brothers' historic flight at Kitty Hawk.
As a kid, I was amazed that two bike ⁵]**mechanics** with high school educations
could achieve something that mankind had dreamed of for *millennia.
C This *feat really ⁶]**sparked** my interest in ⁷]**engineering**.

我希望能目睹萊特兄弟在吉特赫克進行的歷史性飛行。我小時候就對這兩位高中學歷的自
行車技師能實現人類千年來的夢想感到驚奇。這一壯舉確實激發了我對工程學的興趣。

回答
範本

▍寫作重點

A. 呈現出你正面的個人特質。

例如：

—— A1 the proliferation of fake news is the most significant challenge facing the
world today
→點出社會上假新聞氾濫的問題，可能會讓評審覺得你追求真相，心中有
公平正義，不是人云亦云，而是有自己想法的人。「有自己想法」是評
審會看重的人格特質。

—— A2 I worked as a counselor for a summer program that brings overseas
Chinese college students (mostly from North America) to Taiwan to learn
about Chinese language and culture.
→從範本 2 中可看出申請人很有國際觀，至少不畏懼與外國朋友接觸交流。

B. 提出自己專業的看法與想法。

例如：

—— B as the Taiwan presidential election approaches, fake news stories... to
make informed decisions
→提出發現假新聞可能會使選民更難做出明智的決定這件事，表現出申請
者本人對這件事很關心，也算是專業的看法。

C. 利用所問問題體現出自己的專業與熱情。

例如：

—— C This feat really sparked my interest in engineering.
→透過具體的描述，讓審查官對申請人的工程的熱情，有了更清楚的感受。

LESSON 7
Longer Essays
第七話：長篇文章

Vocabulary Bank

1. **obstacle** [ˈɑbstəkəl] (n.) 障礙(物)
   The road to success is full of challenges and obstacles.

2. **encounter** [ɪnˈkaʊntə] (v./n.) (意外、偶然) 遇見，遭遇 (困境)
   Laura was surprised when she encountered her ex-boyfriend at the mall.

3. **fundamental** [ˌfʌndəˈmɛntəl] (a.) 基礎的，基本的
   The Constitution protects our fundamental rights.

4. **setback** [ˈsɛt.bæk] (n.) 挫折，失敗，阻礙
   The project was delayed due to setbacks.

5. **miraculous** [məˈrækjələs] (a.) 奇蹟般的
   The patient made a miraculous recovery.

6. **legend** [ˈlɛdʒənd] (n.) 傳奇，傳說
   The Loch Ness Monster is just a legend.

7. **rally** [ˈræli] (n./v.) 重整旗鼓，重新振作
   The stock market closed higher after a late rally.

8. **umpire** [ˈʌmpaɪr] (n.) 裁判
   The umpire called a foul ball.

9. **furious** [ˈfjʊriəs] (a.) 狂怒的
   My parents were furious when they saw my report card.

10. **consolation** [ˌkɑnsəˈleʃən] (n.) 安慰，慰藉
    Your kind words were a consolation to me.

Q1: The lessons we take from [1]**obstacles** we [2]**encounter** can be [3]**fundamental** to later success. ***Recount** a time when you faced a challenge, [4]**setback**, or failure. How did it affect you, and what did you learn from the experience? (250~650 words)*

問題 1：我們從遇到的障礙中所吸取的教訓，可能會對日後的成功至關重要。請敘述你以往在面臨挑戰、挫折或失敗時如何受到影響，又從經驗中學到什麼？（250～650 字）

▌回答範本

I've loved playing baseball ever since I was a little kid. But somehow, at 15, I still wasn't a very good player. You would think that years of playing on my school team and an older brother who'd been a star player would have ***rubbed off** on me, but you'd be wrong. I mean, I wasn't totally hopeless. I was a fast runner, and I could hit my older brother's fastball about half the time. But I wasn't about to be ***scouted** for a professional team.

我從小就喜歡打棒球，但到了 15 歲時，我依舊不是很優秀的球員。你可能會認為，我在校隊裡打球多年，又有一個明星球員的哥哥，我會因此受到影響，但你這就錯了。我是說，我並非完全無望。我跑步相當快，而且經常能打到我哥哥投出的快速球。但我不足以成為職業球隊物色的人才。

My junior high school team wasn't anything special either. We had one or two talented players, but most, like me, were average at best. But somehow we'd almost made it through the first round of ***playoffs**, with only one game between us and the ***semifinals**. In the last ***inning**, our team had two outs and players on second and third base, and it was my turn at bat.

我國中的校隊也沒什麼特別的。我們有一、兩個有才華的球員，但大部分都像我一樣，充其量是中等程度。但我們也差點打入季後賽第一輪，我們距離半決賽只剩一場比賽了。在最後一局中，我們球隊有兩人出局，二壘和三壘有球員，而且輪到我上壘打擊了。

You may be imagining one of those scenes you see in the movies. The skinny kid who nobody believes in hits a [5]**miraculous** home run, winning the big game for his team and becoming a local [6]**legend**. Except my life wasn't like the movies, and any hope my coach or teammates might have had for a last-minute [7]**rally** to victory were crushed when the [8]**umpire** yelled, "***Strike** three, you're out!"

你或許會想像接下來就像電影中的場景，沒人看重的小瘦子奇蹟般打出全壘打，為自己的球隊贏得重大比賽，成了當地的傳奇人物。只不過我的人生不像電影，當裁判大喊「三振出局」時，我的教練和隊友在最後一刻爭取勝利的希望都破滅了。

回答範本

長篇文章撰寫須知

　　審查官想深入了解你的人格特質、過去經驗，甚至是寫作與說故事能力，是不是學校想要的人才。往往會提供字數限制，記得要把回答說完整，字數也並非越多越好，把從事件中學到的經驗、自我的成長清楚交代，才是最重要的。

I was [9]**furious** with myself after the game. I spent the whole ride home ignoring my parents' words of [10]**consolation**, *reliving my strikeout over and over in my head. For the several days I made myself [11]**miserable** thinking about how, if it hadn't been for me, our team might have been on its way to a [12]**league** victory. Nothing anyone said could convince me that the loss wasn't my fault and my fault alone.

比賽結束後，我相當惱怒自己。乘車回家時，我一路上都沒聽進父母安慰我的話，被出局的情景在我腦海中一再上演。接下來數日我一直苦思，當時若不是因為我，我們球隊或許已經一路走到聯賽勝利。任何人都無法說服我，這場失敗不是我的錯，而且是我一個人的錯。

Around a week later, I got together with some of my friends from the team at the local park. When I arrived, I was surprised to find that nobody seemed to be mad at me. I'd lost us the game, after all, and they must have been disappointed about not making the semifinals. It wasn't until we divided into teams for a *pickup game that I started to realize why no one was angry. Maybe it was the excitement of reaching the playoffs or the pressure of [13]**living up to** my brother's achievements, but sometime during the game, **A** I had [14]**lost sight of** why most of us played baseball. It wasn't to win the [15]**championship**, as awesome as that would have been. It was because we all loved to play the game. I didn't need a [16]**trophy** or a big *comeback win to have fun playing baseball with my friends, but maybe I needed to *strike out at the [17]**critical** moment to remember that.

約一週後，我和球隊的幾個朋友約在當地公園見面。我到了那裡後驚訝地發現沒有人生我的氣。畢竟是我害球隊輸掉比賽，不能打入半決賽，他們一定感到失望。直到我們分組打臨時賽時，我才明白為什麼沒人生氣。或許我是出於快打到季後賽的興奮感，也或許是為了追隨哥哥的成就而感到壓力，但在比賽期間，我忘了我們大多數人打棒球的原因。我們不是為了奪冠軍，儘管能奪冠也很棒。而是因為我們都喜歡打棒球。跟朋友們一起打棒球不需要獎盃或盛大的逆轉勝才會開心，但或許我必須在這個關鍵時刻三振出局才能記住這點。

回答範本

---

11. **miserable** [ˋmɪzəəbəl] (a.)
痛苦的，悲慘的
Thomas felt lonely and miserable after his divorce.

12. **league** [lig] (n.) 聯盟，聯合會
The Yankees are the top team in their league.

13. **live up to** (phr.) 達到，不辜負
Eric tried hard to live up to his parents' expectations.

14. **lose sight of** (phr.) 忘記，忽略
You should never lose sight of your goals.

15. **championship**
[ˋtʃæmpiənˌʃɪp] (n.) 錦標賽，冠軍稱號
The team won a stunning victory in the championship.

16. **trophy** [ˋtrofi] (n.) 獎盃，獎品
The tennis player's living room is filled with trophies.

17. **critical** [ˋkrɪtɪkəl] (a.)
關鍵性的，極為重要的
Steven's leadership skills were critical to his success.

補充字彙

* **recount** [riˋkaʊnt] (v.) 敘述

* **rub off (on)** (phr.) （性格、品質等）感染，影響

* **scout** [skaʊt] (v./n.) （球探）物色、尋找；球探

* **playoff** [ˋpleˌɑf] (n.) 延長賽

* **semifinal** [ˌsɛmiˋfaɪnəl] (n.) 準決賽

* **inning** [ˋɪnɪŋ] (n.) （棒球）局，回合

* **strike** [straɪk] (v.) （棒球比賽中的）揮棒落空

* **relive** [riˋlɪv] (v.) 重溫

* **pickup game** (phr.) 臨時球賽

* **comeback** [ˋkʌmˌbæk] (n.) 東山再起，再度走紅

* **strike out** (phr.) 三振出局，失敗，砸鍋

♫ 019 | 單字

Vocabulary Bank

1. **flip** [flɪp] (v.)（電視、收音機）快速轉台
   I sat there flipping stations while my dad drove.

2. **fascinate** [ˋfæsə͵net] (v.) 著迷，使神魂顛倒
   Roberta has always been fascinated by Asian culture.

3. **mysterious** [mɪsˋtɪrɪəs] (a.) 神祕的
   The coffin is covered with mysterious symbols.

4. **occupation** [͵ɑkjəˋpeʃən] (n.) 佔領，佔據
   The Nazi occupation of Paris lasted four years.

5. **expand** [ɪkˋspænd] (v.) 開拓，擴展
   The company has plans to expand into Asia.

6. **grammar** [ˋgræmə] (n.) 文法
   We did grammar drills in French class today

7. **exception** [ɪkˋsɛpʃən] (n.) 例外
   Every rule has an exception.

8. **pronunciation** [prə͵nʌnsɪˋeʃən] (n.) 發音
   Our English teacher puts a lot of emphasis on pronunciation.

9. **contrast** [ˋkɑntræst] (n.) 對比，in contrast to / with... 為「與⋯形成對比」
   In contrast with his brother, Robert is quite tall.

Q2: Some students have a background, identity, interest, or talent that is so meaningful they believe their application would be incomplete without it. If this sounds like you, then please share your story.

問題 2：有些學生的背景、身分、興趣或才華十分有意義，因此他們相信若沒有這些，申請書就不完整。你若符合這點，就請分享你的故事。

回答範本

Sitting on the couch channel-¹⁾**flipping** one night, I stopped on a Japanese channel, ²⁾**fascinated** by the sounds of the language. I struggled to make sense of the ³⁾**mysterious** words coming out of the characters mouths and immediately knew that Japanese was a puzzle I needed to solve. When I mentioned my interest to my parents, they told me that my grandfather, who had gone to school during the Japanese ⁴⁾**occupation** of Taiwan, was fluent in Japanese even in his later years. I'd never heard him speak the language, and regretted learning about this ***intriguing** fact only after his death.

有天晚上我坐在沙發上隨意轉台，轉到一個日文頻道，被迷人的日語所吸引。在我努力想聽懂從各角色嘴裡說出來的神秘語言時，立刻明白日語是我需要解開的謎團。我告訴父母我有興趣學日語時，他們說我的祖父在日據時代受過日文教育，甚至到了晚年時還能說流利的日語。我從沒聽他說過日語，很遺憾在他過世後才得知這件有趣的事。

I'd been taking ***mandatory** English classes since the third grade, and enjoyed the world of knowledge that opened up to me as I became more fluent. **B** But now that I was in junior high, I had the chance to study a second foreign language, and of course I didn't hesitate to choose Japanese. Since starting Japanese class, I've fallen in love not only with the language, but also the country and culture. In fact, learning Japanese has become part of my identity, and I feel that both English and Japanese have greatly ⁵⁾**expanded** my understanding of the human experience.

我從小學三年級起就開始上英語必修課，英語變得更流利後，也能享受隨之開啟的知識世界。到了國中時，我有機會學習第二外語，當然我也毫不猶豫選擇了日語。自從上日語課以來，我不僅愛上日語，也愛上日本和其文化。其實學日語已經塑造了我的部分人格，而且我認為英語和日語都大幅開拓我對人生的理解。

回答範本

Many of my fellow students started studying Japanese because of their interest in manga or anime, but I find the language itself to be the most interesting aspect of Japanese culture.

C Like the orderly society Japan is famous for, the Japanese language has just a handful of [6]**grammar** [7]**exceptions**, and [8]**pronunciation** is uniform. This is [9]**in contrast to** English, which seems to have more exceptions than rules, and is a challenge to pronounce for Chinese speakers like me. Yet while grammar and pronunciation follow regular rules, Japanese has *three* writing systems: hiragana and katakana, which each contain 46 [10]**syllables**, and kanji, which includes thousands of characters. Luckily, kanji are based on Chinese characters, which gave me a *head start over learners from other countries.

我有許多同學是因為對日本漫畫或動漫有興趣而開始學日語，但我認為日語本身是日本文化中最有趣的一面。就像日本以富秩序的社會而聞名一樣，日語只有少數文法例外，而且發音很規律。這點與英語大大不同，英語似乎例外比規則還多，而且發音對於像我這樣說中文的人來說是一種挑戰。儘管日語在文法和發音上遵循固定規則，但日語有三種書寫系統：各包含 46 個音節的平假名和片假名，以及包含數千個字符的漢字。幸好漢字源自中文，讓我比其他國家的學習者有領先優勢。

Beyond the joy of using the three writing systems to string together orderly sentences, the most *mesmerizing aspect of Japanese culture is the striking *dichotomy of old and new. Last summer, I spent a month living with a *host family in a small Japanese town. On festival days, Japanese teenagers walked the streets in summer [11]**kimono** while texting on the latest smartphones. Although Japan is always at the [12]**cutting edge** of technology, the tea [13]**ceremony**, flower arranging and *archery classes I took were full of locals connecting to their rich traditional culture. In Tokyo, I saw skyscrapers covered in [14]**neon** next to Buddhist temples and Shinto [15]**shrines**. Japan's ability to appreciate its history while constantly looking to the future never [16]**ceases** to amaze me.

除了運用三種書寫系統將句子依序串連起來的樂趣外，日本文化最迷人的一面是截然不同的新舊文化。去年夏天我在日本一座小鎮的寄宿家庭住了一個月。在節慶期間，日本青少年穿著浴衣在街上逛，同時用著最新的智慧手機傳簡訊。雖然日本一直處於科技最前線，但我上的茶道課、花道課和弓道課都看到許多來吸取豐富傳統文化的當地人。在東京，我看到點綴著霓虹燈的摩天大樓，旁邊是佛寺和神社。日本珍視自身歷史的同時，也不斷展望未來的能力，始終令我感到驚奇。

Japanese may not have been a part of my identity growing up in Taiwan, but it has definitely become a part of who I am as a young adult. The more fluent I become in Japanese, and the more I learn about the culture, the more I seem to learn about myself. While English will become much more important to me as I [17]**embark** on the next stage of my [18]**academic** journey in the U.S., I know that wherever my future takes me, my passion for mastering Japanese and learning all I can about the **Land of the Rising Sun** will continue to burn.

日語或許與幼年的我無關，但無疑在我青年時塑造了我的部分人格。我的日語越流利、對日本文化越了解，我對自己的了解似乎也就越多。儘管在我展開人生下一階段的美國求學之旅中，英語對我來說會更重要，但我知道，無論我的未來如何走，我對精通日語和學習一切有關日出之國的熱情將會持續燃燒。

回答範本

---

10. **syllable** [ˈsɪləbəl] (n.) 音節
The word "pilot" has two syllables.

11. **kimono** [kəˈmono] (n.) 和服
The geisha wore a silk kimono.

12. **cutting edge** (phr.) 領先地位，發展前端
The team's research is at the cutting edge of biology.

13. **ceremony** [ˈsɛrəˌmoni] (n.) 儀式，典禮
The wedding ceremony was held at a small church.

14. **neon** [ˈnian] (n.) 霓虹燈
Las Vegas is famous for its neon lights.

15. **shrine** [ʃraɪn] (n.) 神殿，神壇
Thousands of people visit the shrine on religious holidays.

16. **cease** [sis] (v.) 停止
The kids at the next table wouldn't cease their whining.

17. **embark (on)** [ɪmˈbɑrk] (v.) 開始，著手進行
We're embarking on a new project next month.

18. **academic** [ˌækəˈdɛmɪk] (a.) 學術的
Shelly has a good academic record.

補充字彙

* **intriguing** [ɪnˈtrigɪŋ] (a.) 非常有趣的

* **mandatory** [ˈmændəˌtori] (a.) 強制的，義務的

* **head start** (phr.) 先起步的優勢

* **mesmerizing** [ˈmɛzməˌraɪzɪŋ] (a.) 迷人的

* **dichotomy** [daɪˈkɑtəmi] (n.) 對立，強烈對比

* **host family** (phr.) 寄宿家庭

* **archery** [ˈɑrtʃəri] (n.) 射箭

Vocabulary Bank

Land of the Rising Sun
日出之國

是西方人對日本的稱呼,這稱呼起源於中國,對中國來說,日本所在位置是太陽升起的方向,故有此稱呼。

寫作重點

A. 遇到挫折時,不被擊倒,反而學到一課。

例如:

—— A I had lost sight of why most of us played baseball... . It was because we all loved to play the game.

→有些年輕人成長之路一帆風順,一路都是父母牽扶著走,重金捧出國念書,以至於挫折容忍力很低,遇到一點小事就無法承受。本文展現出申請者雖然害球隊輸球,但卻沒被此擊垮,也維持了對打棒球的熱愛。審查官能感受到申請者正面思考的正能量。

B. 展現自己對某事物的熱情,以及投注的心力。

例如:

—— B But now that I was in junior high, ... and of course I didn't hesitate to choose Japanese.

→除了這段以外展現出對日語的熱情之外,後面申請者對日語的種種獨到見解,都說明了他的熱忱與所投注的心力。審查官可能會把此專注的研究精神投射在申請者申請的科系上,感受申請者對喜愛的事,可能會所投注的熱情和心力,因而增加錄取機會。

C. 展現自己的獨特見解。

例如:

—— C Like the orderly society Japan is famous for, ...which includes thousands of characters.

→這裡展現了申請者對日文發音、文法和書寫的獨特觀察。另外前面說「我有許多同學是因為對漫畫或動漫有興趣而開始學日語,但我發現日語本身是日本文化中最有趣的一面。」藉此彰顯申請者和其他申請人的差異,是很不錯的表達方式。

Recommendation Letter
第八話：推薦信

♫ 020 | 單字

Vocabulary Bank

推薦信範本

To whom it may concern,

It is a [1]**privilege** to recommend Mr. Chin-hsiang Lin for admission to the Master of Chemical Sciences program at the University of Pennsylvania. **A** I was [2]**fortunate** to teach Mr. Lin in my *Polymer [3]**Chemistry** course, and was also on the review committee for his [4]**senior** [5]**thesis**. In my contact with him, I found him to be an intelligent, diligent and [6]**articulate** student, and I feel that he is an excellent [7]**candidate** for your program.

B In Polymer Chemistry, Mr. Lin [8]**impressed** me with his ability to quickly grasp [9]**concepts** related to structure, *morphology and synthesis and then apply them in the [10]**laboratory**. He often sat in the front row in class, and his *insightful questions always added to the discussion. [11]**Moreover**, when responding to questions I posed, Mr. Lin showed a thorough understanding of the material and always provided [12]**precise** answers.

As a member of the review committee for Mr. Lin's senior thesis, Synthesis and [13]**Characterization** of *Polystyrene-Poly Diblock Copolymers, **C** I was impressed not only by his [14]**research**, but also his strong [15]**oral** and written [16]**communication** skills, which are often lacking in students in the sciences. He showed a clear logic in his research design, and did a fine job explaining how he used his [17]**theoretical** knowledge and previous [10]**lab** experience to [18]**resolve** problems encountered in the synthesis process.

During one of our discussions, Mr. Lin mentioned his ambition of pursuing a Masters in chemistry at a top university in the United States in preparation for a career as a research [3]**chemist**. Given his diligence, [19]**determination** and strong [20]**foundation** in chemistry, I am confident that he will succeed in these goals. **D** I therefore recommend him to you *wholeheartedly, and strongly encourage you to give his application the [21]**utmost** consideration.

Sincerely,

Wang Ching-fu
Professor of Chemistry
National Tsing Hwa University

（人物為虛構）

英文版本

1. **privilege** [ˈprɪvəlɪdʒ] (n.) 特權，特殊利益
   Driving is a privilege, not a right.

2. **fortunate** [ˈfɔrtʃənɪt] (a.) 幸運的，僥倖的
   We should try to help those who are less fortunate than ourselves.

3. **chemistry** [ˈkɛmɪstri] (n.) 化學，當職業時為 chemist [ˈkɛmɪst] 化學家
   Our professor is a Nobel laureate in chemistry.

4. **senior** [ˈsinjɚ] (n.) 畢業班學生
   Dan dropped out of high school in his senior year.

5. **thesis** [ˈθisɪs] (n.) 論文，畢業論文、製作
   How long did it take to write your master's thesis?

6. **articulate** [ɑrˈtɪkjələt] (a.) 表達清楚的，善於表達的
   Kevin is the most articulate student in his class.

7. **candidate** [ˈkændɪˌdet] (n.) 求職應試者，候選人
   The company is looking for candidates with sales experience.

8. **impress** [ɪmˈprɛs] 給…極深的印象，impressive [ɪmˈprɛsɪv] (a.) 出色的，令人印象深刻的
   I was really impressed by your presentation.

9. **concept** [ˈkɑnsɛpt] (n.) 觀念，概念
   Risk is a difficult concept to understand.

CHAPTER 1

申請學校

Applying to Schools

Vocabulary Bank

10. laboratory [ˋlæbrəˌtɔrɪ] (n.)
研究室，實驗室，檢驗室，簡稱為 lab [læb]

Are your tests back from the lab yet?

11. moreover [morˋovɚ] (adv)
而且，再者

It's illegal to swim here and, moreover, it's dangerous.

12. precise [prɪˋsaɪs] (a.) **精確的，準確的**

Beethoven's precise date of birth is unknown.

13. characterization [ˌkɛrəktərəˋzeʃən] (n.)
特性描述

I was surprised by the film's characterization of the president as a drunk.

14. research [ˋrisɝtʃ / rɪˋsɝtʃ] (n./v.) **(學術) 研究，調查 ／ (n.) researcher** [ˋriˌsɝtʃɚ] **研究者，調查者**

A team of scientists is conducting research on the new virus.

15. oral [ˋorəl] (a.) **口 (部) 的，口頭的，口述的**

Did you pass the oral exam?

16. communication [kəˌmjunəˋkeʃən] (n.) **溝通，傳播**

Good communication skills are important for sales managers.

17. theoretical [ˌθiəˋrɛtɪkəl] (a.) **理論 (上) 的，假設的**

Chloe has a degree in theoretical chemistry.

推薦信重點

　　推薦信是一般申請美國大學、研究所、博士時所需要提供的一份資料。每間學校要求申請人提供的推薦信函數量不等，具體要求可透過申請系統或學校官網得知。推薦信一般都是**請較了解你的任課老師、學校輔導員或實習公司的主管來寫**。選擇推薦人時，切記不要過度看重推薦人的職稱，如果選了一個職稱較高，但對你不了解的人來寫，會造成內容空洞，達不到應有效果。**相反選擇對你熟悉的人來寫**，可以寫出很多關於你的故事及優點。申請人應儘早選擇推薦人，並提供自己相關資料或與推薦人碰面，讓他能夠更了解你。切記，**推薦信須由推薦人撰寫並寄出，不可經由申請人幫忙寄出**（學校會查電腦 IP），因有造假之可能。

敬啟者您好：

很榮幸能推薦林欽祥先生申請賓州大學化學系碩士班的入學許可。我有幸在我的高分子化學課中能教導林先生，也參與了他的畢業論文審核委員會。與他接觸後，我發現他是聰明、勤奮和善於表達的學生，我認為他也是貴系所的優秀申請人。

林先生在高分子化學課程中能快速掌握聚合物結構、形態與合成相關的概念，並應用於實驗室，令我印象深刻。他經常坐在教室前排，他富有深刻見解的問題總是能讓討論更熱烈。此外，林先生在回答我提出的問題時，不但表現出對資料理解透徹，也總是能提供精準的答案。

身為林先生的畢業論文，《聚苯乙烯 - 聚二嵌段共聚物的合成與特徵》審核委員，我對他的研究與出色的口語和書面溝通技巧印象深刻，而理科生通常欠缺這方面技能。他在研究設計中表現出清晰的邏輯，並在解釋如何運用自己的理論知識和先前的實驗室經驗來解決合成過程中遇到的問題方面，表現得相當出色。

在我們的其中一次討論中，林先生提到自己的抱負是想到美國頂尖大學攻讀化學碩士學位，為投入化學研究員的職涯做準備。鑑於他的勤奮、決心和實力堅強的化學基礎，我有信心他能達成目標。因此我竭誠向您推薦他，並強烈鼓勵您盡量考慮他的申請書。

誠摯的

王敬福
化學系教授
國立清華大學

（人物為虛構）

中文版本

寫作重點

A. 表明自己的身分，和申請者的關係

　　A I was fortunate to teach Mr. Lin in my Polymer Chemistry course, and was also on the review committee for his senior thesis.

　　→表明自己是申請者的指導老師，也審查過他的畢業論文。表示此人對申請者有一定的了解，是位可信的推薦人。

B. 有哪些具體的表現，會讓人推薦，請舉出具體的例子

　　B In Polymer Chemistry, Mr. Lin impressed me with his ability to quickly grasp concepts related to polymer structure, morphology and synthesis and then apply them in the laboratory.

　　→透過具體描述，指出了申請人的令人印象深刻的優點。

C. 申請者有哪些和一般申請人不同的地方，會讓推薦人覺得特別突出

　　C I was impressed not only by his research, but also his strong oral and written communication skills, which are often lacking in students in the sciences.

　　→透過舉例說明，讓審查官知道申請人擁有同為理科生所沒有的口語和書面溝通技巧。

D. 最後請重申撰寫這封推薦函想達到的目的

　　D I therefore recommend him to you wholeheartedly, and strongly encourage you to give his application the utmost consideration.

　　→強力推薦申請人，並請求審查官考慮錄取申請人。

18. resolve [rɪˋzɑlv] (v.) 解決

The couple resolved their differences and decided to stay together.

19. determination [dɪ͵tɝməˋneʃən] (n.) 堅毅，決心

Learning to play a musical instrument takes patience and determination.

20. foundation [faʊnˋdeʃən] (n.) 基礎，根據

The course provides the foundation necessary for advanced study.

21. utmost [ˋʌt͵most] (a./n.) 最大的，極度的；極限，最大可能

These instruments should be handled with the utmost care.

補充字彙

∗ **polymer** [ˋpɑlɪmɚ] (n.) 聚合物，聚合體

∗ **morphology** [mɔrˋfɑlədʒɪ] (n.) 形態學

∗ **insightful** [ˋɪn͵saɪtfəl] (a.) 有深刻見解的，有洞察力的

∗ **polystyrene-poly diblock copolymer** (phr.) 聚苯乙烯 - 聚二嵌段共聚物

∗ **wholeheartedly** [͵holˋhɑrtɪdli] (adv.) 全心全意地，全神貫注的

LESSON 9
Statement of Purpose
第九話：讀書計畫

 022 | 單字

Vocabulary Bank

1. **aptitude** [ˈæptɪ,tud] (n.) **資質，才能**
Ethan has a natural aptitude for languages.

2. **motivation** [,motɪˈveʃən] (n.) **動機，原因**
The motivation of a business is to make a profit.

3. **intellectual** [,ɪntəˈlɛktʃuəl] (a.) **知識（分子）的，（需）智力的，intellectual property 為「智慧財產」，簡稱 IP**
Chess is a very intellectual game.

4. **attain** [əˈten] (v.) **達到，獲得**
You need to work hard to attain success.

5. **combination** [,kambəˈneʃən] (n.) **結合，組合，密碼**
Purple is a combination of red and blue.

6. **capital** [ˈkæpətəl] (n.) **資本，資金**
You need capital if you want to start a business.

7. **industrialize** [ɪnˈdʌstriəlaɪz] (v.) **工業化**
England was the first country to industrialize.

8. **innovation** [,ɪnəˈveʃən] (n.) **創新，新想法，形容詞為 innovative** [ˈɪnə,vetɪv] **創新的**
Innovation is the key to success in the global economy.

Statement of Purpose:

*Please describe your **aptitude** and **motivation** for graduate study in your area of specialization, including your preparation for this field of study, your academic plans or research interests in your chosen area of study, and your future career goals. Please be specific about why our school would be a good **intellectual** fit for you.*

讀書計畫：

請敘述在你的專業領域中，你對碩士研究的才能和動力，包括你對該研究領域的準備工作、學術計畫，或在你所選研究領域中的探究興趣，以及你未來的職涯目標。請具體說明為何我們學校在智識發展上適合你。

▌讀書計畫範本

A1 To explain my motivation for **attaining** an ***MBA** in the U.S., it's necessary to go back in time to the Taiwan economic miracle of the 1970s-1980s. With a **combination** of Western **capital** and wise economic policy, my country **industrialized** rapidly, becoming an export ***powerhouse**. In recent decades, however, Taiwan has experienced difficulty moving up the ***value chain** and creating global brands, and now lags behind the other three "***Asian Tigers**."

為了說明我為何想在美國攻讀企業管理碩士學位，就必須要回顧一下 1970 到 1980 年代的台灣經濟奇蹟時期。在結合西方資本和明智的經濟政策下，我的國家迅速工業化，成了出口大國。但在近幾十年，台灣在提升價值鏈和創造全球品牌方面經歷困境，目前在「亞洲四小龍」中敬陪末座。

Some say this is an **innovation** problem, but in fact, on a ***per capita** basis, Taiwan ranks third in the world for **patent** applications. The problem is, most local **manufacturers** do all their R&D *in-house, *hoard their patents even if they don't use them, and make no effort to license outside patents. **A2** The result is that **intellectual property**, whether local or international, isn't **utilized** efficiently by firms in Taiwan, thus keeping them from reaching their full **potential**. *In light of this issue, I intend to pursue an MBA at Georgia Tech and then return to Taiwan and pursue a career in **IP** management.

有人認為這是創新的問題，但事實上，按人均來說，台灣在專利申請方面排名世界第三。大部分本地製造都是在做內部研發，即使不用自己的專利，也不分享出去，更不會積極取得外部專利的授權，這才是問題所在。這一點所造成的結果是，台灣的公司都未有效利用本地或國際的智慧財產，因此無法發揮最大潛力。有鑒於此問題，我計畫在喬治亞科技大學攻讀企業管理碩士，然後回到台灣從事智慧財產管理事業。

回答
範本

什麼是讀書計畫

為 statement of purpose，又可簡稱為 SOP，是申請碩博士學位者需要撰寫的文章之一。這可以說是一篇對申請者來說很重要的文章，因為此文章會告訴招生官你是誰，為什麼要申請本校，為什麼學校要錄取你，跟你未來想做什麼。招生官會閱讀你的讀書計畫，從中找到跟學校最契合的人選。

How did I reach this decision? **B1** During my studies in the College of **Commerce** at National Chingchi University, I gained a solid foundation in business administration. I particularly enjoyed studying ***marketing** management, so when I had the chance to work as a marketing ***intern** at my uncle's small manufacturing company in the summer of my **junior** year, I jumped at the chance. I knew that his leather furniture was made for export, but it wasn't until my ***internship** that I learned it was all contract manufacturing for foreign brands.

我為什麼會做這樣的決定呢？我在國立政治大學商學院就讀時，在企業管理方面打下了紮實的基礎。我特別喜歡研究行銷管理，所以在大三那年暑假，我有機會在我叔叔的小製造公司擔任行銷實習生時，我立刻把握機會。我已知道他公司製造的皮革家具是用於出口，但一直到我擔任實習生時，我才知道工廠全是為外國品牌代理生產。

When I raised the possibility of building his own brand, my uncle said that because his profits were ***razor-thin**, he didn't even have the money to upgrade his products, much less spend on branding. **B2** Given this financial situation, I applied what I learned in marketing class, using free and inexpensive social media advertising tools to help my uncle find new contract clients. After graduating, I was hired by Pacific IP Group as a market **analyst**. While writing tech industry IP market reports, I found that I had an aptitude for market research. I quickly learned that Taiwan's IP market is far from mature, and that there are many challenges in connecting patent holders with the companies that can make the best use of them.

在我提出建立自有品牌的可能性時，叔叔說因為他的利潤微薄，因此根本沒錢提升產品，更別說將錢花在品牌建立上了。在這種財務情況下，我運用了自己在市場行銷課中所學，利用免費和低廉的社群媒體廣告工具，協助叔叔尋找新的代工客戶。畢業後，我被太平洋智慧財產集團聘為市場分析師。在寫科技業智慧財產市場報告時，我發現自己有做市場研究的天賦。我很快得知，台灣的智慧財產市場十分不成熟，而且要幫專利持有者找到能善加運用專利的廠商方面有許多挑戰。

回答
範本

---

9. **patent** [ˈpætənt] (n./v.) 專利
The patent for this device is owned by Apple.

10. **manufacturer** [ˌmænjəˈfæktʃəʊ] (n.) 製造商
Taiwan is home to several of the world's largest computer manufacturers.

11. **utilize** [ˈjutəˌlaɪz] (v.) 使用，利用
Companies are increasingly utilizing robots to perform dangerous jobs.

12. **potential** [pəˈtɛnʃəl] (n./a.) 潛力，可能性；潛在的，可能的
Going to university will help you reach your potential.

13. **intend** [ɪnˈtɛnd] (v.) 想要，打算
How long do you intend to stay in the U.S.?

14. **commerce** [ˈkɑmɝs] (n.) 商業，貿易
Wilbur Ross is currently serving as the U.S. Secretary of Commerce.

15. **junior** [ˈdʒunjɚ] (a./n.) (大學)三年級；三年級生
I worked a part-time job in my junior year.

16. **analyst** [ˈænəlɪst] (n.) 分析師
Darryl works as a financial analyst at a large corporation.

17. **set one's sights on** (phr.) 目標放在…，志在…
Jeremy has set his sights on law school.

18. **renowned** [rɪˈnaʊnd] (a.) 有名的
The history textbook was written by a renowned historian.

19. **emphasis** [ˈɛmfəsɪs] (n.) 強調，重點
The English teacher puts a lot of emphasis on pronunciation.

20. **integrate** [ˈɪntəˌgret] (v.) 整合，結合
The company plans to integrate GPS into all their new watches.

🎵 **023** | 單字

Vocabulary Bank

21. aspect [ˋæspɛkt] (n.) **方面，觀點**

We must consider the various aspects of the problem.

22. curriculum [kəˋrɪkjələm] (n.) **學校全部的課程，（一門）課程**

PE is no longer part of the curriculum.

23. ultimate [ˋʌltəmɪt] (a.) **終極的，最終的，根本的**

The team's ultimate goal is to win the championship.

24. consulting [kənˋsʌltɪŋ] (a.) **提供諮詢的，顧問的**

Ron works in the field of business consulting.

25. devote [dɪˋvot] (v.) **將⋯奉獻給，致力於**

Bill Gates decided to devote the rest of his life to philanthropy.

26. harness [ˋhɑrnəs] (v.) **利用，控制**

We do our best to harness the skills of our employees.

27. enhance [ɪnˋhæns] (v.) **提高（價值），提升（品質）**

The government is working to enhance water quality.

28. competitiveness [kəmˋpɛtɪtɪv͵nɪs] (n.) **競爭力，形容詞為 competitive** [kəmˋpɛtətɪv] **(a.) 競爭激烈的，有競爭力的**

Hong Kong is losing its competitiveness as a financial center.

This is when I **set my sights on** becoming a tech IP manager. B3 I also realized that in order to better understand the complex issues regarding tech IP management in a global business environment, my best path would be to pursue an international MBA degree at a university with close ties to the tech industry. This is why C I have decided to apply to the Scheller College of Business at Georgia Tech, a world-**renowned** research university with an **emphasis** on **integrating** technology into all **aspects** of its **curriculum**.

於是這時我立志成為科技智慧財產經理人。我也明白到，為了更了解全球經商環境中與科技智慧財產管理相關的複雜問題，最好的途徑是在與科技業關係密切的大學攻讀企業管理碩士學位。所以我決定申請喬治亞科技大學的薛勒商學院，這是一所世界知名的研究型大學，著重於在各方面課程中融入科技。

D My **ultimate** goal is to start my own IP management **consulting** firm and **devote** my efforts to helping Taiwanese companies **harness** innovation to **enhance** their **competitiveness** on the international stage. Specifically, I believe that Scheller's course offerings in the areas of IP management, technology **transfer**, **digital** marketing and **venture** creation will give me the tools I need to achieve this goal. I am confident that my academic background and **professional** experience have prepared me for the **rigors** of the Scheller program, and also look forward to sharing my knowledge of Taiwan's tech and export industries with my fellow students.

我的最終目標是創立自己的智慧財產管理諮詢公司，並致力於協助台灣企業運用創新提升自己在國際舞台上的競爭力。具體來說，我相信薛勒商學院在智慧財產管理、技術轉移、數位行銷和創業方面提供的課程，能讓我學到實現此目標所需的工具。我有信心，我的學術背景和工作經驗已讓我準備好攻讀嚴謹的薛勒商學院課程，我也期待能與同學分享我對台灣科技和出口業的知識。

回答
範本

寫作重點

A. 用生動的開頭吸引讀者目光。可以寫一個跟你想要申請的科系有關的經驗、啟示、小故事，並説明這為何讓你產生興趣。

例如：

> **A1** To explain my motivation for attaining an MBA in the U.S., it's necessary to go back in time to the Taiwan economic miracle of the 1970s-1980s...Taiwan has experienced difficulty moving up the value chain and creating global brands, and now lags behind the other three "Asian Tigers."
> →相關小故事，感興趣的源頭

> **A2** The result is that intellectual property, whether local or international, isn't utilized efficiently by firms in Taiwan,.... In light of this issue, I intend to pursue an MBA at Georgia Tech and then return to Taiwan and pursue a career in IP management.
> →為何產生興趣

B. 你的優勢、強項、所具備的技能、上過什麼課、做過什麼事讓你更了解這個領域。説説這些經驗影響了你什麼，為什麼讓你想繼續進修。

例如：

> **B1** During my studies in the College of Commerce at National Chingchi University, I gained a solid foundation in business administration.
> →上過的課

> **B2** Given this financial situation, I applied what I learned in marketing class...to help my uncle find new contract clients.
> →實戰經驗

> **B3** I also realized that in order to better understand the complex issues regarding tech IP management in a global business environment, my best path would be to pursue an international MBA degree at a university with close ties to the tech industry.
> →想繼續進修理由

C. 透過調查學校、系所網站或教授研究興趣等，來展現出你已了解學校、系所的宗旨或願景，並説明這和你要申請的科系有什麼關係。

例如：

> **C** I have decided to apply to the Scheller College of Business at Georgia Tech, a world-renowned research university with an emphasis on integrating technology into all aspects of its curriculum.
> →想申請此校理由

D. 生涯規劃，未來想做什麼？如何應用所學完成目標？

例如：

> **D** My ultimate goal is to start my own IP management consulting firm...to enhance their competitiveness on the international stage.
> →未來目標

---

29. transfer [`trænsfɚ] (n./v.)
轉移，調動，匯款
Education is more than just the transfer of knowledge.

30. digital [`dɪdʒɪtəl] (a.)
數位的
How do you like my new digital watch?

31. venture [`vɛntʃɚ] (n.) 新創事業，投資事業
The business venture ended in bankruptcy.

32. professional [prə`fɛʃənəl] (a.) 專業的，職業的
Cynthia wants to be a professional musician.

33. rigor [`rɪgɚ] (n.) 嚴格，嚴謹
The research paper lacked intellectual rigor.

補充字彙

* **MBA** (n.) 企業管理碩士，即 master of business administration

* **powerhouse** [`pauɚ͵haus] (n.) 強而有力的人事物

* **value chain** (phr.) 價值鏈

* **Asian Tigers** (phr.) 亞洲四小龍，指自 1960~1990 年間，西太平洋四個發展迅速的經濟體：韓國、臺灣、香港及新加坡

* **per capita** (phr.) 人均，按人口平均計算

* **in-house** [`ɪn͵haus] (a.) 在組織內部的

* **hoard** [hɔrd] (v.) 貯藏，囤積

* **in light of** (phr.) 鑑於，根據

* **marketing** [`mɑrkɪtɪŋ] (n.) 行銷，促銷

* **intern** [`ɪntɝn] (n./v.) 實習人員，實習生；作實習生，**internship** [`ɪntɝn͵ʃɪp] (n.) 工作實習

* **razor-thin** [`rezɚ͵θɪn] (a.) 微小的，細微的

LESSON 10
Letter of acceptance
第十話：學校錄取通知

024 | 單字

圖解英文　輕鬆看懂錄取通知

Vocabulary Bank

1. **acceptance** [əkˋsɛptəns] (n.)
錄取，接受
Have you received any acceptance letters yet?

2. **district** [ˋdɪstrɪkt] (n.) 地區，
行政區
Which district of the city do you live in?

3. **rewarding** [rɪˋwɔrdɪŋ] (a.)
獲益良多的，有報酬的，感到充實的
Going to college was a very rewarding experience.

4. **registration** [ˌrɛdʒɪˋstreʃən] (n.) 註冊，登記，動詞為
register [ˋrɛdʒɪstə] (v.) 登記，
註冊
Registration week starts next Monday.

5. **enclose** [ɪnˋkloz] (v.) 隨信附上
Please enclose the following documents with your application.

6. **embassy** [ˋɛmbəsɪ] (n.) 大使館
Documents must be submitted to the embassy for verification.

7. **issue** [ˋɪʃu] (v.) 核發，發行
How long does it take to issue a new passport?

From: Office of Admissions
March 31, 2019
Shu-hui Lin

2 Fl., No. 131, Wufu 4th Road
Yancheng [2]**District**, Kaohsiung City
Taiwan, R.O.C.

Dear Shu-hui,

It's a pleasure to inform you that you have been accepted for admission to Cerritos College. We are pleased you chose Cerritos and look forward to you joining us for fall semester. We hope your experience on campus will prove to be enjoyable and [3]**rewarding**.

Fall semester classes begin on August 26, 2020. You will need to arrive no later than August 1, as indicated on your I-20. When you arrive in the United States, contact the Office of Admissions to schedule an appointment. You must bring your passport, I-94 and payment for the medical insurance. We will advise you on the next steps you need to take before attending Advising and [4]**Registration**.

Your I-20 form is [5]**enclosed**. Please bring your financial documents, passport and I-20 form to the U.S. ***consulate** or [6]**embassy** in your country for processing of the F1 visa, which is required for entrance into the U.S. Your 1-20 form must be signed in blue ink.

If you are unable to attend fall semester, you must return the enclosed I-20 form. A new I-20 form will be [7]**issued** for a [8]**subsequent** semester when we have received the form issued for fall semester and we have current financial ***documentation** on file.

Welcome to the Cerritos [9]**community**!

Sincerely,

Catherine Harris
***Coordinator** of International Admissions

（人物為虛構）

收到錄取通知後，要做什麼？

　　美國大部分的學校都會以 e-mail 通知學生被錄取的資訊，並將後續事宜寫在 e-mail 中，學生若決定就讀此校，則需按照信中要求去做。若已確定不就讀該校，則需儘早回絕，好讓在候補名單中的同學能夠儘早得到錄取通知。學生在收到 e-mail 通知 1-2 禮拜內會收到學校寄來的相關資料，其中 I-20 最為重要。I-20 是美國學校提供給國際學生申請簽證 (F-1 簽證) 時的入學文件，也算是一種入學許可。學生收到 I-20 後，即可持該文件去美國在台協會辦理簽證。

寄件人：入學服務處　　　五福四路 131 號 2 樓
2019 年 3 月 31 日　　　高雄市鹽埕區
林淑慧　　　　　　　　台灣，中華民國

親愛的淑慧：

很高興通知你，你獲得喜瑞都大學錄取。很高興你選擇喜瑞都大學，期待你在秋季學期入學。希望你在本校能有愉快且受益匪淺的體驗。

秋季學期於 2020 年 8 月 26 日開課。按照你的 I-20 所指示，你必須在 8 月 1 日前抵達。抵達美國後，請聯絡入學服務處安排會面。你必須攜帶護照、I-94 和醫療保險費。，我們會通知你在參加諮詢與註冊之前要採取的步驟。

隨信附上你的 I-20 表格。請將財力證明、護照和 I-20 表格帶到你所在國家的美國領事館或大使館辦理進入美國所需的 F1 簽證。你的 I-20 表格必須以藍色墨水簽名。

你若無法在秋季學期入學，則必須退回信中隨附的 I-20 表格。待我們收到秋季學期核發的 I-20 表格，並將目前的財力證明存檔後，將為下一學期核發新的 I-20 表格。

歡迎加入喜瑞都大學！

謹致

凱瑟琳哈里斯
國際招生協調員

（人物為虛構）

---

8. **subsequent** [ˋsʌbsɪkwənt]
   (a.) **隨後的，後續的**
   We'll keep you informed about subsequent developments.

9. **community** [kəˋmjunəti] (n.)
   社群，社區，社會
   The theory quickly won acceptance in the scientific community.

補充字彙

* **consulate** [ˋkɑnsəlɪt] (n.)
   領事館

* **documentation**
   [ˌdɑkjəmənˋteʃən] (n.) **文件證據，證明文件**

* **coordinator** [koˋɔrdəˌnetɚ]
   (n.) **協調員，統籌者**

學期制與學季制

美國大學有分為學期制 (semester) 與學季制 (quarter)。使用學期制的大學較多，使用學季制的大學較少。學期制是不含暑假，一年有兩個學期，一個學期四個月，也就是 18 周。學季制是不含暑假，一年有三個學季，每學季 12 周。學期和學季制都是每年讀 36 周，所花費的時間和金錢也都差不多。如想早點完成學業，也可於暑假繼續修課，不過由於暑假時間較短，而每門課都有規定上課時數，所以每週上課的時間會比普通學期 / 季來得長。

 025 | 單字

Vocabulary Bank

1. **personalized** [ˋpɝsənəˏlaɪzd]
   (a.) 為某人特製的
   All the wedding guests received personalized invitations.

2. **enrollment** [ɪnˋrolmənt]
   (n.) 登記，註冊，入學；動詞為
   enroll [ɪnˋrol] 登記
   Enrollment for the class will begin next week.

3. **fulfill** [fulˋfɪl] (v.) 完成（任務等），執行（命令等）
   The manager was fired for failing to fulfill his duties.

4. **associate** [əˋsoʃɪət] (n.)
   副學士
   I transferred to a four-year college after getting my associate degree.

5. **proficiency** [prəˋfɪʃənsɪ] (n.)
   精通，熟練
   The sales position requires proficiency in Spanish.

6. **cumulative** [ˋkjumjələtɪv]
   (a.) 累積的，漸增的
   The scientists studied the cumulative effect of stress on the body.

7. **institution** [ˏɪnstɪˋtuʃən] (n.)
   機構，制度，習俗
   This university is the largest educational institution in the state.

 圖 解 英 文 輕鬆看懂有條件錄取信

May 12, 2019
Chang Hung-yi

5F, No. 12, Ln. 534, Wanda Rd.
Taipei 108, Taiwan

Dear Mr. Chang,

Congratulations on your *conditional admission to the University of Massachusetts, Dartmouth! We invite you to join our university community recognized as a *vibrant public university, actively engaged in [1]**personalized** teaching and innovative research, and acting as an intellectual *catalyst for regional and global economic, social, and cultural development.

Our offer of conditional admission is based on your [2]**enrollment** at Green River College, and is guaranteed for you to transfer to UMass Dartmouth. To [3]**fulfill** the conditions of your admission you must:

1. Complete an approved transferable [4]**associate**'s degree at Green River College.

2. Submit an approved form of proof of English [5]**Proficiency**, e.g., official TOEFL score of 68 (**iBT**), or a minimum IELTS score of 6.0.

3. Earn a minimum 2.5 [6]**cumulative** grade point average on transferrable credit from all previous [7]**institutions**. Please note that Engineering, [8]**Biology**, Chemistry, and Medical Laboratory Science majors require a minimum cumulative grade point average of 2.7. Students with a cumulative grade point average of 3.25 or higher [9]**qualify** to receive a [10]**merit** scholarship. Please visit www.umassd.edu/financialaid/scholarships/admissions/ for more information.

4. Submit a complete International Application with official copies of all [11]**transcripts** at www.umassd.edu/apply/.

5. *Adhere to UMass Dartmouth's deadlines for application and document submission, and admission policies.

6. Upon full admission, submit all required documents for F-1 student status and SEVIS transfer.

Please note that admission into a specific academic program is not guaranteed and is [12]**dependent on** specific program admission requirements and [13]**capacity**. For additional information, please contact us by e-mail at admissions@umassd.edu or by phone at the Admissions Office: 508-999-8605. We look forward to welcoming you to UMass Dartmouth.

Sincerely,
Ian Day
Vice *Chancellor for Enrollment Management

（人物為虛構）

什麼是 conditional admission（有條件錄取）？

條件式入學是指申請人在申請學校時，托福、雅思、GRE、GMAT、在學成績等，其中一項或多項未達學校要求標準，但學校仍然希望錄取此學生時，會給學生提出條件，並讓其在規定時間內完成後即可正式錄取，若未在規定時間完成，則取消錄取。條件式錄取並非所有學校都有，申請者需自行查詢申請學校是否有此項目。

條件式錄取有兩種：一種是學校會給你條件式的錄取通知，並給你此校 I-20，學生只需在規定時間內達到學校要求即可換取正式錄取。另一種則是學校會給你語言學校 I-20+ 學校錄取信，學生則需要完成學校規定語言課程後（依學校規定不同，有些還需經過學校語言考試或參加托福、雅思考試），方可正式進入大學就讀正式課程。

大部分國際學生收到條件式入學通知都是因為語言成績未達標準。多數學校有開設語言課程來幫助學生提高英語能力，至於一般要上多久，則取決於學生的語言能力。

2019 年 5 月 12 日
張宏毅

108 台灣台北
萬大路 534 巷 12 號 5 樓

親愛的張先生：

恭喜你獲得麻州大學達特茅斯分校的有條件錄取！我們邀請您加入我們的大學，本校是公認活力充沛的公立大學，積極從事個人化教學和創新研究，並為地區和全球經濟、社會與文化發展擔任智識催化劑的角色。

我們根據你在青溪社區大學的入學情況提供有條件錄取，可保證讓你轉學至本校。為了滿足你的錄取條件，你必須：

1. 在青溪大學完成符合轉學資格的副學士學位。

2. 提交合格的英語能力證明，例如托福網路測驗 68 分以上，或雅思 6 分以上的官方成績單。

3. 在先前就讀的所有大專院校中，符合轉學資格的學分累計平均成績達 2.5 以上。請注意，主修工程學、生物學、化學和醫學檢驗技術學的平均成績需達 2.7 以上。累計平均成績達 3.25 以上的學生可獲得優等獎學金。詳情請參考網站：www.umassd.edu/financialaid/scholarships/admissions/。

4. 請在本校網站提交完整的國際申請書，並附上所有官方成績單副本，網址：www.umassd.edu/apply/。

5. 請遵守本校申請書和文件提交的截止日期和入學政策。

6. 正式錄取後，請提交 F-1 學生身分和 SEVIS 轉學所需文件。

請注意，這不保證錄取特定學程，這取決於特定學程的錄取要求和名額。欲知詳情請以電郵聯絡：admissions@umassd.edu，或致電入學服務處：508-999-8605。我們期待並歡迎你就讀本校。

謹致

伊恩戴
入學管理副校長

（人物為虛構）

---

8. **biology** [baɪˋɑlədʒi] (n.) 生物學
Biology is the study of living things.

9. **qualify** [ˋkwɑləˏfaɪ] (v.) 具有資格，具備合格條件
A master's degree qualifies you to teach at the university level.

10. **merit** [ˋmɛrɪt] (n.) 功績，優點（這裡指成績）
Raises at our company are based on merit.

11. **transcript** [ˋtrænskrɪpt] (n.) 成績單，副本，抄本
Official transcripts should be sent directly to the Admissions Office.

12. **dependent (on)** [dɪˋpɛndənt] (a.) 取決於
Starting pay is dependent on your work experience.

13. **capacity** [kəˋpæsəti] (n.) 容量，容積
The stadium has a capacity of 30 thousand.

補充字彙

* **conditional** [kənˋdɪʃənəl] (a.) 有前提條件的

* **vibrant** [ˋvaɪbrənt] (a.) 活躍的，活潑的

* **catalyst** [ˋkætəlɪst] (n.) 催化劑

* **adhere (to)** (v.) [ədˋhɪr] 遵守

* **chancellor** [ˋtʃænsələ] (n.) （大學）校長

TOEFL iBT

托福網路測驗 (TOEFL iBT®) 是現階段北美洲大學入學許可之認證考試，由原先之 TOEFL CBT 電腦型態測驗於 2006 年 9 月停辦後，所改制而成。托福網路測驗 (TOEFL iBT®) 是使用電腦與耳機麥克風，透過網路即時連線至 ETS 進行線上測驗，考試範圍涵蓋「聽、說、讀、寫」四項技能。

LESSON 11
College Acceptance—Thank You Letter
第十一話：回覆錄取通知的感謝信

♫ 026 | 單字

Vocabulary Bank

1. **await** [əˈwet] (v.) 等候，期待
   I eagerly await your reply to my letter.

2. **attach** [əˈtætʃ] (v.) 把…作為電子郵件的附件，貼上，連接
   Remember to attach a photo to your application.

收到錄取通知信後該做什麼？

　　學生們在收到學校錄取通知信後，需儘早回覆是否前往就讀，並依照學校信中回覆方式回覆。有些學校是以 e-mail 方式寄送通知，這類一般會有超連結供學生線上回覆。有些學校則會在寄送的文件中附上一張 enrollment response card 供你填寫，寫好之後請傳真或寄回學校。另外，若都沒有提及，那麼你則需要打一份接受或回絕的信，告知對方你的決定。這是一種比較禮貌的作法，也讓人家知道你是否接受入學。

感謝信範本：

Dear Admissions Committee:

I am very pleased to accept your offer to enroll in the Master of Science in Biology program at the University of San Francisco. I truly appreciate your time and consideration during the admissions process. I look forward to attending your program in fall 2020, and am excited by the opportunities that [1] **await**.
Please find all the required documents [2]**attached** to this letter. If any additional information or documentation is needed, don't hesitate to contact me.

Sincerely,
Rebecca Chao

親愛的入學委員會：

我很高興接受舊金山大學生物科學碩士班的錄取通知。我衷心感謝貴校在錄取過程中撥冗考慮。我期待在 2020 年秋季入學，也為即將到來的機會感到興奮。
所有必須繳交的文件已隨信附上，若需要其他資料或文件，請隨時與我聯絡。

謹致
瑞貝卡趙

（人物為虛構）　範本

NOTE

LESSON 12
Rejection Letter
第十二話：拒絕入學信

 027｜單字

Vocabulary Bank

1. **clinical** [ˋklɪnɪkəl] (a.)
   臨床的，門診的
   The new medicine is still in clinical trials.

2. **psychology** [saɪˋkɑlədʒɪ] (n.)
   心理學
   It's important for coaches to have an understanding of sports psychology.

3. **comment** [ˋkɑmɛnt] (n./v.)
   意見，評論；發表意見
   The politician's comments have caused great controversy.

4. **referee** [͵rɛfəˋri] (n.) 推薦人
   All applicants must provide letters from three referees.

5. **relevant** [ˋrɛləvənt] (a.)
   相關的
   Your comment isn't relevant to the discussion.

6. **faculty** [ˋfækəltɪ] (n.) （高等院校、學系）全體教師（和行政人員）
   Students and faculty are invited to attend the lecture.

7. **exceed** [ɪkˋsid] (v.)
   超出，超過
   The driver was found guilty of exceeding the speed limit.

8. **unfavorable** [ʌnˋfevərəbəl] (a.) 不利的，負面的
   The film received mostly unfavorable reviews.

回絕錄取通知寫作重點：

　　如果申請者同時被多間學校錄取，則需選擇一間，其他則需禮貌性的回絕。因為招生官花了很多時間在你身上審查了你的資料，從禮貌上來說應該要感謝人家。從另外一方面來說，如果你不去的話，應該早點通知學校，把機會讓給在候補名單中的同學，這樣也比較不會影響到學校招生。此外若你決定不去也不回絕，則會給招生官留下負面的印象，這有可能會影響到你之後學弟妹們的申請，也可能會影響到你推薦人的可信度。撰寫回絕信不需要長篇大論，也不需要多做解釋，只需簡單、委婉即可。

回絕錄取通知信範本：

Dear Admissions Committee:

I am writing in response to your offer of admission to the Master's in **Clinical Psychology** program at Drexel University. I appreciate your interest in me, but I regret to inform you that I will not be accepting your offer of admission. Thank you for your time and consideration.

Sincerely,
Chien-ming Tseng

親愛的入學委員會：

謹此回覆卓克索大學錄取我就讀臨床心理學碩士的決定。感謝貴校對我的垂青，但很遺憾通知貴校，我不接受貴校的錄取。感謝貴校撥冗考慮。

謹致
曾建明

（人物為虛構）　範本

9. **endeavor** [ɪnˋdɛvɚ] (n.) **努力，力圖，事業**

I hope you succeed in all your endeavors.

Hui-min Yang
No. 26, Ln. 75, Guoguang St.
Hsinchu City, Taiwan

Dear Ms. Yang,

We regret that we are not able to offer you admission to the *Doctoral** Program in Education at UC Irvine. As you probably know, we look at each application as a whole. Admissions decisions are based on a *composite** of information including your previous academic performance, **comments** from **referees**, **relevant** professional activities, proposed research statements and GRE scores. Your application file was considered in detail by me and by the **faculty** members in your area of interest. The number of applications we received far **exceeded** the number of students we are able to accept, so we had to make very difficult admissions decisions. Each application is considered in relation to other applications in the same area, and only the top applicants are admitted. Your application, considered as a whole, was not as strong as some of the others we received.

Although I must regretfully send you an **unfavorable** response to your application, I appreciate your interest in our program and I certainly wish you the best for your future **endeavors**.

Yours truly,
Sandra Whalen, Ph.D.
Graduate Advisor

（人物為虛構）

補充字彙

* **doctoral** [ˋdɑctərəl] (a.) **博士的**

* **composite** [kəmˋpɑzɪt] (n.) **綜合體**

收到拒絕信，你可以怎麼做？

1. 保持積極的心態，並客觀地分析為何會被拒絕。學校拒絕你一定是有理由的，有時還可透過上訴（appeal）讓學校重新考慮錄取你。

2. 不要灰心喪志，若有申請其他學校，方可選擇去其他學校就讀。其實能滿足你要求的學校還有很多，不必糾結於一間不愛你的學校。

3. 若無申請其他學校或全部被拒絕，則需考慮補申請其他學校，例如社區大學，或推遲半年／一年再出發。

楊慧敏
台灣新竹市
國光路 75 巷 26 號

親愛的楊女士：

很遺憾我們無法錄取妳申請就讀加州大學爾灣分校的教育博士班。正如妳所知，我們是以整體情況審核每位申請者。錄取資格取決於綜合資料，包括妳以前的學業成績、推薦人的意見、相關專業活動、研究計畫書和 GRE 成績等。

妳的申請書是由我和妳所申請領域的教職員仔細審查。我們收到的申請數量遠遠超過所能錄取的名額，所以我們不得不做出非常困難的錄取決定。在考慮每位申請者時，都會與同一領域的其他申請者相比較，而我們只錄取最優秀的申請者。以整體來看，妳的申請書不如我們所收到的其他部分申請書優秀。

儘管我不得不遺憾地為妳的申請做出負面答覆，但仍感謝妳有興趣申請我們的課程，也祝福妳在未來一切順利。

謹致

桑卓華倫博士
碩士班指導教授

（人物為虛構）

PART 2

**完勝國外大學
必備英語**

Essential
English for
Overseas Study

GO

1. 辦理學生簽證

拿到 I-20 後
就可以約時間申請了。

2. 申請宿舍

收到學校寄來的錄取通知後
即可申請，如果不住宿舍，
要及早租屋或尋找寄宿家
庭。

3. 健康保險

學生保險基本上是含在學費
裡面的，不需要特別申請，
除非要另外買保險抵掉學校
保險。那麼在繳學費前做好
就好了。

4. 開帳戶

你需要有自己的帳戶，才能
存取錢。

Preparing

成功收到學校錄取通知 (offer) 好高興，
但這不表示你可以開始上課了。
正式上課前，還有不少要準備的事項，
這章就來告訴你，該做哪些準備工作。

TURN

7. 同學和室友

俗話說：「在家靠父母，出外靠朋友。」國際學生真的只能靠自己和朋友了，別忘了在迎新活動上認識幾個朋友，平常和室友聊聊天，認識一下。

8. 省錢

生活處處都需要錢，你註冊後可以去辦張學生證，用學生證買東西通常都會有折扣，我們也會教你省錢的秘訣喔。

6. 註冊

辦妥以上這些事以後，最重要的就是註冊了，別忘了先研究一下畢業需求，該選哪些課才能畢業，再來選課。

5. 迎新

基本的事情都完成後，應該去參加學校的迎新活動 (orientation)，比較能對學校有全面性的了解，包括熟悉校園、學校特色、社團等。

第二章：開課前準備

or Your Studies

2
CHAPTER

CHAPTER 2
開課前準備

Preparing for Your Studies

LESSON 1

APPLYING FOR A U.S. STUDENT VISA
第一話：申請美國學生簽證

028｜好用句

029｜單字

Vocabulary Bank

1. **scanner** [ˋskænɚ] (n.) **掃描機，掃描器**
   Does this printer have a scanner?
2. **relative** [ˋrɛlətɪv] (n.) **親戚、親屬**
   How often do you get together with your relatives?
3. **graduation** [ˌgrædʒuˋeʃən] (n.) **畢業**
   Are your parents coming to the graduation ceremony?

學生簽證種類

簽證類型	適合哪類人	居留時間
F-1 以學術性為目的，想取得學分及學位。	●從小學至博士留學生 ●語言學校 ●社區大學 ●綜合性大學 ●專科學校	●簽證有效期為 5 年，不過還是要以 I-20 上的日期為準。例如，申請人 4 年能夠從大學畢業並且沒有繼續升學或實習工作 (OPT) 的打算，那麼他的簽證有效期就是 4 年。 ●若 5 年內無法完成學業(延畢、繼續升學)，需申請簽證延期。 ●居留期到期後需在 60 天內離境。
J-1 以訪問、交流、研究、教學、實習、培訓為目的。	交換學生、打工旅遊 (Work and Travel) 學生、教師、教授、研究學者、醫師、政府訪問者等。	J-1 簽證會因各種不同交流訪問項目的不同，居留時間也會不同。一般來說，普通高中、大學交換學生最多 12-18 個月。
M-1 以學習職業技能為目的，而不是為了取得學分及學位。	飛行員、美容師、舞蹈家、廚師等。	●簽證有效期為 1 年，超過 1 年需申請簽證延期，延期時間以課程而定，最長不能超過 1 年（1 年簽證＋1年延期，最多共2年）。 ●居留期到期後需在 30 天內離境。

申請學生簽證流程

Step 1：上網填寫 DS-160 表格。

Step 2：上 USTravelDocs 網站，付申請費用。

Step 3：確認付費後，上 US Travel Docs 網站，預約去 AIT 的面談。

1. Please give me your passport and application form.

   請提供你的護照和申請表。

2. Do you have the form F-1/I-20? I need that, too.

   你有 F-1 / I-20 嗎？
   我還需要那個。

3. Please put your form up on the glass with the photo side facing me, so I can see it.

   請把表格放在玻璃上，
   有照片的那面朝著我，
   這樣我才看得到。

4. Place your left hand fingers on the [1]**scanner** without your thumb.

   請把你的左手手指放在掃描機上，
   大拇指不用。

5. Fingers together and no space in between.

   手指併攏，中間不留空。

6. Now do the same with your right hand.

   右手也做一樣的動作。

7. Stay there and we're done.

   維持這個姿勢，好了，結束了。

8. You can now go to the Interview Section.

   你現在可以去面試區。

Common Phrases | 申請學生簽證面試，你要聽得懂

1. Why do you want to study in the U.S.?

   你為何想來美國念書？

2. Why did you choose this specific school/major?

   你為何選擇這所學校 / 這個主修？

3. Do you have any [2]**relatives** in the U.S.?

   你在美國有親戚嗎？

4. How do you plan to fund your studies?

   你要如何支付學費？

5. What are your plans after [3]**graduation**?

   你畢業後有什麼計畫？

簽證 面談程序

01 資料輸入

● 遞交申請表和護照，若需要其他相關資料（I-20）會再請申請人提供。

02 指紋掃描

● 將申請表格的正面面向官員，並把表格貼靠在玻璃窗上。
● 依照指示，分別將四根手指平放在指紋掃描機上，然後換雙手大拇指。

03 面談

將申請表和護照遞交後，即開始面談。若決定核發簽證，將會把護照收走，並給申請人一張快遞條碼單。

04 辦理快遞手續

收到快遞條碼單後，請離開並填寫快遞申請單。填完後，請至快遞窗口，繳交快遞申請單和條碼單，即可離開。

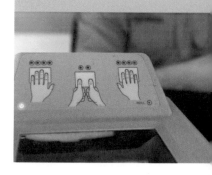

🎵 030 | 好用句＋對話

🎵 031 | 單字

Vocabulary Bank

1. **reputation** [ˌrɛpjəˈteʃən] (n.) 名譽，名聲
   The scandal destroyed the senator's reputation.

2. **career** [kəˈrɪr] (n.) 職業，生涯
   After a long career in journalism, James will be retiring in August.

進階字彙

* **semiconductor** [ˈsɛmikənˌdʌktə] (n.) 半導體

Common Phrases | 申請學生簽證面試，你要會說

1. A U.S. degree will help me find a better job.
   美國學位能夠幫我找到比較好的工作。

2. I hope to work at an international firm in Taiwan.
   我希望未來能在台灣的外商公司上班。

3. The U.S. has the best programs in my field.
   針對我的領域，美國提供最好的課程。

4. The school / program has an excellent [1]**reputation.**
   這間學校／這個課程享有盛名。

5. The school is well known for **research** in my field.
   我的領域在這間學校以學術研究聞名。

6. I have an aunt in Seattle, but we aren't in touch.
   我有個阿姨在西雅圖，但我們沒什麼聯絡。

7. My parents will be funding my studies.
   我的父母會幫我付學費。

8. I plan on returning to Taiwan and starting my [2]**career.**
   我的計畫是回台灣後工作。

Useful Pattern | 形容自己的學校，就這樣說

▶ **I'm really impressed by the _____ at Stanford.**
（我覺得史丹佛大學的 _____ 很棒。）

faculty 師資
facilities 設施、設備（恆用複數）
courses 課程
academics 學科（恆用複數）
research environment 學術環境

SITUATION 1

F-1 Visa Interview F-1
學生簽證面試

Interviewer Why do you want to go to the U.S.

Student I want to go there to get a master's in electrical engineering.

Interviewer OK. Which school will you attend?

Student I'll be going to UC Berkeley.

Interviewer Why did you choose this school?

Student It's one of the top engineering programs in the U.S.

Interviewer What are your plans after graduation?

Student I'll return to Taiwan and find a job in the *semiconductor industry.

Interviewer How will you support your studies in the U.S.?

Student I'll be using my personal savings and money borrowed from my parents.

面試者 你為什麼想要去美國？

學生 我想去那裡取得電機碩士學位。

面試者 好，你念的是哪一所學校？

學生 我要讀柏克萊大學。

面試者 你為什麼選這所學校？

學生 它提供美國數一數二的工程課程。

面試者 你畢業後有什麼計畫？

學生 我會回台灣，從事半導體工作。

面試者 你要如何支付在美國念書的開支？

學生 我會用自己的存款，以及和父母借來的錢支付。

答題技巧

1. 誠實回答面試官所有問題。

2. 避開有移民傾向之回答，例如：嚮往美國生活、環境好、就業機會好等。

3. 所有回答圍繞著「讀書」來說，例如：嚮往美國教育、有個美國學歷回來後比較好找工作等。讓移民官覺得你無移民傾向，畢業後會回國。

4. 面試前請查好，並記好學校相關資料，例如：學校名字、地理位置、歷史、讀科系等。

5. 若有問到畢業之後的計畫，請圍繞著「回國」來說，例如：畢業後要回國工作、想多花時間陪父母。

6. 準備好所有資料以備不時之需，例如：存款證明、父母收入證明等。寧可多帶沒用到，也不要少帶。

7. 若有被拒簽紀錄，也請被問到時誠實回答，並說明原因，例如：準備不足等。

8. 面試前，請記清申請表格DS-160 上所有填寫內容。若有被問到相關內容，比較不會答出錯誤的答案。

CHAPTER

開課前準備

2

Preparing for
Your Studies

LESSON 2

Applying for Campus Housing
第二話：申請宿舍

🎵 032 | 好用句

🎵 033 | 單字

Vocabulary Bank

1. **freshman** [ˈfrɛʃmən] (n./a.)
   (高中、大學) 一年級生；一年級 (生) 的
   My younger sister is a college freshman.

2. **lounge** [laʊndʒ] (n.) **休息室，會客廳**
   Mr. Smith always eats lunch in the teacher's lounge.

3. **facility** [fəˈsɪlətɪ] (n.) **設施，設備**（此定義用複數 **facilities** [fəˈsɪlətiz]）
   Hotel facilities include a restaurant, bar and business center.

4. **furnished** [ˈfɜnɪʃt] (a.) **附家具的，unfurnished** [ʌnˈfɜnɪʃt] 即「未附家具的」
   Are you looking for a furnished or unfurnished apartment?

5. **decoration** [ˌdɛkəˈreʃən] (n.) **裝飾品**
   Where did you buy the decorations for your Halloween party?

6. **prohibit** [prəˈhɪbɪt] (v.) **禁止**
   Smoking is prohibited inside the restaurant.

7. **Internet** [ˈɪntɚˌnɛt] (n.) **網際網路**
   You can find all the information you need on the Internet.

8. **cable** [ˈkebəl] (n.) **有線（電視）**
   The new cable service lets you watch movies and shows on demand.

一般來說，宿舍住宿有哪幾種類型？

美國大學宿舍有分學生公寓型（apartment）跟學生宿舍型（residence hall）。一般分為男女單住，也就是一棟宿舍裡只有男生或女生。另一種常見的是男女混住，也就是一棟宿舍裡有男有女。

男女混住又分幾種：

⚫ 同一棟樓裡有分男生樓層跟女生樓層
⚫ 同一棟樓裡男女都住在同一樓層

	公寓型	宿舍型
房型	單人公寓、雙人公寓、三或四人公寓	單人房、雙人房、三或四人房
房間設備	單獨臥室，住客共用客廳、廚房、衛浴	單人床、衣櫃、書桌等，浴室通常是同一層樓共用，少數學生宿舍的房間可能會附有淋浴裝置及廁所的套房。
性別	男女混住或男女單住	男女混住或男女單住
價位（設備越齊全，人數越少越貴）	高	中
優點	較有私人空間，可自行進行料理。	容易與別房同學進行交流，利於社交。有包含學校伙食，無需自行料理。
缺點	無包含學校伙食，需自行料理或需交比宿舍學生價格稍高的學校伙食費。	需與室友公共房間，較無私人空間。無客廳、廚房，室友共用房間，廁所衛浴整層樓共用。

● 請在看完馬修挑選宿舍的條件 (criteria) 後，從以下三棟宿舍中，為他選出最符合需求的宿舍：

Matthew is an incoming college [1]**freshman** who is looking for a two-bed room. He wants to stay in a *co-ed a residence with a [2]**lounge** area and shared kitchen for $3,500 per semester or less. Which of the following is best suited to his needs?

1) Davis Residence	2) Harrison Hall	3) Connelly Apartments
1. Sex: men only	1. Type: M/F	1. Sex: M/F
2. Floor plan: single and double rooms	2. Floor plan: double *occupancy rooms	2. Floor plan: 3-BR apartments
3. Price: $3,400 per semester	3. Price: $3,600 per semester	3. Price: $4,200 per semester
4. *Amenities: free laundry, study area	4. Amenities: shared private restrooms, cooking [3]facilities	4. Amenities: 24-hour security, full kitchen

解答：2) Harrison Hall
翻譯請見 p. 212

Common Phrases | 詢問宿舍相關問題，你要會說

1. Is it possible to request a *roommate? 　是否可指定室友？

2. Can I request a specific residence hall? 　是否可指定特定宿舍大樓？

3. Do the apartments come [4]**furnished**? 　公寓是否附家具？

4. Is it possible to change rooms after I sign a contract? 　簽訂合約後是否能換房間？

5. What personal items and [5]**decorations** are permitted/ [6]**prohibited** in the dorms? 　宿舍裡允許/禁止哪些個人物品和裝飾品？

6. Is there a damage deposit? 　是否有損壞押金？

7. Do you provide [7]**Internet** and [8]**cable** TV services? 　是否提供網路和有線電視服務？

補充字彙

* **co-ed** [ˋko͵ɛd] (a.) 男女混合（同校）的

* **amenity** [əˋmɛnəti] (n.) 便利設施，生活福利設施（此定義用複數 amenities [əˋmɛnətiz]

* **occupancy** [ˋɑkjəpənsi] (n.) 居住，占用

房屋配備

· **high-speed Internet** 高速上網
· **cable television** 有線電視
· **air-conditioning** 冷氣
· **heat** 暖氣
· **extra-long beds** 床鋪加長
· **movable furniture** 活動家具
· **free laundry 24/7** 全天候免費洗衣房
· **community lounge & study space** 社區會客室和閱覽室
· **card-access entry system** 門禁卡進出系統
· **24/7 front desk** 全天候櫃臺服務
· **shared private bathrooms** 共用私人浴室

挑選室友

學生數量多，宿舍量少，越早申請越能申請到自己理想的宿舍。學校會盡可能的按照你的要求去為你選擇室友以及房型，不過不一定每個人都能分配到完美的室友及房型。另外，美國是個多種族的國家，所以填申請表時不要有種族歧視，像是不能寫「不想和⋯人住」，只能針對生活習慣、個性等方面去填寫。

🎵 **034** | 好用句

🎵 **035** | 單字

Vocabulary Bank

1. **preference** [ˈprɛfərəns] (n.)
   喜好，愛好
   I have a preference for spicy food.

2. **appliance** [əˈplaɪəns] (n.)
   家電，用具
   The store sells kitchen and bathroom appliances.

3. **triple** [ˈtrɪpəl] (a.) **三倍的**
   Becky ate a triple scoop of ice cream.

4. **-oriented** [ˈɔrɪəntɪd] (字尾)
   以…為目標的，以…為導向的
   Kate wants to date a guy who is career-oriented.

5. **socialize** [ˈsoʃəˌlaɪz] (v.)
   交際，參加社交活動
   Martha is so busy with work that she has no time to socialize.

6. **outgoing** [ˈaʊtˌgoɪŋ] (a.)
   開朗的，外向的
   Tom's outgoing personality made him popular at school.

7. **overnight** [ˌovəˈnaɪt] (a./adv.) **過夜的，夜間的**
   We took the overnight train to Venice.

Common Phrases | 詢問宿舍相關問題，你要看得懂

1. Roommate requests are allowed, but students must be in same academic college.
   可以指定室友，但學生必須就讀同一間學院。

2. You may request a specific hall, but there is no guarantee you will receive your [1]**preference**.
   可以指定特定大樓，但不保證能如願申請到。

3. Apartments come furnished and equipped with major [2]**appliances**.
   公寓附有家具，並配備主要電器。

4. It's possible to change rooms, but availability may be limited.
   可以換房間，但可供更換的房間有限。

5. All normal personal items are allowed, but ***flammable** items are not permitted.
   允許所有一般個人物品，但禁止可燃物品。

6. There is a $300 deposit that is refunded when the student moves or graduates.
   有 300 美元押金，學生遷出或畢業時可退回。

7. All rooms come with Internet service and basic cable.
   所有房間都有網路服務和基本有線電視。

圖解英文 | 輕鬆看懂室友偏好表

① **Major** | 主修
② **I am applying for a** | 要申請的房型
③ **Contract length** | 合約期限
④ **Roommate preferences** | 室友偏好（可複選）
⑤ 我可以接受和以下何種性別同住
⑥ **Do you smoke?** | 你抽菸嗎？
⑦ 你可以接受與抽菸者同住？
⑧ **What do you do for fun?** | 你的娛樂活動是什麼？
⑨ **Academic & intellectual interests** | 學術或智識興趣

⑩ **What qualities are important to you in a roommate?** | 室友的哪種素質對你來說很重要？
⑪ **Room Care and Use** | 房間管理和使用：對於房間「髒亂」的容忍度、房間的用途與溫度
⑫ **Sleep Habits** | 睡覺習慣：作息時間、睡眠深淺、習慣窗戶開或關
⑬ **Study Habits** | 讀書習慣：在哪讀書、讀書時間、習慣的背景聲音
⑭ **My Personality** | 我的個性：個人空間、音樂喜好
⑮ **Overnight Guests** | 過夜客人

翻譯請見 p. 212

Roommate Preference Sheet

If you are a new student or don't have a roommate at the time of residence hall room selection, please complete this form to assist campus staff in assigning a *compatible roommate.

Name:_____ ❶ Major: _____ Gender: _____ Phone: _____
E-mail: _____

❷ I am applying for a: ☐ double room ☐ ³⁾triple room
❸ Contract length: ☐ year ☐ fall ☐ spring

❹ Roommate preferences (check all that apply): ☐ new student
  ☐ returning student ☐ international student ☐ *LGBTQ student

❺ I would be comfortable living with someone of the following gender identity
  (check all that apply):
  ☐ male ☐ female ☐ *transgender ☐ *non-binary

❻ Do you smoke? ☐ yes ☐ no
❼ Are you comfortable with a roommate who smokes? ☐ yes ☐ no

❽ What do you do for fun? _____
❾ Academic & intellectual interests _____
❿ What qualities are important to you in a roommate? _____

⓫ Room Care and Use:
My room at home is: ☐ always clean and organized ☐ fairly clean and neat
                    ☐ *cluttered and messy
I want my room to be: quiet and study-⁴⁾oriented
                    ☐ a place to ⁵⁾socialize ☐ a combination of quiet/social
I want the temperature to be: ☐ cold ☐ cool ☐ warm ☐ very warm

⓬ Sleep Habits:
What time do you prefer to go to bed? _____ What time do you get up? _____
I consider myself a: ☐ light sleeper ☐ heavy sleeper
                     ☐ I can sleep through anything
When I sleep I: ☐ snore ☐ *sleepwalk/talk ☐ windows open
                ☐ windows shut

⓭ Study Habits:
I prefer to study: ☐ inside room ☐ outside room
                   ☐ both inside and outside room
I plan to study: ☐ in morning ☐ in afternoon ☐ in evening
                 ☐ late at night
When I study I: ☐ listen to music ☐ need total quiet
                ☐ don't have preference

⓮ My Personality:
I consider myself: ☐ shy ☐ ⁶⁾outgoing ☐ relaxed ☐ energetic
I require: ☐ very little private time ☐ a little private time
           ☐ a lot of private time
Musical preferences: ☐ classical ☐ jazz ☐ rock ☐ country ☐ rap
                     ☐ R&B

⓯ ⁷⁾Overnight Guests:
  ☐ I am comfortable with overnight guests
  ☐ I am not comfortable with overnight guests

補充字彙

* **roommate** [ˋrum͵met] (n.)
  室友

* **flammable** [ˋflæməbəl] (a.)
  易燃的

* **compatible** [kəmˋpætəbəl]
  (a.) 相容的，可共存的

* **LGBTQ** [͵ɛldʒibitiˋkju] (a.)
  多元性別，由 lesbian（女
  同性戀者）、gay（男同性戀
  者）、bisexual（雙性戀者）、
  transgender（跨性別者）、
  queer（自由性別者）這幾個字
  組成

* **transgender**
  [trænzˋdʒɑndə] (n.) 跨性別者

* **non-binary** [nɑnˋbaɪnə͵i] (a.)
  非二元性別的

* **cluttered** [ˋklʌtəd] (a.) 雜亂
  的，塞滿的

* **sleepwalk** [ˋslip͵wɑk] (v.)
  夢遊

LESSON 3
Student Health Insurance Plan
第三話：學生健保計畫

 036 | 好用句

 037 | 單字

Vocabulary Bank

1. **dental** [ˈdɛntəl] (a.) **牙齒的，牙科的**

   Does your company provide dental insurance?

2. **prescription** [prɪˈskrɪpʃən] (n.) **處方，（眼鏡）度數，動詞為 prescribe** [prɪˈskraɪb] (v.) **開藥，開處方**

   I need a refill of this prescription.

3. **coverage** [ˈkʌvərɪdʒ] (n.) **保險涵蓋範圍，當動詞為 cover 指「給⋯保險，承保，包括，足夠支付」**

   Which company provides better health coverage?

4. **annual** [ˈænjuəl] (a.) **一年一次的**

   He won the annual tennis tournament three years in a row.

5. **medication** [ˌmɛdɪˈkeʃən] (n.) **藥物，藥物治療**

   A prescription is required for this medication.

補充字彙

* **inpatient** [ˈɪnˌpeʃənt] (n.) **住院病人，outpatient** [ˈaʊtˌpeʃənt] 為「門診病人」

* **copay** [ˈkoˌpe] (n.) **掛號費，定額手續費（被保險人用於就醫或配藥所支付的小額費用）**

* **deductible** [dɪˈdʌktəbəl] (n.) **自付額**

國際學生健保

　　學生健康保險是強制性的，大部分學校會將國際學生自動納入學校的學生保險方案中，若你能提供替換的保險單證明，也是可以退出學校保險的。但有些學校為了保險起見，也會強制要求國際學生保學校的方案，以防萬一。

　　雖然美國政府並未在國際學生相關法條中規定國際學生必須要有健康保險，也不會因為你沒有出示健康保險證明就取消你的簽證。不過學校卻可能會因為你沒有健康保險而不讓你註冊拿學分（美國政府規定國際學生每學期需最少拿 12 個學分），這結果會導致你學生簽證失效。不過值得慶幸的是，國際學生和美國當地學生所支付的費用是一樣的。

學校健保包含項目

　　學校健保通常有包括一般醫療，例如，住院、醫生門診、急診、處方藥、身體檢查等。有些學生保險還有包括牙科、眼科等。每間學校所提供的健保方案不同，包含的項目越多，保費越高。加入學校健保後，學生會獲得學生健保卡，上面有學生的姓名、年齡、地址、保險號碼等資訊，學生需妥善保管並隨身攜帶，以便不時之需。

Common Phrases | 健保問題，你要會說

1. Are international students required to enroll in your health insurance plan?

   國際學生是否規定要參加你們的健保計畫？

2. Does the health insurance plan cover ***inpatient** and ***outpatient** medical care?

   健保計畫是否包含住院和門診醫療？

3. Does the health plan cover vision and 1)**dental**?

   健保計畫是否包含眼科和牙科？

4. Will I be covered when I go out of state?

   到外州是否能使用健保？

5. How much are ***copays** and ***deductibles**?

   掛號費和自付額是多少？

6. Are 2)**prescription** drugs included in the health insurance plan?

   健保計畫是否給付處方藥？

7. When does my 3)**coverage** begin and end?

   保單從何時開始，到何時結束？

Common Phrases | 健保問題，你要聽得懂

1. Yes. International students are automatically enrolled in our health insurance plan.

   是的。國際學生會自動加入我們的健保計畫。

2. Yes. Inpatient, outpatient and emergency room care are all covered.

   是的。住院、門診和急診醫療全都包含。

3. The plan covers one 4)**annual** eye exam and dental care for injury to natural teeth.

   健保計畫包含一年一次眼科檢查和天然牙齒受損的醫療。

4. Yes. As long as care is provided by an in-network provider.

   是的。只要是由網內醫療機構提供的服務都可使用健保。

5. There is an annual deductible of $300 and no copays for in-network care.

   一年自付額是 300 元，網內醫療服務不需付掛號費。

6. Yes. Most prescription 5)**medications** are covered.

   是的。大部分處方藥可給付。

7. Coverage for the coming year begins on 08/19/2020 and ends on 08/18/2021.

   下一年保單從 2020 年 8 月 19 日開始至 2021 年 8 月 18 日結束。

學生健保的建議

在美國沒有保險是很危險的一件事情，美國醫療很貴，若你沒保險生病或發生意外，所花費的金額可能會讓你傾家蕩產。美國有很多不同類型的健康保險，如果願意花時間研究，說不定能找到物美價廉的保險。如果不願意花時間，學校保險也是個不錯的選擇，但缺點就是保費相對稍高，因為他是針對所有學生集體提出的保險方案。學生保險的另一個缺點是，很多學校是會按照學期來幫學生購買保險的，也就是說，若你某學期沒有註冊上學，那麼你就會沒有保險。例如，很多學生在暑期會選擇不上學，但留在美國旅遊或實習，那麼因為你沒有註冊，所以這段時間你將會失去保險保護。

 038 | 單字

Vocabulary Bank

1. **maximum** [ˋmæksəməm]
   (a./n.) **最大的，對多的;最大量、
   數等**

   The maximum sentence for
   murder is life in prison.

2. **benefit** [ˋbɛnəfɪt] (n.) **福利，
   (如醫療保險、人壽保險等) 給
   付項目**

   Our company offers excellent
   wages and benefits.

3. **addiction** [əˋdɪkʃən] (n.)
   成癮，癮頭

   The star admitted his drug
   addiction in a TV interview.

4. **device** [dɪˋvaɪs] (n.) **器具，裝
   置，設備**

   Our store sells all the latest
   wireless devices.

5. **preventive** [prɪˋvɛntɪv] (a.)
   預防性的，亦作 preventative
   [prɪˋvɛntɛtɪv]

   The government has
   announced a new preventive
   health program.

6. **chronic** [ˋkrɑnɪk] (a.) **(尤指
   疾病或不好的事物) 慢性的，長
   期的**

   Greg suffers from chronic back
   pain.

7. **cavity** [ˋkævətɪ] (n.) **(牙齒的)
   蛀洞**

   Sue needs to go to the dentist
   to get a cavity filled.

📖 Reading Quiz | 閱讀測驗

● 請在看完學生健保保單概要後，回答下面問題：

STUDENT HEALTH INSURANCE COVERAGE SUMMARY, 2020-2021

PLAN *PREMIUM & DEDUCTABLE	School Plan
Type of plan	Individual
Annual premium	$4,566
Annual deductible	$500

PLAN REQUIREMENTS (under *Affordable Care Act)	School Plan Benefits
Annual out-of-pocket [1]**maximum** must be =/< $7,900	$1,500
Treatment for pre-existing conditions	Yes
ESSENTIAL HEALTH [2]**BENEFITS**	
Outpatient care	Yes
Emergency services	Yes
Inpatient care	Yes
Mental health services and [3]**addiction** treatment	Yes
Prescription drugs	Yes
***Maternity** and newborn care	Yes
***Rehabilitative** services and [4]**devices**	Yes
Laboratory services	Yes
Inpatient mental health care	Yes
[5]**Preventive** services and [6]**chronic** disease treatment	Yes
***Pediatric** services	Yes
Coverage for medical ***evacuation** and ***repatriation** expenses •Required for all F1 / J1 students •Required for all other students ONLY when they will be studying / traveling / doing research out of the United States during the current academic year	Yes
Active coverage from the day student arrives on campus through August 31, 2021 or the end of their academic program (whichever comes first)	Yes

1. What is the price per year of student health insurance?

(A) $500
(B) $1,500
(C) $4,566
(D) $7,900

2. Which of the following is NOT covered by the health plan?

(A) Treatment for children
(B) Medicine prescribed by a doctor
(C) A hospital stay
(D) Getting a [7]**cavity** filled

3. What would happen if a student became critically ill while outside the U.S.?

(A) They would receive medical treatment abroad.
(B) They would be transported to the U.S. for treatment.
(C) They would have to pay for their own treatment.
(D) They would lose their health insurance coverage.

解答：1. (C) 2. (D) 3. (B)
翻譯請見 p. 212

解說
1. 學生的保費為每年 $4566，一年自付額 $500 會根據學生的使用額度來判斷是否要再酌收。
2. 選項中只有 (D) 齲齒補牙未涵蓋在保單內。

補充字彙

* **premium** [ˈprimiəm] (n.) 保險費
* **affordable** [əˈfɔrdəbəl] (a.) 負擔得起的
* **maternity** [məˈtɜnəti] (a./n.) 孕婦的，產科的；母性
* **rehabilitative** [ˌrihəˈbɪləˌtetɪv] (a.) 復健的，康復的
* **pediatric** [ˌpidiˈætrɪk] (a.) (醫) 小兒科的
* **evacuation** [ɪˌvækjuˈeʃən] (n.) 避難，疏散
* **repatriation** [rɪˌpetriˈeʃən] (n.) 遣送回國，調回本國

LESSON 4
Air Travel for Overseas Students
第四話：留學生美國出入境

🎵 039 | 對話

🎵 040 | 單字

Vocabulary Bank

1. **immigration** [ˌɪmɪˈɡreʃən]
   (n.) **入境（檢查），移民**
   Going through immigration
   was a nightmare.

2. **customs** [ˈkʌstəmz] (n.) **海關**
   Did they check your luggage
   when you went through
   customs?

3. **declare** [dɪˈklɛr] (v.) **申報（納稅品等）**
   All fruits and vegetables must
   be declared to a customs
   officer.

補充字彙

∗ **paperwork** [ˈpepɚˌwɝk] (n.)
   資料，檔案

▎入境文件

做為一個拿學生簽證的學生，入境需要準備包括護照、I-20、入境申請表、海關申請表。如果是首次拿學生簽證入境，則需多準備包括學校錄取通知書、存款證明、學歷證明（高中成績單／畢業證書）等來備用以便不時之需。學生需要注意的是，千萬不能把這些文件放入托運行李裡，需隨身攜帶，托運行李只能在出海關後領取。另外，學生還需檢查 I-20 的日期，首次入境者，只能在開學前 30 天內入境，不可提前。而非首次拿 I-20 入境者則需在離開美國前檢查 I-20 的到期日，若 I-20 會在你離開美國中到期，則需先到學校國際學生服務處辦理 I-20 更新。

▎獲得學生簽證就一定能入境美國？

不一定。所有類的簽證都只是能讓你到美國海關而已，至於讓不讓你入境，則是取決於海關。若你資料準備不齊全或海關覺得你可疑，他們是有權利拒絕你入境，並原機遣返。

▎入境必備知識

學生到美國是為了進行學業進修，所以入境時需先了解自己即將就讀學校的各種信息。例如，學校名字、地理位置、就讀科系、大概學費，以及美國居住地址等。

[1]Immigration
入境

Officer	What is the purpose of your visit?
Student	I'm here to attend graduate school. Here's my *paperwork.
Officer	All right. Everything appears to be in order. What will be your major?
Student	I'll be majoring in electrical engineering.

移民官	你這次造訪的目的是什麼？
學生	我是來就讀研究所。這是我的文件。
移民官	好。文件看起來都很齊全。你主修什麼？
學生	我主修電機工程學。

At [2]customs
過海關

Officer	Do you have anything to [3]declare?
Student	Just some instant noodles and a package of mushrooms.
Officer	Are the mushrooms fresh or dried?
Student	They're dried.
Officer	OK. That's fine.

海關	你有什麼要申報的嗎？
學生	只有幾包泡麵和一包香菇。
海關	香菇是新鮮的還是乾燥的？
學生	是乾燥的。
海關	好，那就沒問題。

其他可能問題與建議回答方式

Q1 若你不是從學校所在地入境的話，可能會被問到為何從這邊入境？

回答重點：可回答因為這邊有朋友，想先過來探望一下。

Q2 你帶了多少現金、支票？（入境美國攜帶超過 $10,000 美金需申報）如何繳交學費？

回答重點：照實回答。建議先準備好至少第一學期的學費。

Q3 你在大學都拿哪些課程？拿了多少學分？

回答重點：清楚了解你在學校的所有計畫細節。

🎵 041 | 好用句

🎵 042 | 單字

Vocabulary Bank

1. **sponsor** [ˈspɑnsə] (v.) 資助，贊助
   The conference was sponsored by the local government.

2. **profession** [prəˈfɛʃən] (n.) （受過專門訓練的）職業
   I'm considering a career in the legal profession.

補充字彙

* **partner** [ˈpɑrtnə] (n.) （公司的）合夥人

Common Phrases | 入境問題，你要聽得懂

1. Have you visited the U.S. before? | 你以前來過美國嗎？

2. How many schools were you accepted to? | 有幾所學校錄取你？

3. How long will you study in the U.S.? | 你會在美國讀幾年？

4. Where did you complete your undergraduate degree? | 你在哪裡完成大學學位？

5. What are your TOEFL and GRE scores? | 你的托福和 GRE 成績是多少？

6. Do you want to stay in the U.S. after you graduate? | 你畢業後想留在美國嗎？

7. Who is [1]**sponsoring** your studies and what is their [2]**profession**? | 是誰資助你念書，他們的職業是什麼？

8. Do you plan on working while you're here? | 你留在這裡時打算工作嗎？

Common Phrases | 入境問題，你要會說

1. Yes. I came to study English last summer. | 是的，我去年夏天來這裡學英語。

2. Two—Cal State East Bay and UC Santa Cruz. | 有兩所。加州州立大學東灣分校和加州大學聖塔克魯茲分校。

3. My master's degree will take two years to finish. | 我的碩士學位需要兩年才能完成。

4. I graduated from National Yang-Ming University in Taipei. | 我畢業於台北的國立陽明大學。

5. My TOEFL score is 88 and my GRE score is 325. | 我的托福成績是 88 分，GRE 成績是 325 分。

6. No. I plan on returning to Taiwan and starting my career. | 不，我打算回台灣工作。

7. My father. He's a ***partner** at an accounting firm. | 我父親。他是一間會計事務所的合夥人。

8. No. I want to devote my full time to my studies. | 不，我想專心當全職學生。

❶ **Name** │ 姓名：Last 填上「姓氏」，First 填上「名字」

❷ **Birth date** │ 生日

❸ **Number of Family members traveling with you** │ 同行家庭成員人數

❹ **U.S. Street Address** │ 在美地址（旅館或目的地地址）

❺ **Passport issued by** │ 護照發行國家

❻ **Passport number** │ 護照號碼

❼ **Country of Residence** │ 居住國家

❽ **Countries visited on this trip prior to U.S. arrival** │ 此次旅行在抵達美國前去過的國家

❾ **Airline/Flight No.** │ 航空公司 / 飛機班次

❿ 若這次旅行目的是出差，勾選 Yes。

⓫ 不可攜帶任何農產品或以家禽製成的原物料進入美國。若有攜帶，一定要據實勾選。

⓬ 若有跟家禽類有接觸，勾選 Yes。

⓭ 若攜帶總值超過美金一萬元的「貨幣」currency 或「金融票據」monetary instruments，勾選 Yes。「金融票據」指「支票、匯票、匯款單」等。

⓮ 若攜帶「商品」commercial merchandise，勾選 Yes。

⓯ 若攜帶物品總值超過 1400 美金，須將重要物品條列於背面「物品清單」Description of Articles。

⓰ I have read the above statements and have made a truthful declaration. │ 我已閱讀完上面所有注意事項，並已誠實申報。（在下面簽名，並註明日期）

Customs Declaration

FORM APPROVED
OMB NO.1651-0009

19 CFR 122.27, 148.12, 148.13, 148.110, 148.111, 19 USC 1498; 31 CFR 5316

Each arriving traveler or responsible family member must provide the following information (only ONE written declaration per family is required). The term "family" is defined as "members of a family residing in the same household who are related by blood, marriage, domestic relationship, or adoption."

1 Family **Name**

First (Given)　　　　　　　　　Middle

2 **Birth date**　Month　　　Day　　　Year

3 Number of **Family members** traveling with you

4 (a) U.S. Street Address (hotel name/destination)

(b) City　　　　　　　　(c) State

5 **Passport issued by** (country)

6 **Passport number**

7 Country of **Residence**

8 **Countries visited** on this trip prior to U.S. arrival

9 **Airline/Flight No.** or **Vessel Name**

10 The primary purpose of this trip is **business**:　Yes　No

11 I am (We are) bringing

(a) fruits, vegetables, plants, seeds, food, insects:　Yes　No

(b) meats, animals, animal/wildlife products:　Yes　No

(c) disease agents, cell cultures, snails:　Yes　No

(d) soil or have been on a farm/ranch/pasture:　Yes　No

12 I have (We have) been in close proximity of **livestock**:　Yes　No

(such as touching or handling)

13 I am (We are) carrying **currency or monetary instruments** over $10,000 U.S. or foreign equivalent:　Yes　No

(see definition of monetary instruments on reverse)

14 I have (We have) **commercial merchandise**:　Yes　No

(articles for sale, samples used for soliciting orders, or goods that are not considered personal effects)

15 RESIDENTS—the total value of all goods, including commercial merchandise I/we have purchased or acquired abroad, (including gifts for someone else but not items mailed to the U.S.) and am/are bringing to the U.S. is:　$

VISITORS—the total value of all articles that will remain in the U.S., including commercial merchandise is:　$

Read the instructions on the back of this form. Space is provided to list all the items you must declare.

16 I HAVE READ THE IMPORTANT INFORMATION ON THE REVERSE SIDE OF THIS FORM AND HAVE MADE A TRUTHFUL DECLARATION.

X

Signature　　　　　　　　　Date (month/day/year)

CBP Form 6059B (11/16)

LESSON 5
Bachelor and Master's Degree Graduation Requirements
第五話：學士和研究生畢業需求

♫ 043 | 句型

♫ 044 | 單字

Vocabulary Bank

1. **bachelor** [ˋbætʃələ] (n.) 學士，單身漢

   Kelly has a bachelor of arts in economics.

2. **architecture** [ˋɑrkɪ,tɛktʃə] (n.) 建築，建築學

   The city of Aberdeen in Scotland is famous for its Gothic architecture.

3. **biological** [,baɪəˋlɑdʒɪkəl] (a.) 生物的，與生命過程有關的

   The country was accused of developing biological weapons.

4. **mechanical** [məˋkænɪkəl] (a.) 機械的

   Our flight was delayed due to mechanical problems.

5. **nutritional** [ˋnutrɪʃənəl] (a.) 營養（學）的

   Most fast food has poor nutritional value.

6. **philosophy** [fɪˋlɑsəfi] (n.) 哲學

   There aren't many career options for philosophy majors.

7. **physics** [ˋfɪzɪks] (n.) 物理學

   Einstein made many important discoveries in physics.

8. **sociology** [,soʃiˋɑlədʒi] (n.) 社會學

   Sociology is the study of human society.

Useful Pattern | 想取得的科系和學位，就這樣說

▶ **I want to pursue a/an ① (in) ② .**

我想要取得②（系）的①（學位）。

①常見學位縮寫

學士主修

B.A. = [1]**Bachelor of Arts** 文學學士
B.S. = **Bachelor of Science** 理學學士
B.F.A. = **Bachelor of *Fine Arts** 藝術學士
AA = **Associate of Arts** 專校文學文憑

碩士學位

M.A. = **Master of Arts** 文學碩士
M.S. = **Master of Science** 理學碩士
M.F.A. = **Master of Fine Arts** 藝術碩士

博士學位

Ph.D.

②常見科系

Accounting 會計系
Anthropology 人類學系
[2]**Architecture** 建築系
[3]**Biological Sciences** 生物科學系
Chemistry 化學系
Criminal Justice 刑事司法系
Civil Engineering 土木工程學系
Communications 傳播系
Computer Science 資訊工程學系
Economics 經濟學系
Education 教育系
Electrical Engineering 電機工程系
English 英文系
Finance 財務金融學系
Geography 地理系

History 歷史系
Industrial Engineering 工業工程系
***Linguistics** 語言學系
Management 管理系
Marketing 行銷系
Mathematics 數學系
[4]**Mechanical Engineering** 機械工程系
Music 音樂系
[5]**Nutritional Sciences** 營養科學系
[6]**Philosophy** 哲學系
[7]**Physics** 物理系
Political Science 政治系
Psychology 心理系
[8]**Sociology** 社會系
Statistics 統計學系

補充字彙

* **fine arts** (phr.) 美術，純藝術
* **linguistics** [lɪnˋgwɪstɪks] (n.) 語言學

我想了解更多各校系所資訊，該上哪裡找？

大部分學校系所網站都有提供「選課型錄」(General Catalog/Course Catalog) 供學生查詢，裡面會有包括課程介紹、畢業標準、必修、選修課程等說明。學生可先透過查詢了解此學校與系所所提供之課程是否是你想學到的東西，再以此資訊來挑選學校。

畢業需求通常包括哪些？

畢業需求主要包括 General Education Requirements（通識教育課程需求）、College、Major Requirements（學院與主修科系需求）。學生需達到 GPA 2.0（全部課程都達到及格標準 C 以上成績）及完成學校規定的 Unit Requirements（學分數量要求），各校的學院及系所要求學分數不盡相同，請自行上系所官網查詢，或和學校 counselor 確認。上述要求也適用與轉學生，不過轉學生一般都已經在社區大學拿完通識課程，所以轉學後不必再拿通識課程，除非有缺少課程學分才需補齊。

怎麼知道畢業需求為何？

一般來說學校網站上的 General Catalog 都有寫，也可和學校 counselor 約見面討論確認。

---

department 和 program 有什麼不同？

Department 是系，指的是大學內的教學單位。而 Program 是帶領你拿到學位或證書的課程，例如，物理學士課程、應用物理學士課程、碩士課程、博士課程等…。

碩士該選哪一種課程？

碩士課程有兩種，一種是 thesis program，也就是需要寫論文的，這種一般是為了將來要成為學者或者是想繼續升學拿到博士學位的人設計的。而另一種是 non-thesis program，也就是不寫論文的，這種一般是為了那些畢業後想直接投入工作的學生設計的，但因為不需要寫研究論文，所以大部分需要有額外的實習時數做為畢業要求。學生在申請時可自行選擇要哪一種，並在之後自行尋找研究項目及指導老師或實習工作。

♪ **045** │ 圖解

♪ **046** │ 單字

Vocabulary Bank

1. **credit** [ˋkrɛdɪt] (n.) **學分，信用**

   Most language classes are five credits.

2. **core** [kor] (n.) **核心，基礎課程**

   I'm taking three core classes this semester.

3. **elective** [ɪˋlɛktɪv] (n.) **選修課**

   How many electives are you taking this quarter?

4. **consultation** [͵kɑnsʌlˋteʃən] (n.) **諮商，諮詢**

   I scheduled a consultation with my lawyer tomorrow.

補充字彙

* **liberal arts** (phr.) 人文科學

* **syntax** [ˋsɪntæks] (n.) 語法

* **semantics** [səˋmæntɪks] (n.) 語義學

* **phonology** [fəˋnɑlədʒɪ] (n.) 音韻學

* **subspecialty** [͵sʌbˋspɛʃəltɪ] (n.) 次專業，附屬專業

* **articulatory** [ɑrˋtɪkjələ͵tɔrɪ] (a.) 發音的

* **acoustic** [əˋkustɪk] (a.) 聲學的

* **phonetics** [fəˋnɛtɪks] (n.) 語音學

圖解英文　**輕鬆看懂畢業需求**

---

❶ Undergraduate Programs of Study

Major

❷ Major in Linguistics (Bachelor of Arts)

❸ Requirements

❹ The Bachelor of Arts with a major in linguistics requires a minimum of 120 [1]**credits**, including 30 credits of work for the major. ❺ Students must maintain a GPA of at least 2.00 in all courses for the major. ❻ They also must complete the College of *__Liberal Arts__ and Sciences General Education [2]**Core**.

❼ The major in linguistics prepares students to do basic language analysis in *__syntax__-*__semantics__ (sentence patterns and their relation to meanings) and *__phonology__ (sound patterns). [3]**Elective** courses in a variety of *__subspecialties__ enable students to tailor the program to their own interests.

The B.A. with a major in linguistics requires the following course work.

Courses	⑩ Hours
❽ **Major Courses**	15
❾ **Electives**	15
Total Hours	30

❶ **Undergraduate Programs of Study**│大學學程

❷ **Major in Linguistics**│主修科系

❸ **Requirements**│需求

❹ 畢業至少須完成的學分數，至少需有多少學分來自主修

❺ GPA 學業成績要求

❻ 必須完成的核心課程

❼ 完成這個學位後，學生將習得的技能

❽ **Major Courses**│主修課程

❾ **Electives**│選修課程

❿ **Hours**│時數，一種常見的學分計算方法是與該科目的每星期上課的小時數目掛鉤，如每星期上 3 小時課即為 3 學分。

concentration 是什麼？

concentration [ˌkɑnsənˋtreʃən] 是你專攻的領域，也就是比主修科系更細分。一般大學主修科系學的東西都是比較籠統、基礎的知識，到了研究所，就開始細分領域了。例如，你大學時主修心理學系，到了研究所你專攻犯罪心理學，這個犯罪心理學就是你的 concentration。

Major Courses

❶ Students must complete no fewer than 15 credits of requirements for the major, including LING:3001: Introduction to Linguistics, LING:3005 ***Articulatory** and ***Acoustic*****Phonetics**, LING:3010 Syntactic Analysis, and LING:3020 Phonological Analysis.

❷ The course LING:1003 English Grammar does not count toward the linguistics major.

❸ Code	❹ Title	Credits
❺ **All of these:**		
LING:3001	Introduction to Linguistics	3
LING:3005	Articulatory and Acoustic Phonetics	3
LING:3010	Syntactic Analysis	3
LING:3020	Phonological Analysis	3
❻ **One of these:**		
A course in language history, such as LING:3080		3
A course in an old language (Classical Greek, Latin, Old English, Sanskrit)		3

Electives

Electives are chosen in ⁴⁾**consultation** with a faculty advisor (15 credits), bringing the total credits in the major to 30.

❶ 至少須完成的學分數，必修課有哪些
❷ 特別要注意的事項
❸ **Code**｜課程代碼
❹ **Title**｜課程名稱
❺ **All of these**｜有時候除了選課的文字敘述外，還有表格，**All of these** 指的是「以下所有皆為必修課」
❻ **One of these**｜要選其中一堂，這也是必修課，只是給予學生選擇權，可依自己的喜好選一堂

翻譯請見 p. 213

LESSON 6
Registration: Adding and Dropping Courses
第六話：註冊：加退選課程

🎵 **047** | 好用句

🎵 **048** | 單字

Vocabulary Bank

1. **instructor** [ɪnˋstrʌktɚ] (n.)
   教員，指導者，教練
   My golf instructor has really helped me improve my game.

2. **guarantee** [ˌgærənˋti] (v./n.)
   保證，保障
   The refrigerator is guaranteed for two years.

3. **drop** [drɑp] (v.) （課程）退選
   I'm thinking of dropping my Psych 101 class.

4. **withdraw** [wɪðˋdrɔ] (v.) 退出，撤回
   Will withdrawing from a class affect my GPA?

5. **waiting list** (phr.) 候補名單
   There aren't any tables available, but I can put you on the waiting list.

6. **refund** [ˋriˏfʌnd] (n./v.) 退款
   Keep the receipt in case you need to get a refund.

補充字彙

* **microeconomics** [ˌmaɪkroɛkəˋnɑmɪks] (n.)
  微觀經濟學

* **behavioral** [bɪˋhevjəəl] (a.)
  （關於）行為的

* **macroeconomics** [ˌmækroɛkəˋnɑmɪks] (n.)
  宏觀經濟學，總體經濟學

* **audit** [ˋɔdɪt] (v.) 旁聽

圖解英文　輕鬆看懂課程敘述

Saint Mary University
Course Catalog ❶

Subject ❷▲	Title ❸	Day, Time ❹
ECON 10A	Principles of Economics *Microeconomics	**M, W, F** 10:30a.m.-11:45a.m.
ECON 20	Introduction to data Analysis	**Tu, Th,** 10:30a.m.-11:45a.m.
ECON 980Z	*Behavioral Finance	**Tu,** 12:00p.m.-2:45p.m.
ECON 1310	The Economy of China	**M, W,** 1:30p.m.-2:45p.m.
ECON 1550	International *Macroeconomics	**Tu, Th,** 2:45p.m.-4:00p.m.

❶ **Course Catalog** | 課程目錄

通常是課程列表，點入課程名稱，便可看到課程詳細介紹。

❷ **Subject** | 科目

是表示該科目的縮寫加編號，例如 ECON 表示此科目是經濟學類的學科。數字表示級別程度，例如，100 代表大一程度、200 代表大二程度、500 以上一般代表研究所程度課程，而課號越小，例如個位或十位數則代表課程程度越基礎。編號最後的少數字母則表示同一名稱課程的等級或特殊課程。例如，ECON 10A 可能代表這是經濟學概論第一級，後面可能還有 10B（經濟學概論第二級）、10C（經濟學概論第三級）等。

❸ **Title** | 名稱

是該科目的名字，多數課程可從名稱中看出該課的內容，不過還是要仔細看課程介紹來了解更詳細的資訊。

❹ **Day, Time** | 日期、時間

代表上課的日期與時間，學生需看好時間與日期，不要選到衝堂的課程，另外也可把上課時間都集中安排在某幾天，這樣就不用每天跑學校上課了。

翻譯請見 p. 213

Common Phrases | 詢問註冊相關問題，你要會說

1. What are the general education requirements for psychology majors?
心理學主修的通識教育必修課有哪些？

2. How do I know if there is space available in a course?
我如何知道某個課程是否還有名額？

3. What is the minimum/maximum number of courses I can register for?
我最少／最多可以註冊幾堂課？

4. How do I get [1]**instructor** permission if it's required to register for a course?
若註冊課程需要老師批准，我要如何取得批准？

5. If I receive permission from the instructor to enroll in a class, does it [2]**guarantee** me a spot?
我若取得老師批准註冊課程，這是否能保證我的註冊名額？

6. How do I know if a course requires a discussion/lab section?
我如何知道課程是否規定要上討論／實驗班？

7. How do I change my class to pass/no pass or *audit?
我要如何將課堂改為及格／不及格或旁聽？

Common Phrases | 詢問加退選相關問題，你要會說

1. What is the deadline for adding/[3]**dropping** a class?
加／退課的截止日期是什麼時候？

2. What's the difference between dropping and [4]**withdrawing** from a course?
退課和停修課程有什麼分別？

3. How do I change the discussion/lab section for a course I'm registered for?
如何替已註冊的課程更改討論／實驗班？

4. If the class I want is full, how can I get on the [5]**waiting list**?
如果我想修的課程已額滿，我要怎麼列入候補名單？

5. How do I know if an instructor has added me to a class?
我如何知道老師是否已將我加入某堂課？

6. What happens if I miss the deadline for adding and dropping classes?
我若是錯過加／退課的截止日期該怎麼辦？

7. Will I receive a [6]**refund** for courses I withdraw from?
我停修課後能退款嗎？

如何選課？

現在基本上都線上化了，大多數的學校都有線上選課系統，需先註冊後，等待學校分配給你的選課時間再去選課。學生可在選課前先仔細閱讀各個課程介紹，及排好想選科目後，待選課時間到達後直接上線選課。千萬不要選課時間後才上線慢慢挑選，因為熱門課程很快就會被搶光了。

關於課程

說到選課，就不得不提到課程編號。課程編號是大學課程的一個代稱，一般由 4 位以內的英文字母（課程簡寫）加 3-4 位數字組合而成。例如 MATH 代表數學、PSYC 代表心理學、MUS 代表音樂等等的。而數字一般表示課程的級別程度，例如，100 代表大一程度、200 代表大二程度、500 以上一般代表研究所程度課程。而課號越小，例如個位或十位數則代表課程程度越基礎。（以上內容不一定適用於所有學校，部分學校可能不同）

課程有分很多種，差別在哪裡？

比較常見的課程一般有 lecture、seminar、lab 等。lecture 就是一般的演講型上課，教授會在課堂中教導課程知識。seminar 是專題研討會，學生們與教授聚在一起研究討論相關課程題材。lab 是實驗課程，在課堂上會做實驗，一般 lab 都是會搭配 lecture 一起上的。例如物理課一個禮拜三堂，其中兩堂是 lecture，一堂是 lab。

049 | 單字

Vocabulary Bank

1. **economist** [ɪˋkɑnəmɪst] (n.)
   經濟學家，經濟學者
   Economists predict that the economy will improve next year.

2. **algebra** [ˋældʒəbrə] (n.)
   代數學
   We learned how to solve equations in algebra class.

3. **demand** [dɪˋmænd] (n./v.)
   需求，要求
   The demand for face masks continues to grow.

4. **limitation** [ˌlɪməˋteʃən] (n.)
   限制
   The country signed an agreement on the limitation of arms exports.

5. **statistic** [stəˋtɪstɪks] (n.)
   統計數字，（複數）統計學
   Statistics show that women in the area live longer than men.

6. **motivate** [ˋmotɪˌvet] (v.)
   激勵，激發
   Bonuses are a good way to motivate employees.

7. **illustrate** [ˋɪləˌstret] (n.)
   （尤指用例子）說明，闡明
   The speaker gave an example to illustrate his point.

8. **seminar** [ˋsɛməˌnɑr] (n.)
   研討會，專題討論會
   All employees are required to attend the training seminar.

9. **asset** [ˋæsɛt] (n.) 資產，財產
   The company owns over a billion dollars in assets.

圖解英文 輕鬆看懂課程介紹

Saint Mary University
Course Catalog

| **ECON 10A** | ② **Principles of Economics (Microeconomics)** | ③ **4 units** |

④ [1]**Economists** study human behavior using a combination of models and data. ECON 10A introduces students to economic models by using *intuitive discussions, *graphical analysis and, in some cases, very basic [2]**algebra**. The models study individual decision-making and markets, and range from classical approaches like supply and [3]**demand** to more recent approaches that consider informational [4]**limitations** and behavioral mistakes.

Saint Mary University
Course Catalog

| **ECON 20** | **Introduction to Data Analysis** | **4 units** |

This course will introduce students to data analytic methods useful for answering social science questions. The course will cover the fundamentals of *probability and [5]**statistics** while introducing students to *causal inference, *quasi-experimental methods, and *regression analysis. All the methods studied in the course will be [6]**motivated** and [7]**illustrated** with real-world applications.

Saint Mary University
Course Catalog

| **ECON 980Z** | **Behavioral Finance** | **3 units** |

This [8]**seminar** will provide an overview of theoretical and *empirical research on [9]**asset** pricing that adopts a "behavioral" [10]**perspective**, i.e. that considers the joint [11]**consequences** of: (i) investors who have either less than fully [12]**rational** beliefs or non-standard preferences; and (ii) various *impediments to *arbitrage.

Saint Mary University
Course Catalog

ECON 1310	The Economy of China	4 units

This course critically examines China's remarkable economic performance in the post-Mao era and places this performance in historical and [13]**comparative** [14]**context**. Topics covered include China's economic structure, institutions, ***inequality**, trade, population, and public policy.

❶ 課程簡寫
❷ 課程名稱
❸ 學分數
❹ 課程細部，包含教學方式，可看出偏理論還是應用，課程涵蓋主題等。學生可在選課前先了解課程內容與方向。

翻譯請見 p. 212

選課技巧

　　選課需以自己能力去做分配，若一學期選 5 門課，可選擇 2-3 門較難課程，其餘安排較輕鬆的課程，另外部份課程有 prerequisite 的要求，需先上完 prerequisite 課程後才可修該課程。學生選課時可先把自己無法上課的時間先剔除，選擇跟自己時間對得上的課程。學生選課時需把教室步行距離算入考量，若課與課的時間較近，而教室離得較遠的話，可能造成慣性遲到，給教授留下不好的印象。另外學生也可把課程集中安排在某幾天，例如選課程都在禮拜二、四的，這樣就不一定每天都要到學校了。

如何了解更多課程相關資訊

　　現在是網路的世代，各大院校都會有 Facebook 社團或論壇，學生們可在此找到很多相關資訊，也可直接詢問學長姊們關於課程資訊、教授評價等。另外學生也可上 Rate My Professors 的網站上查詢教授評價，此網站擁有美國幾乎所有學校的教授評價，而所有評價都是由上過課的學生所評分撰寫的，不過需注意不要太過依賴此網站，有時候可能會踩到地雷，學生們可在第一堂課時先去課堂了解此教授風格及拿教授的課程大綱，這樣可更進一步了解教授與課程，若覺得課程太困難，可在規定時間內退選。

---

10. **perspective** [pɚˋspɛktɪv] (n.) 角度，觀點
The mountain looks taller from this perspective.

11. **consequence** [ˋkɑnsəˌkwɛns] (n.) 後果，結果
Drunk driving can have serious consequences.

12. **rational** [ˋræʃənəl] (a.) 合理的，理性的
I'm sure there's a rational explanation for the strange sounds you heard.

13. **comparative** [kəmˋpɛrətɪv] (a.) 比較的，對比的
Shelly teaches a course in comparative literature.

14. **context** [ˋkɑntɛkst] (n.) 上下文，(事情發生的) 背景、來龍去脈
The meaning of the word depends on its context.

補充字彙

* **intuitive** [ɪnˋtuətɪv] (a.) 直覺的

* **graphical** [ˋgræfɪkəl] (a.) 圖像的，用圖的

* **probability** [ˌprɑbəˋbɪlətɪ] (n.) 可能性

* **causal inference** (phr.) 因果推論

* **quasi-experimental** [ˌkwɑzɪɪkˌspɛrəˋmɛntəl] (a.) 準實驗性的

* **regression** [rɪˋgrɛʃən] (n.) 迴歸

* **empirical** [ɪmˋpɪrɪkəl] (n.) 以經驗 (或實驗) 爲依據的

* **impediment** [ɪmˋpɛdmənt] (n.) 妨礙，阻止

* **arbitrage** [ˋɑrbɪˌtrɑʒ] (n.) 套利，套匯

* **inequality** [ˌɪnɪˋkwɑlətɪ] (n.) 不平等，不均等

LESSON 7
Orientation and Introductions
第七話：迎新、自我介紹

Vocabulary Bank

1. **highlight** [ˋhaɪˌlaɪt] (n.) 最精采、有趣的一部分

   Visiting Venice was the highlight of our trip to Italy.

2. **orientation** [ˌorɪənˋteʃən] (n.) 新生訓練，入學輔導

   I made a lot of new friends during orientation week.

3. **auditorium** [ˌɔdɪˋtorɪəm] (n.) 禮堂，會堂

   There is no smoking in the auditorium.

4. **refreshment** [rɪˋfrɛʃmənt] (n.)（恆用複數）小吃、飲料，茶點

   Refreshments will be served after the lecture.

5. **beverage** [ˋbɛvərɪdʒ] (n.) 飲料

   What's your favorite beverage?

補充字彙

* **student union** (phr.) 學生活動中心

* **head start** (phr.)（競賽或賽跑中）先起步的優勢

* **dean** [din] (n.)（大學）學院院長，教務長

* **giveaway** [ˋgɪvəˌwe] (n.)（給顧客的）贈品

Listening Quiz ｜ 聽力測驗

● 聽完校園迎新導覽之後，回答下列問題：

1. Who is the talk addressed to?

   (A) Graduate students
   (B) Undergraduates
   (C) Orientation leaders
   (D) Faculty

2. What is NOT included in the tour?

   (A) A bookstore
   (B) The tutoring center
   (C) The Student Union
   (D) Fun activities

解答：1.（B）　2.（D）

▌聽力測驗原文

Hello! My name is Amy Smith, and I'm the Freshman Orientation Program Director. We're going to have lots of fun activities today so you can meet your classmates and faculty members, and then our student orientation leaders will take you on a tour of campus resources. **Highlights** include visits to the ***Student Union**, the Main Library, the Campus Bookstore, where you'll be purchasing textbooks for your courses, and the tutoring center, where you can get help with academic writing and tutoring in any subject. And of course we'll visit the Registration Office so you can get a ***head start** on enrolling for classes.

大家好！我叫艾美史密斯，我是大一新生訓練計畫主任。今天我們將舉辦許多有趣的活動，讓大家可以認識同學和教職員，然後我們的新生訓練隊長將帶大家參觀校園資源。重點包括參觀學生活動中心、總圖書館、校園書店，你們可以在這裡購買課堂用的教科書，還有輔導中心，你們可以在這裡尋求學術寫作的協助和各科目的輔導。當然我們會參觀註冊處，這樣就可以搶先註冊課程。

● 請在看完迎新海報後，回答下列問題：

1. Which of the following is NOT included in the orientation?

(A) Snacks
(B) Drinks
(C) Prizes
(D) Tour

2. Where is the orientation being held?

(A) Outdoors
(B) In a library
(C) In a hall
(D) In a faculty lounge

解答：1. (D) 2. (C)
翻譯請見 p. 213

CHAPTER

開課前備

2

Preparing for
Your Studies

🎵 **052** | 對話＋好用句

🎵 **053** | 單字

Vocabulary Bank

1. **chip** [tʃɪp] (n.) （電腦的）晶片
   Computer chips are made of silicon.

2. **circuit** [ˋsɝkɪt] (n.) 電路，回路
   The circuit board in the camera had to be replaced.

3. **get involved (in)** (phr.) 投入，介入
   Have you ever gotten involved in a political campaign?

4. **ID** [ˏaɪˋdi]，全名為 **identification** [aɪˏdɛntəfɪˋkeʃən] (n.) 身分證明
   To open an account, two forms of ID are required.

5. **badminton** [ˋbædˏmɪntən] (n.) 羽毛球運動
   I'm thinking of trying out for the badminton team.

6. **facility** [fəˋsɪlətɪ] (n.) 設施，設備（此定義用複數 **facilities** [fəˋsɪlətiz]）
   Hotel facilities include a restaurant, bar and business center.

補充字彙

* **portal** [ˋpɔrtəl] (n.) 入口網站

* **robotics** [roˋbɑtɪks] (n.) 機器人學

* **molecular** [məˋlɛkjələ] (a.) 分子的

Asking questions
詢問問題

Orientation Leader	Does anyone have any questions?
Student	Yes. Where can we find information about campus activities?
Orientation leader	There's a big bulletin board in the lobby of the Student Union, and you can also find information about activities on the ETU web *portal.
Student	OK. That's good to know.

新生訓練隊長	誰還有問題嗎？
學生	有，我們要到哪裡找校園活動的資訊？
新生訓練隊長	學生活動中心的大廳有一個大型公告板，你也可以在東德大學網站上找到活動資訊。
學生	好的，太好了。

Chatting about majors
聊聊主修

Freshman 1	Excuse me. I just heard you're majoring in electrical engineering. I'm an EE major too.
Freshman 2	Oh, cool. Have you started thinking about a concentration yet?
Freshman 1	Well, I want to work in ¹⁾**chip** design, so I'm considering ²⁾**Circuits** and Systems. How about you?
Freshman 2	I'm not sure yet, but I'm interested in *robotics.

新生 1	不好意思，我剛聽說你的主修是電機工程，我的主修也是電機。
新生 2	噢，酷。你開始考慮要專攻哪方面領域了嗎？
新生 1	呃，我想從事晶片設計，所以我在考慮電路與系統，你呢？
新生 2	我還沒確定，但我對機器人有興趣。

Common Phrases | 新人介紹，你要會說

1. My name is Allan Lin, and I'm a Business freshman.

   我叫艾倫林，我是企管系的新生。

2. I'm majoring in Business with a concentration in Marketing.

   我主修企管，專攻行銷領域。

3. I'm here to pursue a master's in *Molecular Biology.

   我是來攻讀分子生物學的碩士學位。

4. I'm from Kaohsiung, which is a port city in southern Taiwan.

   我來自高雄，那是南台灣的海港城市。

5. I'm a transfer student in the Economics Department.

   我是經濟系的轉學生。

6. I'm really excited about living and studying in the U.S.

   我很興奮能在美國生活和求學。

7. I can't wait to ³⁾get involved in campus activities.

   我等不及要參加校園活動了。

Common Phrases | 迎新活動，你要會問

1. Do you know where the College of Business is?

   你知道商學院在哪裡嗎？

2. Are there any stores near campus that sell used textbooks?

   校園附近有商店在賣二手教科書嗎？

3. Do we need to bring our own photos for the student ⁴⁾ID?

   我們申請學生證時需要自己準備大頭照嗎？

4. Are there any good restaurants or cafés on campus?

   校園內有什麼好餐廳或咖啡廳嗎？

5. What is the nightlife like around here?

   這附近的夜生活如何？

6. I'm into ⁵⁾badminton. Is there a badminton club?

   我喜歡打羽毛球，這裡有羽球社嗎？

7. Can you tell us more about the campus gym/sports ⁶⁾facilities?

   你能多介紹校園裡的健身房 / 運動設施嗎？

Useful Pattern | 形容自己的個性，就這樣說

▶ People say I'm a/an _____ person.

大家都說我是 _____ 的人。

adventurous 愛冒險
affectionate 溫柔親切
ambitious 雄心壯志
anxious 焦慮
assertive 武斷
bubbly 活潑
chatty 健談
cheerful 開朗
considerate 體貼
dependable 可靠
easy-going 隨和
enthusiastic 熱情
extroverted 外向
fearless 大膽
friendly 友善
funny 有趣
generous 慷慨
helpful 熱心助人
honest 誠實
humorous 幽默
impulsive 衝動
industrious 勤勞
introverted 內向
kind 親切
laid-back 悠閒
lazy 懶散
loyal 忠誠
moody 喜怒無常
neat 愛整潔
nervous 易緊張
outgoing 外向
passionate 熱情
patient 有耐心
persistent 堅持不懈
quiet 文靜
reliable 可靠

LESSON 8

Campus and the Community

第八話：校園和校區

♫ 054 │ 單字

Vocabulary Bank

1. **track and field** (phr.) 田徑運動

   Does your school have a track and field team?

2. **softball** [ˋsɑft.bɔl] (n.) 壘球 (運動)

   Karen played softball in high school.

3. **conference** [ˋkɑnfərəns] (n.) 會議，討論會，聯盟

   Who will be speaking at the conference?

補充字彙

* **permit** [ˋpɝmɪt] (n.) 許可證，執照

* **complex** [ˋkɑmplɛks] (n.) 複合式建築，綜合設施

* **computer science** (phr.) 電腦科學，資工，可簡稱為 CS

熟悉校園建築位置

　　大部分學校佔地都很大，從一棟樓到另一棟樓可能需要花上 15-20 分鐘不等。所以看懂學校地圖很重要，以免在學校迷路找不到上課的教室而遲到。另外了解學校地圖也跟選課息息相關，因為下課時間有限，需要計算自己的腳程看看是否能趕得上下一堂課，若教室與教室間離得太遠，就需考慮放棄其中一堂或選擇其他時間。此外，了解學校地圖也方便自己利用學校各種設施，知道什麼問題應該到哪裡解決。

📖 Reading Quiz │ 閱讀測驗

● 請根據以下學校地圖，回答下列問題：

1. If you were an Education student, which would be the most convenient place to live?

(A) Lucretia Kennard Residence Hall
(B) Towers Residence Hall
(C) Dwight Holmes Residence Hall
(D) Harriet Tubman Residence Hall

2. If you were going to attend a football game, which would be a better place to park?

(A) Parking Lot G
(B) Parking Lot H
(C) Parking Lot P
(D) Parking Lot N

3. Which direction would one walk in to get from the James E. Proctor Jr. Building to the Career Center?

(A) Northeast
(B) Northwest
(C) Southeast
(D) Southwest

解答：1. (D) 2. (B) 3. (C)

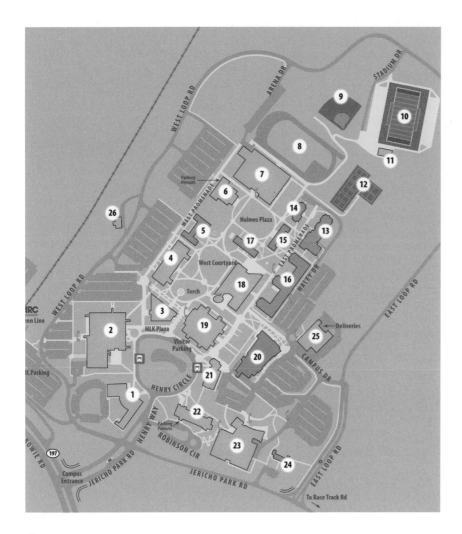

① Center for Business and Graduate Studies
② Martin Luther King Jr. Communication Arts enter
Myers Auditorium
③ William E. Henry Administration Building
Admissions
Financial Aid
Student Accounts
④ James E. Proctor Jr. Building
College of Education
⑤ Harriet Tubman Residence Hall
⑥ Theodore McKeldin Gymnasium
Campus Police
Parking *Permits
⑦ Leonidas S. James Physical Education *Complex
⑧ [1]**Track and Field**
⑨ [2]**Softball** Field
⑩ Bulldog Football Stadium
⑪ Field House
⑫ Tennis and Basketball Courts
⑬ Alex Haley Residence Hall

⑭ Towers Residence Hall
⑮ Dwight Holmes Residence Hall
⑯ Christa McAuliffe Residential Community
⑰ Lucretia Kennard Residence Hall
⑱ Center for Natural Sciences, Mathematics and
Nursing
⑲ Thurgood Marshall Library
⑳ Student Center
Bookstore
Career Center
[3]**Conference** Services
㉑ ***Computer Science** Building
College of Arts and Sciences
㉒ Charlotte Robinson Hall
Campus Police
Human Resources
㉓ Fine & Performing Arts Center
㉔ Goodloe Apartments
㉕ Facilities Management Building

地圖摘錄自 Bowie State University 的網站，部分建築名稱已經過修改

翻譯請見 p. 212

CHAPTER 2

開課前準備

Preparing for
Your Studies

🎵 055 │ 對話＋好用句

🎵 056 │ 單字

Vocabulary Bank

1. **up ahead** (phr.) 前方
   There's a sharp turn up ahead.

2. **pick up** (phr.) 購買，取得某物
   Where did you pick up that cool watch?

3. **worth of** (phr.) 值，價值…的…
   How far can you drive on a dollar's worth of gas?

4. **ATM** (phr.) 全名為
   automated teller machine，
   自動提款機
   I need to find an ATM and withdraw some money.

5. **grab a bite** (phr.) 簡單吃點東西
   Do we have time to grab a bite before the movie?

6. **shuttle (bus)** [ˈʃʌtəl] (n.) 接駁車
   How often does the shuttle come?

7. **hang a left/right** (phr.) 左轉，右轉
   You need to hang a left at the next intersection.

SITUATION 1

Asking for directions
詢問方向

DIALOGUE 1

Freshman	Excuse me. I seem to be lost. I'm trying to find the campus bookstore.
Junior	Let's see, that's in the Student Union. Do you see that white building [1]**up ahead**?
Freshman	Yes. Isn't that the Main Library?
Junior	Yep. If you walk past it and make a left, the Student Union will be the second building on your right.

新生	不好意思，我好像迷路了。我想找校園書店。
大三生	我看看，書店在學生活動中心裡，你看到前面的白色大樓了嗎？
新生	看到了，那不是總圖書館嗎？
大三生	對，你經過圖書館後左轉，學生活動中心就是右邊第二棟大樓。

DIALOGUE 2

Freshman	Hey, Stan. Do you know where the nearest grocery store is?
Senior	If you just want to [2]**pick up** milk or something, there's a Walgreens on Telegraph and Bancroft.
Freshman	I actually want to get a week's [3]**worth of** groceries.
Senior	In that case, you'll want to go to the Safeway on College. You can get there on the 51B bus.

新生	嘿，史丹，你知道最近的超市在哪裡嗎？
大四生	如果你只是想買牛奶之類的，電報街夾班克洛街有沃格林藥妝店。
新生	我其實想買一星期的食品量。
大四生	這樣的話，你可以到大學街的喜互惠超市，你可以搭 **51B** 號公車到那裡。

Common Phrases | 詢問位置，你要會說

1. Is there an [4]**ATM** around here?　這附近有提款機嗎？

2. Can you tell me how to get to the Computer Science Building?　你能告訴我電腦科學大樓怎麼去嗎？

3. Is there somewhere I can get my hair cut on campus?　校內有剪頭髮的地方嗎？

4. Is there a café on campus where I can [5]**grab a** quick **bite**?　校內有可以買輕食的咖啡廳嗎？

5. So the Student Center is across from the library?　所以學生中心是在圖書館對面嗎？

6. Where is the nearest subway station/bus stop?　最近的地鐵站／公車站牌在哪裡？

7. Can you show me where to catch the campus [6]**shuttle**?　你能告訴我在哪裡搭校內接駁車嗎？

Common Phrases | 詢問位置，你要聽得懂

1. Actually, I'm going that way too. I can show you where it is.　其實我也要去往個方向，我可以帶你去。

2. Sorry, but I'm new here too.　抱歉，但我也是新生。

3. You're going the wrong way. The Administration Building is in that direction.　你走錯方向了，行政大樓是在那個方向。

4. Green Library is between Hoover Tower and Meyer Green.　格林圖書館是在胡佛塔樓和梅爾廣場之間。

5. If you walk this way for around three minutes, you'll see the tennis courts on your right.　你若是從這邊走大概三分鐘，就會在右手邊看到網球場。

6. The stadium is on the other side of campus. The quickest way to get there is on the shuttle bus.　體育館是在校園的另一頭。去那裡的最快方法是搭接駁車。

7. To get to the gym, [7]**hang a left** at the fountain up ahead, then walk for about 50 yards.　去健身房要在前面的噴水池左轉，然後走大概 50 碼。

CHAPTER
開課前準備

2

Preparing for
Your Studies

LESSON 9
Opening an Account and Using Money
第九話：開帳戶和使用金錢

🎵 057 | 對話

🎵 058 | 單字

Vocabulary Bank

1. **funds** [fʌndz] (n.) 存款，現款，財源

   I'd like to lend you the money, but I'm low on funds.

2. **interest** [ˈɪntrəst] (n.) 利息

   How much interest do you earn on your savings?

3. **go with** (phr.) (口) 選擇，接受

   I think I'll go with the lasagna.

4. **native** [ˈnetɪv] (a.) 本土的，天生的

   Are you a native speaker of Chinese?

5. **sum** [sʌm] (n.) 金額，一筆

   You should be careful when withdrawing large sums from an ATM.

Opening an account
開帳戶

Customer	Hi, I'm an international student. Would it be possible for me to open an account here?
Teller	Of course. I'll just need to see your passport, another form of ID with your local address on it, and a copy of your student visa.
Customer	OK. Can I use my student ID?
Teller	Sure. Would you like to open a checking account or a savings account?
Customer	What's the difference?
Teller	A checking account allows you to write checks and take out [1]**funds** as often as you like, and has a low minimum balance. A savings account has a higher minimum balance, but also provides a higher [2]**interest** rate.
Customer	I'll [3]**go with** a checking account then. Will it be possible to apply for a credit card too?
Teller	I'm afraid you need a Social Security number for that, but accounts come with a VISA debit card that can be used anywhere credit cards are accepted.

顧客	你好，我是國際學生。我可以在這裡開戶嗎？
行員	可以，請給我你的護照，另外一個有當地地址的證件，以及學生簽證影本。
顧客	好的，學生證可以嗎？
行員	可以，你想開活期存款帳戶還是儲蓄帳戶呢？
顧客	這兩種有什麼不同？
行員	活期存款帳戶讓你可以開支票和隨時提款，最低餘額要求也比較低。儲蓄帳戶最低餘額要求比較高，但提供的利息也較高。
顧客	那我開活期存款帳戶好了，我可以順便申辦信用卡嗎？
行員	恐怕需要提供社會安全號碼才行，但我們會提供每個帳戶 VISA 簽帳卡，所有接受信用卡的地方也會接受這張卡。

Withdrawing cash
提款

Teller	Hello. How may I help you?
Customer	I'd like to withdraw some money from my account. I have a withdrawal slip here, but I'm sorry—my [4]**native** language isn't English. Could you please help me fill it out?
Teller	Yes, of course. This space is for your bank account number, and the space next to it is for the [5]**sum** you want to withdraw.

行員	您好，有什麼能為您效勞的嗎？
顧客	我想要從我的帳戶提款，這邊有一張提款單，不過很不好意思，英文不是我的母語。你可以協助我填單嗎？
行員	好的，沒問題。這格是要填您的銀行帳戶號碼，旁邊這格則是您要提款的金額。

圖解英文　輕鬆看懂提款單

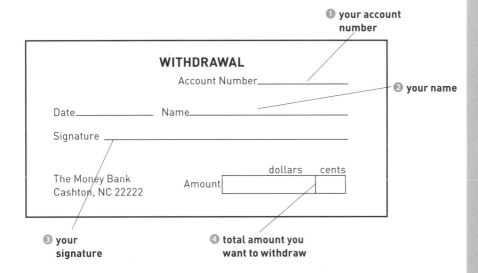

❶ your account number

❷ your name

❸ your signature

❹ total amount you want to withdraw

❶ **fill in your account number**｜填入帳戶號碼
❷ **name**｜填上全名
❸ **signature**｜簽名
❹ **amount**｜填上欲提款金額

CHAPTER 2

開課前準備

Preparing for
Your Studies

 059 | 對話＋好用句

 060 | 單字

Vocabulary Bank

1. **incoming** [ˈɪnˌkʌmɪŋ] (a.)
   進來的，**outgoing** [ˈaʊtˌɡoɪŋ]
   (a.) **外出的**
   All incoming and outgoing calls
   will be recorded.

2. **check** [tʃɛk] (n.) **（餐廳）帳單**
   Whose turn is it to pay the
   check?

3. **charge** [tʃɑrdʒ] (n./v.) **刷卡**，
   用信用卡付費
   Will that be cash or charge?

4. **decline** [dɪˈklaɪn] (v.) **拒絕**，
   （信用卡）刷不過
   When I tried to pay, both of my
   credit cards were declined.

5. **unfortunately** [ʌnˈfɔrtʃənɪtli]
   (adv.) **遺憾地，可惜**
   Unfortunately, I won't have
   time to do any sightseeing
   while I'm in Paris.

補充字彙

* **remittance** [rɪˈmɪtəns] (n.)
   匯款，匯款額

 Wire transfer
匯款

Customer	Hi, I'm here to check on a wire transfer. Here's my passbook.
Teller	Thank you. Is that an [1]**incoming** or [1]**outgoing** transfer?
Customer	Incoming. I should be receiving a ***remittance** from Taiwan.
Teller	OK, let me look that up for you. Yes, here it is. Your transfer arrived yesterday. There's a 16 dollar fee for the transfer. Would you like me to deduct it from your account?
Customer	Yes. That's fine.

顧客	你好，我要查看一筆匯款，這是我的存摺。
行員	謝謝。請問是匯入還是匯出？
顧客	匯入。我應該會收到一筆來自台灣的匯款。
行員	好，我來幫你查一下。沒錯，查到了。款項是昨天匯入的，有 16 元的手續費，你要我從你的戶頭裡扣除嗎？
顧客	好的，沒問題。

 Paying by credit card
信用卡付款

Customer	That was a wonderful meal. Waiter, may I have the [2]**check**, please?
Waiter	Here you are. And how will you be paying—by cash or credit card?
Customer	I'd prefer to pay by credit card. Do you take MasterCard?
Waiter	Yes. We accept all major cards. I'll just run your card through the machine and bring back your receipt for you to sign.

顧客	真是美味的一餐。服務生，請幫我買單。
服務生	這是您的帳單。您要怎麼付款，現金還是信用卡？
顧客	我用信用卡好了，你們收萬事達卡嗎？
服務生	嗯，我們收各大銀行信用卡。刷完卡後，我會將收據拿回來給您簽名。

圖解英文 | 輕鬆看懂信用卡

① **issuer** ｜ 發卡機構（銀行）
② **EMV chip** ｜ EMV 晶片
③ **account number** ｜ 卡號
④ **card type** ｜ 信用卡別
⑤ **expiration date** ｜ 有效期限
⑥ **name of card holder** ｜ 持卡人名字
⑦ **magnetic strip** ｜ 信用卡磁條
⑧ **signature panel** ｜ 持卡人簽名欄
⑨ **security code** ｜ 信用卡安全碼

Common Phrases ｜ 付款及退換貨，你要會說

1.	Do you accept mobile payment?	可以用行動支付付款嗎？
2.	Can I pay with this debit card?	可以用這張簽帳卡付款嗎？
3.	Will that be cash or ³⁾**charge**?	付現還是用信用卡呢？
4.	How would you like to pay for that?	您想用什麼方式付款呢？
5.	I'm sorry, we don't accept checks.	不好意思，我們不收支票。
6.	I'm sorry, your card was ⁴⁾**declined**/denied.	抱歉，您的卡片刷不過。
7.	I'm afraid your credit card didn't go through.	恐怕您的卡片刷不過。
8.	Here's your receipt.	這是您的收據。
9.	Please sign the receipt here.	請簽收據。
10.	Is there an ATM around here?	這附近有提款機嗎？
11.	I'd like a refund for this.	我想退貨。
12.	⁵⁾**Unfortunately**, all sales are final.	真抱歉，貨物既出，概不退換。

LESSON 10
Apartment Rental
第十話：海外租屋

🎵 **061** | 對話

🎵 **062** | 單字

Vocabulary Bank

1. **move in** (phr.) 移入，住進新居

   Is the apartment ready to move in?

2. **tenant** [ˋtɛnənt] (n.) 房客

   The landlord is threatening to evict the tenant.

3. **studio** [ˋstudɪo] (n.) 套房，工作室

   I'm looking for a studio apartment with hardwood floors.

4. **landlord** [ˋlænd.lɔrd] (n.) 房東，地主

   The landlord decided to raise our rent.

5. **furnished** [ˋfɝnɪʃt] (a.) 附家具的

   Are you looking for a furnished or unfurnished apartment?

6. **twin bed** (n.) 單人床

   The room is only big enough to fit a twin bed.

補充字彙

* **finder** [ˋfaɪndɚ] (n.) 探測器，發現者

* **nightstand** [ˋnaɪt.stænd] (n.) 床頭櫃

* **coin-operated** [ˋkɔɪn.ɑpə.retɪd] (a.) 投幣式的

📖 **Reading Quiz** | 閱讀測驗

● 請在看完租屋廣告後，回答下列問題：

Apartment *Finder

Furn room for rent in 3 BR 1½ BA apt with a/c, balc, shared kitch and LR. Room incl pvt ½ BA. Rent is $600/mo. util incl. [1]**Move in** cost is fmr/lmr + 1 mo sec. Bldg is close to campus and has elev, pool, lndr.

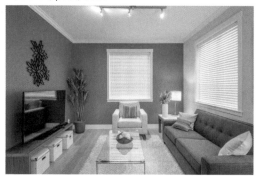

1. Which of the following is NOT included in the attached bathroom?

(A) Toilet
(B) Shower
(C) Mirror
(D) Sink

2. How much will the [2]**tenant** have to pay to move in?

(A) $600
(B) $1,200
(C) $1,800
(D) $2,400

解答：1. (B) 2. (C)
翻譯請見 p. 214

解說

(1) 1½ BA 指的是半套衛浴（只有馬桶和洗臉盆），所以表示沒有淋浴設備。

(2) Move in cost is fmr/lmr + 1 mo sec. 遷入時需支付第一個月和最後一個月租金，以及一個月押金，各 $600，所以總共是 $1,800。

Apartment hunting
找房子

Student	Hi, I'm calling about the [3]**studio** apartment you have advertised. Is it still available?
[4]**Landlord**	Yes. Several people have come by to look at it, but it's still available.
Student	Great. The ad said it's close to campus. Is it close enough to walk?
Landlord	Yes. It's just two blocks from campus. There's also a supermarket within walking distance.

學生	嗨,我打來詢問關於你廣告的套房,現在還空著嗎?
房東	是的,有幾個人來看過,但還是空著。
學生	太好了。廣告上說近校園,是在步行距離內嗎?
房東	對,距離校園只有兩個街區。還有一間超市也在步行距離內。

Amenities
屋況與設施

Student	Does the room come fully [5]**furnished**?
Landlord	Yes. It comes with a [6]**twin bed**, *****nightstand**, dresser, desk and chair, and has a full closet.
Student	Perfect. And does the apartment have a washer and dryer?
Landlord	No, but the building has a laundry room with *****coin-operated** machines.

學生	房間有包含完整家具嗎?
房東	是的,有一張單人床、床頭櫃、斗櫃、書桌和椅子,還有一間衣帽間。
學生	太好了,公寓裡有洗衣機和烘衣機嗎?
房東	沒有,但大樓裡有一間洗衣房,有投幣式洗衣機。

▌學生租屋資訊

　　大部分學校都有設立一個部門幫助學生租屋,裡面會有很多租屋相關資訊,學生們到美國後可先到租屋部門或國際學生部門尋找相關資訊。另外,學生們也可以透過參加 orientation 來尋找室友或是互相交換租屋資訊。許多學校或學校所在地區也在 Facebook 上擁有專門的租屋 (housing) 社團,裡面會有很多租屋資訊,學生們可加入社團尋找相關資訊或室友。其他還有一些租屋網站,像是 Realtor.com、Zillow、Rent.com、Apartments.com、Craigslist 都是美國人很愛的租屋網站,但裡面有一些案件是詐騙的,所以各位在使用時一定要多加小心。

租屋廣告常見縮寫

- **½ bath:** 半套衛浴(只有馬桶和洗臉盆)
- **ba = bathroom** 衛浴
- **sq ft: square feet** 平方英尺
- **a/c: air-conditioning** 空調
- **appl: appliances** 家電
- **avail: available** 空房
- **balc: balcony** 陽台
- **br: bedroom** 臥室
- **bkyd: backyard** 後院
- **bldg: building** 大樓
- **bsmt: basement** 地下室
- **d/w: dishwasher** 洗碗機
- **dr: dining room** 餐廳
- **dup: duplex** 雙層樓公寓
- **dep: deposit** 押金
- **elec: electricity** 電費
- **elev: elevator** 電梯
- **fmr: first month's rent** 第一個月租金
- **flr: floor** 樓層
- **fp: fireplace** 壁爐
- **furn: furnished** 含家具
- **inc: includes** 包括
- **lndr: laundry** 洗衣房
- **lr: living room** 客廳
- **lmr: last month's rent** 最後一個月租金
- **mo: month** 月
- **pvt ba: private bathroom** 私人衛浴
- **refs reqd: references required** 需要推薦人
- **rm: room** 房間
- **sec: security deposit** 押金
- **util incl: utilities included** 月租金包含水電瓦斯費
- **w/d: washer/dryer** 洗衣機 / 烘衣機
- **yd: yard** 院子

🎵 063 | 對話＋好用句

🎵 064 | 單字

Vocabulary Bank

1. **deposit** [dɪˋpɑzɪt] (n.) 押金，訂金，**security deposit** 為 (租屋等的) 押金

   The damage to the apartment was deducted from my security deposit.

2. **penalty** [ˋpɛnəltɪ] (n.) 罰款，處罰

   If you cancel your plane ticket, you have to pay a 20% penalty.

3. **utility** [juˋtɪlətɪ] (n.) 公共事業，如水電、瓦斯等 (的費用)

   Are utilities included in the rent?

4. **electricity** [ɪˌlɛkˋtrɪsətɪ] (n.) 電能，電力

   The power company is sending someone to turn on our electricity today.

5. **option** [ˋɑpʃən] (n.) 選項，可選擇的東西

   You should explore your options before you choose a major.

6. **screening** [ˋskrinɪŋ] (n.) 檢查，過濾

   The company has a screening policy for all job applicants.

7. **grace period** (phr.) (還款等的) 延緩期，寬限期

   Is there a grace period for loan payments?

補充字彙

* **guarantor** [ˌgærənˋtɔr] (n.) 擔保人，保證人

 SITUATION 3

Rental rates
租金

DIALOGUE 1

Student	$800 a month is really reasonable for this studio. Is there a **security** [1]**deposit**?
Landlord	No, but tenants are required to pay first and last months' rent when they move in.
Student	OK. Is there a minimum lease term?
Landlord	Yes—one year. There's a one-month [2]**penalty** if you break the lease.

學生	這間套房一個月八百美元相當合理，要付押金嗎？
房東	不用，但房客遷入時需要付第一個月和最後一個月的租金。
學生	好，有規定最短租期嗎？
房東	有，最短一年，違約會有一個月租金的罰款。

DIALOGUE 2

Student	Are [3]**utilities** included in the rent?
Landlord	Water and gas are included, but [4]**electricity** is separate.
Student	How about cable and Internet?
Landlord	That's separate too, but you can get a basic cable and Internet package for about $40 a month.

學生	租金包含水電瓦斯費嗎？
房東	包含水費和瓦斯費，但不含電費。
學生	有線電視和網路呢？
房東	也不包含在內，但你可以訂基本有線電視和網路套餐，一個月約 40 元。

Common Phrases | 尋找租屋處，你要會說

1. I am looking for a studio close to a subway station.
   我在找靠近地鐵站的套房。

2. What's included in the rent?
   租金包含什麼？

3. What's the typical monthly cost for utilities?
   每月的水電瓦斯費通常多少錢？

4. Is there parking available in the building?
   大樓裡有停車位嗎？

5. Would it be possible to sign a six-month lease?
   我可以只簽半年的租約嗎？

6. Will the security deposit be returned when the lease ends?
   租約到期後會歸還押金嗎？

7. Do tenants have the [5]**option** to renew their lease?
   房客可以續約嗎？

Common Phrases | 看房租屋，你要聽得懂

1. I'm looking for a roommate to share a two-bedroom apartment.
   我在找一位室友合租兩房公寓。

2. No smoking or pets are allowed in the building.
   大樓內禁菸和禁養寵物。

3. You'll need to fill out an application and pay a $35 [6]**screening** fee.
   你需要填申請表，並付 35 美元審查費。

4. We run a credit check and background check on all potential tenants.
   我們要對所有可能簽約的房客進行信用和背景審查。

5. Rent is due on the first of the month, and there's a five-day [7]**grace period**.
   租金每月一號支付，有五天寬限期。

6. You'll need a ***guarantor** to co-sign your lease.
   你需要一位保證人一起簽租約。

7. As long as there is no damage, your security deposit will be returned with interest.
   只要沒有損壞，你的押金會和利息一起歸還。

CHAPTER
開課前準備

2

Preparing for
Your Studies

LESSON 11
Meal Plans
第十一話：餐點方案

♫ **065** | 好用句

♫ **066** | 單字

Vocabulary Bank

1. **carry over** (phr.) (錢、福利等) 挪到下一段時間使用

   Can vacation time be carried over from one year to the next?

2. **location** [loˋkeʃən] (n.) 所在地，地點，位置

   The resort was built in a beautiful location.

3. **vending machine** (phr.) 自動販賣機

   I think the vending machine is out of order.

補充字彙

* **dining dollars** (phr.) 儲值餐費

📖 **Reading Quiz** | 閱讀測驗

● 請在看完下面學生的餐點方案和用餐習慣後，幫下面學生選出適合他的方案：

Freshman Meal Plan Options			
Meal Plan	Bonus Meals	*Dining Dollars	Price Per Semester
Any Meal / Any Time	10	100	$3,175
19 Meals Per Week	15	150	$2,950
14 Meals Per Week	20	200	$2,695
10 Meals Per Week	25	250	$2,405

Tom is a freshman who wants to have 3 meals a day on campus on weekdays, two a day on weekends, and buy snacks and coffee a few times a week. Which plan would meet his needs at the lowest cost?

(A) Any Meal / Any Time
(B) 19 Meals Per Week
(C) 14 Meals Per Week
(D) 10 Meals Per Week

解答：(B)
翻譯請見 p. 214

解說

一天吃三餐，週末一天吃兩餐，週間不定時購買點心和咖啡，相當於每周固定 19 餐，另外還有 15 頓餐點和 150 元的餐費，是最符合湯姆需求，且價格也最低的方案。

1. How do I pay for my meal plan?   餐點方案如何付款？

2. Can I [1]**carry over** unused meals to the next semester?   我可以將沒用到的餐數挪到下學期嗎？

3. Where can Dining Dollars be spent?   儲值餐費可以在哪裡花費？

4. How can I check my Dining Dollars balance?   我要怎麼查看我的儲值餐費餘額？

5. Is it possible to change my meal plan?   我可以更換餐點方案嗎？

6. Can I use my dining card to pay for a guest's meal?   我可以用我的餐點卡支付賓客餐點嗎？

7. Can my dining card be used off-campus?   我的餐點卡能在校外使用嗎？

Common Phrases | 餐點方案，你要聽得懂

1. Students can pay for meal plans at the Housing Office or through the Office's web portal.   學生可在住宿事務處或透過事務處網站支付餐點方案。

2. No. So you should be careful in choosing the plan that best fits your eating habits.   不能。所以你應該謹慎選擇最適合你的用餐習慣的方案。

3. Dining Dollars can be used at all on-campus dining [2]**locations** and [3]**vending machines**.   儲值餐費可在校內所有用餐地點和販賣機使用。

4. The balance is printed on your receipt each time you make a purchase.   每次付帳後，儲值餐費餘額會列印在收據上。

5. Yes. Meal plan changes are accepted during the first week of each semester.   可以。每學期第一週可以更改餐點方案。

6. Yes, but only if you have a meal plan that includes guest meals.   可以，但只有包含賓客餐點的方案才能使用。

7. Meals can only be used on-campus, but some off-campus restaurants accept Dining Dollars.   餐點數只能在校內使用，但有些校外餐廳會接受儲值餐費。

大多數學校的餐點方案

美國大多數學校的 meal plan 都是以自助餐為主，學生需向學校購買符合自己需求的方案後，使用自己的學生證或消費卡進入學校餐廳用餐。有些學校可重複刷同一張卡帶朋友進入餐廳用餐，但也有學校規定一張卡同一個時間只能刷一次。此外，多數學校的 meal plan 除了可以在餐廳使用之外，還可以在學校咖啡廳、超市等地使用。購買學校 meal plan 的同學們需注意的是，大多數學校都有規定在學期末前需要把卡內的點數或錢全班用光，否則將自動作廢，不可退費或留到下學期使用。所以若學期末將近，還剩不少點數的話，可到學校咖啡廳、超市等地購買零食、飲料、礦泉水等。

Vocabulary Bank

1. **no wonder** (phr.) 難怪，並不
   讓人驚訝，並不奇怪
   No wonder you're hungry—you
   didn't eat breakfast.

2. **access** [ˋæksɛs] (n./v.) 使用，
   進入
   You need fast Internet access
   to play online games.

補充字彙

＊ **unlimited** [ʌnˋlɪmɪtɪd] (a.)
   無限制的，無限量的

Asking for advice
詢問餐點方案建議

Student	Hi. I'm having trouble deciding which meal plan to choose.
Clerk	Well, how many dining hall meals do you plan on having per day?
Student	Just lunch and dinner during the week. Oh, and I'll also be away for two weeks this semester.
Clerk	In that case, the 10 meals a week plan is your best option.

學生	嗨，我在猶豫要怎麼選擇餐點方案。
職員	這樣啊，你預計一天要吃幾餐？
學生	週間只要午餐和晚餐。噢，這學期我還會請假兩星期。
職員	這樣的話，一星期十餐的方案是最適合你的選擇。

Discussing meal plans
討論餐點方案

Student A	Wow, you're really piling the food on your plate there.
Student B	Ha, yeah. I'm on the off-campus meal plan that includes 25 meals a semester, so I try to make the most of every meal.
Student A	[1]**No wonder.** I'm on the all-[2]**access** plan, so I just eat whenever I'm hungry.
Student B	I don't think *unlimited meals would work for me. I'd probably gain 20 pounds a semester!

學生 A	哇，你的盤子裝得真多。
學生 B	哈，對，我的是校外餐點計畫，一學期包含 25 餐，所以我每餐會多拿點。
學生 A	難怪，我的是吃到飽方案，只要餓了隨時都能吃。
學生 B	我不覺得無限制餐數方案適合我。這樣我一學期可能會增重 20 磅！

Asking about meal plans
詢問餐點方案

Student	Hi. Do you accept dining cards here?
Cashier	Yes, of course. What would you like to order?
Student	Um, let's see. Can I use one of my meals here?
Cashier	No, but you can use your dining dollars to order anything you like.
Student	Oh, I see. So you just deduct dining dollars from my card when I order?
Cashier	Yes, that's right.
Student	OK. Give me a second to look at the menu.

學生	嗨,這裡接受餐點卡嗎?
收銀員	當然接受,你想點什麼?
學生	嗯,我看看,我能用我的餐數嗎?
收銀員	不能,但你可以用儲值餐費點任何東西。
學生	這樣啊,所以我點餐後,你就直接從我卡裡扣餐費?
收銀員	對,沒錯。
學生	好,等我看一下菜單。

餐點方案選擇建議

大家在選擇餐點方案前可先大概計算自己會在學校吃幾次飯,然後以這個為基準去選擇適合你的方案。如果每天3餐都打算在學校吃的話,那麼就需要購買最完整,也是最貴的一個方案,好處是可以不用每天煩惱吃什麼,肚子餓就去學校餐廳吃,不過壞處是學校餐廳大部分都是以自助餐為主,很容易吃膩,所以如果沒有每天每餐吃的話就很容易造成浪費。所以大家可以以自己的情況來購買最適合自己的方案。

LESSON 12
Homestay Family
第十二話：寄宿家庭

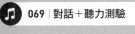

 069 | 對話＋聽力測驗

 070 | 單字

Vocabulary Bank

1. **yogurt** [ˋjogɚt] (n.) 優格，乳酪，酸奶
   What's your favorite flavor of yogurt?

2. **make it** (phr.) 趕上，成功抵達
   The climbers never made it to the top of the mountain.

3. **in time** (phr.) 及時，來得及
   If we don't hurry, we won't arrive in time to catch the train.

4. **takes turns** (phr.) 輪流
   We take turns feeding the cat.

5. **cracker** [ˋkrækɚ] (n.) 薄脆鹹餅乾
   Crackers and cheese make a great snack.

6. **den** [dɛn] (n.) 電視間，休息室
   The kids are watching TV in the den.

補充字彙

* **notepad** [ˋnot͵pæd] (n.) 記事本

* **linen** [ˋlɪnɪn] (n.) 床單，亞麻製品

* **load** [lod] (n.) 一次洗衣機、洗碗機等的量

---

1 SITUATION
Meeting the host family
首次見面

Student	Hi. I'm Michael.
Host Mother	Hi, Michael. I'm Becky. Welcome to our home. You must be tired from your flight.
Student	Yes. I got some sleep on the plane, but it was a long flight.
Host Mother	Well, let me introduce you to everyone. This is my husband Rick, this is my son Tom, and this is my daughter Lisa.
Student	Hi, everybody. It's great to meet you!
Host Mother	OK, now let me show you to your room so you can get some rest.

學生	嗨，我叫麥可。
寄宿家庭媽媽	嗨，麥可，我叫貝琪，歡迎你來我們家。你坐飛機一定累了。
學生	對，我在飛機上睡了一下，但那是長途飛行。
寄宿家庭媽媽	嗯，我介紹大家給你認識。這是我丈夫李克，我兒子湯姆，我女兒麗莎。
學生	大家好，很高興認識你們！
寄宿家庭媽媽	好，我帶你去看你的房間，好讓你休息一下。

2 SITUATION
Showing the room
參觀房間

Host Mother	Here's your room. I just put clean sheets on the bed, and there are towels in your bathroom, which is over there. Just tell me if you need any more.
Student	OK, thank you. Is there Internet I can use?
Host Mother	Yes. We have WiFi in every room. I wrote our password on that *notepad on the desk.
Student	Great. I want to get in touch with my family and let them know I've arrived safely.

寄宿家庭媽媽	這是你的房間。我已經換上乾淨的床單，浴室有毛巾，就在那裡。你還需要毛巾的話就跟我說一聲。
學生	好，謝謝。有網路可以用嗎？
寄宿家庭媽媽	有，我們每個房間都有無線網路。我已經把密碼寫在書桌上的記事本裡了。
學生	太好了。我要跟我家人聯絡一下，讓他們知道我平安到達了。

Listening Quiz | 聽力測驗

● 請在聽完 home 媽説明寄宿家庭生活常規後，回答下面問題：

1. What meals will the homestay student have to wash dishes for?

(A) Breakfast
(B) Dinner
(C) Breakfast and dinner
(D) Lunch and dinner

2. What type of laundry is the student expected to do?

(A) Towels
(B) Clothes
(C) Sheets
(D) Linens

解答：1. (C) 2. (B)

聽力測驗原文

We usually have two meals at home—breakfast and dinner. We each make our own breakfast and wash our own dishes. There's always milk, juice, eggs and [1]**yogurt** in the refrigerator. There's also cereal and bread for toast. Either Allen or I make dinner. We usually eat at 6:30. If you can't [2]**make it** [3]**in time**, just call us and we'll save you a plate of food. Everybody [4]**takes turns** washing the dinner dishes. We also have snacks like cookies, [5]**crackers**, chips and fruit in the kitchen—feel free to help yourself. You're welcome to use all of the downstairs rooms—the kitchen, dining room, living room, [6]**den**. The washer and dryer are in the basement. I wash all the towels and *linens, but you can do a *load of clothes anytime you like.

我們通常在家吃兩餐，早餐和晚餐。我們各自會自己做早餐，自己洗碗。冰箱裡會常備牛奶、果汁、雞蛋和優格。還會有穀片和土司麵包。晚餐由我或艾倫來做。我們通常在六點半吃飯。你若無法準時用餐，只要打電話給我們，我們會留一盤菜給你。大家要輪流洗晚餐的碗盤。廚房裡也有甜餅乾、鹹餅乾、洋芋片和水果之類的點心，請隨意取用。樓下所有房間都可以使用，例如廚房、餐廳、客廳和電視間。洗衣機和烘衣機在地下室。我會洗所有毛巾和床單，但你也可以隨時洗衣服。

如何挑選優良的寄宿家庭

需先了解他們是否有以下條件：

1. 是否有犯罪紀錄，家庭、家長是否品行端正
2. 是否有愛心與責任心
3. 是否有良好的家庭氛圍
4. 是否願意與學生做交流溝通
5. 是否有足夠時間、精力照顧住宿學生

只要能滿足上述 5 個條件就能算是優良的 homestay 了！學生或家長可上網查詢欲住宿 homestay 的情況，也可用 e-mail 和視訊跟對方進行溝通對談，對談時觀察 homestay 環境以及家長的責任心。如果有時間，也可預先到備選 homestay 參觀，感受真實情況。

CHAPTER 2

開課前準備

Preparing for Your Studies

♫ 071 | 對話＋好用句

♫ 072 | 單字

Vocabulary Bank

1. **central heating** (phr.) **中央 暖氣系統**

   Does your house have central heating?

2. **theft** [θɛft] (n.) **竊盜**

   There have been several thefts in the building lately.

3. **oatmeal** [ˋot͵mil] (n.) **燕麥片、 粥**

   I like to put milk and brown sugar in my oatmeal.

4. **porch** [pɔrtʃ] (n.) **門廊**

   We like to sit on the porch on summer evenings.

補充字彙

* **space heater** (n.) **室內電暖 器**

* **humidifier** [hju ˋmɪdə͵faɪɚ] (n.) **空氣加濕器**

* **thermostat** [ˋθɝmə͵stæt] (n.) **恆溫器，溫控器**

humidifier 加濕器

SITUATION 3

Communicating an issue
溝通狀況

Student It's a little cold in my room. Would it be possible to turn the heat on?

Host Mother We don't have [1]**central heating**, but I have a *space heater** you can put in your room.

[later]

Student The heater works great, but it's making the air really dry.

Host Mother Oh, a *humidifier** would help with that. We don't have one, but you could pick one up cheap at Costco. I can take you if you like.

學生 我的房間有點冷，可以開暖氣嗎？

寄宿家庭媽媽 我們沒有中央暖氣，但我有一個室內電暖器，可以放在你的房間。

[稍後]

學生 暖氣很好用，但會讓空氣變得很乾燥。

寄宿家庭媽媽 噢，可以用加濕器，我們沒有，但在好市多可以買到便宜的，需要的話我可以帶你去。

SITUATION 4

Responding to an invitation
回應邀約

`DIALOGUE 1`

Tom Hey, Michael. Do you like playing video games?

Student Yeah. I have a PlayStation back in Taiwan.

Tom I have an Xbox. Do you want to play Grand [2]**Theft** Auto with me?

Student Sure. I'm not used to playing on the Xbox though, so you'll probably beat me, ha-ha.

湯姆 嘿，麥可，你喜歡打電玩嗎？

學生 喜歡，我在台灣有 PlayStation。

湯姆 我有 Xbox。你想跟我一起玩俠盜獵車手嗎？

學生 好啊，但我不習慣在 Xbox 上玩，所以你應該會擊敗我，哈哈。

DIALOGUE 2

Host Mother The whole family is going to church on Sunday morning. Would you like to come with us?

Student Thanks for asking, but I'm not really religious.

Host Mother Oh, OK. We're also going out for hamburgers afterwards. If you like, we could come by and pick you up.

Student Sure. That sounds great!

寄宿家庭媽媽 我們全家週日早上會上教堂，你想跟我們一起去嗎？

學生 謝謝你的邀請，但我沒信教。

寄宿家庭媽媽 噢，好，之後我們也會去吃漢堡。你想去的話，我們可以回來接你。

學生 好啊，聽起來很不錯！

Common Phrases | 詢問問題，你要會說

1. Is it OK if I invite friends over?   我可以邀請朋友過來嗎？

2. Would it be possible to have hot [3]**oatmeal** for breakfast?   早餐可以有熱麥片嗎？

3. Can I use the kitchen to cook my own meals?   我能用廚房自己煮飯嗎？

4. Would it be all right if I turned up the ***thermostat** a little?   我可以將暖氣稍微調高嗎？

5. Could you please show me how to use the washer and dryer?   可以請你教我怎麼用洗衣機和烘衣機嗎？

6. Do you mind if I smoke in the yard/on the [4]**porch**?   你介意我在院子／門廊上抽菸嗎？

7. I was thinking of buying a bicycle. Is there somewhere I could put it?   我在考慮買腳踏車，有地方可以讓我放嗎？

hot oatmeal

1. homestay 就像你在國外的家庭，所以你要和父母交代的事，在 homestay 也要做到，像是出門要講一聲，用餐時，若不回去用餐，要提早說，對方才能提早做調整。

2. 盡量配合住宿家庭作息時間，如果住宿家庭習慣早睡，學生最好在晚上 9 點後不要發出大聲響，例如，用電話跟家人朋友聊天，洗澡時發出很大聲音（盡量不要在人家睡覺後洗澡），也不要太晚回家，以免影響到住宿家庭作息，如要晚歸，請先通知住宿家庭。

3. 有什麼問題就問住宿家庭，不要自作聰明，更不要聽不懂就隨便答 Yes，以免造成誤會，如果聽不懂他們說什麼，可以請他們解釋或用簡單方式在說一次。

4. 入住時先詢問適合自己洗澡的時間，並盡量減短洗澡時間。

5. 如有朋友來訪或邀請朋友來訪前，需先獲得住宿家庭的同意，且不能留朋友下來過夜。

6. 使用住宿家庭的東西時，要遵守規定，東西用完要物歸原位。

7. 飲食部分若有不習慣或不吃的東西，請先跟住宿家庭溝通好，以免造成誤會與不快。

8. 除了自己房間要保持乾淨外，也主動幫忙做家事。例如，洗碗、收拾桌子、打掃房子衛生等。

CHAPTER
開課前準備

Preparing for
Your Studies

2

LESSON 13
Housing Safety
第十三話：居住安全

🎵 073 | 對話

🎵 074 | 單字

Vocabulary Bank

1. **assess** [əˋsɛs] (v.) **對…進行評估**

   It's wise to assess the real estate market before buying a house.

2. **plow** [plaʊ] (v./n.) **耕地，犁，剷（雪）**

   The farmer used an ox to plow the field.

3. **route** [rut / raʊt] (n.) **路徑，路線**

   Which route do you usually take to work?

4. **burglary** [ˋbɝgləɪ] (n.) **入室盜竊（罪），burglar** [ˋbɝglə] (n.) **為「入室竊賊」**

   There was a burglary at our house last week.

5. **report** [rɪˋport] (n./v.) **舉報，告發**

   I'd like to report a hit and run.

6. **dispatch** [dɪˋspætʃ] (v.) **發送，派遣**

   An ambulance was dispatched to the scene of the accident.

7. **escort** [ˋɛskɔrt] (n./v.) **護送（員），護航，陪同**

   That area is too dangerous to visit without an escort.

Noise complaint
投訴噪音

Student	Hi. I'd like to make a noise complaint. My upstairs neighbors are having a party and the music is really loud.
Operator	Have you asked them to turn it down?
Student	Yes, but they just turned it up again a few minutes later.
Operator	OK. Can you give me your address, please?
Student	I'm at 930 Cranbrook Court, Apartment 122.
Operator	All right. We'll send out an officer to [1]assess the situation within 30 minutes.

學生	嗨，我想舉報噪音。我樓上的鄰居在開派對，音樂開太大聲了。
接線生	你有請他們轉小聲點嗎？
學生	有，但他們過幾分鐘後又轉大聲。
接線生	好，請把你的住址給我好嗎？
學生	我住在克蘭布克巷 930 號 122 室。
接線生	好，我們會在 30 分鐘內派警察過去評估狀況。

Too much snow
大雪通報

Student	Hi. There's over a foot of snow in front of my house, and I need to drive to school soon. Can you tell me when the street will be [2]**plowed**?
Operator	Sure. What street do you live on?
Student	I'm on Constitution Ave.
Operator	OK, that's a primary snow [3]**route**, so a plow should be coming by within half an hour.

學生	嗨，我家門前的積雪已超過一英尺，我等一下要開車去學校。可否告訴我街道何時會剷雪？
接線生	好，你住在哪條街？
學生	我在憲法大道。
接線生	好，那是主要積雪路線，所以剷雪車應該會在半小時內過去。

[4]**Burglary**
住宅入室竊盜

Student	Hello. I'd like to [5]**report** a burglary. I'm at 1503 Elm Street.
Operator	Are you inside your home?
Student	No. I'm on the front porch. The window next to the front door is broken, and I hear sounds coming from inside.
Operator	OK. Don't attempt to enter your house. I'm [6]**dispatching** officers now. Please wait on the corner until they arrive.

學生	你好,我想舉報入室竊盜案,我住在榆樹街 1503 號。
接線生	你現在在家中嗎?
學生	沒有,我在前門廊,前門旁邊的窗戶破了,我聽到屋子裡有聲音。
接線生	好,不要進屋子。我立刻派警察過去,請在街角等候警察。

Safety [7]**escort**
要求護送

Operator	BearWalk. How can I help you?
Student	Hi. I'd like to request a safety escort.
Operator	Sure. Where are you located, and where are you headed?
Student	I'm at Moffit Library, and I'm going back to my apartment at College and Haste.
Operator	OK. An escort will meet you at the library entrance in 15 minutes.

接線生	這裡是金熊護送隊,有什麼能為你效勞嗎?
學生	嗨,我想請安全護送員來接我。
接線生	好,你的位置在哪裡,要去什麼地方?
學生	我在莫菲特圖書館,我要回大學街夾海斯特街的公寓。
接線生	好,護送員會在 15 分鐘內到圖書館入口處與你會合。

Useful Pattern | 通報案件,就這樣說

▶ **I want to report a case of** _____.
　我想舉報_____。

robbery 搶劫	**domestic violence** 家暴
burglary 入室竊盜	**child abuse** 虐待兒童
(car) theft (汽車)竊盜	**assault** 攻擊
arson 縱火	**intimidation** 恐嚇
(sexual) harassment (性)騷擾	**vandalism** 破壞公物
rape 強暴	**Identity theft** 身份竊盜
stalking 跟蹤	**hit and run** 肇事逃逸

校外安全建議

1. 盡量不要到危險的區域,有時寧願繞一點路也不要路過危險區域。

2. 不把貴重物品(包包、筆電、GPS、相機…)放在車內明顯處,請盡量全部帶下車。如不方便帶下車,請在到達目的地前先放入後車廂,切勿到達後在開後車廂置放。

3. 隨時提高警覺注意周圍情況,不一邊走路一邊看手機。搭公車、地鐵時,請保護好你的貴重物品(手機、包包),最好也不要玩手機,如果一定要玩,請握好它,很多搶匪會在下車前搶了就跑。

4. 如果不幸遇到持武器搶劫,請果斷放棄你的物品,沒有東西會比你的生命更重要。

5. 請遠離非法毒品,外出吃飯喝酒時,視線請勿離開自己的飲料,以免有心人士下藥。另外,喝酒後,請不要太晚回家,以免發生危險。

6. 外出時請盡量讓家人、朋友知道你的動向,例如,去哪裡,大概什麼時候回來。

7. 如遇到危險情況,請撥打 911 報警。

Vocabulary Bank

1. **suspicious** [sə`spɪʃəs] (a.)
   可疑的，多疑的

   The villagers are very
   suspicious of strangers.

2. **hang tight** (phr.) (口) 稍候，
   稍安勿躁

   Just hang tight for a minute
   and I'll be right back.

3. **laptop** [`læp,tɑp] (n.) **筆記型
   電腦**

   I always take my laptop with
   me when I travel.

4. **anonymous** [ə`nɑnɪməs] (a.)
   不具名地，匿名地

   The crime was reported by a
   witness who wishes to remain
   anonymous.

5. **rack** [ræk] (n.) **架子**

   We put a ski rack on our car.

6. **self-defense** [,sɛlfdɪ`fɛns]
   (n.) **自我防護，防身術**

   The woman's lawyer claims
   she shot her husband in self-
   defense.

7. **steering wheel** (phr.) **方向
   盤**

   You should always keep both
   hands on the steering wheel.

補充字彙

* **footage** [`fʊtɪdʒ] (n.) **一段影
   片，片段**

Reporting [1]suspicious people
通報可疑人物

Operator	Campus police.
Student	Hi. I'd like to report some suspicious behavior. There's a man walking around the student parking lot. He has some kind of tool in his hand, and I'm afraid he may be a car thief.
Operator	OK. [2]**Hang tight** and don't try to approach him. An officer should be there within ten minutes.

接線生	這裡是校警。
學生	嗨，我要舉報可疑行為。有一個人在學生停車場周圍徘徊，他手上拿著某種工具，我擔心他可能是汽車竊賊。
接線生	好，請稍安勿躁，別靠近他，警察會在十分鐘內趕到。

Theft
偷竊

Student	Excuse me. I just went to use the restroom, and when I got back my [3]**laptop** was gone.
Librarian	Oh dear. We'd better inform the campus police. I'll make the call.
Student	Thank you. I really hope I can get it back. I just bought it.
Librarian	No problem. While we're waiting, we can take a look at the security camera ***footage**.

學生	不好意思，我剛剛去廁所，等我回來時，我的筆電不見了。
圖書館員	天啊，我們最好通知校警，我來打電話。
學生	謝謝，我真的很希望能把筆電找回來，我才剛買的。
圖書館員	沒問題，在等警察來之前，我們先來看看監視器畫面。

Common Phrases | 安全相關問題，你要會說

1. Is my report [4]**anonymous**?
   我的舉報是匿名的嗎？

2. I just had my wallet/purse stolen.
   我的皮夾 / 手提包剛剛被偷了。

3. Is it safe to ride the subway late at night?
   深夜搭地鐵安全嗎？

4. Are there safety escorts available here?
   這裡有安全護送隊嗎？

5. Do you know where I can buy pepper spray around here?
   你知道這附近哪裡可以買到辣椒噴霧嗎？

6. Are there [5]**racks** on campus where I can lock my bike?
   校園裡有可供上鎖的自行車架嗎？

7. Does the school offer [6]**self-defense** classes?
   學校有提供防身術課程嗎？

Common Phrases | 安全相關問題，你要聽得懂

1. Please remember to lock all the doors and windows when you leave.
   請記得離開時要鎖好所有門窗。

2. Here is the security code for the burglar alarm.
   這是防盜警報器的密碼。

3. If you're walking outside after dark, it's best to walk with a friend.
   如果天黑後要出門，最好和朋友結伴同行。

4. Always walk in well-lit areas after dark.
   天黑後務必走在有燈光的地方。

5. If you're alone, you can request a safety escort to walk with you.
   如果你是獨自一人，可以請安全護送員陪你同行。

6. Be sure to put chains on your car when the roads are icy.
   道路結冰時，請務必在輪胎裝上雪鏈。

7. There are a lot of car thefts around here, so you should use a [7]**steering wheel** lock.
   這附近有很多汽車竊盜案，所以你應該要用方向盤鎖。

steering wheel lock

校內安全建議

1. 美國校園內都設有緊急電話，請先了解它們在哪，如遇到危險，可前往撥打。

2. 知道學校校警電話號碼。每間學校都會有警察進駐，在學校遇到或看到危險，撥打校警電話會比撥打 911 要快。

3. 盡量結伴同行，尤其是晚上。

4. 如必須單獨行走，建議攜帶防身武器（防狼噴霧、電擊棒…）

5. 夜晚可利用學校提供的安全護送。多數學校都會提供需晚歸的學生安全護送服務，會有專人前往你的所在地陪你走路或接送。

LESSON 14
Getting to Know Your Roommates
第十四話：和室友混熟

🎵 077｜對話

🎵 078｜單字

Vocabulary Bank

1. **in charge of** (phr.) 負責，照護

   The senior vice president is in charge of company operations.

2. **be into** (phr.) 熱中於…

   Jason's really into heavy metal.

3. **rusty** [ˋrʌstɪ] (技術) 生疏的，荒廢的

   My French is a little rusty.

4. **shoot hoops** (phr.) 打籃球

   Wanna shoot some hoops after class?

5. **stay in shape** (phr.) 保持體適能

   Practicing yoga is a great way to stay in shape.

6. **guideline** [ˋgaɪd͵laɪn] (n.) 準則，指導方針

   We follow strict guidelines on the protection of personal information.

7. **split** [splɪt] (v.) (使) 分開

   We always split the bill when we eat out.

補充字彙

* **housewarming (party)** [ˋhaʊs͵wɔrmɪŋ] (n.) 喬遷慶宴

*Housewarming party invitation
入住派對邀請

Student 1	Hey, what do you think about having a housewarming party so everybody can get to know each other better?
Student 2	That's a great idea. I just bought a case of beer, so that should help break the ice.
Student 1	Ha-ha. I'm not sure if Randy and Bruce drink, so I'll pick up some soda and juice.
Student 2	I guess Randy and Bruce are ¹⁾**in charge of** pizza and snacks then. I'll let them know when I see them later.

學生 1	嘿，來辦個喬遷派對，讓大家互相熟悉一下，你覺得怎樣？
學生 2	好主意。我剛買了一箱啤酒，應該可以炒熱一下氣氛。
學生 1	哈哈。我不確定蘭迪和布魯斯喝不喝酒，所以我會買些汽水和果汁。
學生 2	我想就讓蘭迪和布魯斯負責買披薩和點心。等一下看到他們時我再跟他們說。

Chatting
閒話家常

Student 1	My name is Robert, but my friends all call me Bobby. How about you?
Student 2	Well, my Chinese name is hard to pronounce. You can just call me Jason.
Student 1	Cool. ²⁾**Are** you **into** sports? I'm a big football fan.
Student 2	I'm into baseball. It's the national sport in Taiwan. I also like to play basketball.
Student 1	Oh yeah? Me too. I'm a little ³⁾**rusty** though. Maybe we can ⁴⁾**shoot** some **hoops** sometime.
Student 2	Sounds great. It's a good way to ⁵⁾**stay in shape**.

學生 1	我叫羅伯特，但我的朋友都叫我鮑比。 你呢？
學生 2	呃，我的中文名字很難發音，你可以叫我傑森。
學生 1	酷。你喜歡運動嗎？我是美式足球迷。
學生 2	我喜歡棒球，這在台灣是全民運動，我也喜歡打籃球。
學生 1	是嗎？我也是。不過我有點生疏了，也許我們哪天可以打一下。
學生 2	聽起來不錯，這是保持體適能的好方法。

Setting [6]guidelines
訂立守則

Student 1　Since we're gonna be living together, I guess we should set some house rules, right?

Student 2　Yeah. We're both engineering students, so we'll be studying a lot. How about quiet time after ten?

Student 1　Sounds good. I'm gonna do most of my studying at the library, but I get up early. Do you think we should shop together and [7]**split** the costs or just buy food separately?

Student 2　I think separate is better. I don't do much cooking anyway, so you can have two shelves in the fridge if you like.

Student 1　OK, cool. How about cleaning? Should we just clean up after ourselves?

Student 2　Sure. But we should probably take turns cleaning the common areas like the living room and the bathroom.

Student 1　That seems fair. How do you feel about having friends over?

Student 2　That sounds fine, as long as things don't get too noisy. I'm OK with overnight guests too, but only on the weekends.

學生 1　既然我們要一起生活，我想我們應該要訂立一些生活公約吧？

學生 2　對，我們都是工程系學生，所以要經常念書。十點後保持安靜怎麼樣？

學生 1　聽起來不錯。我大部分時候會在圖書館念書，但我會早起。你覺得我們應該一起採購並分攤費用，還是各自採購食物？

學生 2　我覺得分開比較好。反正我不常做飯，所以冰箱你可以用兩層。

學生 1　好，酷。清潔方面呢？我們各自用完就各自清潔嗎？

學生 2　好。但我們應該輪流打掃客廳和浴室等公共區域。

學生 1　這樣挺公平的。你覺得帶朋友來怎麼樣？

學生 2　我覺得沒關係，只要不會太吵。朋友來過夜我也覺得沒關係，但只限週末。

學生們入住第一天最好跟室友們坐下來聊一聊，互相了解各自的生活習慣以及需要注意的事情等，並制訂生活公約，千萬不要覺得不好意思。

生活公約內建議包括：

1. **睡覺時間：**
   每個人的作息都不同，有人習慣早睡，有人是夜貓子，所以需先跟室友商量好各自的睡覺時間以及解決的辦法。例如：早睡的可以戴眼罩、耳塞，晚睡的盡量不要發出聲響。

2. **是否可以帶朋友回來住？需要幾天前先徵得大家同意？**
   很多美國人喜歡帶朋友到家裡玩，如果只是待一下就走，應該沒有什麼問題，只要不要影響到你，或是碰你的東西就好了。但如果要住下來的話，應該需要先徵得大家同意，以免尷尬。

3. **房屋清潔衛生由誰做？**
   大家同住一個屋簷下，一定需要先商量分配好公共區域的家事，以免以後發生糾紛。

除了生活公約外，跟國外室友相處還需謹記下列幾點：
1. 有什麼問題或不滿，一定不能憋著，要說出來跟室友溝通。如果不說，室友可能會覺得你可以接受這件事而繼續做下去。

2. 與室友溝通時，最好用詞委婉，盡量不要讓人感覺你在指責他。

3. 跟室友達成「借用東西時一定要先詢問」的共識。

4. 尊重彼此的隱私、文化差異。

5. 購買家裡共用家具時，一定不要分攤，以免發生搬出時物品歸屬糾紛。大家可先商量什麼東西由誰購買，搬出時就由購買人帶走。

6. 如果真的遇到壞室友，無法忍耐，請果斷找舍監／房東換宿或退租。

Vocabulary Bank

1. **headphones** [ˋhɛd.fonz] (n.)
   耳機

   Can you recommend a good
   pair of headphones?

2. **cleanser** [ˋklɛnzɚ] (n.) **清潔
   劑，去汙劑，洗面乳**

   Remember to use cleanser
   when you clean the sink.

補充字彙

✱ **finale** [fɪˋnæli] (n.) （影集）**最
   後一集，表演的終場**

📖 Reading Quiz │ 閱讀測驗

● 請先看完以下的生活公約，再回答下列問題：

House Rules

Expenses
Common expenses like rent, utilities, toilet paper and cleaning
supplies will be split 50/50.

Shopping
A shopping trip will be made each Sunday, with each roommate
paying for own groceries.

Guests
Friends and boyfriends can visit at any time, but must leave before
11:00 p.m. A relative or friend from out of town can spend the night
with advance notice.

Private and common spaces
Living room, kitchen and bathroom are common areas, but
bedrooms are private and shouldn't be entered without permission.

Cleaning
Each person is responsible for cleaning up after themselves and
keeping their bedroom clean. Roommates will take turns cleaning
common spaces.

Food and cooking
Each roommate will keep their food on their own refrigerator and
cupboard shelves. There will be no borrowing of others' food without
asking. Each roommate will cook their own food and wash their own
dishes.

Quiet time
Quiet time begins at 9:00 p.m. and ends at 8:00 a.m. [1]**Headphones**
should be used if you want to listen to music during quiet time.

Bathroom use
Showers should be limited to five minutes and bathroom time to 15
minutes when the other roommate is home.

---

1. Which of these guests would be allowed to spend the night?
(A) A study partner
(B) A college classmate
(C) A visiting parent
(D) A boyfriend or girlfriend

2. Which one of these expenses will not be shared?
(A) Food
(B) Electricity
(C) [2]Cleanser
(D) Rent

解答：1. (C) 2. (A)
翻譯請見 p. 214

Common Phrases | 和室友溝通，你要會說

1. Today is Wednesday, so it's your turn to take out the trash.

   今天是星期三，輪到你倒垃圾了。

2. Do you mind if I watch The Bachelor? It's the season *finale.

   你介意我看《鑽石求千金》嗎？今天是這季最後一集。

3. Could you make sure to check the drain after you take a shower? I found hair in it again.

   你洗完澡以後，可以記得把頭髮從排水口撿起來嗎？我又發現裡面有頭髮了。

4. Please remember to keep your showers short. I just ran out of hot water when I was taking a shower.

   請記得縮短淋浴時間，我剛剛洗澡時熱水用完了。

5. Didn't we agree that boyfriends had to leave by 11:00?

   我以為我們對於 11 點後，男友需要離開這件事有共識。

6. Would you mind turning the music down a little? I have a report due tomorrow.

   你可以把音樂聲關小聲點嗎？我有份報告明天要交。

7. There's something spilled on the kitchen counter. Could you please remember to clean up when you're done?

   有東西撒在廚房流理台上。你使用後可以記得順手清理一下嗎？

Useful Pattern
想委婉溝通，
就這麼說

▶ **I couldn't help but noticing that _____.**

（我忍不住注意到 _____。）

last night's dirty dishes are still in the sink
昨夜的髒碗盤還在水槽裡

you forgot to take the garbage out last night
你昨晚忘了倒垃圾

someone ate one of my bagels without asking
有人沒問過我，就吃了我的一個貝果

you didn't clean the bathroom yesterday
你昨天沒有清理浴室

you left dirty laundry in the washing machine
你把髒衣服留在洗衣機裡

the front door wasn't locked when I came home
我回家時，發現大門沒鎖

you were playing music at 11:00 last night
你昨天晚上 11 點還在放音樂

LESSON 15
Tips on Saving Money
第十五話：省錢妙招

 081 | 對話

 082 | 單字

Vocabulary Bank

1. **coupon** [ˈkupɑn] (n.) 折價券，優惠券

   Betty always clips coupons before she goes grocery shopping.

2. **outlet** [ˈaʊtlɛt] (n.) 暢貨中心，批發商店

   I buy most of my clothes at the local outlet mall.

3. **racket** [ˈrækɪt] (n.) 敲詐，騙局，非法勾當

   That gang runs a protection racket.

4. **help** [hɛlp] (v.) （與 can、could 連用）避免，阻止

   I can't help laughing when you tickle me.

5. **disorganized** [dɪsˈɔrgəˌnaɪzd] (a.) 雜亂無章的

   How can you stand having your desk so disorganized?

6. **brand name** (phr.) 品牌，名牌

   I can't afford to buy brand name basketball shoes.

7. **sign up** (phr.) 註冊，報名

   If you want to go on the field trip, you need to sign up by Friday.

 SITUATION 1

Savings at the supermarket
超市省錢作戰

Student 1 I clipped some [1]**coupons**. We can use them when we go to Safeway later. I don't buy anything unless there's a discount.

Student 2 I guess that's a good way to save money, but what if the food you want isn't on sale?

Student 1 Then I don't eat it, ha-ha.

Student 2 If you really want to save money, we should go to Grocery [2]**Outlet**. All their groceries are 40 to 70% off.

學生 1 我剪了一些折價券，我們等一下去喜互惠超市時可以用。我只買有折扣的東西。

學生 2 我想這是省錢的好方法，但如果你想買的食物沒折扣怎麼辦？

學生 1 那我就不吃了，哈哈。

學生 2 如果你真的想省錢，我們應該去暢貨超市，那裡的食品雜貨都打三到六折。

 SITUATION 2

Buying used textbooks
買二手課本

Student 1 I was just at the campus bookstore and I couldn't believe how expensive textbooks are.

Student 2 I know. It's a [3]**racket**. I never buy textbooks new if I can [4]**help** it.

Student 1 I hear there's a couple bookstores near campus that sell used textbooks.

Student 2 Yeah. You can try those, but they usually go pretty fast. There's also a textbook exchange for Cal students on Facebook, and you can find used textbooks on online bookstores like Amazon too.

學生 1 我剛剛到校園書店，簡直不敢相信課本會這麼貴。

學生 2 就是啊，簡直像敲詐，如果可以的話，我都不會買新課本。

學生 1 我聽說校園附近有幾家書店會賣二手課本。

學生 2 對，你可以去找找，但通常很快賣完。臉書上也有讓柏克萊學生交易課本的社群，你也可以在亞馬遜之類的網路書店找二手課本。

Dress for less
買折扣衣服

Student 1 So what do you think of Ross? It has a huge selection of clothes, right?

Student 2 Yeah, and the prices are low. But it's so ⁵¹**disorganized**. I don't really know what to buy.

Student 1 Well, they have plenty of mirrors, so we can start matching things and see what looks good.

Student 2 True. How about this blouse and these *slacks?

學生 1 你覺得羅斯百貨怎麼樣？這裡有很多衣服可選吧？

學生 2 對，而且價格便宜，但擺設很亂，我真的不知道該怎麼買。

學生 1 這裡有很多鏡子，所以我們可以邊看邊搭配，看有哪些不錯的。

學生 2 沒錯，這件上衣配這件休閒褲怎麼樣？

Student discounts
學生優惠

Student 1 If you want to save money on all kinds of ⁶¹**brand name** stuff, one of the best ways is to use your student ID.

Student 2 You mean I can get discounts in stores by just showing my ID?

Student 1 Sometimes. But the best way is to ⁷¹**sign up** to sites like Student Beans and UNiDAYS. After they *verify your ID, you can get discounts for Calvin Klein, Nike, H&M, Under Armour....

Student 2 Wow, that sounds awesome! Is that just for online purchases?

Student 1 Mostly. But some companies offer discounts for *in-store purchases too.

學生 1 如果你想在各種名牌商品上省錢，最好的辦法是用學生證。

學生 2 你是說只要在商店出示學生證就能獲得折扣？

學生 1 有時候可以，但最好的方法是先在 Student Bean 和 UNiDAYS 之類的學生優惠網站註冊，等他們驗證你的學生證後，你可以獲得 Calvin Klein、Nike、H&M、Under Armour 等品牌的折扣。

學生 2 哇，聽起來很棒！那只能用在網路購物嗎？

學生 1 大部分是，但有些公司也提供店內折扣。

補充字彙

* **slacks** [slæks] (n.) （休閒）長褲

* **verify** [ˋvɛrəˌfaɪ] (v.) 證明，證實

* **in-store** [ˋɪnˌstɔr] (a.) 店內的

學生相關的優惠

1. **食**：美國很多速食餐廳、學校附近餐廳都有學生優惠價，但一般店家不會主動告知，學生需主動詢問並出示學生證才能獲得打折。學生們還可自行尋找關注各個餐廳的 happy hour（Happy Hour 一般指某時間的酒類打折）以及促銷活動。

2. **購物**：美國很多商店也都有學生打折的優惠，但店家們不會主動告知，學生需主動詢問並出示學生證才能獲得打折。有些可能需要先上一些認證網站 UniDAYS、Student Beans 註冊才可以獲得折扣。

3. **住**：如不住宿舍，學生可租離學校較近的地方，方便寒暑假不住時可以暫時轉租他人，節省房租。

4. **行**：在美國開車、養車很貴，如果能不開車就盡量不要開車。美國很多大學都有跟當地公車公司合作，學生只要到學校申辦公車卡即可無限次搭乘當地公車。此外有些地方還有免費接駁車可以搭乘，大家可以詢問學校做確認。

5. **育樂**：美國一些電影院、博物館都有學生票，只需出示學生證即可購買。此外，多數學校的健身房都可供學生免費使用。學生們還可多參加學校舉辦的免費活動，有時可以免費吃喝玩樂、拿贈品。

♫ 083 | 對話＋好用句

♫ 084 | 單字

Vocabulary Bank

1. **mattress** [ˈmætrɪs] (n.) 床墊
   Soft mattresses are bad for your back.

2. **donate** [ˈdonet] (v.) 捐助
   Michael donated some of his old clothes to the church.

3. **charity** [ˈtʃærəti] (n.) 慈善，慈善事業
   John donates 15% of his annual salary to charity.

4. **ride** [raɪd] (n.) (口) 交通工具，車輛
   That's a sweet ride you have there.

5. **percent** [pəˈsɛnt] (n.) 百分比，部分
   The electronics store is having a twenty percent off sale.

6. **clearance** [ˈklɪrəns] (n.) 清倉大拍賣，也稱作 clearance sale
   Everything at the clearance is half price.

補充字彙

* **loveseat** [ˈlʌvˌsit] (n.) 雙人沙發

* **coffee table** (phr.) 茶几

* **end table** (n.) 邊桌

* **vanity** [ˈvænəti] (n.) 梳妝台

📖 Reading Quiz | 閱讀測驗

Student Moving Sale

Graduating student moving house, all furniture must go
***Loveseat**, ***coffee table**, TV stand, ***end table**, computer desk & chair, small bookcase, single bed frame & [1]**mattress**, nightstand, four-drawer dresser, ***vanity** & bench
Furniture will be available for viewing this weekend, June 15th and 16th
All reasonable offers accepted, unsold items will be [2]**donated** to [3]**charity**
Address: 3667 Main St, Apt# 27, Springfield

If you wanted something to store your clothes in, which would you buy at the sale?

(A) End table
(B) Vanity
(C) Nightstand
(D) Dresser

解答：1. (D)
翻譯請見 p. 214

⑤ Car insurance discount
汽車保險折扣

Student 1	Hey, I like your new ⁴⁾**ride**. Did you get a good student discount when you bought insurance?
Student 2	No. I didn't even know there was such a thing. How good do your grades have to be?
Student 1	I think it depends on the company, but a B average is usually good enough. You can get a 15 or 20 ⁵⁾**percent** discount.
Student 2	Wow, that's a lot. I'll have to ask for that when I renew next year.

學生 1	嘿，我喜歡你的新車。你買汽車保險時有獲得好學生折扣嗎？
學生 2	沒有，我根本不知道有這種折扣。成績要多好才會有？
學生 1	我想這要看公司，但通常平均 B 以上就夠了，可以獲得八折或八五折的折扣。
學生 2	哇，好多，明年續約時我一定要申請。

Common Phrases | 詢問折扣，你要會說

1. Do you offer a student discount?　是否提供學生折扣？

2. How long is the discount available?　折扣期限有多久？

3. Is this coupon still valid?　這張折價券還有效嗎？

4. Is everything in the store 20 percent off?　店內所有商品都打八折嗎？

5. It said on the shelf that this item is 30 percent off.　架上寫說這商品打七折。

6. Do you have a ⁶⁾**clearance** section?　你們有商品出清區嗎？

7. Can you give me a better price?　你能給我優惠嗎？

loveseat

coffee table

end table

vanity

其他非學生相關優惠

除了學生優惠外，美國也有很多其他不同優惠。例如，尋找收集折價卷、到折扣商店（Ross、T.J. Maxx、Michaels）購物、到跳蚤市場或 garage sale 撿便宜、打折節假日掃貨、使用返利網站線上購物、使用福利較好信用卡累積點數等等⋯

LESSON 16
Student ID
第十六話：學生證

🎵 **085** │對話

🎵 **086** │單字

Vocabulary Bank

1. **you name it** (phr.) 凡是你說得出的；應有盡有
   You name it, we sell it!

2. **check out** (phr.) 借出
   How many books can I check out at a time?

3. **log onto/into (on/in)** (phr.) (電腦、帳號等) 登入
   Could you show me how to log onto this computer?

補充字彙

* **flex dollars** (phr.) 小額付款，通常當作電子錢幣使用，運作方式和儲值卡類似

* **deactivate** [di`æktə,vet] (v.) 使無效，使失效

* **reactivate** [ri`æktə,vet] (v.) 使重新啟動，使重新起作用

Applying for a student ID
申請學生證

DIALOGUE 1

Student	Excuse me. Could you tell me how to apply for my student ID?
Clerk	Sure. You need to go to the Campus Card Office. It's on the first floor of the Palace Road Building.
Student	Thanks. Do you know what I need to bring with me?
Clerk	Yes. You'll need a valid photo ID, a passport photo and your student identification number.

學生	不好意思。可以請你告訴我如何申請學生證嗎？
職員	可以。你要到校園學生證辦事處，就在宮殿街大樓的一樓。
學生	謝謝。你知道我需要帶什麼去嗎？
職員	嗯，你要帶附照片的有效身分證件、證件照和學生識別號碼。

DIALOGUE 2

Student	What can my student ID be used for?
Clerk	[1]**You name it.** You can use it to access the gym, the residence halls, the computer labs, student parking. You also use it for meals if you have a meal plan, and you can spend *flex dollars at campus stores and restaurants.
Student	How about the libraries?
Clerk	You can use it to [2]**check out** books at most libraries, and also for printing and copying.

學生	學生證可以用來做什麼？
職員	很多事情，你可以用來進出健身房、宿舍、電腦教室、學生停車場。你若有參加餐點方案，也可以用來付餐費，也可在校園商店和餐廳做小額付款。
學生	那圖書館呢？
職員	你可以在大部分圖書館當作借書證，也可以用來列印和複印。

Losing a student ID
學生證遺失

Student	What if I lose my student ID?
Clerk	If it's lost or stolen, you should immediately [3]**log onto** the student card website and ***deactivate** your account.
Student	OK. And how do I get a new card?
Clerk	You need to come to our office to ***reactivate** your account and get your replacement card. There's a 10 dollar replacement fee.

學生	我要是遺失學生證怎麼辦？
職員	如果遺失或被竊，你應該立刻登入學生證網站停用帳號。
學生	好，我要怎麼辦新學生證？
職員	你要來我們辦事處重新啟用帳號，然後補辦學生證，補辦費是十美元。

Dorm access
進出宿舍

Student 1	Hey, did you just let that guy in with your card?
Student 2	Yeah. He said he forgot his card, so I opened the door for him. I forget my card too sometimes.
Student 1	But the card access system is there to make sure people who don't belong here can't get in.
Student 2	Yeah, I get it. But I know him. He lives across the hall from me.

學生 1	你剛剛是不是讓那個人用你的卡進來？
學生 2	對，他說他忘了帶卡，所以我幫他開門，我有時也會忘記帶卡。
學生 1	但磁卡出入系統就是為了防止外人進入。
學生 2	對，我懂，但我認識他，他就住在我對面的房間。

學生證基本上是一個讓在校學生作為身分證明的一個證件。除此之外很多學校會對學生證添加很多不同的功能，例如：

- 進入學校非開放場地：實驗室、圖書館、健身房、宿舍、電腦室等。
- 使用學校物品：借書證、電腦、列印機等。
- 使用交通工具：公車卡、停車卡、腳踏車租借卡等。
- 電子錢包：學校食堂吃飯付款、學校商店購物付款等。
- 出勤紀錄卡等等。

以上功能依學校而異，並非所有學校都有上述功能。

  087 | 對話＋好用句

088 | 單字

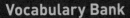
Vocabulary Bank

1. **wear out** (phr.) 用壞，穿破
   Skechers are comfortable, but they wear out really fast.

SITUATION 4

Free shuttle bus
接駁車免費搭乘

Student 1	Excuse me. Are you a Cal student?
Student 2	Yes. Why do you ask?
Student 1	I just saw you pay the shuttle fare, but it's free for students. All you have to do is show your Cal Card.
Student 2	Oh, thanks. I didn't know that. The fare is cheap, but free is better!

學生 1	不好意思，請問你是柏克萊學生嗎？
學生 2	對，怎麼了？
學生 1	我剛剛看到你付接駁車的錢，但學生可以免費搭乘，你只要出示學生證就好。
學生 2	噢，謝謝，我不知道。車票錢很便宜，但免費更好！

SITUATION 5

Bike rental
租借腳踏車

Student	Hi, I'd like to check out a bike.
Clerk	OK, I'll need to see your Cat Card. Would you like a single-speed or a seven-speed?
Student	Here you go. I'll take a single-speed, please. When do I need to return the bike by?
Clerk	No later than 4:00 p.m. tomorrow. Here's your key.

學生	嗨，我想借腳踏車。
職員	好，我要看你的學生證，你要單速還是七速？
學生	學生證在這裡。我要單速，謝謝。我什麼時候要還腳踏車？
職員	明天下午 4 點以前。這是你的鑰匙。

1. May I see your student ID, please?　　　我能看你的學生證嗎？

2. You need to hold your card closer so the scanner can read it.　　　你要把學生證拿近一點，掃描器才能讀取。

3. If your card is lost or stolen, please report it immediately.　　　你的學生證若是遺失或被竊，請立刻報失。

4. Never loan your campus card to anyone.　　　千萬不要將學生證借給任何人。

5. You can use most major credit cards to add funds to your ID card.　　　你可以用大部分信用卡將金額轉入學生證。

6. Which buildings can I access with my student card?　　　我可以用學生證進出哪些校舍？

7. You can view your transaction history by logging into your student account.　　　你可以登入學生帳戶查看交易紀錄。

Common Phrases | 關於學生證，你要會說

1. What should I do if I lose my student ID card?　　　我若遺失學生證該怎麼辦？

2. Are there any discounts for using my student ID?　　　用學生證能享有折扣嗎？

3. Can I pay here with my student ID?　　　我能用學生證付帳嗎？

4. How do I use the printer with my student card?　　　怎麼使用學生證操作印表機？

5. How long is my ID card valid for?　　　學生證的有效期限有多久？

6. How can I add money to my campus card?　　　我要怎麼將錢轉入學生證？

7. If my card is [1]**worn out**, is there a charge to replace it?　　　學生證若破舊了，換新需要手續費嗎？

學生證還可以怎麼說

大部分學校的學生證都是叫 campus card 或 student ID，但有些學校喜歡在學生證上冠上自己學校的簡稱、暱稱或學校吉祥物的名字，例如：UC Berkeley 的學生證就叫做 Cal 1 Card、University of Arizona 的學生證就叫做 Cat Card。

LESSON 17
Services for International Students
第十七話：對國際學生的服務

Vocabulary Bank

1. **expiration** [ˌɛkspəˈreʃən] (n.) 到期，期滿
   I always look at the expiration date when I buy milk.

2. **duration** [dʊˈreʃən] (n.) （時間的）持續、持久，持續期間
   You should slowly increase the duration of your workout.

3. **status** [ˈstætəs] (n.) 身分，狀態，地位
   What is your current immigration status?

4. **division** [dɪˈvɪʒən] (n.) 級，部分，部門
   Are you taking any upper division courses?

5. **adapt** [əˈdæpt] (v.) 適應，改變
   Children usually adapt easily to new environments.

6. **isolated** [ˈaɪsəˌletɪd] (a.) （被）孤立的，（被）隔離的
   The isolated village has little contact with the outside world.

7. **culture shock** (n.) 文化衝擊（指去異國或異地時產生的困惑感）
   Did you experience any culture shock when you studied in France?

8. **get used to** (phr.) 習慣
   I'll never get used to waking up early.

SITUATION 1 International Student Office
國際學生服務處

Student	Hi. I was wondering if I could ask you a question about my I-94.
Clerk	Sure. What seems to be the problem?
Student	For the [1]**expiration** date, it says, "D/S." I'm not sure what that means.
Clerk	It stands for "[2]**duration** of [3]**status**," which means it's valid until you complete your studies.
Student	Oh, I see. Thanks. That's really helpful.
Clerk	My pleasure. We also advise international students on tax, legal and housing issues. Feel free to *drop by any time.

學生	嗨，我在想我能不能問你關於 I-94 的問題。
職員	可以，有什麼問題？
學生	到期日期上寫著「D/S」，我不知道那是什麼意思。
職員	那是「身分有效期」的意思，這表示有效期一直到你完成學業為止。
學生	原來如此，謝謝，真的幫了我大忙。
職員	我的榮幸。我們也會協助國際學生瞭解稅務、法律和住宿問題，儘管隨時來詢問。

SITUATION 2 Academic adviser
學術輔導員

Student	I haven't decided on a major yet, so I'm having trouble deciding what classes to take.
Advisor	Have you thought about possible directions yet?
Student	I'm thinking about either psychology or criminology, but I'm not sure. Can you recommend any general courses to take?
Advisor	Sure. Lower [4]**division** courses like Psych 1, Socio 1 and Stat 5 will help prepare you for either major.

學生	我還沒決定主修，所以不知道該怎麼選課。
指導員	你有考慮過哪些可能的方向嗎？
學生	我在考慮心理學或犯罪學，但我不確定。你能建議我修哪些通識課程嗎？
指導員	好，心理學 1、社會學 1 和統計學 5 之類的入門課都適合當這兩個主修的先修課。

The counseling center
諮詢處

SITUATION 3

DIALOGUE 1

Student I'm having trouble [5]**adapting** to life here. I feel lonely and [6]**isolated**.

Counselor It sounds like you're experiencing [7]**culture shock**. It takes time to [8]**get used to** a new environment.

Student Yes. I also miss my life in Taiwan, and it's hard for me to communicate in English.

Counselor I'm sure your English will improve quickly. In the [9]**meantime**, surrounding yourself with familiar things can improve your mood. There's a Taiwanese restaurant near campus, and a Taiwanese student [10]**association** you can join.

學生 我不太能適應這裡的生活，我感到寂寞孤獨。

輔導員 看來你正經歷文化衝擊。適應新環境是需要時間的。

學生 對，我也想念台灣的生活，而且用英語溝通對我來説很難。

輔導員 我相信你的英語會進步很快。在這段時間接觸熟悉的事物能改善你的心情。校園附近有台灣菜餐館，你也可以加入台灣學生會。

DIALOGUE 2

Student I've been working hard to improve my English, but writing [11]**papers** is still really difficult for me.

Counselor You should take advantage of our writing [12]**tutorial** services then. They're completely free.

Student That sounds like just what I need. How do I sign up?

Counselor You just make an [13]**appointment** online and show up at the Tutorial Center at the scheduled time.

學生 我一直努力提升英語，但寫報告對我來説還是很難。

輔導員 那你可以利用我們的寫作輔導服務，這是完全免費的。

學生 看來這就是我需要的，我要怎麼報名？

輔導員 你只要上網預約，然後按排程時間到輔導中心報到就好。

9. **meantime** [ˋmin.taɪm]
   (adv.) 期間 / (phr.) **in the meantime** 在…期間，在…之前
   Kelly wants to be a reporter, but in the meantime she's working as an editor.

10. **association** [ə.sosiˋeʃən]
    (n.) 協會，聯盟
    Have you joined any student associations?

11. **paper** [ˋpepɚ] (n.) 論文，報告
    I stayed up all night finishing my history paper.

12. **tutorial** [tuˋtɔrɪəl] (n.)
    教學單元，個別指導 (v./n.)
    tutor [ˋtutɚ] 教導；家教
    Lots of free tutorials are available online.

13. **appointment** [əˋpɔɪntmənt]
    (n.) 約會
    Be sure and set your alarm so you aren't late for your appointment.

補充字彙

＊ **drop by** (phr.) 順道去拜訪

國際學生服務處提供的服務

國際學生服務處可以說是國際學生很好的一個窗口，他們不僅可以幫你辦 I-20 和簽你暫時離開美國所需文件，他們還可以針對你需要的幫助，引導你去對的地方找對的人。另外，國際學生服務處還有提供協助國際學生找房子、找工作/OPT 質詢、醫療保險、轉學、如何保持有效學生身分等眾多服務。如果你學習上有困難，例如需要額外的幫助或考試需要多點時間，國際學生服務處人員也可幫你跟教授溝通商討。

國際學生可使用的資源

‧ 英文學習相關資源
‧ 國際學生活動與社團

091 │ 對話＋好用句

092 │ 單字

Vocabulary Bank

1. **frustrating** [ˋfrʌ͵stretɪŋ] (a.)
   使人感到挫折的，使人氣餒、煩惱的
   Using this software is such a frustrating experience.

2. **fit in** (phr.) 適應環境，相處融洽
   I'm having trouble fitting in at my new school.

3. **authentic** [ɔˋθɛntɪk] (a.) 道地的，純正非假冒的，正宗的
   That restaurant serves authentic Cantonese food.

補充字彙

* **mentor** [ˋmɛntɔr/ˋmɛntɚ] (n.)
  良師益友，精神導師

* **show sb. the ropes** (phr.) 給（某人）指點竅門，教（某人）如何工作

DIALOGUE 3

Student	I often don't understand what people say, so I keep repeating, "Pardon me? Excuse me?" And then they start talking louder and louder.
Counselor	That must be [1]**frustrating**. But I'm sure things will get better as your English improves.
Student	I just worry that I won't be able to [2]**fit in** and make friends here.
Counselor	It's natural to have these feelings at first. Give it time.

學生	我常聽不懂別人說什麼，所以我一直重複說：「抱歉？不好意思？」然後他們就開始越說越大聲。
輔導員	那一定很令人感到挫折，但我相信隨著你英語能力進步，情況就會好很多。
學生	我只是擔心我無法在這裡適應和交朋友。
輔導員	剛開始有這種感覺是很自然的，過段時間就好了。

SITUATION 4
International Student Mentor Program
國際學生輔導計畫

Counselor	If you need support, we can partner you with a **mentor* from our International Student Mentor Program.
Student	Do you have any mentors who speak Chinese?
Counselor	All the mentors are international students like yourself, so I'm sure we can find you one.
Student	OK. It would be nice to have someone to *show me the ropes*.

輔導員	你若需要支援，我們可以透過國際學生計畫幫你找學長姐。
學生	你們有會說中文的學長姐嗎？
輔導員	所有學長姐都跟你一樣是國際學生，所以一定可以幫你找到。
學生	好，如果有人可以請教會很好。

Common Phrases | 聽不太懂對方的話時，你要會說

1. I beg your pardon?　　　　　　　　抱歉你説什麼？

2. Excuse me?　　　　　　　　　　　　不好意思？

3. Could you say that again, please?　　請再説一次好嗎？

4. Could you repeat that?　　　　　　　可以再説一次嗎？

5. Could you please speak more slowly?　能請你説慢一點嗎？

6. What do you mean by "***"?　　　　你説的「XX」是什麼意思？

7. I'm sorry. I didn't catch that.　　　　抱歉，我沒聽清楚。

Common Phrases | 想家時，你要會說

1. I really miss my friends and family back home.　　　　我很想念家鄉的朋友和家人。

2. I wish my family could be here with me.　　我希望家人能在這裡陪我。

3. I talk to my family on Skype/Line, but it's not the same as being there.　　我用 Skype/Line 跟家人聊天，但跟在家鄉的感覺不一樣。

4. I miss my boyfriend/girlfriend back in Taiwan so much.　　我很想念在台灣的男／女友。

5. I'm flying back to visit my family on winter break.　　寒假時我會飛回家看家人。

6. There's a Taiwanese restaurant here, but it's not very [3]**authentic**.　　這裡有台灣菜餐館，但不是很道地。

7. Drinking bubble tea reminds me of home, but it's so expensive here!　　喝珍珠奶茶讓我想起家鄉，但這裡的珍珠奶茶好貴！

PART 2
**完勝國外大學
必備英語**

Essential
English for
Overseas Study

課堂
Classroom

課堂上最重要的，不外乎是課程與教授了，同學可以在選課前先上網查查教授評價，在第一堂課時，了解課程大綱，認識幾個同學，好好完成作業，若課堂上有任何不清楚，或需要請教授補充的，記得要發言和提問。

但可惜的是，一切並不會那麼順利，
你可能會遇到的問題：

Q1 期末要交書面報告，
但你的英文作文不夠好。

Q2 課堂中我有個地方聽不太懂，但班上人數很多，
不希望因為我問了「蠢問題」，而浪費所有人的
時間。

這時就要了解
學校有哪些資源可以應用了。

不管是去美國就讀大學、研究所,還是博士班,
世界各地慕名而來的學生要搞定哪些事呢?
我們認為,主要分為「課堂」和「資源」兩種。

資源
Resources

學校很多大樓裡都有電腦可以運用,通常也提供 wifi 可以
讓學生免費上網,圖書館裡也有大量的實體書和電子書可
以運用。

回答你上面的問題:

A1 一般來說,學校通常會有免費的寫作諮詢服務
(Writing Tutorial Service),不管是當地人或
是國際學生都可預約使用,可以協助你完成書
面報告。

A2 只要是有建設性的問題,都還是歡迎在課堂
上發問。只是課堂上動輒幾百人,如果不好
意思提出,也可以在助教 (TA) 帶領的小班制
discussion group 上提出,或是在教授的辦公
時間 (Office hours) 去找他就可以了。

第三章:**上課囉!**

Going to Class

3
CHAPTER

CHAPTER

上課囉！

Going to Class

3

LESSON 1
Course Syllabus
第一話：課程大綱

093 | 單字

Vocabulary Bank

1. **perception** [pə`sɛpʃən] (n.)
   認知，看法

   There is a public perception that the government is corrupt.

2. **interaction** [.ɪntə`rækʃən]
   (n.) 互動，交流

   The activity is designed to encourage student interaction.

3. **nurture** [`nɜtʃə] (n./v.) (後天)
   栽培，養育

   Is our character affected more by nature or nurture?

4. **free will** (phr.) 自由意志

   Do you believe in free will?

5. **evidence** [`ɛvədəns] (n.) 證
   據，物證

   The police were accused of destroying evidence.

6. **evaluate** [ɪ`vælju.et] (v.)
   評估，名詞為 **evaluation**
   [ɪ.vælju`eʃən]

   We need to evaluate our options.

7. **section** [`sɛkʃən] (n.) (大學)
   討論課

   I'll see you in section tomorrow.

8. **participation** [pɑr.tɪsə`peʃən]
   (n.) 參與

   Class participation will account for ten percent of your grade.

圖 解 英 文　**輕鬆看懂教學大綱**

Course *Syllabus

❶ Psych 101 (Introduction to Psychology)

❷ Instructor: Prof. Michael Palmer
❸ Office: 290B Psychology Building
❹ Hours: Tu/Th 10-11 a.m.

❺ TAs: Laura Cosby, Carl Manning
Office: 280 Psychology Building
Hours: *TBA

❻ Texts: (1) Kosslyn, Rosenberg: *Introducing Psychology: Brain, Person, Group* (2) Marcus: *Norton Psychology Reader*

❼ Course description:
This course is an introduction to the scientific study of human nature, including how the mind works and how the brain supports the mind. Topics include the mental and *neural bases of [1]perception, emotion, learning, memory, *cognition, child development, personality, mental illness and social [2]interaction. Students will consider how such knowledge relates to debates about nature and [3]nurture, [4]free will, consciousness, human differences, self and society.

❽ Course goals:
Teach students to think critically about psychological [5]evidence, and to [6]evaluate its validity and its relevance to important issues in human life.

❾ Grading:
There will be four exams (three during the semester and one during finals week), two writing assignments and weekly TA-led discussion [7]sections. Grades will be based 60% on exams, 30% on papers and 10% on discussion section [8]participation.

翻譯請見 p. 214

什麼是教學大綱

　　通常在第一堂課時，教授會發下教學大綱，從教學大綱中，可看出教授對課程的目標（希望學生可以學會什麼）、他的評分標準、期望學生可以做到的事，學生了解教授的具體目標後，也能朝一致的目標努力學習，避免困惑。

課程大綱上通常會包含下列各項：

❶ **課程名稱**，一般會寫上課程編號或名稱。例如：Math 101（Calculus）、History 205（World History）等。

❷ **Instructor｜教授姓名**：在課綱上一般會印上教授全名，寫 essay（報告）時，應在首頁填上教授全名。不過在信件或口語上，應使用教授的 last name（姓）並加上 Mr./Ms.，如：Mr. Foden。

❸ **Office｜教授辦公室**：讓你知道教授的辦公室位置，方便學生造訪。

❹ **Hours｜辦公室時間**：教授在辦公室的時間。如有任何問題，可在這時間去找他。如時間不合，可與教授另約時間。

❺ **TA｜助教**：為 teaching assistant 的簡稱。

❻ **Textbooks｜教科書**：課程所需課本會列於此，需自行購買。

❼ **Course description｜課程大綱**：課程什麼時候會教些什麼？會回答哪些問題？

❽ **Course goals｜課程目標**：你將會從課程中學到什麼？

❾ **Grading｜評分標準**：課程中各項事務比例。例如：出席 (20%)、作業 (30%)、期中考 (25%)、期末考 (25%) 等。

註：有些科目會有 **prerequisite**（先修課程）：修課前必須滿足的條件。例如：修微積分 2 前，需先修過微積分 1 或有相等知識。

學生於教授的辦公室時間 (office hours) 詢問問題

TA（助教）

TA 用中文來說就是助教，基本上是由學校的碩、博士生所擔任。TA 的人選可能由教授直接指定，或由學院根據學生們的專長來分配擔任。在大學內，並不是所有的課程都會有 TA，一般來說，只有那些除了理論課程外還需綁實際討論或操作的課程才會需要 TA。TA 一般會幫助學生解決問題、帶領學生的實驗課、討論課等。

TA 協助學生電腦操作問題

♫ 094 | 聽力測驗

♫ 095 | 單字

Vocabulary Bank

1. **shed light (on)** (phr.) 照亮，使…明朗，曝光

   The investigation shed light on government corruption.

2. **perceive** [pɚˋsiv] (v.) 理解，看待，意識到

   How do the British perceive the French?

3. **adulthood** [əˋdʌlt‚hʊd] (n.) 成年（時期）

   Most Americans move out when they reach adulthood.

補充字彙

∗ **infancy** [ˋɪnfənsɪ] (n.) 嬰兒時期

Listening Quiz | 聽力測驗

● 聽完教授對課程的介紹後，回答下列問題：

1. Which of the following are prerequisites to the course?

(A) High school biology
(B) High school physics
(C) Statistics
(D) None of the above

2. Who does the professor suggest should leave the room?

(A) Those who arrived late
(B) Those who entered by mistake
(C) Those who haven't taken the prerequisites
(D) Those who didn't prepare for class

解答：1. (D) 2. (B)

聽力測驗原文

Good afternoon. Congratulations to everybody on making it through the snow to get here! My name is Michael Palmer and this is Introduction to Psychology. If you're in the wrong room, now is the time to leave, ha-ha. Let me start by saying this is a course about you. It's about what we understand in a scientific way about human nature—how people's minds work, how people's brains work. It's about understanding how people feel, think and act in the world. Since this is an introductory course, there are no specific prerequisites, but high school biology and physics, and a basic understanding of statistics, will probably help you get more out of the course. What we're going to focus on this semester is where the scientific method has [1]**shed light**—through experiments and evidence—on what makes people behave the way they do. As we go through the semester, we'll talk about the brain; how we [2]**perceive** the world—how we see, how we hear, how we think, how we feel; personality; development from ***infancy** and childhood through [3]**adulthood** and old age; social interaction, how we behave in groups and think about other people; and mental illness—something that affects so many people in their lives.

午安，恭喜各位克服下雪天前來上課！我叫麥可帕莫，這堂課是心理學概論。如果你走錯教室，現在應該要離開了，哈哈。首先，我要說這堂課是與你息息相關，我們要以科學方式了解人性──人的思想如何運作、人的大腦如何運作。這堂課要了解人在這世上如何感受、思考和行動。因為這是入門課，所以不需要特定的先修課，但若上過高中生物和物理，並對統計學有基本的了解，或許更能幫你從這堂課中獲益。這學期的重點是以科學方法──即透過實驗和證據──闡明人類行為的原因。在本學期中，我們會討論大腦；我們如何理解這世界──我們如何看、聽、思考和感受；人格；從嬰兒時期和兒童時期到成人時期和老年時期的發展；社交互動，我們在群體中的行為，對他人如何思考；以及影響到許多人生活的精神疾病。

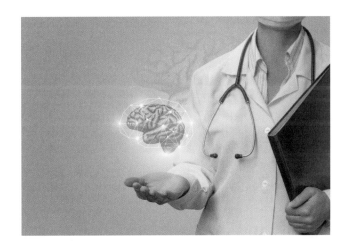

一般第一堂課主要就是教授會和學生說明 course syllabus，需注意聽的是教授授課方式、評分標準及出勤的部分。你可從教授授課方式了解這位教授以及這堂課是否真的適合你，如 syllabus 上寫將會有 3 次口頭報告，而你剛好不喜歡上台，那麼除非沒得選，不然就不要拿這位教授的課。評分標準也是看點之一，你可以教授評分比例來看自己是否適合這節課，例如你不喜歡上台，不過上台的評分比例只有 5%，那麼這堂課就還可以考慮。另外在美國出勤也會算在你的成績內，例如你不喜歡上課、喜歡遲到，那就不要選對出勤率看的很重的教授。

LESSON 2
Getting to Know Your Classmates
第二話：認識同學

♫ 096 | 對話

♫ 097 | 單字

Vocabulary Bank

1. **content** [ˋkɑntɛnt] (n.) **內容**
   The film contains adult content.

2. **catch** [kætʃ] (v.) **聽到**
   I didn't catch what you said.

3. **percentage** [pɚˋsɛntɪdʒ] (n.) **百分比，部分**
   A large percentage of voters support the president.

4. **midterm** [ˋmɪd.tɜm] (n.) **期中考試，中期**
   I got a B+ on the midterm.

5. **final** [ˋfaɪnəl] (n.) **期末考，結業考**
   Are you ready for the Psych final?

6. **totally** [ˋtotəli] (adv.) 表「完全同意」，**徹底，非常**
   Is Steve an idiot? Totally!

7. **skip** [skɪp] (v.) **略過，跳過**，**skip class** 為「翹課」
   I skipped class to go to an interview.

SITUATION 1

Asking about lecture [1]content
詢問講課內容

Student 1	Excuse me. Did you [2]**catch** what [3]**percentage** of our grade the [4]**midterm** and [5]**final** count for?
Student 2	Um, let's see. Let me check my notes. Yeah, here it is. The midterm is 15 percent and the final is 25 percent.
Student 1	Thanks. I need to take better notes, ha-ha. I'm Ryan, by the way.
Student 2	Nice to meet you. I'm Cynthia.

學生 1	不好意思，你有聽到期中考和期末考各佔總成績多少比例嗎？
學生 2	嗯，我想想，我看一下我的筆記。有，在這裡。期中考是 15％，期末考是 25％。
學生 1	謝謝。我要加強記做筆記了，哈哈。對了，我叫萊恩。
學生 2	很高興認識你，我叫辛蒂亞。

SITUATION 2

Borrowing notes
借筆記

Student 1	Hey, Cindy. I missed class on Friday. Do you mind if I borrow your notes?
Student 2	I don't really like to lend my notes out, but I don't mind if you copy them during class.
Student 1	How about if I take pictures of them with my phone?
Student 2	Yeah, I guess that's OK. But don't give them to anyone else.

學生 1	嗨，辛蒂，我星期五沒來上課，我能跟你借筆記嗎？
學生 2	我不太喜歡把筆記借給別人，但我不介意讓你在上課時抄。
學生 1	那我能用手機拍下你的筆記嗎？
學生 2	好，我想應該可以。但不要把筆記給別人。

Chatting with a classmate
和同學閒聊

Student 1	You look really familiar. Do you live in Brittany Hall?
Student 2	Yeah. I think I'm down the hall from you.
Student 1	No wonder. So you're taking Econ 101 too?
Student 2	Yep. I'm thinking of majoring in Econ. How about you?
Student 1	I'm thinking of Econ or Business. Hey, we can share notes if one of us misses class.
Student 2	Yeah, [6]**totally**. Not that I plan on [7]**skipping** class, ha-ha.

學生 1	你看起來很眼熟,你住在布列塔尼樓嗎?
學生 2	對,我想我是住在跟你同一層的走廊盡頭。
學生 1	難怪,所以你也修經濟學 101 嗎?
學生 2	對,我在考慮主修經濟學,你呢?
學生 1	我在考慮經濟學或企管。嘿,如果我們有人沒來上課,可以分享筆記。
學生 2	好啊,沒問題。我並不是想蹺課,哈哈。

**為什麼多認識些
同學很重要?**

在課堂上多認識些同學可以確保
自己沒去上課時有人可以詢問功
課或借筆記。如果自己上課時有
什麼沒聽懂或沒聽到的資訊,也
可詢問認識的同學。另外,大家
也可相約一起念書學習討論。

 098 | 對話＋好用句

 099 | 單字

Vocabulary Bank

1. **contact** [ˋkɑntækt] (n.) 聯絡人，熟人
   I'm meeting with a business contact later.

2. **social media** (n.) 社群媒體
   I waste too much time on social media.

3. **lecture** [ˋlɛktʃɚ] (n./v.) 演講，講課
   The professor gave a lecture on Russian literature.

4. **handout** [ˋhænd͵aʊt] (n.) 講義，傳單
   I'll be passing out a handout after class.

補充字彙

* **joint** [dʒɔɪnt] (n.) (口) 小餐館，小吃店

 Adding [1]contacts on [2]social media
加熟人到社群媒體上

Student 1	Hey, aren't we in the same Bio 121 class too?
Student 2	Yeah. It looks like we have two classes together.
Student 1	Actually, I think we have three classes together. Aren't you taking Chem 101 too?
Student 2	Yes. I didn't see you there, but that [3]**lecture** hall is pretty big.
Student 1	Since we have so many of the same classes, we should be study partners.
Student 2	Yeah, for sure. Let's add each other on Facebook.
Student 1	OK, but I don't really use Facebook that much. Are you on WhatsApp?
Student 2	Yes. Let me add you to my contacts now.

學生 1	嘿，我們不是也一起上生物學 121 嗎？
學生 2	對，看來我們有兩堂課是一樣的。
學生 1	其實我們有三堂課是一樣的，你不是也上化學 101 嗎？
學生 2	對，我在那堂課沒看到你，不過講堂很大就是了。
學生 1	我們既然有那麼多堂課一起上，我們應該成為學習伙伴。
學生 2	對，好啊，我們互加臉書吧。
學生 1	好，但我不太用臉書，你用 WhatsApp 嗎？
學生 2	有，我現在就把你加入我的聯絡人。

 Grabbing a bite
出去吃點東西

Student 1	Hey, how's it going? I'm Stan.
Student 2	I'm Steve. What's up?
Student 1	I was wondering if there are any good restaurants around here.
Student 2	There's a good burger ***joint** on High Street.
Student 1	Cool. Could you tell me how to get there?
Student 2	I'm actually heading there now. We can go together.

學生 1	嘿，你好嗎？我叫史丹。
學生 2	我叫史帝夫，你好嗎？
學生 1	我在想這附近有沒有什麼好吃的餐廳。
學生 2	高街有一家好吃的漢堡店。
學生 1	酷，你能告訴我怎麼走嗎？
學生 2	我其實正要去哪裡，我們可以一起去。

我要如何認識同學？

要認識同學其實沒有什麼特別的技巧，就是要不害羞，主動跟對方搭話。可以在上課前跟前後左右的同學們搭話，可以先從說 Hi 以及自我介紹開始。如果錯過上課前這個時機，也可在下課後再跟同學搭話，因為已經經過上課的過程，所以可以藉著一些課堂上的疑問來跟對方詢問或聊天。

Common Phrases | 認識同學，你要會說

1. You look familiar. Are we in the same dorm?
   你看起來很眼熟，我們住在同一棟宿舍嗎？

2. Hi, Ashley. You're taking this class too?
   嗨，艾席莉，你也修這堂課嗎？

3. Did you understand the part about...?
   你懂不懂這一部分…？

4. I think we're in the same Econ section.
   我們好像上同一堂經濟學。

5. I forgot to bring my textbook. Can we share?
   我忘了帶課本，我們可以一起看嗎？

6. Excuse me. What page are we on?
   不好意思，現在講到哪一頁？

7. Would you like to be study partners?
   你願意當我的學習伙伴嗎？

Common Phrases | 認識同學，你要聽得懂

1. Do you mind if I sit here?
   你介意我坐在這裡嗎？

2. Is this seat taken?
   這座位有人坐了嗎？

3. I'm considering dropping this class.
   我在考慮退掉這堂課。

4. Which section are you in?
   你上哪一節討論課？

5. Did you get the reading list 4)**handout**?
   你有拿到閱讀清單講義嗎？

6. Are you taking this class for your major?
   你上這堂課是因為主修嗎？

7. Would you mind watching my stuff for me? I'll be right back.
   你能幫我顧一下東西嗎？我很快就會回來。

8. I'm organizing a study group. Would you like to join?
   我在召集學習小組，你想加入嗎？

LESSON 3
Discussing Classes and Professors
第三話：討論課程與教授

♫ 100 │ 對話

♫ 101 │ 單字

Vocabulary Bank

1. **lost** [lɑst] (a.) 聽不懂，不知所措

   I was lost during the lecture today.

2. **accountant** [ə`kaʊntənt] (n.) 會計，會計師

   We hired an accountant to do our taxes.

3. **professor** [prə`fɛsə] (n.) 教授

   The professor gave a lecture on Russian literature.

4. **tough** [tʌf] (v./a.) 堅持，忍受、忍耐；嚴格的，**tough it out** 為「勇敢地承受，堅持到底」

   When the hurricane hit, we stayed in our home and toughed it out.

補充字彙

* **calculus** [`kælkjələs] (n.) 微積分

SITUATION 1

Talking about courses
談論課程

DIALOGUE 1

Student 1	What kinds of electives are you taking?
Student 2	Mostly just subjects I'm interested in. I'm taking a course on art history, and one on classical music. Next semester I'm gonna take a psychology class.
Student 1	Those sound really interesting. You'll have to tell me how they go.
Student 2	Sure. I'll be sure to let you know.
學生 1	你在修哪些選修課？
學生 2	大部分是我有興趣的科目，我在修一堂藝術史課，一堂古典音樂課，下學期我會修一堂心理學課。
學生 1	聽起來真有趣，你要告訴我上課的情況如何。
學生 2	好，我一定會告訴你。

DIALOGUE 2

Student 1	I thought I was pretty good at math, but I'm totally [1]**lost** in my accounting class.
Student 2	Oh no. Didn't you say you wanted to major in accounting?
Student 1	Yeah. I was thinking about it. There's high demand for [2]**accountants**, and the pay is good.
Student 2	Well, maybe you should consider another business-related major. How about marketing?
學生 1	我以為我的數學還不錯，但會計課完全聽不懂。
學生 2	不會吧，你不是說你想主修會計？
學生 1	對，我本來是在考慮，會計師的需求很大，薪水也不錯。
學生 2	這樣啊，也許你該考慮其他商學相關的主修，行銷怎麼樣？

Talking about [3]professors
談論教授

SITUATION 2

DIALOGUE 1

Student 1　So what do you think of the professor?

Student 2　I really like him. He's great at explaining the material, and I appreciate his clear grading criteria. I don't think my math foundation is strong enough though, so I'm thinking of dropping the class.

Student 1　That's too bad. He's a great teacher. Maybe you can enroll again later.

Student 2　Yeah, definitely...after I take a *calculus course.

學生 1　你覺得這個教授怎麼樣？

學生 2　我很喜歡他，他的教材解說得很棒，我也喜歡他明確的評分標準。但我覺得我的數學基礎不夠強，所以我在考慮退課。

學生 1　那太可惜了，他是很棒的老師，也許你之後可以再重修。

學生 2　對，一定會…先等我修完微積分。

DIALOGUE 2

Student 1　Did you say you have Rogers for Econ 101?

Student 2　Yeah. Why?

Student 1　I had him last year and I couldn't stand him. He was never prepared for class, and his lectures were completely disorganized.

Student 2　Uh-oh. The deadline for dropping classes was last week. I guess I'll just have to [4]tough it out—and give him a negative evaluation if he's really bad.

學生 1　你說你經濟學 101 是跟上羅傑斯教授上的嗎？

學生 2　對，怎麼了？

學生 1　我去年有修他的課，我受不了他，他從不備課，他的講課內容完全雜亂無章。

學生 2　哎呀，退課的截止日期是上星期，看來我只能咬緊牙關撐過去，他若是真的很糟，只好給他負評。

選課後，不喜歡的課可以退選嗎？

可以，大部分學校都是只要在開學後兩個禮拜內都可以免費、不留紀錄的退選，開學後一個月至一個半月內都可以留紀錄、不留成績的退選（詳細時間請參考學校行事曆）。若要退選重選其他課的要儘早，否則錯過太多堂課會跟不上。

學術人員怎麼說

行政人員 (administration)

dean 院長
department chair 系主任
vice president 副校長
president 校長
librarian 圖書館員

教職人員 (faculty members)

professor 教授
associate professor 副教授
assistant professor 助理教授
lecturer 講師
adjunct professor/lecturer 兼任教授／講師
instructor 指導老師
TA (teaching assistant) 助教

🎵 **102** | 對話＋好用句

🎵 **103** | 單字

Vocabulary Bank

1. **multiple** [ˈmʌltəpəl] (a.) **多重的，不只一個的，multiple choice 為「選擇題」**
   The secretary made multiple copies of the document.

2. **part-time** [ˈpɑrtˈtaɪm] (a.) **兼職的，部分時間的**
   Kevin got a part-time job after school to earn pocket money.

3. **reading** [ˈridɪŋ] (n.) **閱讀，讀物**
   The course provides instruction in basic reading and writing.

4. **accent** [ˈæksɛnt] (n.) **口音，腔調**
   Larry is good at imitating foreign accents.

補充字彙

* **lenient** [ˈliniənt] (a.) **寬厚的，寬容的**

* **workload** [ˈwɜkˌlod] (n.) **工作量，工作負荷**

DIALOGUE 3

Student 1 You're taking Business Statistics with Peters, right? How is it?

Student 2 I like it. Peters is good at making the subject interesting. But he's a pretty *tough grader, and there's *lots* of homework. I'll be lucky if I get a B.

Student 1 Well, it sounds like you're learning a lot—which is what's important, right?

Student 2 Yes, that's true. And it's required for my major anyway.

Student 1 Same here. Anyway, thanks for the info. I'll be sure to take the class with Peters.

學生 1 你在修彼得斯教授的商業統計，對吧？這堂課怎麼樣？

學生 2 我挺喜歡，彼得斯擅長把這科目講得很有趣，但他評分很嚴格，還有好多作業，我如果能拿 B 就很幸運了。

學生 1 聽起來你能學到很多，這也是重點吧？

學生 2 對，沒錯，而且這是我主修的必修課。

學生 1 我也是，總之謝謝你分享的資訊，我一定會修彼得斯的課。

 **Asking for advice
詢問建議**

Student 1 You have classes with Edwards and Sanchez don't you? Which do you like better?

Student 2 Well, let's see. Edwards is good at teaching complex concepts, but Sanchez is a more *lenient grader. All his tests are [1]multiple choice and the tests count for 60 percent of the grade.

Student 1 Hmm. Edwards sounds great, but I have a [2]part-time job, so I have less time to study than I'd like.

Student 2 In that case, it sounds like Sanchez would suit your needs better.

學生 1 你有修愛德華和桑奇斯的課吧？你比較喜歡誰？

學生 2 我想想，愛德華擅長講授複雜的概念，但桑奇斯的評分比較寬鬆，他的考試都是選擇題，而且考試佔總成績的 60%。

學生 1 嗯，愛德華感覺很棒，但我有在打工，所以我能念書的時間不多。

學生 2 這樣的話，感覺桑奇斯比較適合你。

Common Phrases | 討論課程，你要會說

1. Does Bio 240 have any prerequisites? | 生物學 240 需要先修課嗎？

2. I'm using the pass/fail option for all my electives. | 我所有選修課都選擇及格／不及格的計分方式。

3. I wanted to take Geography 105, but it was full when I registered. | 我想修地理 105，但等我選課時已經額滿。

4. Is there a term paper for Comm 110? | 傳播學 110 需要寫學期報告嗎？

5. The *workload in Phys 221 is really heavy. | 物理 221 的課業很重。

6. Are you taking a full course load this semester? | 這學期你是上全日制課程嗎？

7. There's so much required [3]reading for my philosophy class. | 我的哲學課有好多課文要念。

Common Phrases | 討論教授，你要會說

1. Professor Simmons expects students to participate in class. | 賽門斯教授要求學生在課堂上參與發言。

2. How strict is Professor Lee about attendance? | 李教授對出席的要求有多嚴格？

3. Professor Richardson teaches from the textbook. | 李查森教授是按課本內容授課。

4. Does Professor Schwartz **grade on a curve**? | 史瓦茲教授是用拉曲線的方式評分嗎？

5. I have trouble understanding Professor Gupta's [4]**accent**. | 我聽不太懂古普塔教授的口音。

6. Harrison is really helpful during office hours. | 哈里森的諮詢時間很有幫助。

7. Professor Freeman's lectures are really dry and boring. | 弗里曼教授的講課很枯燥無聊。

如何知道教授評價

學生們在選課時，授課的教授名字會出現在課堂名稱後面，學生可依這個名字上全美大學教授評分網站 ratemyprofessors.com 查詢參考各學期學生們給教授的評分以及感想。學期結束後也可上此網站給教授留下評分以及感想供後面的學生們參考。

教授對成績的影響有多大

教授是給你成績的人，選擇到給分寬鬆的教授，可以讓你這門課輕鬆通過，選擇到給分嚴厲的教授，會讓你需要付出更多時間、精力去學習這門課，以達到教授要求。

grade on a curve 成績分佈曲線

成績分佈曲線稱為 grade on a curve，是指在學校的考試成績不是按照固定的分數來給分。例如，普通評分方式是以 100 分為滿分，100-90 分是 A、89-80 分是 B、79-70 分是 C、69-60 分是 D、59 分以下是 F。而 grade on a curve 是按照所有學生考試的成績，來給出一個成績分佈曲線，再按學生的成績在這個曲線上的位置給分。例如，分數級別有 A、B、C、D、F，而老師要讓 15% 的學生得 A、20% 的學生得 B、30% 得學生得 C、30% 的學生得 D、5% 的學生得 F，如果滿分是 100 分，學生有 100 人，那麼考試成績排名第 15 的學生就算考試成績是 60 分，也能得 A。相反的，如果考試題目較簡單，第 100 名的同學就算考 80 分，也是 F 不及格。

LESSON 4
Speaking Up and Asking Questions in Class
第四話：在課堂上發言、提問

♫ 104 | 聽力測驗＋對話

♫ 105 | 單字

Vocabulary Bank

1. **presentation** [ˌprɛzənˈteʃən] (n.) 報告，演講

   Did you use visual materials in your presentation?

2. **crucial** [ˈkruʃəl] (a.) 關鍵的，決定性的

   This election is crucial to the country's future.

3. **respectively** [rɪˈspɛktɪvli] (adv.) 分別地，個別地

   Melissa and Kathy are 24 and 26 years old, respectively.

4. **self-conscious** [ˌsɛlfˈkɑnʃəs] (a.) 害羞扭捏的，不自在的

   Michael is very self-conscious about his braces.

5. **speak up** (phr.) 發聲，大聲地說

   You need to speak up so I can hear you.

6. **fluid** [ˈfluɪd] (n.) 液體，流體

   The doctor removed the fluid from the patient's lungs.

補充字彙

＊ **viscosity** [vɪˈskɑsəti] (n.) 黏性，黏度，形容詞為 **viscous** [ˈvɪskəs] 黏性的，黏的

Listening Quiz | 聽力測驗

● 請先聽完以下教授給分標準，再回答下面問題：

1. What percentage of the grade does class participation count for?

(A) 10
(B) 20
(C) 25
(D) 30

2. What percentage of the grade is the final [1]**presentation** worth?

(A) 10
(B) 20
(C) 30
(D) 40

聽力測驗原文

OK, I'd like to talk a little about grading policy. Since this is a small seminar course—there are only 25 of you here—attendance and participation are [2]**crucial**. Attendance is mandatory, and all students are required to actively participate in discussions. Attendance will count for 10 percent of your grade, and participation for 20. There will be two presentations—one mid-term and one at the end of the semester, worth 30 and 40 percent, [3]**respectively**.

好，我想談一下評分標準。因為這是小型研討課，只有 25 名學生，所以出席和參與討論都至關重要。出席是強制規定，所有學生都必須積極參與討論。出席佔總成績的 10%，參與討論佔 20%。有兩次口頭報告，一次是期中報告，另一次是期末，分別佔 30%和 40%。

解答：1. (B) 2. (D)

1 SITUATION
Answering questions
回答問題

Professor What are some of the problems **ESL** students may encounter when using English?

Student 1 They may worry that their grammar is incorrect.

Professor Yes, good. Anyone else?

Student 1 They may be [4]**self-conscious** about their accent.

教授 ESL 學生使用英語可能遇到哪些問題？

學生 1 他們可能會擔心文法使用不正確。

教授 對，很好，還有呢？

學生 2 他們可能對自己的口音感到不自在。

2 SITUATION
[5]Speaking up
發言

Professor Does anybody have any questions about the reading assignment?

Student Yes. On page 247, it says that "for liquids the *****viscosity** *usually* decreases with increasing temperature." Does this mean that there are exceptions?

Professor Good question. Yes, there are exceptions.

Student Could you give us an example?

Professor Sure. There are certain non-Newtonian [6]**fluids** that actually become more *****viscous** when heated.

教授 關於閱讀作業，還有誰有問題？

學生 有，第 247 頁上寫的「液體黏性通常隨著溫度上升而下降」，這表示有例外嗎？

教授 好問題，對，會有例外。

學生 能請你舉例嗎？

教授 好，某些非牛頓液體在加溫後反而會更有黏性。

發言的重要性

一般來說，演講類型的大課堂，教授比較不會有設定發言分數，因為人數太多。一般都是小班制課堂或研討課的教授才會有設定發言分數，因為教授想讓每位學生都能參與課堂、發表意見，發言分數一般 10-20% 不等，看教授怎麼設定。在課堂上多發言除了為了分數之外，還可以加深教授對你的印象，未來找工作或升學需要推薦信時，可請對方幫忙撰寫。

發言的小技巧

發言最忌諱的就是「害怕」，很多英文非母語人士最害怕的就是講錯或問了蠢問題。套一句美國老師們最喜歡說的話：There's no such thing as a stupid question.「沒有任何問題是蠢問題。」美國的老師是很鼓勵大家踴躍參與跟發言的。所以同學們不需要害怕，有什麼問題就提問，有什麼想法就說出來。

CHAPTER 3

上課囉！

Going to Class

106 | 對話＋好用句

107 | 單字

Vocabulary Bank

1. **margin** [`mɑrdʒɪn] (n.) 頁邊，空白，白邊
   I made a few notes in the margin.

2. **in principle** (phr.) 基本上，原則上
   We agree with the plan in principle.

3. **make up** (phr.) 組成，構成
   Women make up almost half of the workforce.

4. **take sth. into consideration** (phr.) 把某事考慮進去
   We'll take your suggestion into consideration.

5. **comment** [`kɑmɛnt] (n./v.) 意見，評論；發表意見
   If you have any comments, please raise your hand.

6. **point of view** (phr.) (思考的) 角度，著眼點
   Everyone has their own point of view.

7. **be under the impression** (phr.) 以為，誤以為
   I was under the impression that admission was free.

8. **concrete** [`kɑnkrit] (a.) 具體的
   The police have concrete evidence that the woman killed her husband.

Asking questions
提問

DIALOGUE 1

Professor Just to remind everyone, term papers will be due on December 15th. Any questions?

Student Yes. Is there a length requirement? I didn't see anything about *word count in the syllabus.

Professor There's no specific word count, but papers should be eight to ten pages, single-spaced, with one-inch [1]**margins**.

教授 提醒各位，學期報告的截止日期是 12 月 15 日，還有問題嗎？

學生 有，報告有長度規定嗎？我在教學大綱上沒看到字數相關的規定。

教授 沒有特別的字數規定，但報告通常是八到十頁，單行間距，邊距一英吋。

DIALOGUE 2

Student I have a question about our research reports. My grade on this one was a little low, and I was wondering if I got a better grade on the second one, would that count more toward my final grade?

Professor Well, [2]**in principle**, the two reports each [3]**make up** 20% of your grade, but I will [4]**take** improvement **into consideration**.

Student OK, thanks. I also have questions about some of the [5]**comments** you wrote on my report.

Professor For individual questions, you can come to my office hours, Tuesdays and Thursdays from 10:00 to 11:00.

學生 關於研究報告我有一個問題，我這次報告成績有點低，我在想如果我的第二份報告能拿高一點的分數，能不能拉高佔總成績的比重？

教授 基本上，兩份報告各佔總成績的 20%，但如果成績有進步，我會考慮。

學生 好的，謝謝，我還有一些問題是關於你寫在我報告上的評語。

教授 有個人問題的話，可以在我的辦公時間來找我，每週二和週四上午 10 點到 11 點。

補充字彙

∗ word count (phr.) 字數

Common Phrases | 在課堂發言，你要會說

1. In my (personal) opinion,....　　　　　我個人認為…

2. From my [6]**point of view**,....　　　　　以我的角度來看…

3. In my experience,....　　　　　　　　以我的經驗來看…

4. It seems to me that....　　　　　　　在我看來…

5. I [7]**was under the impression** that....　　我以為…

6. I would argue that....　　　　　　　我的主張是…

7. I agree/disagree with the author's conclusion.　　我認同 / 不認同作者的結論。

Common Phrases | 在課堂提問，你要會說

1. What does the term "..." mean?　　　「…」這個詞是什麼意思？

2. Can you please explain "..." in greater detail?　　能請你詳細解釋「…」嗎？

3. Could you explain the relationship between A and B?　　能請你解釋 A 和 B 的關係嗎？

4. Could you give us a [8]**concrete** example of "..."?　　能請你給我們「…」的具體例子嗎？

5. Can you suggest any other reading materials on this topic?　　你能建議這個主題的其他閱讀資料嗎？

6. Will "..." be covered on the quiz/test/exam/final?　　小考 / 考試 / 期末考會包括「…」嗎？

7. When will the exam results be available?　　考試結果何時出爐？

LESSON 5
Computers, Internet and Printing
第五話:電腦資源、網路、影印

🎵 108 | 對話

🎵 109 | 單字

Vocabulary Bank

1. **connect** [kə`nɛkt] (v.) 連線,連接,名詞為 **connection** [kə`nɛkʃən]
   I'm having trouble connecting to the Internet.

2. **PC** [`pi`si] (n.) 個人電腦,**personal computer** 的縮寫
   What operating system do you have on your PC?

3. **quota** [`kwotə] (n.) 定額,限額
   The U.S. has strict immigration quotas.

4. **locker** [`lɑkə] (n.) 置物櫃
   Are there lockers in the subway station?

補充字彙

* **WiFi** [`waɪ,faɪ] (n.) 無線寬頻連線

* **desktop** [`dɛsk,tɑp] (n.) 桌上型電腦

* **mobile** [`mobəl] (a.) 可以在行動電話 (或小型電腦) 上提供的

* **icon** [`aɪkɑn] (電腦) 圖示

* **Mac** [mæk] (n.) Mac 電腦,蘋果電腦

* **workstation** [`wɜk,steʃən] (n.) (電腦) 工作站

* **ringer** [`rɪŋə] (n.) (手機等) 鈴聲

1 SITUATION Getting connected
連線

Student	Hi. Could you please tell me how to [1]**connect** to campus *WiFi?
Operator	Sure. Are you using a *desktop or a *mobile device?
Student	I'm using my laptop.
Operator	OK. Click on the WiFi *icon at the bottom right of your screen, select Mwireless and click connect. Next, enter your student login ID and password, click OK and you're done.

學生	嗨,能請你告訴我怎麼連接到校園無線網路嗎?
接線生	沒問題,你是用桌上電腦還是行動裝置?
學生	我用的是筆電。
接線生	好,點擊你螢幕上右下角的 WiFi 圖示,選擇 Mwireless,然後點擊連接。接下來輸入你的學生帳號和密碼,點擊 OK 就行了。

2 SITUATION Looking for a computer
尋找電腦

Student	Excuse me. I need a computer to type up an essay I have due tomorrow.
Clerk	We have three open computer labs on campus. The nearest one is in Harrison Hall, Room 200. They have [2]**PC** and *Mac *workstations, and they're open till 7:00 p.m.
Student	Great. Are there printers there I can use too?
Clerk	Yes, there's a printing station there, and you can use the printing [2]**quota** on your student I.D.

學生	不好意思,我需要一台電腦打明天要交的報告。
職員	校園有三間開放電腦室,最近的一間在哈利森樓 200 室。那裡有 PC 和 Mac 電腦工作站,開放到晚上 7 點。
學生	太好了,那裡也有印表機可用嗎?
職員	有,那裡有列印室,你可以用學生證裡的列印配額。

Mobile charging stations
手機充電站

Student	Hi. Is there somewhere around here I can charge my phone?
Clerk	Yes. There are free charging stations at all of the libraries on campus. The Fine Arts Library is closest. They have charging [4]**lockers** there too.
Student	Charging lockers? How do they work?
Clerk	You can lock your phone inside and leave it there to charge. You just have to make sure you turn your *****ringer** off, and you can't leave your phone in the locker overnight.
Student	OK. That's really convenient. Oh, I don't have my charging cable with me. Is that a problem?
Clerk	No. All the charging stations have cables you can use.

學生	嗨，這附近有手機的充電插座嗎？
職員	有，校園所有圖書館都有免費充電站。美術圖書館是最近的，那裡也有手機充電櫃。
學生	手機充電櫃？那要怎麼用？
職員	你可以將手機鎖在裡面，放在裡面充電。你只要確定有將鈴聲關掉，也不能將手機放在裡面一整夜。
學生	好，那真的很方便。哦，我沒帶充電線，這會有問題嗎？
職員	不會，所有充電站都有充電線讓你使用。

學校網路

現在美國的大學普遍都有提供免費的 WiFi 供學生使用，每間學校使用登入的方法會有所不同，有的學校會需要學生在使用前先輸入自己的學生號碼作為登入的帳密，而有些學校會請學生先上網登記註冊帳密之後才能使用。使用學校網路時要注意千萬不要用來做一些非法的事情，例如，下載盜版影片等，因為很容易被抓到。

學生論壇

美國大學可能不像台灣有 PTT，大部分學生都是使用 Facebook 社團來互相聯繫，交換資訊。Facebook 上有許多學校專門的社團是只有擁有本校學生 e-mail 才能申請加入的。

charging lockers 手機充電櫃

CHAPTER 3

上課囉！

Going to Class

🎵 **110** | 對話＋好用句

🎵 **111** | 單字

Vocabulary Bank

1. **inquire** [ɪnˋkwaɪr] (v.) 詢問
   I called the theater to inquire about tickets.

2. **journalism** [ˋdʒɚnəl.ɪzəm] (n.) 新聞學系，新聞業
   After a long career in journalism, James will be retiring in August.

3. **software** [ˋsɔft.wɛr] (n.) (電腦) 軟體
   What software do you have on your computer?

4. **website** [ˋwɛb.saɪt] (n.) (電腦) 網站
   Does your company have a website?

5. **projector** [prəˋdʒɛktɚ] (n.) 投影機，放映機
   Remember to set up the projector before the meeting.

6. **secure** [sɪˋkjʊr] (a.) 安全的，無危險的
   You should store your valuables in a secure place.

7. **install** [ɪnˋstɔl] (v.) 安裝，裝置
   We're having an air conditioner installed tomorrow.

---

 [1] **Inquiring about software**
詢問軟體

Student 1	Have you decided what to do for your [2]**journalism** project yet?
Student 2	I'm thinking of doing a short film, but I don't have iMovie on my *MacBook.
Student 1	The computer labs have lots of [3]**software** available for students to use. You should check the library [4]**website**.
Student 2	Good idea. Let's see...oh, here we go—they have it on the Macs at the Main Library.

學生 1	你的新聞專題製作決定主題了嗎？
學生 2	我在考慮做一部短片，但我的 Mac 筆電沒有 iMovie。
學生 1	電腦室有很多軟體讓學生使用，你應該查一下圖書館網站。
學生 2	好主意，我看看…噢，在這裡，總圖書館的 Mac 電腦有。

 A *Tech-savvy school
高科技學校

Student 1	I'm really impressed by our schools tech resources.
Student 2	Oh yeah? Like what?
Student 1	All you need to do is show your student ID at any of the library service desks and you can borrow laptops, tablets, [5]**projectors**... even **maker** tools like 3D scanners.
Student 2	Wow, that *is* impressive. I had no idea.

學生 1	我們學校的科技資源真的很棒。
學生 2	是嗎？比如說呢？
學生 1	你只要在任何圖書館的服務櫃臺出示學生證，就可以借筆電、平板、投影機，甚至 3D 掃描器等製作工具。
學生 2	哇，真棒，我都不知道。

Common Phrases | 討論校園網路,你要會說

1. The WiFi in the dorms is really slow.　　宿舍的 WiFi 速度很慢。

2. The WiFi in the Main Library is the fastest.　　總圖書館的 WiFi 速度是最快的。

3. I always use a *wired connection when I play online games.　　我玩線上遊戲時都用有線網路。

4. Do you know how to connect to the eduroam network?　　你知道怎麼連接 eduroam 網路嗎?

5. Is there a map of WiFi *hotspots?　　有 WiFi 熱點的地圖嗎?

6. How [6]secure is the campus network?　　校園網路的安全性如何?

7. Can guests connect to the wireless network?　　訪客可以連接無線網路嗎?

Common Phrases | 討論電腦資源,你要會說

1. Which computer lab has the newest computers?　　哪個電腦室有最新的電腦?

2. Do any of the computer labs have Macs?　　哪間電腦室有 Mac 電腦?

3. The computer lab at the Main Library has printers and scanners.　　總圖書館的電腦室有印表機和掃描器。

4. Could you show me how to use this software?　　你能教我怎麼用這個軟體嗎?

5. Can I have the software [7]installed on my own laptop/PC?　　我能將這軟體安裝在我的筆電 / PC 嗎?

6. If you have a problem, you can call campus tech support.　　你如果有問題,可以打給校園技術支援。

7. Can I borrow a projector for my presentation?　　我能借投影機讓我在口頭報告時使用嗎?

校園科技

美國多數學校有提供學生或教授可以借取上課、學習所需工具,例如,筆電、平板、投影機等。多數學校也有設置列表機供學生免費或是付費列印,以及有提供部分軟體供學生免費安裝。

maker 創客

「創客」這個名稱來自於英文的 maker,是一群熱愛科技、熱愛實踐,不以利益為目的,把各種創意轉化為現實的人。創客文化是源自美國的車庫文化,在美國,很多人把自己家的車庫或地下室改造成家庭工作室或實驗室,例如:賈伯斯、比爾蓋茨等人就都是在車庫把創意化為現實的。創客文化除了「創造」之外,另一個特點就是「分享」,於是有了一個叫 Maker Faire 的創造嘉年華,供創客們展示與分享自己的作品。

LESSON 6
Using Library Resources
第六話：使用圖書館資源

♫ 112 | 對話

♫ 113 | 單字

Vocabulary Bank

1. **circulation** [ˌsɝkjəˋleʃən] (n.)
   流通，傳播，**circulation desk**
   為借還書櫃台
   You can return books at the
   circulation desk.

2. **at once** (phr.) 同時
   Everyone started talking at
   once.

3. **renew** [rɪˋnu] (v.) 續借，續
   約，展期，名詞為 **renewal**
   [rɪˋnjuəl]
   Are you going to renew your
   lease?

4. **put a hold (on)** (phr.) 預約
   I'm afraid somebody's already
   put a hold on that book.

5. **retired** [rɪˋtaɪrd] (a.) 退休的
   My parents are retired now.

6. **juvenile** [ˋdʒuvə,naɪl] (a./n.)
   青少年的；青少年
   There has been a rise in
   juvenile crime.

SITUATION 1

At the [1]circulation desk
在借還書處

Librarian	Hi. How can I help you?
Student	I was wondering what your hours are.
Librarian	We're open 7:00 a.m. to 9:00 p.m. Monday through Friday, and 9:00 a.m. to 9:00 p.m. on weekends.
Student	OK. I was also wondering how many books I could borrow [2]**at once**.
Librarian	You can borrow up to 10 books at a time.
Student	And how long can I borrow them for?
Librarian	The loan period is 21 days, and you can [3]**renew** twice after that as long as nobody [4]**puts a hold** on the book.

圖書館員	嗨，我能為你效勞嗎？
學生	我想知道你們的開放時間。
圖書館員	我們從週一到週五早上 7 點開放到晚上 9 點，週末從早上 9 點到晚上 9 點。
學生	好，我也想知道我一次能借幾本書。
圖書館員	一次最多可借十本。
學生	我可以借多久？
圖書館員	借書期限是 21 天，只要沒有人預約，你就能續借兩次。

📖 Reading Quiz | 閱讀測驗

● 請先看完以下借閱規則，再回答下面問題：

Loan Periods and Renewals

	Undergraduates, Staff, [5]Retired Faculty	Faculty & Graduate Students
Books Renewals	28 days five 28 day **renewals**	56 days five 56 day renewals
[6]**Juvenile books** Renewals	28 days Five 28 day renewals	56 days Five 56 day renewals
Videos Renewals	7 days One 3 day renewal	7 days Two 3 day renewals
Music CDs Renewals	7 days One 7 day renewal	7 days Two 7 day renewals
Reserve materials Renewals	2 hours No renewals	2 hours No renewals

1. What is the maximum amount of time a professor could borrow a book for?

(A) 28 days
(B) 56 days
(C) 168 days
(D) 336 days

2. How long can a university employee renew a DVD for?

(A) 3 days
(B) 6 days
(C) 7 days
(D) 14 days

解答：1. (D) 2. (A)
翻譯請見 p. 215

解說

1. professor 屬於 faculty，每次可借 56 天，可借五次，然後可再續借 56 天，56*5+56=336。

翻譯請見 p. 215

圖書館使用規則

學生們在校內借書時，需出示自己的學生證，並嚴守圖書館的借還規則，以免逾期受罰。大學圖書館內有很多書籍是只能在館內閱讀，不能外借的，而有些書籍則是有規定只能借閱幾個小時而已。有些學校有提供甲地借書，乙地歸還的服務，甚至可能還會有提供線上預約，送到學校某指定圖書館拿取的服務，不過並不是每間學校都有上述服務，學生需自行詢問圖書館。

圖書館趣事

大部分大學的圖書館都是有閉館時間的，不過很多學校的圖書館會在期末時，24 小時開放學生在館內讀書。其中加州大學柏克萊分校、UCLA 等校有團體會組織不定時的在圖書館內裸奔快閃。

密西根大學法學院圖書館，為全美 10 大最美圖書館之一。

114 | 對話＋好用句＋聽力測驗

115 | 單字

Vocabulary Bank

1. **hit** [hɪt] (n.) 搜尋結果，（網站的）點擊

   My website isn't getting very many hits.

2. **publication** [ˌpʌblɪ`keʃən] (n.) 出版，出版物，刊物

   The author became famous after the publication of his first novel.

3. **turn in** (phr.) 歸還，繳交

   Have you turned in your paper yet?

4. **lost and found** (n.) 失物招領處

   Is there a lost and found at the station?

5. **session** [`sɛʃən] (n.) 會議，集會，（大學）學期

   This course is only offered in the fall session.

6. **archive** [`ɑr͵kaɪv] (n.) 檔案（館、庫），紀錄

   Many old movies are stored in the film archive.

7. **cram** [kræm] (v.) （為應考）K書、死背

   I'd like to go with you, but I have to cram for an exam.

8. **designated** [`dɛzɪg͵netɪd] (a.) 指定的，委派的

   Who wants to be the designated driver?

9. **slash** [slæʃ] (n.) 斜線

   You forgot the slash in the website address.

SITUATION 2

Search methods
搜尋方法

Student	Excuse me. I was searching the ***database** for articles on the 2008 financial crisis, but I'm getting too many [1])**hits**. Is there any way to narrow my search down?
Librarian	Yes. You can use search ***limiters** to limit your results to just what you need. For example, you can limit your search by date of [2])**publication** or publication type—magazine, newspaper, ***scholarly** journal....
Student	OK, thanks. Where can I find the search limiters?
Librarian	You'll find them underneath the database search box.

學生	不好意思，我在資料庫裡找 2008 年金融危機的文章，但我找到太多筆資料，有什麼辦法能縮小搜尋範圍嗎？
圖書館員	有，你可以用索引限制功能，將搜尋結果限制在你所需的範圍。例如你可以限制搜尋出版日期或出版類型，如雜誌、報紙、學術期刊等。
學生	好，謝謝。我在哪裡能找到搜尋限制功能？
圖書館員	就在資料庫的搜尋框下面。

Common Phrases | 詢問借書與館藏，你要會說

1. How do I find an article by ***citation**? 　　我要怎麼利用引文找到文章？

2. Could you tell me how to search for e-books? 　　你能告訴我怎麼搜尋電子書嗎？

3. How do I request materials using ***Interlibrary** Loan? 　　我要怎麼用館際互借申請資料？

4. Can I return materials to any campus library? 　　我可以將書歸還到任何校園圖書館嗎？

5. I'd like to put a hold on a book. 　　我想預約一本書。

6. Can you tell me how to renew a book I've checked out? 　　你能告訴我怎麼續借一本書嗎？

7. Is it possible to request a book/article that's not in the collection? 　　我能申請館藏中沒有的書籍/文章嗎？

● 請在聽完圖書館員的導覽之後，回答下列問題：

1. Where would materials on the university's history be located?

(A) At the circulation desk
(B) On the 2nd floor
(C) On the 3rd floor
(D) On the library's website

2. What floor would you go to if you wanted to [3]**turn in** a lost item?

(A) The 1st floor
(B) The 2nd floor
(C) The 3rd floor
(D) The 4th floor

聽力測驗原文

Hi, everybody. Welcome to the Main Library. We'll start our tour at the first floor circulation desk. This is where you'll check out books, reserve materials, pay fines or just ask your general library questions. It's also where our [4]**lost and found** is located. Next, on the second floor, is the Grand Reading Room, which is a great place to study or work with your group. As you can see, we have group study rooms too, which are available for all students to use. You can reserve a room online for a maximum of three hours per [5]**session**. Here on the third floor you'll find Special Collections and [6]**Archives**. You'll have access to things like the Sonoma Valley Historical Collection and the University Archives. And there's more. If you need a place to [7]**cram** for a test, our first, fifth and sixth floors are [8]**designated** quiet floors. Want to know more about library services? Visit us at www dot svu dot edu [9]**slash** library.

大家好，歡迎來到總圖書館。我們先從一樓的借還書處開始導覽，這是你們借閱書籍、預約參考資料、付罰款或詢問一般圖書館問題的地方，也是失物招領處所在地。接下來是二樓，這是大閱覽室，是適合念書和小組討論的地方。正如各位所見，我們也有小組討論室，所有學生都可使用。你可以線上預約討論室，每次可使用三小時。三樓是特殊館藏和檔案處。你可以在這裡找到索諾瑪谷歷史館藏和大學檔案之類的資料。不只如此，你若需要一個考前抱佛腳的地方，我們的一樓、五樓和六樓是指定安靜樓層。想知道更多圖書館服務嗎？請造訪圖書館網站，網址是 www.svu.edu/library。

解答：1. (C) 2. (A)

補充字彙

* **database** [ˈdetəˌbes] (n.)
  資料庫

* **limiter** [ˈlɪmɪtɚ] (n.)
  限制器

* **scholarly** [ˈskɑləli] (a.)
  學術性的，scholarly journal 為「學術期刊」

* **citation** [saɪˈteʃən] (n.)
  引文，引述

* **interlibrary** [ˌɪntɚˈlaɪˌbrɛri] (n.)
  館際之間

如何有效使用圖書館資源

多數學校圖書館都有設置網頁，學生們可先上網輸入關鍵字查詢自己需要的書籍，再前往借取或詢問圖書館管理員協助。學校除了有實體書之外，還有很多電子書籍、期刊、論文等，學生可直接上網，登入學校圖書館系統搜尋調閱。

何時會需要使用圖書館資源

學生們在需要讀書、寫論文、做研究、找尋資料時都可以使用圖書館資源來協助。此外，部分學校也有提供討論室供學生們做小組討論。

美國大學圖書館也有隔間式桌子（cubicle desks），許多學生會在考前來這裡念書。

LESSON 7
Writing and Academic Assistance
第七話：寫作與課業協助

🎵 116｜對話＋好用句

🎵 117｜單字

Vocabulary Bank

1. **draft** [dræft] (n./v.) 草稿；草擬

   Have you finished the final draft of your paper?

2. **feedback** [ˈfid͵bæk] (n.) 意見，反應

   Jim asked for feedback from the audience after his presentation.

3. **paragraph** [ˈpɛrə͵græf] (n.) （文章的）段，段落

   A paragraph should include at least three sentences.

4. **thesis** [ˈθisɪs] (n.) 論點，thesis statement 為「論述」

   What is the thesis of your essay?

5. **concise** [kənˈsaɪs] (a.) 簡潔的，簡明的

   This dictionary has very concise definitions.

6. **punctuation** [͵pʌŋktʃuˈeʃən] (n.) 標點符號，標點符號用法

   The teacher said I need to improve my punctuation.

7. **version** [ˈvɝʒən] (n.) 版本

   Which version of Windows do you have on your computer?

8. **suggestion** [səgˈdʒɛstʃən] (n.) 建議

   If anyone has any suggestions, feel free to speak up.

SITUATION 1 **At Writing Tutorial Services**
在寫作諮詢服務處

DIALOGUE 1

Student	Hi. I brought a rough [1]**draft** of a paper I'm working on. I was hoping you could give me some [2]**feedback**.
Tutor	Sure. Let's take a look. OK, looking at your first [3]**paragraph**, it seems like you're lacking a clear [4]**thesis** statement.
Student	OK. What can I do to improve it?
Tutor	Well, the topic is the use of computers in the classroom. If you ask the question, "What are the benefits of computers in the classroom," and then answer that in a [5]**concise** sentence, that'll make a strong thesis statement.
Student	All right, I'll do that. I also feel like I'm having trouble organizing my ideas.
Tutor	Yes, your paragraphs are a little disorganized. It would help if you have a clear topic sentence at the start of each paragraph.
Student	OK. Do you have any other *pointers for me?
Tutor	Let's see. I'm seeing some grammar and [6]**punctuation** errors, so be sure to use the grammar *checker in Word.

學生	嗨，我把我正在寫的論文草稿帶來了，希望你能給我一些建議。
輔導老師	沒問題，我們來看看。好，看一下你的第一段，看來你缺少清楚的論述。
學生	好，我該怎麼做才能改進？
輔導老師	嗯，這個主題是教室裡的電腦利用。如果你提個問題：「教室裡設電腦的好處是什麼」，然後以一句簡明扼要的句子回答這個問題，這就是一個有力的論述。
學生	好，我會這麼做。我也覺得我不太會組織我的想法。
輔導老師	對，你的段落有點混亂。如果你每段開頭都有一個明確的主題句，這會有幫助。
學生	好，你還有其他建議嗎？
輔導老師	我想想，我看到有些文法和標點錯誤，所以務必用 Word 裡頭的文法檢查功能。

Student　　Here's the latest [7]**version** of my paper. I used the [8]**suggestions** you made to [9]**revise** it.

Tutor　　Let's take a look. OK, your thesis is clearer now, and your ideas are much better organized.

Student　　Are there any other improvements I can make?

Tutor　　The [10]**transitions** between paragraphs could be a little **smoother**, and there are a few *****run-on sentences**.

學生　　這是我的論文最新版本，我照你的建議修改了。

輔導老師　　我們來看看。好，你的論述現在清楚了，你的想法也組織得比較好了。

學生　　還有哪些地方是我可以改進的呢？

輔導老師　　段落之間的轉換可以再順暢一點，還有幾個比較拖沓的句子。

Common Phrases | 形容自己的寫作問題，你要會說

1. I don't think my outline is clear enough.　　我想我的概述不夠清楚。

2. I'm having trouble writing a conclusion.　　我不太會寫結論。

3. I can't figure out which verb [11]**tense** to use.　　我想不出要用哪個動詞時態。

4. Could you [12]**proofread** my paper for me?　　你能幫我校對論文嗎？

5. My professor said I need to avoid using [13]**clichés**.　　我的教授說我要避免使用陳腔濫調。

6. I'm not sure which citation style to use.　　我不確定要用哪種文獻引用格式。

7. I need to work on my grammar and punctuation.　　我需要練習文法和標點符號。

9. **revise** [rɪ`vaɪz] (v.) 修改，修正
   I revised my paper before turning it in.

10. **transition** [træn`zɪʃən] (n./v.) 轉變，轉換，轉折
    The country made a smooth transition to a market economy.

11. **tense** [tɛns] (n.) （動詞的）時態
    "Made" is the past tense of "make."

12. **proofread** [`pruf.rid] (v.) 校對
    I asked my dad to proofread my essay.

13. **cliché** [kli`ʃe] (n.) 陳腔濫調，老套的話
    This article is full of clichés.

補充字彙

* **pointer** [`pɔɪntə] (n.) 提示，建議

* **checker** [`tʃekə] (n.) 檢查器

* **run-on** [`rʌn.ɑn] **sentence** (n.) 缺乏連接詞或標點符號的長句

寫作協助

在美國無論是社區大學還是四年制大學，幾乎都有寫作協助的服務，有些學校叫 writing tutorial service(s)，有些學校叫 writing center。這種寫作協助基本上是免費提供給全校學生使用的，無論你的母語是否為英文者都可以使用，只要你有任何關於寫作上的問題，都可以前往尋求幫助。裡面的輔導員會指導你寫作，教你構思等方法。在使用服務前，有些學校需事先預約，而有些學校可以直接過去。

♫ 118 | 對話＋聽力測驗

♫ 119 | 單字

Vocabulary Bank

1. **assigned** [ə`saɪnd] (a.) 指定的，已分配的，動詞為 assign [ə`saɪn] 分配，分派

   Does this class have assigned seating?

2. **genetics** [dʒə`nɛtɪks] (n.) 遺傳學

   The team of scientists is studying monkey genetics.

3. **vaccine** [væk`sin] (n.) 疫苗

   This vaccine protects against several types of bacteria.

4. **measure** [`mɛʒɚ] (n.) 方法，措施

   Stronger measures are needed to fight crime.

5. **epidemic** [ˌɛpɪ`dɛmɪk] (n.) 流行病，瘟疫

   The government must be prepared for the next flu epidemic.

6. **dispose of** (phr.) 清除，處理

   Please dispose of your trash properly.

7. **bin** [bɪn] (n.) 垃圾箱

   Did you empty the waste bin?

8. **rinse** [rɪns] (v.) 漱，沖（洗）

   Leave the conditioner in your hair for two minutes before rinsing.

9. **glassware** [`glæs,wɛr] (n.) 玻璃器皿

   The glassware is in that cabinet.

Answering the TA's questions
回答助教的問題

TA	How many of you did the [1]**assigned** reading? Let's see a *show of hands*. OK, Michael—what did you learn about the latest *epidemiology* research?
Student 1	Um...that advances in [2]**genetics** are making it easier to create new [3]**vaccines**.
TA	Good. How about you, Rachael?
Student 2	That effective response [4]**measures** are still the most important part of fighting [5]**epidemics**.

助教	你們有多少人唸完指定的閱讀作業？舉手讓我們看一下。好，麥可，你從最新的流行病學研究中學到什麼？
學生 1	呃…遺傳學的進步讓製造新疫苗變得更容易。
助教	很好，瑞秋，你呢？
學生 2	有效的應對措施仍是對抗流行病最重要的部分。

Asking the TA questions
詢問助教問題

TA	Does anybody have questions about the quiz we took last week? Yes?
Student 1	I was wondering if it was graded on a curve.
TA	No. The section quizzes are mainly used to assess your progress. The midterm and final will be graded on a curve though. Yes?
Student 2	So the quizzes won't be a big part of our grade?
TA	No. Just five percent.

助教	有人對上週的小考還有問題嗎？有嗎？
學生 1	我想知道這是不是以拉曲線的方式評分？
助教	不是，討論課的小考主要是用來評估你們的進度。不過期中考和期末考是以拉曲線的方式評分。還有嗎？
學生 2	所以小考不會佔總成績太多比例嗎？
助教	不會，只有 5%。

Listening Quiz | 聽力測驗

● 請聽助教説明實驗室安全守則後，回答下面問題：

1. Where should broken glass be [6]**disposed of**?

(A) A lab trash can
(B) A special [7]**bin**
(C) The ***hazardous** waste bin
(D) A ***dustpan**

2. Which type of shoes should NOT be worn in the lab?

(A) Tennis shoes
(B) Cowboy boots
(C) ***Open-toed shoes**
(D) ***Dress shoes**

聽力測驗原文

Before we start this semester, let's talk a little about lab safety. To protect our eyes, safety ***goggles** should be worn at all times in the lab. If your eyes ever sting or feel uncomfortable at all, use the eye wash to [8]**rinse** your eyes immediately. Lab coats and gloves should also be worn at all times. And you need to wear ***close-toed shoes** to protect your feet. And if you have long hair, make sure to tie it up. If you break any [9]**glassware**, don't try to pick it up with your hands. Always use a broom and dustpan. And there's a special bin for broken glass—don't put it in the lab trash cans. Finally, when you're done using hazardous materials, always make sure to dispose of them in the proper hazardous waste bin.

在本學期開始之前，我們先稍微談一下實驗室安全。為了保護眼睛，在實驗室時須全程配戴護目鏡。如果眼睛感到刺痛或有任何不舒服，請立刻沖洗眼睛。實驗室袍和手套也要全程穿戴，而且要穿包鞋以便保護雙腳。如果你有留長髮，務必挽起頭髮。如果弄碎玻璃器皿，不要用手撿起，務必用掃帚和畚箕，並丟進專門放碎玻璃的垃圾桶，請勿丟進實驗室垃圾桶。最後，用完危險材料後，務必丟進適當的危險廢棄物垃圾桶內。

解答：1. (B) 2. (C)

補充字彙

* **show of hands** (phr.) 舉手表決

* **epidemiology** [ˌɛpədimiˈɑlədʒi] (n.) 流行病學

* **hazardous** [ˈhæzədəs] (a.) 危險的

* **dustpan** [ˈdʌstˌpæn] (n.) 簸箕

* **open-toed shoe** (n.) 露趾鞋，close-toed shoe 為「包鞋」

* **dress shoe** (n.) 皮鞋

* **goggles** [ˈɡɑɡəlz] (n.) 護目鏡，泳鏡

為何有 TA 制度

會出現 TA 制度是因為一般大學的演講型課堂都有上百人以上的學生，而教授沒時間也無法自己去關注到每位學生，從而出現 TA 來協助教授。

TA 的職責

TA 一般負責回答同學們的問題、再細講教授上課時所講的內容、改作業、改考卷、監考等輔助教授工作的事務都是 TA 的工作。另外，不同科系的 TA 也會帶領學生進行不同的附加課程，例如：化學系的 TA 可能需要帶領學生做實驗；數學系的 TA 可能需要為學生講解教授規定習題；歷史系 TA 可能需要帶領一個小班，針對課堂上提到的文獻進行討論，我們稱這種課程為 discussion section。discussion section 一般都是跟教授的 lecture 綁在一起的，但課堂是由 TA 帶領，以小班制進行，是強制參加，並且課堂表現、成績都是算在 lecture 名下的。所以如果所上課程有綁 discussion section 的話，選課時需注意，不要和其他課衝堂。

LESSON 8
Participating in Group Projects
第八話：**參與小組專題研究**

🎵 **120** | 對話

🎵 **121** | 單字

Vocabulary Bank

1. **set up** (phr.) **安排，計劃**
   I'll have my secretary set up a meeting.

2. **read up (on)** [rid ʌp] (phr.) **研讀，仔細研究**
   We should read up on Thailand before our trip.

3. **retail** [ˈri.tel] (n.) **零售（業），retailer** [ˈri.telə] (n.) **零售商**
   Our products are only sold in retail stores.

4. **after all** (phr.) **畢竟，終究**
   I don't like him, but he is, after all, our president.

補充字彙

∗ **sustainable** [səˈstenəbəl] (a.) **無法維持的，無法支撐的**

∗ **the Great Depression** (phr.) **大蕭條時期**

∗ **automation** [ˌɑtəˈmeʃən] (n.) **自動化，自動操作**

Joining a group
加入小組

Student 1	Have you joined a group for the group project yet?
Student 2	Yeah. We chose ∗**sustainable** development for our project topic.
Student 1	Ooh, that sounds really interesting. Is your group full yet?
Student 2	We actually need one more member, so you're welcome to join us.

學生 1	你有找到小組專題報告的組員了嗎？
學生 2	有，我們選了「永續發展」作為報告主題。
學生 1	喔，聽起來真有趣，你們小組的人數滿了嗎？
學生 2	其實我們還需要一個人，所以歡迎你加入我們。

Arranging a time to meet
約討論時間

Student 1	Hey, guys. We should 1)**set up** a time to discuss our project.
Student 2	Yeah, good idea. I have free time on Thursday afternoons.
Student 1	Sorry. That doesn't work for me. I have class all afternoon on Thursday.
Student 3	How about Tuesday afternoon? I'm free from 12:00 to 2:00.
Student 2	OK, sure. I'm free from 1:00 to 2:00. How about you, Lisa?
Student 4	Yeah, that's fine. Let's make it next Tuesday at 1:00.
Student 3	We should all 2)**read up** on ∗**the Great Depression** before we meet. That way, we'll have a better idea of what to discuss.

學生 1	嗨，各位，我們該約個時間討論報告。
學生 2	對，好主意，我每週四下午都有空。
學生 1	抱歉，我不行，我週四下午都有課。
學生 3	那週二下午呢？我從中午到 2 點有空。
學生 2	好，可以，我 1 點到 2 點有空。麗莎，妳呢？
學生 4	好，沒問題。我們就約下週二 1 點。
學生 3	我們見面前每個人該好好研究一下經濟大蕭條，這樣才能比較知道要討論什麼。

Discussing the topic
討論主題

Student 1	So, our topic is "how technology is changing [3]**retail**." How do you think we should approach it?
Student 2	Well, I don't think we should just emphasize the technology aspect. Shopping is a human activity, [4]**after all**.
Student 3	So you mean we should focus on the shopping experience, and how technology is improving it?
Student 2	Yes. And also how [3]**retailers** are using technology to adapt to social trends—like using ads on social media to attract shoppers.
Student 4	And we should also talk about how traditional retailers are struggling to keep companies like Amazon from stealing all their customers.
Student 1	These are all good ideas. We should also discuss how *__automation__ is changing both types of business.

學生 1	所以我們的主題是「科技如何改變零售業」。大家覺得我們該怎麼處理？
學生 2	呃，我想我們不該只強調科技方面，購物畢竟是人類活動。
學生 3	所以你是說我們該將重點放在購物體驗，還有科技如何提升購物體驗？
學生 2	對，還有零售商如何利用科技因應社會趨勢，例如利用社群媒體廣告吸引買家。
學生 4	我們也該討論傳統零售商如何努力對抗亞馬遜之類的公司搶走他們的顧客。
學生 1	這些主意都不錯，我們也該討論自動化如何改變這兩種類型的商業。

如何尋找組員

學生們可大膽詢問周圍同學是否可以跟自己組隊，或可否加入其他人的小組。若有小組已經有決定主題，學生可先詢問人家大概想做什麼主題後，看自己是否有興趣再決定是否加入。

如何參與討論

在美國，基本上就是要大膽，自己有什麼想法就要勇敢說出來跟大家討論。如果英文沒有很好的話，可先跟組員說，請求他們讓你負責不那麼困難的部分，不過因為美國人很講求公平，所以能參與討論的部分就盡量參與，不要一句話都不說，因為他們會因此而判斷你的貢獻程度低。

CHAPTER 3

上課囉！

Going to Class

🎵 122 | 對話＋好用句

🎵 123 | 單字

Vocabulary Bank

1. **divide (up)** [dɪ`vaɪd] (phr.) 分（攤）
   Let's divide up into groups now.

2. **make sense** (phr.) 形容某事說得通、很合理
   Does this sentence make sense to you?

3. **conduct** [kən`dʌkt] (v.) 進行，管理
   A team of scientists is conducting research on the new virus.

4. **write up** (phr.) 整理成文章
   Have you written up your results yet?

5. **nominate** [`nɑmə,net] (v.) 提名，推薦
   The star was nominated for three Oscars.

6. **brainstorm** [`bren,stɔrm] (v.) 腦力激盪，集思廣益
   Let's brainstorm and see if we can find a creative solution.

7. **differ** [`dɪfɚ] (v.) 意見不同，beg to differ 即「不敢苟同」
   The two politicians differ on the trade agreement.

8. **feasible** [`fizəbəl] (a.) 可行的，行得通的
   Sending humans to Mars is not feasible at this time.

補充字彙

＊ **crunch time** (phr.) 艱難時刻，關鍵時刻

 SITUATION 4

Assigning tasks
工作分配

Student 1　OK, how should we [1]**divide** up the work for our project?

Student 2　We could all do some research and see which part of the topic we're most interested in.

Student 3　I think we should assign tasks based on each person's abilities.

Student 4　That [2]**makes sense**. I was on the debate team in high school, so I could be in charge of the presentation.

Student 1　I agree. I'm majoring in marketing, so I could [3]**conduct** the survey. How about you, Allen?

Student 3　Well, I'm good at writing, so I can [4]**write up** our findings.

Student 2　OK, I guess I'm in charge of the research then.

學生 1　好，我們該怎麼替我們的報告分配工作？

學生 2　我們可以各做點研究，然後看每個人對主題的哪部分最有興趣。

學生 3　我覺得我們該根據每個人的能力分配工作。

學生 4　有道理，我曾在高中參加辯論隊，所以我可以負責口頭報告。

學生 1　我同意，我主修行銷，所以我可以進行調查。艾倫，你呢？

學生 3　我擅長寫作，所以我可以將我們的調查結果寫成報告。

學生 2　好吧，看來我要負責做研究。

Common Phrases | 提出見解，你要會說

1. We should all exchange contact information so we can keep in touch.

   我們該交換聯絡訊息，這樣就可以保持聯絡。

2. Let's vote to choose a group leader.

   我們投票選出組長。

3. I [5]**nominate** Greg to be the project leader.

   我提名葛瑞格當報告組長。

4. Let's get together and [6]**brainstorm** ideas for the project.

   我們聚一下，為報告做集思廣益。

5. Everybody needs to **pull their own weight**.

   大家都要各盡其責。

6. It's ***crunch time**—our presentation is on Monday.

   現在時間緊迫，週一就要口頭報告了。

7. We need to work as a team if we want a good grade.

   我們如果想得到好成績，就要團隊合作。

Common Phrases | 表達不同想法，你要會說

1. I don't agree/I disagree.

   我不同意。

2. I beg to [7]**differ**.

   我不敢苟同。

3. I'm afraid I don't share your view.

   恐怕我的意見跟你不一樣。

4. I don't think that idea is [8]**feasible**.

   我認為這辦法不可行。

5. I reached a different conclusion.

   我的結論不一樣。

6. I see what you're saying, but....

   我懂你的意思，但是…

7. I see your point, but in my opinion....

   我懂你的意思，但我認為…

pull one's weight 盡到責任

只要想像工作是在「做牛做馬」，就很容易了解 pull one's weight 是什麼意思了，因為 weight 是「重量」，pull one's weight 字面上的意思就是「拖著該負擔的重量走」，也就是盡到一個人該負的責任。

A: It seems like Ron's really been slacking off lately.
看來朗恩快要被裁員了。

B: Yeah. If he doesn't start **pulling his weight**, he's gonna get fired.
是啊。如果他再不開始負起責任，他就要被開除了。

若遇到組員意見分歧時，該怎麼做

在小組內有不同意見是常有的事，大家應該盡量提出自己的觀點、看法來跟對方討論，找出最適合小組的方案。

可以表達不同意見嗎？

可以。美國的教育就是要讓大家都能有不同的想法，可以獨立思考。所以每個人都可以表達不同的意見，再說，有不同的意見，大家才能討論，才能碰撞出更好的東西。

LESSON 9
Talking to Professors
第九話：和教授談

♫ 124 | 對話

♫ 125 | 單字

Vocabulary Bank

1. **so far** (phr.) 到目前為止
   How much money have we raised so far?

2. **development** [dɪˋvɛləpmənt] (n.) 開發，研製，**developer** 即「開發者，開發商」
   I hope to pursue a career in video game development.

補充字彙

* **programming** [ˋproˏɡræmɪŋ] (n.) （電腦的）程式

* **cyber** [ˋsaɪbɚ] (n.) 電腦的，與電腦有關的，網路的（尤指網際網路）

Introducing yourself
自我介紹

Student	Hi, Dr. Williams. I'm Matt Smith. I'm taking your International Business class.
Professor	Hi, Matt. Nice to meet you. What can I do for you today?
Student	I have a few questions about the syllabus I was hoping you could answer.
Professor	Of course. What would you like to know?

學生	嗨，威廉斯博士，我是麥特史密斯，我在修你的國際商業課。
教授	嗨，麥特，幸會。今天有什麼需要幫忙的？
學生	我有幾個關於教學大綱的問題，希望你能回答。
教授	當然，你想知道什麼？

Asking questions about a lecture
詢問講課相關問題

Student	Hi, Professor Martin. I really liked your lecture on the Austrian School.
Professor	Thanks. It's one of my favorite topics.
Student	I'd like to learn more about Austrian economics. Are there any books you could recommend?
Professor	Sure. Holcombe's *Introduction to the Austrian School* is a good place to start. And after that, I'd recommend Mises' *Human Action*.

學生	嗨，馬丁教授，我很喜歡你在奧地利經濟學派方面的講課。
教授	謝謝，那是我最喜愛的主題之一。
學生	我想學更多關於奧地利經濟，有什麼書可以推薦嗎？
教授	有，霍爾科比的《奧地利經濟學派導論》是不錯的入門書，看完之後我建議讀米塞斯的《人類行為》。

Seeking advice
尋求建議

DIALOGUE 1

Student: Hi, Mr. Stockton. I need to maintain a 3.0 GPA to keep my scholarship, and I was wondering if you could give me some tips on improving my grade in your class.

Professor: Let's see...you have a B+ [1]**so far**. If you got an A on the final, you could get an A- or an A for the course.

Student: I studied really hard for the midterm, but I still only got a B. Is there anything I can do to prepare better?

Professor: Well, 20% of the grade will come from material in the textbook that wasn't covered in class, so you could spend more time reviewing the textbook.

學生: 嗨,史德頓老師,我必須將 GPA 維持在 3.0 以上才能繼續領取獎學金,我在想你是不是能給我一些訣竅,能提升我在你班上的成績。

教授: 我想想…你目前的成績是 B+,如果你能在期末考拿 A,這堂課的總成績就能拿到 A- 或 A。

學生: 我很努力準備期中考,但我還是只拿了 B,有什麼辦法能準備得更好嗎?

教授: 嗯,20%的考題來自課堂上不會提到課本內容,所以你可以花更多時間複習課本。

DIALOGUE 2

Student: I'm really enjoying your *Programming Languages class, Mr. Evans. Could you recommend any other courses for me to take?

Professor: Well, I guess that depends on your interests.

Student: I'm hoping to pursue a career in software [2]**development**. I'm especially interested in *cyber security.

Professor: In that case, I'd recommend CS 492: Computer Security and CS 493: Secure Software Systems.

學生: 我很喜歡你的程式語言課,艾凡斯老師,你能推薦其他課程給我嗎?

教授: 呃,我想這要看你的興趣。

學生: 我希望從事軟體開發工作,我對網路安全特別有興趣。

教授: 這樣的話,我會推薦 CS492 電腦安全,和 CS493 安全軟體系統。

要讓教授對你有好印象就需要做到以下幾點:

1. **課前先做好預習**:好處是你能夠聽得懂教授在說什麼,上課時可以跟教授互動。而且先預習,如有疑問,可以帶著疑問到課堂上問教授,讓教授知道你有在用心上他的課,這樣也會給教授留下一個好的印象。

2. **上課不遲到**:不遲到是對教授以及其他同學的尊重,遲到不僅會容易影響教授對你的觀感,而且遲到還會影響到教授上課。

3. **盡量往前坐**:教授一般都會早到教室,而這段時間,他們會喜歡跟坐的比較近的學生們聊聊天,先了解一下,感情其實就是這樣培養起來的。

4. **認真上課,多問問題跟教授做好互動**:沒有人喜歡死氣沈沈的教室,所以上課不僅要好好做好筆記之外,還要盡量跟教授互動,讓教授感覺到你的熱情,覺得你是真的很認真想學習這些東西。

5. **下課後跟教授簡單介紹自己**:下課後不要急著走,可以留下來跟教授聊聊天,介紹一下你自己,這樣能夠加深教授對你的印象。

6. **去 office hours**:除了上課要跟教授互動外,下課也要盡量去跟教授互動。每位教授都有被學校要求設置 office hours 讓學生能夠去問問題,這是一個很好跟教授拉近關係的時間,可以讓他覺得你很有心要學習,就算沒有問題,也可以去跟他聊天,反正他們那個時間必須要待在那裡。

7. **勿觸碰到教授隱私問題**:在美國,幾乎什麼問題都可以問,但就是不要去問人家的隱私,例如:年紀、家庭、收入等,因為美國人是很在乎隱私的。

CHAPTER 3

上課囉!

Going to Class

 126 │ 對話＋好用句

 127 │ 單字

Vocabulary Bank

1. **investment** [ɪnˋvɛstmənt]
   (n.) 投資 (額、標的) / 動詞為
   invest [ɪnˋvɛst] 投資
   Stocks can be good long term investments.

2. **impact** [ˋɪmˏpækt] (n.) 影響，衝擊
   The book had a huge impact on my thinking.

3. **acquisition** [ˏækwəˋzɪʃən]
   (n.) 獲得，取得，習得
   The goal of education is the acquisition of knowledge.

4. **cite** [saɪt] (v.) 引用，引述
   The student cited several studies in his paper.

補充字彙

* **plagiarism** [ˋpledʒəˏrɪzəm]
   (n.) 剽竊，抄襲

* **paraphrase** [ˋpɛrəˏfrez] (v.)
   意譯，改述

* **footnote** [ˋfʊtˏnot] (n.) 註腳

* **correlation** [ˏkɔrəˋleʃən] (n.)
   相互關係

 SITUATION 4

Requesting a recommendation letter
要求提供推薦函

Student	Hi, Professor Jones. I was wondering if you'd be willing to write a letter of recommendation for me.
Professor	Sure. I'd be glad to. Are you applying to an MBA program?
Student	I'm actually applying for an internship at an [1]**investment** bank.
Professor	Oh, that's great. Just send me an e-mail including what your goals are for applying, the name and address of the bank, and the application deadline.

學生	嗨，瓊斯教授，我在想你是否願意替我寫推薦函。
教授	當然，我很樂意，你要申請工商管理碩士研究所嗎？
學生	我其實是要在投資銀行申請實習工作。
教授	噢，太好了，你就寄一封電郵給我，告訴我你的申請目標是什麼，銀行的名稱和地址，還有申請期限。

Common Phrases │ 討論論文，你要會說

1. How do I avoid ***plagiarism**? 我要如何避免剽竊？

2. Should I only use peer-reviewed sources? 我只能使用同儕審查的資源嗎？

3. I'm not sure which citation style to use. 我不確定要使用哪種引用格式。

4. Should I quote or ***paraphrase**? 我應該引用文章還是釋義？

5. How do I learn about writing in MLA format? 我要如何學習以 MLA 格式寫作？

6. Can you recommend any scholarly articles on this topic? 你能推薦關於這個主題的學術文章嗎？

7. Should I include ***footnotes** in my paper? 我應該在論文中加入註釋嗎？

Research papers
研究論文

Professor	So have you chosen a topic for your research paper yet?
Student	Yes. I want to write about the [2]**impact** of English learning on students' native language in Taiwan.
Professor	I see. That sounds interesting. Have you been able to find enough relevant research data on the subject?
Student	Yes. I've found several studies on the effect of English learning on native language [3]**acquisition**. In specific, I'll be using data from a study on primary school students at two different schools in Taiwan.
Professor	Was a negative ***correlation** found?
Student	Yes. The more time spent learning English, the stronger the impact on their Chinese writing skills. Does this subject sound suitable?
Professor	Yes. Just be sure to clearly [4]**cite** your sources when you write your paper.

教授	你選好研究論文的主題了嗎？
學生	是的，我想寫關於英語學習對台灣學生母語的影響。
教授	這樣啊，聽起來很有趣，你針對這主題找到切題的研究數據了嗎？
學生	是的，我已經找到一些關於英語學習對母語習得的影響的幾項研究。具體來說，我會用台灣兩所不同學校的小學生研究數據。
教授	有發現負相關嗎？
學生	有，從中文翻譯成英文的時間越長，對中文寫作技巧的影響就越大。這個主題聽起來合適嗎？
教授	是的，你只要確保在寫論文時清楚註明來源。

如何有效率的撰寫研究論文

要撰寫出讓教授滿意的研究論文，第一個要做的是就是先了解教授的口味。學生可先初步做一些研究、找一些資料後，去詢問教授意見。多數教授會給你一些建議，你再往他期望的方向去撰寫。在寫完要提交前，也可再去找教授幫你看一下，再給你一些建議讓你修改。

同儕審查 (peer-reviewed)

同儕審查文章是經過相同領域的專家評審和批准的期刊文章。有些學術期刊經過同儕審查，有些則沒有。這些文章的作者通常是研究人員或學者，而不是學生。

MLA 論文格式

MLA 論文格式是美國現代語言學會編定的一套學術論文格式，是英文論文寫作最常用的一種參考文獻格式。MLA 論文格式比起其他一般論文的格式有很大的不同，使用前需先了解清楚 MLA 格式的規則與結構。

娛樂
Entertainment

娛樂設施

既然已經付了高昂的學費，當然要先了解學校有哪些娛樂設施是免費，或是相對便宜的，抽空去游泳池、健身房、運動場問一問，了解一下。另外校外也有美術館、博物館、百老匯等，可以在閒暇之餘，充實身心靈。

社團

「大學就是要玩社團！」如果你在台灣曾經參加過社團，那在美國何不繼續參加，順便比較一下有什麼不同。記住，你不做，永遠不會知道！

校園活動

美國大專院校基本上每天都有很多活動，有學術性的（和某科系相關）、藝術性質的（如詩歌朗讀）、就業相關的等，基本上你想得到的活動都有。

校內體育活動

和台灣大專校院不同的是，美國校園很熱中體育活動，不但有體育社團，還有校隊等。他們認為體育訓練可培養青年堅毅品格、忍耐精神、團隊協作，所以校園裡有許多體育活動。適當參與體育活動，也能更增進對美國文化的認識。

去美國念書，你不能只會讀書，還要融入校園生活，才算是真正體驗美式生活。否則花大錢念了幾年書，回頭想想，只剩下一張畢業證書，就可惜了。

交朋友、約會
Friends & Dating

朋友

前面已經強調過很多次了，有機會請多交朋友吧！不管是室友的朋友，社團朋友，台灣朋友，還是國外朋友，只要品行好，不偷不搶，都可以結交。有可能會成為你一生的好友，只要你願意跨出友善的一步。

感情

雖然有句話說：「大學就應該修戀愛學分」，但由於跨了海，交往的對象還是華人，或是外國人，是繼續還是結束，可能也因時間和空間而變得複雜。如果決定談場異國戀，彼此價值觀的不同，在溝通時可能造成的誤解也請小心。

工作
Work

工作

去國外唸書的學生大多是希望對未來就業可以加分，基於這點在當地打工是個不錯的選擇，再加上對於學費不無小補。不一定要和所學有直接相關，不過至少可和未來雇主證明你具備某些相關技能，如：敢和外國人對話、人際關係能力等。

Campus Recreation Facilities
第一話：校園娛樂設施

♪ 128 | 對話

♪ 129 | 單字

Vocabulary Bank

1. **yoga** [ˈjogə] (n.) 瑜珈術
   I'm taking a yoga class at the gym.

2. **thanks to...** (phr.) 多虧
   Thanks to your dedication, we were able to finish the project on time.

3. **pass** [pæs] (n.) 乘車證，出入證
   How much does a bus pass cost?

4. **full-time** [ˈfʊlˈtaɪm] (a.) 全職的
   All full-time employees at the company receive health insurance.

補充字彙

* **alumni** [əˈlʌmnaɪ] (n.) （複數）校友，單數為 alumnus [əˈlʌmnəs]

* **lap swim** (phr.) 來回游泳

* **open swim** (phr.) 開放游泳

* **single-use** [ˈsɪŋgəlˈjus] (a.) 一次性的

1 SITUATION

General inquiries
一般詢問

Student	Excuse me. Which gym facilities are free to use?
Clerk	Current students have free access to all gym facilities. All you need to do is present your student ID.
Student	OK. How about group exercise classes?
Clerk	All [1]**yoga** classes are free, [2]**thanks to** an *alumni donation. Other classes have small fees.

學生	不好意思，健身房哪些設施是免費使用的？
職員	在學學生可免費使用所有健身房設施，你只要出示學生證就好。
學生	好，那團體運動課程呢？
職員	所有瑜伽課都是免費的，這要感謝校友的捐款。其他課程要收取小額費用。

2 SITUATION

Exercise class fees
運動課程費用

Student	How much do exercise classes cost?
Clerk	It depends on the class. Usually between 30 and 70 dollars.
Student	Oh, that's pretty reasonable.
Clerk	Actually, if you plan on taking a lot of classes, your best option is to buy a Flex [3]**Pass**. For just 100 dollars a year, you can take unlimited classes.

學生	運動課程怎麼收費？
職員	要看是哪堂課，通常是 30 到 70 美元。
學生	喔，這相當合理。
職員	其實你如果打算參加很多課程，你最好買通用票，一年只要一百元，就可以無限量參加課程。

● 請在看完游泳池時間表與門票方案後，回答下列問題：

Pool Hours

*Lap Swim:

Monday - Friday
5:30 – 8 a.m. (large or small pool)
11a.m. – 2 p.m. (large pool)
5 – 7 p.m. (large pool)

Saturday
9 a.m. – 12 p.m. (large pool)

*Open Swim:

Monday & Wednesday
7:15 - 9:15 p.m. (small pool)

Friday
5 – 9 pm. (small pool)

Saturday
12 – 3 p.m. (small pool)

*Both pools closed on Sunday

Pool Pass Options

4)**Full-time Students-** Free w/valid student ID
Faculty/Staff- Free w/valid student ID
Children of Students- Free w/parent's valid student ID (Open Swim times only)
Children of Faculty/Staff- $2 *single-use pass (Open Swim times only)
Alumni, Community-
$2 children single-use pass (17-) (Open Swim times only)
$3 adult day pass (18+)
$50/monthly membership
$125/semester membership

1. What would be the best option for a non-student who wanted to use the pool every day for two months?

(A) A *single-use pass
(B) A day pass
(C) A monthly pass
(D) A semester pass

2. When could a student take their kid to the pool with them?

(A) Monday at 7:00 a.m.
(B) Wednesday at 7:30 p.m.
(C) Saturday at 11:00 a.m.
(D) Sunday at 2:00 p.m.

解答：1. (C) 2. (B)
翻譯請見 p. 215

解說
2. 由於學生的孩子只能在 Open Swim（戲水泳池）時段使用，符合 Open Swim 時段的時間只有 (B)。

PART 3
課外活動
Extracurricular Activities

♪ 130 | 對話＋好用句

♪ 131 | 單字

Vocabulary Bank

1. **reserve** [rɪˋzɝv] (n.) 預訂，
   預約，名詞為 **reservation**
   [ˌrɛzɚˋveʃən]
   I'd like to reserve a room with
   an ocean view.

2. **recreation** [ˌrɛkrɪˋeʃən]
   (n.) 消遣，娛樂，**recreation
   center** 為「娛樂中心」，簡稱
   為 **rec center**
   Shopping is my main form of
   recreation.

3. **in advance** (phr.) 預先，事先
   If you want to get a seat on
   the train, you should buy your
   ticket in advance.

4. **equipment** [ɪˋkwɪpmənt] (n.)
   設備，器材，動詞為 **equip
   (with)** [ɪˋkwɪp] 具有能力、工
   具、裝備等
   The new equipment increased
   the efficiency of the factory.

5. **combination** [ˌkɑmbəˋneʃən]
   (n.)（打開密碼鎖的）對號密碼
   I forgot the combination to my
   safe.

補充字彙

* **racquetball** [ˋrækɪtˌbɑl] (n.)
  短柄牆球

* **squash** [skwɑʃ] (n.) 壁球

* **sole** [sol] (n.) 腳底，鞋底

* **weight** [wet] (n.) 重訓器材

 SITUATION 3

Fitness center facilities
健身中心設施

Student   Are showers and towels available in the gym?

Clerk   Yes, of course. Towel service is included in the locker rate, which is fifty dollars per semester.

Student   Is it necessary to rent a locker for a whole semester?

Clerk   No. We also have day lockers, but towels aren't included. You can purchase towel service for 20 dollars a semester.

學生   健身房裡有淋浴設備和毛巾嗎？

職員   當然有，置物櫃費用已包含毛巾服務，每學期是 50 元。

學生   整個學期都必須租置物櫃嗎？

職員   不用，我們也有日租型置物櫃，但不包含毛巾。你可以每學期花 20 元購買毛巾服務。

SITUATION 4

Court reservations
球場預約

Student   Hi. Could you tell me how to [1]**reserve** a badminton court?

Clerk   There's a [1]**reservation** page on the [2]**Recreation** Center website.

Student   OK, thanks. How long [3]**in advance** do I need to make a reservation?

Clerk   You can make a reservation as late as an hour in advance. But the courts go fast, so a day or two in advance is best.

學生   嗨，你能告訴我怎麼預約羽毛球場嗎？

職員   娛樂中心網站上有預約網頁。

學生   好，謝謝，我需要提前多久預約？

職員   你最晚可以在一小時前預約。但球場很快就會預約額滿，所以最好是提前一、兩天。

Common Phrases | 詢問校園娛樂設施，你要會說

1. Do I need to bring my own lock for the locker?
   我需要自己帶鎖來使用置物櫃嗎？

2. Can I get towel service without renting a locker?
   我不租置物櫃也可使用毛巾服務嗎？

3. Are reservations required for the *racquetball/*squash courts?
   短柄牆球／壁球場需要預約嗎？

4. Can I check out/rent sports 4)equipment?
   我能借／租運動器材嗎？

5. Is there parking available at the 2)Rec Center?
   娛樂中心有停車場嗎？

6. Will I still have gym access if I don't enroll in summer classes?
   我若沒註冊暑期班的話，還能用健身房嗎？

7. Are day passes available for non-students?
   非學生可買一日票嗎？

Common Phrases | 詢問校園娛樂設施，你要聽得懂

1. All of the lockers are 4)equipped with 5)combination locks.
   所有置物櫃都配有密碼鎖。

2. With a student ID, you can access all recreational facilities on campus.
   憑學生證可使用校內所有娛樂設施。

3. Only shoes with non-marking *soles are allowed in the gym.
   健身房內只能穿無痕橡膠底鞋。

4. Please return *weights and equipment to their proper place after use.
   重訓等器材用完後請放回原位。

5. Store all personal items in a locker—Campus Rec is not responsible for lost or stolen items.
   將所有個人物品放在置物櫃，校園娛樂中心不負責遺失或失竊物品。

6. If you're not taking summer classes, you can buy a rec membership.
   你若沒修暑期班，可以購買娛樂中心會員。

7. Students and members can purchase guest passes at the front desk.
   學生和會員可在櫃臺購買訪客票。

---

squash 和 racquetball 的差別

壁球 (squash) 是一項室內球拍型運動。運動是由兩到四個人在一個封閉式的場地進行。這個遊戲的目標就是，每位參賽者必須運用場中除了天花板以外的牆壁，以網拍把彈跳的球打到牆上，使得對方無法在球著地兩次之前擊打回來。而打短柄牆球時，則可將球打到天花板。

短柄牆球 (racquetball) 和壁球的差別在於短柄牆球的球較大，且有彈力。壁球的球較小，缺乏彈力。

短柄牆球顧名思義手把部分較短，而壁球的手把較長。

壁球球拍和球

使用校園娛樂設施的好處

學生們每天除了埋頭讀書之外，也應該要多運動、活動筋骨，這不僅能夠讓你的身體變得更健康，壓力大時可以舒緩壓力。有時候做研究、寫論文卡關時，出來運動一下，呼吸新鮮空氣後會表現得更好喔！此外，使用校園娛樂設施還能夠認識到不同的新朋友，以此來增強你的人際關係。其實校園的娛樂設施是種學生福利，而你繳的學費其實就有包含這些使用費了，所以大家可多利用這些設施來讓自己的大學生活變得更健康、更多采多姿。

LESSON 2
Joining Clubs and Organizations
第二話：參與社團和組織

🎵 132 | 對話

🎵 133 | 單字

Vocabulary Bank

1. **inclusive** [ɪnˋklusɪv] (a.)
   包容性的，沒有歧視的
   Our company has inclusive hiring policies.

2. **competition** [ˌkɑmpəˋtɪʃən] (n.) 競賽，競爭
   Evan won second prize in the design competition.

3. **controversial** [ˌkɑntrəˋvɝʃəl] (a.) 有爭議的
   Gun control is a very controversial subject

4. **every other** (phr.) 每隔一個的，所有其他的
   Maria goes to the gym every other day.

補充字彙

* **a cappella** [ˌɑkəˋpɛlə] (n.)
  無配樂合唱

* **karaoke** [ˌkɛriˋoki] (n.)
  卡拉 OK

* **bi-monthly** [ˌbaɪˋmʌnθli] (a./ adv.) 一個月兩次的，兩個月一次的

1 SITUATION

Choosing Clubs
挑選社團

Student	Wow, there are so many clubs to choose from that I'm having trouble deciding which to join.
Clerk	Well, you could pick an activity that you do regularly, or something that you're really interested in trying.
Student	Hmm, let's see. I like to play ping-pong. Is there a club for that?
Clerk	Yes—the Table Tennis Club. They meet in the Student Union basement on Tuesday and Thursday evenings.

學生	哇，有這麼多社團可選，我很難決定要加入哪個。
職員	呃，你可以選一個你會定期做的活動，或是你很有興趣嘗試的。
學生	嗯，我想想，我喜歡打桌球，有相關的社團嗎？
職員	有，桌球社，他們週二和週四晚上都在學生活動中心的地下室聚會。

2 SITUATION

Chatting about clubs
談論社團

Student 1	Didn't you say you like to sing? You should join Pitch Perfect.
Student 2	What's that? Is it a student choir?
Student 1	It's the campus *a cappella group. We sing a cappella versions of all kinds of popular songs.
Student 2	Wow. I'm not sure if I'm good enough to sing a cappella. I'm more of a *karaoke singer, ha-ha.
Student 1	Don't worry. We're an [1]**inclusive** group. You should come to our next practice session.

學生 1	你不是説過你喜歡唱歌嗎？你該加入完美音調團。
學生 2	那是什麼？學生合唱團嗎？
學生 1	那是校園的無伴奏合唱團，我們唱各種流行歌曲的無伴奏版。
學生 2	哇，我不確定我是不是夠格唱無伴奏歌，我比較常唱卡拉 OK，哈哈。
學生 1	別擔心，我們社團包容性很高，下次我們練習時你應該來參加。

📖 Reading Quiz | 閱讀測驗

● 請看下列社團敘述後，回答問題：

HawkTrade
HawkTrade meets every week to discuss current news and events as they relate to the financial markets. The organization also holds "paper trading" [2]**competitions** as a way to learn about trading strategies.

The Daily Iowan
An independent daily serving Iowa City and the campus community. It has won a number of awards and is generally regarded as one of the finest student newspapers in the country.

Debate Club
Debate Club is a place where we get together every Friday to discuss interesting and [3]**controversial** topics. If you want to improve your debate skills, or just hear different perspectives, then this is the club for you!

Sales & Consulting Club
The Sales & Consulting Club is a student organization that aims to prepare students for future careers in sales and consulting. We typically have *__bi-monthly__ meetings in which we discuss related topics.

1. Which of the following organizations meets once [4]**every other** week?

(A) HawkTrade
(B) The Daily Iowan
(C) Debate Club
(D) Sales & Consulting Club

2. Which organization would provide the most valuable experience to a journalism student?

(A) HawkTrade
(B) The Daily Iowan
(C) Debate Club
(D) Sales & Consulting Club

解答：1. (D) 2. (B)
翻譯請見 p. 215

希臘組織 (Greek system)

又稱做 Greek community，是美國大學裡特有的社交組織—兄弟會 (fraternity [frə`tɜnəti]) 和姐妹會 (sorority [sə`rɔrəti])。很多想加入這些組織的人稱為 pledge，這些組織還會有特定一個星期專門舉辦招會員的活動，就是 rush week，入會前還需經過一連串的考驗 (hazing)，直到被學長姐認同後才算正式加入，常被認為是只會喝酒玩樂的社團。但其實並不全然都是娛樂性質，也有純學術或是興趣同好的類型。

密西根大學的姐妹會

134 | 對話＋好用句

 135 | 單字

Vocabulary Bank

1. **dues** [duz] (n.) 會費
   （恆為複數）
   What's the deadline for paying
   membership dues?

2. **webpage** [ˋwɛbˌpedʒ] (n.)
   網頁，亦作 web page
   Could you send me the link to
   that webpage?

補充字彙

* **chapter** [ˋtʃæptə] (n.)
  地方分會

* **treasurer** [ˋtrɛʒərə] (n.)
  總務，財務主管，會計

* **bookkeeping** [ˋbʊkˌkipɪŋ]
  (n.) 簿記，記帳

* **chip in** (phr.) 集資，捐助

 SITUATION 3

Joining a professional organization
加入專業協會

Student 1	I'd like get involved in student activities, but I want to do something related to my major.
Student 2	You're studying mechanical engineering, right? You should join the American Society of Mechanical Engineers.
Student 1	But isn't that a professional association?
Student 2	Yes, but they have a *chapter on campus. It's a great way to make connections and learn more about the profession.

學生 1	我想參加學生活動，但希望是跟我主修有關的活動。
學生 2	你在學機械工程，對吧？你該加入美國機械工程師協會。
學生 1	但那不是專業協會嗎？
學生 2	對，但他們在校園也有分會，這是建立人脈和進一步學習這個專業的好方法。

 SITUATION 4

Becoming a club officer
成為社團幹部

Student 1	Hey, Kelly. You're majoring in accounting, right? How would you like to be club *treasurer?
Student 2	Well, I don't really have any experience.
Student 1	It's not hard—just basic *bookkeeping, keeping track of club funds. I can show you the ropes.
Student 2	OK. I guess this is a good chance to put what I'm learning to use.

學生 1	嘿，凱莉，妳是主修會計吧？妳想擔任社團的總務嗎？
學生 2	呃，我其實沒什麼經驗。
學生 1	這不難，只是基本簿記、記錄社團的資金，我可以教妳怎麼做。
學生 2	好，我想這是我學以致用的好機會。

Common Phrases | 詢問社團資訊，你要會說

1. How often does the group meet? | 社團多久聚會一次？

2. Does the club have membership [1]**dues**? | 社團有會員費嗎？

3. Are there any organizations for international students? | 有國際學生的組織嗎？

4. What do I need to do to start a student club? | 我要怎麼成立學生社團？

5. Are there any requirements for joining your club? | 加入你的社團有什麼要求嗎？

6. Where can I find a list of student clubs and organizations? | 在哪裡能找到學生社團組織的清單？

Common Phrases | 社團資訊，你要聽得懂

1. We meet twice a week—Tuesdays and Thursdays at 7:00 p.m. | 我們每週聚會兩次，週二和週四晚上 7 點。

2. There are no dues, but everybody ***chips in** to cover event costs. | 沒有會費，但每個人都要分擔活動費用。

3. There are many student associations for international students. | 有許多國際學生的學生協會。

4. To start a club, you need to find at least five members and submit a proposal to the Student Affairs Office. | 要成立一個社團，你需要至少找到五名成員，並向學生事務處提出申請。

5. Anyone who's a current student can join our club. | 在校學生都可加入我們社團。

6. There's a list of student groups on the Campus Activities [2]**webpage**. | 校園活動網頁上有學生社團清單。

PART 3
課外活動
Extracurricular Activities

LESSON 3
Chatting with Friends
第三話：和朋友聊天

 136 | 對話

 137 | 單字

Vocabulary Bank

1. **hit the books** (phr.) 用功學習，準備功課
   You better hit the books if you want to pass the exam.

2. **tons (of)** [tʌnz] (a.) (口) 大量，許多
   There are tons of new shows on Netflix.

3. **look up** (phr.) 查找
   You can look up the lyrics to the song online.

4. **comprehension** [ˌkɑmprəˈhenʃən] (n.) 理解力，領悟能力
   How did you do on the English comprehension test?

5. **stunt** [stʌnt] (n.) 特技，驚險動作
   Evel Knievel was famous for his daring motorcycle stunts.

6. **tag along** (phr.) 跟著 (出去玩樂)，當跟班
   My younger brother always wants to tag along with me and my friends.

7. **gap** [gæp] (n.) 間斷，間隔
   We waited for a gap in the traffic to cross the street.

補充字彙

* **buddy** [ˈbʌdi] (n.) 好朋友，夥伴

* **real-life** [ˈriəlˈlaɪf] (a.) 真實生活的，現實生活的

 1 SITUATION **1**

Balancing studies and social life
在學業和社交生活間尋找平衡

Student 1   How are things going? Are you getting used to living and studying here?

Student 2   OK, I guess. I'm spending most of my time studying, so I feel a little lonely sometimes.

Student 1   You can't spend all your time [1]**hitting the books**. You need to go out and have some fun.

Student 2   Yeah. But things like restaurants and movies are so expensive here, and I'm on a tight budget.

Student 1   You should join a club—there are [2]**tons of** clubs on campus. And there are all kinds of free activities too.

學生 1   都還好嗎？你在這裡生活和讀書習慣了嗎？

學生 2   還可以吧，我大部分時間都在念書，所以有時覺得有一點孤單。

學生 1   你不能整天都在念書，你也要出去玩一下。

學生 2   對，但這裡的餐廳和電影都好貴，我的預算很有限。

學生 1   你該加入社團，校園有很多社團，也有各種免費的活動。

2 SITUATION **2**

Improving your English
增進英文能力

Student 1   Your English is really good. Do you have any tips on how I can improve mine? I often don't understand what the professor is saying in class.

Student 2   Actually, I had the same problem when I first got here.

Student 1   So what did you do to improve your listening skills?

Student 2   I made sure to do the reading before class, and [3]**looked up** words I didn't know. I also watched YouTube lectures on related topics. That really helped with my [4]**comprehension**.

學生 1   你的英語真好，你有什麼訣竅能幫我增進英語嗎？我上課時經常聽不懂教授在說什麼。

學生 2   其實我剛來的時候也有同樣的問題。

學生 1   那你是怎麼提升聽力的呢？

學生 2   我一定會在上課前先預習課本，查好我不懂的單字。我也會在 YouTube 上看相關主題的講課，這真的對我的理解力很有幫助。

Local activities
當地活動

Student 1	Hey, Mike. What are your plans for the weekend?
Student 2	Me and some *buddies are going to the Hot Wheels **Monster Trucks** Live Show.
Student 1	Wow. I don't even know what that is.
Student 2	It's a show where *real-life versions of Hot Wheels toy trucks perform all kinds of [5]stunts. I have an extra ticket, so you can [6]tag along if you like.
Student 1	Sure—that would be great. It sounds awesome!

學生 1	嘿，麥克，你這週末有什麼計畫？
學生 2	我和幾個朋友要去看風火輪怪獸卡車現場表演。
學生 1	哇，我連那是什麼都不知道。
學生 2	那是真實版的風火輪玩具卡車表演各種特技，我還有多一張門票，你要的話可以跟我們一起去。
學生 1	好，太好了，聽起來很棒！

Time management
時間管理

Student 1	I'm finding it hard to manage my time effectively.
Student 2	Oh yeah? How so?
Student 1	On Monday, Wednesday and Friday, I have three-hour [7]gaps between classes.
Student 2	You should use that time to study and do homework. That way you'll have more free time in the evenings.

學生 1	我發現我很難有效安排時間。
學生 2	是嗎？怎麼説？
學生 1	每週一、週三和週五，我每堂課之間都有三小時空檔。
學生 2	你可以利用這段時間念書和做功課，這樣你晚上就會有更多空閒時間。

 138 | 對話＋好用句

 139 | 單字

Vocabulary Bank

1. **service** [`sɝvɪs] (n.) 禮拜，宗教儀式

   When will the funeral service be held?

2. **convert** [kən`vɝt] (v.) 改變信仰，皈依

   Sean was raised as a Catholic but later converted to Islam.

3. **democracy** [dɪ`mɑkrəsi] (n.) 民主制度，民主國家，形容詞為 **democratic** [ˌdɛmə`krætɪk]

   The number of democracies in the world is on the rise.

4. **scenery** [`sinəri] (n.) 風景，景色

   The scenery in New Zealand is magnificent.

5. **consist (of)** [kən`sɪst] (v.) 組成，構成

   The salad dressing consists of oil, vinegar, salt and pepper.

6. **ice hockey** (phr.) 冰上曲棍球

   Ice hockey is a very dangerous sport.

補充字彙

* **Buddhist** [`budɪst] (n./a.) 佛教徒，佛教的

* **legalize** [`ligəˌlaɪz] (v.) 使合法化

* **breadbasket** [`brɛdˌbæskɪt] (n.) 糧食的主要產地

 Being invited to church
邀約上教堂

Student 1 If you miss the taste of home, you should come to church with me on Sunday. It's a Taiwanese American Church, and they serve an authentic meal after the [1]**service**.

Student 2 Hmm, I don't know. My parents are *****Buddhist**, and I'm not really religious. They won't try to [2]**convert** me, will they?

Student 1 No, don't worry. Everybody's really nice. You can practice your English and make new friends. There's no pressure at all.

Student 2 Well, I guess I can give it a try.

學生 1 你若是懷念家鄉味，你可以週日和我一起上教堂。那是台裔美人教會，他們在禮拜後會提供道地餐點。

學生 2 呃，我不知道，我父母是佛教徒，我沒有宗教信仰，他們不會想對我傳教吧？

學生 1 不會，別擔心，大家都很親切。你可以練習英語交新朋友，不會有壓力。

學生 2 嗯，我想我可以去看看。

Talking about Taiwan
談論台灣

Student 1 Are you from China?

Student 2 No. I'm from Taiwan.

Student 1 Isn't Taiwan part of China?

Student 2 No. China and Taiwan are two different countries. We have our own government, our own president, and our own flag.

學生 1 你是從中國來的嗎？

學生 2 不是，我來自台灣。

學生 1 台灣不是中國的一部分嗎？

學生 2 不是，中國和台灣是兩個不同的國家，我們有自己的政府、總統和國旗。

Common Phrases | 介紹台灣，你要會說

1. Taiwan is an island with a population of 23 million.

   台灣是一座島嶼，有 **2300** 萬人口。

2. Unlike China, Taiwan is a [3]**democracy**.

   跟中國不同的是，台灣是民主國家。

3. Taiwan is famous for its high-tech industry.

   台灣以高科技業聞名。

4. Taiwan is off the coast of China, between Japan and the Philippines.

   台灣位於中國沿海，在日本和菲律賓之間。

5. Taiwan has beautiful [4]**scenery** and the tallest mountains in East Asia.

   台灣風景秀麗，有東亞最高的山脈。

6. We have a low crime rate, but lots of earthquakes and typhoons.

   我們的犯罪率很低，但有很多地震和颱風。

7. We were the first country in Asia to *legalize same-sex marriage.

   我們是亞洲第一個同性婚姻合法化的國家。

Common Phrases | 介紹美國，你要聽得懂

1. America is a country built on immigration.

   美國是以移民為基礎的國家。

2. Most of the country's population lives on the East and West Coasts.

   美國大部分人口住在東西兩岸。

3. The Midwest is America's *breadbasket.

   中西部是美國的糧倉。

4. The U.S. is the world's biggest economic and military power.

   美國是世上最大的經濟和軍事強國。

5. The United States [5]**consists** of 50 states and five overseas territories.

   美國包含 **50** 州和五個海外領土。

6. The U.S. capital is Washington D.C., but it was originally New York City.

   美國首都是華盛頓特區，但最初是紐約市。

7. Football is America's most popular sport, followed by baseball, basketball and [6]**ice hockey**.

   美式足球是最受歡迎的運動，其次是棒球、籃球和冰上曲棍球。

請避免聊到這些話題

雖然跟美國人什麼都可以聊，但美國人是很重視自己隱私的，所以跟美國人聊天時，請盡量避免涉及個人隱私的問題，例如，年齡、體重、個人成績、收入、宗教或政治傾向等。

PART

課外活動

Extracurricular
Activities

3

LESSON 4

Internship vs. Co-op

第四話：**實習和在校生實習**

🎵 140 | 對話

🎵 141 | 單字

Vocabulary Bank

1. **stand for** (phr.) 是…的縮寫，
   代表
   TEFL stands for Teaching
   English as a Foreign Language.
2. **binder** [ˋbaɪndə] (n.) 活頁夾
   I keep all my notes in a binder.

co-op 和 internship 的相同差異處比較

	co-op（在校生實習）	internship（實習）
時間靈活性	不彈性：需在學期間，工作隨學期開始、結束。	彈性：任何時候都可開始，可學期開始、學期中、暑假、畢業後。
工作時間	全職工作，工作時暫時休學。需課程與工作穿插進行。不可一邊上課，一邊實習。	可全職、可半工半讀，無需休學，可一邊上課，一邊實習。上學期間每週工作 20 小時以下，暑假可全職。
申請所需求學階段	大學兩年以上	大學兩年以上
國際學生可否申請	可（需申請 CPT）	可（需申請 CPT 或 OPT）
好處	公司、職位由學校安排，且能參與全職工作，深入了解專業領域知識。	不用和學校生活完全脫節，可在短時間內嘗試不同職位。
實習長度	4 個月	3-12 個月
注意事項	• CPT 總數不可超過 12 個月，若超過 12 個月，畢業後會自動喪失 OPT 資格。 • 需通過學校同意，不可自行找工作。	
是否支薪	是	不一定，多數否。
是否影響畢業時間	是	否

Internships for international students
國際學生實習

DIALOGUE 1

Student Hi. I'm an international student on an F-1 visa. Would it be possible for me to pursue an off-campus internship?

Clerk Yes. As long as you've completed two full academic semesters here, you're eligible for a CPT internship.

Student What's a CPT internship?

Clerk CPT [1]**stands for** Curricular Practical Training. It's a type of internship for international students arranged by the school.

學生 嗨,我是拿 F-1 簽證的國際學生,我是否能申請校外實習工作?

職員 可以,只要你在這裡完成兩學期學業,你就有資格參加 CPT 實習。

學生 CPT 實習是什麼?

職員 CPT 是課程實踐培訓的縮寫,那是由學校為國際學生安排的實習工作。

DIALOGUE 2

Student Excuse me. I was wondering how to tell which internships are available to international students.

Clerk We have a special [2]**binder** with listings for international students. You can also find the list on our Career Center website. What type of internship are you looking for?

Student I'm an econ major, and I was hoping for something related to finance.

Clerk OK. We have a number of listings for internships in the financial services industry.

學生 不好意思,我想知道哪種實習工作可讓國際學生申請。

職員 我們有為國際學生提供專門的活頁夾,裡面有清單,你也可以在職業中心網站找到這份清單,你想找哪種實習工作?

學生 我主修經濟學,希望能找到金融相關的機會。

職員 好,我們有許多金融服務業的實習機會。

每所學校、每個 program,都提供 co-op 或是 internship 嗎?

不一定,但現在很多學校都有跟一些公司有建教合作的協議,不過目前大部分有提供 co-op 或是 internship 的都是以工程類專業為主,大部分學校都會在學校官網說明自己學校是否有提供 co-op 或 internship 的機會。對於未來想在當地找工作或實習的學生,最好在選擇學校時,先查詢學校是否有提供 co-op 或 internship。對於 co-op 跟 internship 來說,一般都是從大三或大四開始,不過 co-op 要求學生要上課和實習穿插進行,而且是隨著學期的開始而開始,學期的結束而結束。internship 就沒有這種硬性規定了,可以暑假開始,也可以是學期進行到一半開始。

如何找 co-op 或是 internship?

國際學生可以從學校的 international student office 或 career center 開始,這兩個地方會提供你相關資訊,並輔導你進行申請。

PART 3

課外活動

Extracurricular Activities

 142 │ 對話＋好用句

 143 │ 單字

Vocabulary Bank

1. **supervisor** [ˋsupɚˌvaɪzɚ] (n.) **主管，上司**
   Can I speak to your supervisor, please?

2. **human resources** (n.) **人力資源 (部)，簡稱為 HR**
   I hear Katherine works in human resources now.

3. **network** [ˋnɛtˌwɝk] (v./n.) **建立、經營人脈；關係網絡，社群**
   Job fairs are great places to network.

4. **colleague** [ˋkɑlig] (n.) **同事，同僚**
   I'd like you to meet my colleague, Ed Roberts.

5. **initiative** [ɪˋnɪʃətɪv] (n.) **積極舉動，進取心**
   It takes energy and initiative to succeed in sales.

6. **dress code** (phr.) **穿著規定**
   The principal made an announcement about the new dress code

補充字彙

＊ **hands-on** [ˋhændzˋɑn] (a.) **（經驗、訓練等）實際操作的**

DIALOGUE 3

Student	I'm an electrical engineering major, and I'm worried that my spoken English isn't good enough for my internship.
Advisor	I wouldn't worry too much. A lot of the employees at tech companies are here on H-1B visas these days.
Student	I'm afraid my listening skills aren't very good either. Do you have any tips?
Advisor	Well, it would help to read up on the company you'll be interning at, and also the duties you'll be performing in your internship position.

學生	我主修電機工程，我擔心我的英語口語能力不夠好，無法勝任實習工作。
輔導員	不必太擔心這問題，近來這裡的科技公司有許多員工是拿 H-1B 簽證的。
學生	恐怕我的聽力也不太好。你有什麼訣竅嗎？
輔導員	嗯，仔細研究你要去實習的公司會有幫助，以及你實習職務的職責。

First day as an intern
實習第一天

[1]**Supervisor**	Hi, you must be our new intern. Welcome to Smithco.
Intern	Thank you. Here's the paperwork from my school.
Supervisor	OK, let's see. You're a senior in [2]**Human Resources**—excellent. Let's set you up with a desk. You must be eager to get started.
Intern	Yes! I can't wait to get some ***hands-on** experience.

主管	嗨，你一定是我們的新實習生，歡迎來到史密斯科公司。
實習生	謝謝，這是我學校的文件。
主管	好，我看看，你是人資系四年級，很好，我們來安排你的辦公桌，你一定迫不急待開始了。
實習生	對！我等不及想獲得一些實際經驗。

Common Phrases | 身為實習生，你要做這 8 件事

1. Do your homework before you start your internship. 　實習開始前先做功課。

2. Dress for success. 　致勝穿著。

3. Treat your internship like a real job. 　把實習工作當正式工作。

4. Practice good time management. 　做好時間管理。

5. Find a mentor to learn from. 　尋找一位導師學習。

6. [3]**Network** with your new [4]**colleagues**. 　與新同事建立關係。

7. Take [5]**initiative**, but accept guidance. 　積極主動，但要接受指導。

8. Ask for feedback. 　徵求回饋意見。

Common Phrases | 身為實習生，你要會說

1. I'm so excited to be part of your team. 　我很高興能成為你們團隊的一員。

2. Is there a [6]**dress code** at the office? 　辦公室有服裝規定嗎？

3. I'll have the report on your desk first thing tomorrow. 　我明天第一件事會把報告放到你的辦公桌上。

4. Just let me know if you have any other tasks for me. 　如果你還有其他任務要派給我，請告訴我。

5. Could you please show me how to use this software? 　能請你教我怎麼用這個軟體嗎？

6. I'd love to learn more about your experience in the field. 　我很想多聽聽你在這個領域的經驗。

7. Would you be willing to be my mentor? 　你願意當我的導師嗎？

H-1B visa

H-1B visa 是美國簽發給在美從事專業技能工作的外籍人士的工作簽證，是美國最主要的工作簽證類別。這種簽證必須要由雇主為外籍應徵者申請，簽證持有後可以在美國工作三年，之後可再申請延長三年，六年期滿後，若持有者的身分沒有轉換，就必須離開美國。

找實習機會的建議

很多留學生會害怕自己英文不夠好或有口音而小看自己，但其實不用太擔心，因為美國人的包容心是很大的，只要你能虛心受教，勇於表達自己的想法、看法，那麼就不用太擔心。另外，國際學生因為除了英文之外，還會另外一種語言，所以在找工作時也會比較吃香一點。

3

Extracurricular Activities
第五話：校內和社團體育活動

lacrosse 袋棍球

 144 | 對話

♫ 145 | 單字

Vocabulary Bank

1. **recruit** [rɪ`krut] (v.) 招募，招收，名詞為 **recruiter** [rɪ`krutə] 招募者
   The company recruited new employees at the job fair.

2. **athletic** [æθ`lɛtɪk] (a.) (動作) 活躍、敏捷、有力的，運動 (性) 的
   Frank attended college on an athletic scholarship.

3. **try out** (phr.) 選拔，嘗試
   Steve wants to try out for the football team.

4. **collector** [kə`lɛktə] (n.) 收藏家，**collector's item** 即「收藏品」
   My uncle is an antique collector.

補充字彙

* **lacrosse** [lə`krɑs] (n.) 長曲棍球

* **jersey** [`dʒɝzi] (n.) 運動衫，球衣

[1]Recruiting for the *lacrosse club team
袋棍球社團隊招募新血

[1]**Recruiter**	Hey, would you be interested in joining our lacrosse team?
Student	I'm sorry. I don't know what that is.
Recruiter	It's kind of like ice hockey, but it's played on a field. And the stick has a net on the end you can catch and throw the ball with.
Student	Wow, it sounds really difficult. I'm afraid I'm not very [2]**athletic**.

招募者	嘿，你有興趣加入我們的袋棍球隊嗎？
學生	抱歉，我不知道那是什麼。
招募者	這有點像冰上曲棍球，不過是在球場上玩。而且長棍尾端有個網子，可以讓你接球和扔球。
學生	哇，聽起來很難，我恐怕沒什麼運動細胞。

The badminton club team
羽球社團隊

Student 1	I just joined the badminton team. We play twice a week and it's great exercise. You should come [3]**try out**.
Student 2	I like badminton, but I don't think I'm good enough to play on the school team.
Student 1	It's a club team, not the official school team. We compete against clubs at other schools, but you don't have to be a top athlete or anything.
Student 2	That does sound like fun. I think I will try out.

學生 1	我剛加入羽毛球隊，我們每星期打兩次球，是很好的運動，你應該來參加選拔。
學生 2	我喜歡羽毛球，但我想我不夠格加入校隊打球。
學生 1	這是社團球隊，不是正式的校隊。我們會跟其他學校的社團比賽，不過你不一定要是頂尖運動員之類的。
學生 2	聽起來確實很好玩，我想我會去參加選拔。

SITUATION 3

Reasons for playing sports
參與運動的原因

Student 1	How come so many students here play sports? Shouldn't they spend more time studying?
Student 2	Well, you know what they say—healthy body, healthy mind.
Student 1	I guess you have a point. But why not just work out at the gym a couple times a week?
Student 2	Sports have lots of other benefits too. They can teach leadership and teamwork skills, and create stronger ties between schools.

學生 1	為什麼這裡有這麼多學生參加體育活動？他們不是該花更多時間念書嗎？
學生 2	你知道俗話說，有健康的身體才有健康的頭腦。
學生 1	我想你說的有道理，但何不每星期到健身房運動幾次就好？
學生 2	體育活動也有很多其他好處，可以教導領導能力和團隊合作技巧，為學校之間建立更堅固的關係。

 SITUATION 4

Sports *jerseys
球衣

Student 1	I'm not really into sports, but the Cal jerseys are pretty cool.
Student 2	Yeah, I know. I'm collecting them. I have a Bears baseball jersey, basketball jersey, hockey jersey, football jersey.
Student 1	Wow, you must really be a fan. Those things aren't cheap!
Student 2	Well, I think of it as an investment too. They'll probably become 4)**collector**'s items.

學生 1	我不太喜歡運動，但柏克萊的球衣很酷。
學生 2	就是說啊，我有在收集。我有金熊棒球衣、籃球衣、曲棍球衣、美式足球衣。
學生 1	哇，你一定是超級球迷，那些球衣可不便宜！
學生 2	嗯，我也把它當成一種投資，那些球衣可能會變成收藏品。

參與國外大學運動活動，很重要嗎？

其實並不是很重要，因為並不是人人都熱愛運動，不過因為美國多數人喜歡運動，所以如果想要交到外國朋友或有較多共同話題，去參與一些運動活動是個不錯的選擇。

Intramural Sports, Club Sports, Collegiate Sports 有什麼不同

intramural sports 屬於比較自由、非正式的業餘娛樂型團體，他們提供多種運動項目，且不會要求每個人每一次的比賽或活動都要出席。自己可以依照自己的時間來參與。

club sports 是屬於競技型的社團球隊，隊員是需要經過選拔之後才能加入，並且有專業的教練為隊員們做訓練，而且常會跟不同學校進行比賽交流。

collegiate sports 屬於專業校隊，是有學校或企業贊助的，通常比賽會經過電視轉播或售票入場。他們都是經過嚴格的甄選及訓練，很多選手畢業後有機會成為職業選手。

PART 3

課外活動

Extracurricular Activities

Vocabulary Bank

1. **tackle** [ˈtækəl] (v.)（美式足球等球類）擒抱，撲倒

   The player was tackled before he could catch the ball.

2. **recreational** [ˌrɛkrɪˈeʃənəl] (a.) 休閒的，消遣的，娛樂的

   The summer camp offers a variety of recreational activities.

3. **opposition** [ˌɑpəˈzɪʃən] (n.) 對手

   The opposition scored a goal in the last second of the game.

4. **choke** [tʃok] (v.)（運動比賽等關鍵時刻因喪失信心而）失敗，怯場

   The player choked and missed an easy shot.

補充字彙

* **on fire** (phr.) 勢如破竹，形容某人的表現很好，且氣勢越來越旺

* **have a shot (at)** (phr.) 有機會成功、達到目標

* **get one's hopes up** (phr.) 抱（太）大希望

* **down** [daʊn]（美式足球）進攻，起跑

* **touchdown** [ˈtʌtʃˌdaʊn] (n.) 達陣（持球過球門線得分）

* **intramural** [ˌɪntrəˈmjʊrəl] (a.) 學校內的

 Watching American Football
看美式足球賽

SITUATION 5

DIALOGUE 1

Student 1	Hey, Tom. Are you going to the football game on Saturday?
Student 2	Of course! I wouldn't miss it. It looks like the Buckeyes may win the division this year.
Student 1	Yeah, they're really *on fire. They may even *have a shot at the conference title.
Student 2	That would be awesome. I don't want to *get my hopes up too much though. One game at a time.

學生 1	嘿，湯姆，你星期六要去看美式足球賽嗎？
學生 2	當然！我不會錯過的，看起來七葉樹隊今年可能會贏得區冠軍。
學生 1	對，他們真的勢如破竹，可能甚至有機會贏得聯賽冠軍。
學生 2	那就太棒了，但我不想抱太高的期望，一步步慢慢來。

DIALOGUE 2

Student 1	Whoa, did you see that pass? It must've been 30 yards!
Student 2	And the receiver is still running! Go Lions!
Student 1	Oh no—[1]**tackled** on the 15-yard line!
Student 2	It's only the second *down. We can still get a *touchdown.

學生 1	哇，你看到剛剛那個傳球了嗎？一定有 30 碼！
學生 2	而且接球員還在跑！獅子隊加油！
學生 1	糟了，在 15 碼線上被撲倒！
學生 2	這只是第二次進攻，我們還有機會達陣得分。

Common Phrases | 討論體育活動，你要會說

1. Do you have to try out to join the *intramural team?

   要參加選拔才能加入校內球隊嗎？

2. Who is eligible to play intramural sports?

   誰有資格參加校內運動？

3. Are there any fees to play on a club team?

   參加社團球隊需要付費嗎？

4. Is there a student discount for Cal football tickets?

   柏克萊的美式足球門票有學生折扣嗎？

5. Where can I find a list of the intramural sports available?

   哪裡可以找到校內運動的清單？

6. Is it possible to play on more than one team?

   可以不只參加一支球隊嗎？

7. Is your club team competitive or ²⁾**recreational**?

   你們社團球隊是競賽型還是娛樂型？

Common Phrases | 看美式球賽，你要會說

1. We're gonna crush the ³⁾**opposition**!

   我們要痛宰對方！

2. That was an awesome pass!

   那球傳得好！

3. We have a chance to make it to the playoffs.

   我們有機會進決賽。

4. Our team is ⁴⁾**choking** out there.

   我們這隊在場上失利。

5. Go Tigers!

   老虎隊加油！

6. Eagles unite, Fight, Eagles, fight!

   老鷹隊團結一心！老鷹隊，加油！

7. First and ten, let's do it again!

   前進十碼一次到位，如法炮製再來一次！

（編註：美式足球規則當中，一隊能在四次起跑以內向達陣區前進十碼，就可以再得到一次往達陣區跑四次的機會，但若四次起跑未能前進十碼，就換另一隊持球向反方達陣區起跑。）

美國大學運動文化

美國大學的運動文化舉世聞名，很多學校也喜歡重點招收體育生，這是因為背後有龐大的金錢利益。當一間學校擁有一支強隊，他們曝光的機會也就多，而且還可與很多聯盟、體育頻道簽約轉播來獲利，再加上門票、周邊等商品的獲利更是可觀。除此之外，專家也認為「體育訓練是培養青年堅毅品格、忍耐精神、團隊協作和忠誠度的有效途徑。所以，體育屬於包括校園文化在內的美國社會文化的一部分。」因此，在美國，學生運動員很受歡迎，是人人稱羨的對象。

LESSON 6
Dating
第六話：約會

 148 | 對話

 149 | 單字

Vocabulary Bank

1. **recycling** [ˌriˋsaɪkəlɪŋ] (n.)
   回收利用，重複使用
   Which one is the recycling bin?

2. **bring up** (phr.) 談到，提及
   If you're concerned about your weight, you should bring it up with your doctor.

3. **mystery** [ˋmɪstərɪ] (n.) 懸疑電影，懸疑、推理作品
   Ann liked reading mysteries when she was a teenager.

go for it 儘管去做
go 有「追尋某個目標」的意思，it 是代名詞，代表前面所說想做的事情。下次再有人猶豫不決，你就可以說 Go for it! 鼓勵他囉。

A: I'm thinking of trying out for cheerleading, but I hear it's really hard to get in.
   我正在考慮去參加啦啦隊徵選，但聽說非常難考進去。

B: I think you should **go for it**!
   我認為你應該放手一試！

Same here. 我也是。
想要表達自己也有一樣想法時，除了 Me too. 和 So do/am I 之外，也可以用 Same here. 來表示認同。

A: I'm so hungry, I could eat a horse!
   我餓到可以吞下一匹馬！！

B: **Same here**.
   我也是。

SITUATION 1
Saying hi
打招呼

Student 1	Hey, do you see that girl sitting at the table over there?
Student 2	Yeah, she's pretty cute. Do you know her?
Student 1	No, but I'm thinking of going over and saying hi.
Student 2	You should totally go for it. What've you got to lose?

學生 1	嘿，你看到那一桌的女孩了嗎？
學生 2	看到了，她很可愛，你認識她嗎？
學生 1	不認識，但我想過去打聲招呼。
學生 2	你應該要過去，你還能有什麼損失呢？

SITUATION 2
Making an approach
搭訕

Student 1	Hey, aren't we in the same Ecology 101 section? I'm Dylan.
Student 2	Oh, yeah. I thought you looked familiar. I'm Jessica.
Student 1	Hi, Jessica. I really liked that [1]**recycling** idea you [2]**brought up** in class the other day. Say, I'm sitting over there with a friend. Would you like to join us?
Student 2	I actually have class in ten minutes. It was nice meeting you though.
Student1	Same here. See you later.

學生 1	嘿，我們不是上同一堂生態學 101 嗎？我叫迪倫。
學生 2	噢，對，我就覺得你很眼熟，我叫潔西卡。
學生 1	嗨，潔西卡，妳那天在課堂上提出的回收想法我很喜歡。對了，我跟朋友坐在那裡，妳要加入我們嗎？
學生 2	我其實十分鐘後有課，但很高興認識你。
學生 1	我也是，再見。

Asking for a phone number
要電話號碼

Student 1   Well, it was nice talking to you.

Student 2   Yeah. I guess I'll see you in class next week.

Student 1   Yes. Hey, we should exchange phone numbers. Maybe we can have coffee sometime or something.

Student 2   Yeah, sure. Here, let me put my number in your phone.

學生 1   嗯，跟你聊天很愉快。

學生 2   是啊，那就下星期課堂上見囉。

學生 1   對，嘿，我們該交換電話號碼，也許我們哪天可以相約喝咖啡之類的。

學生 2   好，手機給我，我幫你輸入我的電話號碼。

Asking someone out
邀約約會

Student 1   Hey, Sandy. Are you doing anything on Saturday night?

Student 2   I don't really have any plans. Did you have something in mind?

Student 1   I was thinking of seeing Knives Out. Would you like to join me?

Student 2   Sure. I love murder 3)**mysteries**! What time does it start?

Student 1   It starts at 8:00. How about I pick you up at 7:30?

Student 2   OK. It's a date.

學生 1   嘿，珊蒂，週六晚上妳有事嗎？

學生 2   我沒什麼計畫，你有什麼想法嗎？

學生 1   我想去看《鋒迴路轉》，妳要跟我一起去嗎？

學生 2   好啊，我喜歡兇殺懸疑片！電影幾點開始？

學生 1   8 點開始，我 7 點半去接你如何？

學生 2   好，就這麼說定了。

如何描述某人的感情狀態

如果她 / 他已經名花 / 草有主，我們會說：

· He / She is taken. 他 / 她死會了。

· He / She has a girlfriend / boyfriend. 他 / 她有女 / 男朋友。

形容兩人正在交往的片語可以說

· He / She is dating someone. 他 / 她正在和某人交往。

· He / She is seeing someone/ going out with someone. 他 / 她正在和某人交往。

在歐美文化中，還有一種所謂的「開放關係」，意即雖然我有男 / 女朋友，但我和我的另一半都不介意有其他的性伴侶，這英文的說法是：

· We're in an open relationship. 我們目前是開放關係。

· I'm dating someone, but we're not exclusive. 我有交往對象，但彼此還可以跟別人約會。

另外，若兩人正在「冷靜期」的階段，則可以說：

· We're on a break. 我們目前暫時分開冷靜一下。

PART 3

課外活動

Extracurricular Activities

 150 | 對話＋好用句

 151 | 單字

Vocabulary Bank

1. **exclusive** [ɪk`sklusɪv] (a.) 獨有的，唯一的，（關係）專一的
   Are you and Karen exclusive?

2. **go steady** (phr.) 穩定交往
   Are you and Rebecca going steady?

3. **committed** [kə`mɪtɪd] (a.) 忠誠的，堅定的 / (v.) commit [kə`mɪt] 許諾，承擔義務，
   Bob is a committed member of the Democratic Party.

take a rain check 改天吧
面對別人的邀約，回覆現在無法答應，但也許改天可以。
A: Wanna see a movie tonight?
   你今晚想看電影嗎？
B: I'd like to, but I have to study. Can I **take a rain check**?
   想啊，但是我要念書。可以改天約嗎？

on the same page 意見一致
表示雙方對某事有共識，想法一致。
A: Why are we having another meeting? We just had one yesterday!
   我們為什麼要再開一次會？我們昨天才剛開過啊！
B: The boss wants to make sure everybody's **on the same page**.
   老闆想確定大家的想法全都一致。

Relationship status
感情狀態

DIALOGUE 1

Student 1	Hey, Becky. Would you like to have lunch with me?
Student 2	Thanks, but I already have lunch plans with Ryan. Can I **take a rain check**?
Student 1	Sure. So you guys aren't dating?
Student 2	No, we're just friends. I'm free for lunch tomorrow.
Student 1	OK, great. There's this new Italian place that's supposed to be good.

學生 1	嘿，貝琪，妳要跟我一起去吃午餐嗎？
學生 2	謝謝，但我已經跟萊恩約好吃午餐了，我可以跟你約改天嗎？
學生 1	好，所以你們不是在約會嗎？
學生 2	不是，我們只是朋友，我明天午餐時有空。
學生 1	好，太好了，有一家新意大利餐廳聽說很好吃。

DIALOGUE 2

Student 1	We've been out a few times now, and I was just wondering if we're [1]**exclusive**.
Student 2	Well, I'm not dating anybody else. You're the only one I'm interested in.
Student 1	Good to see we're on the same page. I don't really believe in open relationships.
Student 2	I guess we're [2]**going steady** then, ha-ha.

學生 1	我們已經約會幾次了，我在想我們算不算在交往。
學生 2	嗯，我沒有和其他人約會，我只對你感興趣。
學生 1	很高興知道我們有共識，我不太認同開放關係。
學生 2	那我想我們就定下來吧，哈哈。

Common Phrases | 追求對象，你要會說

1. Do you have a boyfriend/girlfriend? 你有男友 / 女友嗎？
2. Are you seeing anyone? 你有交往對象嗎？
3. We should get coffee sometime. 我們哪天可以一起去喝咖啡。
4. I'd like to ask you out sometime. 我想哪天能約你出去。
5. Are you free this Friday/Saturday evening/afternoon? 你這個週五 / 六晚上 / 下午有空嗎？
6. Do you have any plans for the weekend? 你這週末有什麼計畫嗎？
7. Will you be my girlfriend/boyfriend? 你願意當我女友 / 男友嗎？

Common Phrases | 表達想法，你要會說

1. I'm not seeing anyone at the moment. 我現在沒有交往對象。
2. I'm in a [3]**committed** relationship. 我有（固定）交往對象。
3. I don't have time for a relationship right now. 我現在沒時間談戀愛。
4. I'd love to go out with you. 我願意跟你約會。
5. I'm busy on Saturday, but I have free time on Sunday. 我週六很忙，但我週日有空。
6. I'm not ready for anything serious right now. 我現在還沒準備好要認真定下來。
7. Sorry, but you're not my type. 抱歉，但你不是我喜歡的類型。

大學生談戀愛注意事項

在美國大學談戀愛是自由的，但絕對禁止師生戀。不僅是教授，連 TA 也不能跟自己的學生談戀愛，甚至發生性關係。

和美國男女溝通

美國人很講究公平，就算是男女朋友，一起出去約會或吃飯，也不要期待對方會買單，大家都是各付各的。此外，對剛認識或剛交往的另一半，也最好不要問對方的工作以及收入。在感情方面，美國人基本上不會一見面就詢問對方感情狀態或直接告白，他們會經過幾次的出遊或約會，確定對方感情之後才會正式詢問對方是否願意交往。

LESSON 7
Getting a Job On-campus
第七話：申請校內工作

♪ 152 | 對話

♪ 153 | 單字

Vocabulary Bank

1. **aside from** (phr.) **除…以外**
   Aside from tuition, are there any additional fees?

2. **pay off** (phr.) **清償**
   Steven is working two jobs to pay off his debts.

3. **cashier** [kæˋʃɪr] (n.) **收銀員，出納員**
   I think the cashier gave me the wrong change.

4. **head** [hɛd] (v.) **（朝特定方向）前往**
   Where are you headed right now?

補充字彙

* **extrovert** [ˋɛkstrəˌvɝt] (n.) **性格外向的人**

SITUATION 1

TA positions
助教職務

DIALOGUE 1

Student	I'm interested in finding a TA position. Can I ask how you found yours?
TA	My position was advertised on the department bulletin board, and the campus HR Office also has TA listings.
Student	Were there any specific requirements for the position?
TA	Because I'm an international student, I had to meet the English proficiency requirement. There's no specific requirement for grades, but the positions are competitive, so having good grades helps.

學生	我有興趣找助教職位，我能請教你是怎麼找到這工作的嗎？
助教	我是在系所布告欄上看到招聘廣告的，校內人事室也有助教職位清單。
學生	這職位有什麼特別要求嗎？
助教	因為我是國際學生，我必須符合英語能力要求。成績方面沒有特別要求，但由於這職位有很多人申請，所以成績優秀會有幫助。

DIALOGUE 2

Student	So what qualities does it take to be a TA?
TA	Well, [1]**aside from** good English skills and good knowledge of the subject, having an outgoing personality really helps, because you have to lead discussions and talk to the students a lot.
Student	Hmm, I'm not really an *extrovert. I could really use the extra income to [2]**pay off** my student loans though.
TA	Well, I felt a little shy at first. Maybe you just need a little public speaking experience.

學生	那麼當助教需要具備什麼特質？
助教	呃，除了良好的英語能力和科目知識外，個性外向確實有幫助，因為你要經常帶領討論並與學生交談。
學生	這個嘛，我其實並不外向，但我真的需要額外收入還學生貸款。
助教	嗯，我一開始也有點害羞，也許你只是需要一點在大眾面前講話的經驗。

Talking about part-time jobs
談論兼職工作
SITUATION 2

DIALOGUE 1

Student 1	Didn't you say you were looking for a part-time job? I saw an ad for a [3]**cashier** at the Student Union café.
Student 2	Really? I'm an accounting major, so that would be great experience. I better hurry up and put my résumé together.
Student 1	You probably don't even need a résumé. They'll just have you fill out a job application.
Student 2	OK. I'm [4]**heading** over there right now!

學生 1	你不是說你在找兼差嗎？我在學生活動中心的咖啡店看到招聘收銀員的廣告。
學生 2	真的？我念會計系，所以那會是很棒的經驗，我最好趕快將我的履歷表整理好。
學生 1	你應該連履歷表都不需要，他們只會要你填工作申請表。
學生 2	好，我現在就過去！

Submitting a résumé
提交履歷
SITUATION 3

Student	Hi. I saw on the campus job site that you're looking for a student web developer.
Librarian	Yes. Are you interested in applying for the position? We're accepting applications and résumés all week.
Student	I filled out the application online and printed it out. And here's my résumé.
Librarian	OK, thank you. We'll inform you by e-mail if we want you to come in for an interview.

學生	嗨，我在校園求職網站上看到你們在招聘學生網頁開發工程師。
圖書館員	對，你有興趣應徵這個職位嗎？我們這一整週接受申請表和履歷表。
學生	我已經在網路上填好並列印出申請表，這是我的履歷表。
圖書館員	好，謝謝，我們若需要你過來面試，會再用電郵通知你。

何時可以申請校內打工

學生在入學時就可以開始尋找、申請校內打工了，但需要先經過學校管理國際學生的部門同意，並申請 Social Security Number。

國際學生可以從事的校內工作

國際學生可以從事的校內工作有包括到圖書館服務台或整理書籍、到學校食堂打掃或收銀、到學校書局、便利商店打工、學校辦公室事務員、TA 等。

如何得知校內工作資訊

想要獲得校內工作資訊，主要有三個管道：

1. 學校的公佈欄：學校公佈欄常會貼有很多工作機會

2. Career Center：這個部門會幫助學生尋找適合的工作

3. 詢問周圍學長姊或有打工經驗的同學

154 | 對話＋好用句

 155 | 單字

Vocabulary Bank

1. **administrative**
[əd`mɪnə͵stretɪv] (a.) **行政管理的**
This software can help reduce administrative costs.

2. **communications**
[kə͵mjunə`keʃəns] (n.) **通訊，傳訊，傳媒**
Paul hopes to work in the communications industry after he graduates.

3. **in person** (phr.) **親自**
The first time you apply for a passport, you must apply in person.

補充字彙

* **follow up** (phr.) 追蹤，採取進一步行動

* **attire** [ə`taɪr] (n.) （尤指特定樣式或正式的）服裝，衣著

 SITUATION 4

*Following up
後續追蹤

Clerk Hi, Student Affairs. How can I help you?

Student Hi. My name is Steve Lee, and I'm applying for the [1]**Administrative** Assistant position. I e-mailed my résumé yesterday, and I wanted to see if you'd received it.

Clerk Uh, one moment. Let me check. Yes, we have it. We'll be making a decision by next Friday, and will send you an e-mail the same day if you're chosen. If you don't receive one, that means we've chosen another candidate.

職員 嗨，這裡是學生事務處，有什麼需要幫忙的？

學生 嗨，我叫史蒂夫李，我要應徵行政助理的職位，我昨天用電郵寄出我的履歷，我想知道你們是否有收到。

職員 嗯，請稍等，我查一下。是的，我們收到了。我們會在下週五前做決定，如果你被選中，我們會在當天寄電郵通知你。你若沒收到電郵，表示我們選了其他候選人。

SITUATION 5

Interview appointment
面試預約

Clerk Hello, is this Jessica Chang?

Student Yes, speaking.

Clerk Hi. This is Michael at Social Sciences Staff HR. We've chosen you to come in and interview for the [2]**Communications** Assistant position. Does Friday at 3:00 p.m. work for you?

Student Yes. That's fine. I'll be there. Thank you for the opportunity.

Clerk Of course. Oh, be sure to wear office ***attire** to the interview. And if you can't make it for some reason, please let us know at least a day in advance.

職員	喂，請問是潔西卡張嗎？
學生	是的，我是。
職員	嗨，我是社會科學系所人事室的麥可，我們選擇妳來參加傳訊助理職位的面試，妳可以週五下午 3 點過來嗎？
學生	可以，沒問題，我會準時到，謝謝你們給我這個機會。
職員	沒問題，喔，記得穿辦公室服裝前來面試，妳若因故無法前來，請至少提前一天通知我們。

Common Phrases | 詢問校內工作，你要會說

1. Is the Biology 101 TA position still available?
   生物學 101 的助教職位還有空缺嗎？

2. Can international students apply for this position?
   國際學生可以應徵這個職位嗎？

3. Is the position open to students on F-1 visas?
   這個職位開放給持 F-1 簽證的學生嗎？

4. Do I need a **Social Security Number** to be paid?
   我需要社會安全號碼才能支薪嗎？

5. Is the Research Assistant job a **work-study** position?
   研究助理這個職缺是屬於聯邦獎助學金攻讀的職位嗎？

6. My visa only allows me to work 20 hours per week.
   我的簽證只能讓我每星期工作 20 小時。

7. Is the position for a semester or the whole year?
   這職位只能做一學期還是一整年？

Common Phrases | 校內工作答覆，你要會聽

1. I'm afraid that position has already been filled.
   這職位恐怕已經沒空缺了。

2. Please submit your résumé by e-mail or [3]**in person**.
   請用電郵或親自提交你的履歷表。

3. International students aren't eligible for work-study positions.
   國際學生不符合工讀職位的資格。

4. Yes. You need a Social Security Number in order to be paid.
   對，你需要社會安全號碼才能支薪。

5. Please bring a **cover letter** and résumé with you to the interview.
   面試時請攜帶求職信和履歷表。

6. Why do you think you're qualified for this position?
   你為何認為你符合這職位的資格？

7. Can you commit to at least 15 hours per week?
   你能每星期工作至少 15 小時嗎？

國際學生校內打工

國際學生只要持 F-1 簽證就可以在校內打工，且無需繳所得稅，但要注意的是在學期時每個禮拜不能工作超過 20 個小時，不過在寒暑假期間可全職工作。學生要打工前必須先申請 Social Security Number，因為只有獲得 SSN 才能被支付薪水。

Social Security Number 社會安全號碼

Social Security Number (SSN) 是美國聯邦政府發給本國公民、永久居民、臨時工作居民的一組九位數號碼。主要是用來報稅跟進行任何和稅務相關的活動，例如：申請信用卡、租屋、申請駕照等。一旦擁有 SSN，它就會跟你的信用紀錄連結，開始建立你的信用分數，而這個分數會是你以後申請信用卡、租房 / 車、貸款等的重要依據。每一個美國公民和綠卡者都會有一組 SSN，但 SSN 並不是每一個留學生都可以申請的，只有那些在美國有工作的人才可以申請。

cover letter 求職信

cover letter 是一封伴隨著履歷一起投遞給招聘人員的信，主要是用來向招聘人員簡單介紹一下自己以及應徵該職位的動機。

Federal Work-Study Program 美國聯邦獎助學金攻讀計劃

美國聯邦獎助學金攻讀計劃是提供有經濟困難的大學生、研究生打工機會的方案，其目的是讓他們透過在校內打工，來幫助他們支付一部分學費。這種工作只提供給美國公民跟綠卡學生，而國際學生是不可以申請的。在學校內也有很多工作是明文規定只能給 work-study student 的。

PART 3
課外活動

Extracurricular
Activities

LESSON 8
Campus Activities
第八話：校園活動

 156 | 對話

157 | 單字

Vocabulary Bank

1. **celebration** [ˌsɛləˋbreʃən]
   (n.) 慶祝活動，慶典
   We're planning on going to the
   National Day celebration.

2. **tap into** (phr.) 善加利用
   Our company is trying to tap
   into the Asian market.

3. **discipline** [ˋdɪsəplən] (n.)
   學科，紀律
   Scholars from many different
   disciplines attended the
   conference.

4. **obtain** [əbˋten] (v.) 取得，
   獲得
   You can obtain this form from
   the head office.

補充字彙

✱ **alma mater** [ˋɑlmə ˋmɑtə]
   (phr.) 母校

SITUATION 1

Homecoming
校友返校日

DIALOGUE 1

Student 1   It says on that poster that Homecoming starts next week. What exactly is homecoming?

Student 2   It's an annual [1]**celebration** where alumni come back to visit their ✱**alma mater**.

Student 1   I don't get it. Why's it such a big deal?

Student 2   Well, the main event is a football game, and you know how much they love football here.

學生 1   那張海報上寫說返校日從下週開始，返校日到底是什麼？

學生 2   那是讓校友回來拜訪母校的年度慶祝活動。

學生 1   我不懂，為什麼這件事會這麼重要？

學生 2   嗯，美式足球賽是主要活動，你也知道在這裡大家都熱愛美式足球。

DIALOGUE 2

Student 1   It says "Homecoming Week," so there must be other events too, right?

Student 2   Yes, of course. People vote for Homecoming King and Queen, there's a parade, fireworks, a concert....

Student 1   So the football game is at the end of the week?

Student 2   Yeah. And before the game there's a big tailgate party.

Student 1   What's a tailgate party?

Student 2   It's a party they have in the stadium parking lot. Everybody drinks and barbecues and has a great time.

學生 1   上面寫著「返校週」，所以一定還有其他活動吧？

學生 2   對，當然，大家會票選出舞王和舞后，還有遊行、煙火、音樂會等等。

學生 1   所以美式足球賽是在這一週結束時舉行嗎？

學生 2   對，在球賽前還會有一場大型的車尾派對。

學生 1   車尾派對是什麼？

學生 2   那是在體育場的停車場舉行的派對，大家會喝酒烤肉，盡情玩樂。

● 請在看完活動介紹後，回答下列問題：

How to Build Faculty Connections for Undergraduate Students

Date: October 15, 2020
Time: 12:00 p.m.
Sponsor: The College
Location: Faculty Club

Join Faculty Advising Fellows Sylvia Myers and Roger Gordon for an informal lunch and discussion about how you can build faculty connections, which is the best way to get future recommendations and access to opportunities. It's never too early to start thinking about grad school and your future career. Why just depend on your academic advisor when you can [2]**tap into** the knowledge and experience of educators both inside and outside of your [3]**discipline**.

1. What would be the most likely motivation to attend this event?

(A) To [4]**obtain** a faculty position
(B) To network
(C) To ask for a recommendation letter
(D) To eat free food

2. The word "discipline" in the last sentence is closest in meaning to which of the following?

(A) education
(B) practice
(C) field
(D) department

解答：1. (B) 2. (C)
翻譯請見 p. 215

homecoming 校友返校日

校友返校日是美國高中及大學的傳統，通常在九月底或十月初舉行，該段期間會舉辦一系列的活動。通常最重要的活動是運動比賽，比如常見的美式足球賽，或是籃球、冰上曲棍球賽 (ice hockey)，還會有舞會及其他藝文活動，而在舞會中所選出來的舞王和舞后，就叫做 homecoming king 及 homecoming queen，一般來說是以最高年級的學生 (senior) 為主要候選人。

路易斯安那大學拉法葉分校 2017 年校友返校日遊行

tailgate party 車尾派對

tailgate party 的 tailgate [ˈtel.get] 這個字是名詞「後擋板，尾門」，在美國，tailgate party 已經不只是美式足球開賽前舉行，舉凡演唱會、棒球賽等等大型活動，這些表演場或體育館停車場內，都可以看到 tailgate party 的蹤跡。通常以掀背式車尾的車款最適合舉辦這種派對，不過很多人現在就算他的車子沒有車尾，也是照辦不誤。他們會打開後車廂後門吃烤肉、牛排、熱狗、漢堡和喝啤酒。

🎵 **158** │ 對話＋好用句

🎵 **159** │ 單字

Vocabulary Bank

1. **workshop** [ˈwɜk.ʃɑp] (n.)
   研討會，工作室

   I'm going to a drama workshop
   on Saturday.

2. **idiom** [ˈɪdɪəm] (n.) 俚語，
   慣用語

   I try to learn a new English
   idiom every day.

3. **grill** [grɪl] (v.) （用烤架）燒烤

   Let's grill some steaks for
   dinner.

4. **symphony** [ˈsɪmfəni] (n.)
   交響樂，交響曲

   What is your favorite Beethoven
   symphony?

5. **orchestra** [ˈɔrkəstrə] (n.)
   管弦樂團

   Matt plays cello in the school
   orchestra.

6. **exhibit** [ɪɡˈzɪbɪt] (n.) 展覽，
   展覽品

   Would you like to go to the
   Picasso exhibit with me?

補充字彙

✳ **condiment** [ˈkɑndəmənt] (n.)
   調味品，佐料

SITUATION 2 — English language [1]workshop
英語學習坊

Student 1	Hey, check this out. There's a weekly English language workshop that uses articles from the student paper for discussions about American culture and [2]**idioms**. We should go!
Student 2	Hmm, I'm not sure if I want to go or not.
Student 1	It also says here that lunch is provided.
Student 2	Why didn't you say so? I'm game!

學生 1	嘿，看一下這個，有每週英語學習坊，用學生報紙上的文章討論美國文化和俚語，我們應該去參加！
學生 2	呃，我不確定想不想去。
學生 1	這裡也寫說會提供午餐。
學生 2	怎麼不早說？那我肯定要去！

SITUATION 3 — Alumni Q&A session
校友問答講座

Student 1	Next Tuesday morning there's gonna be a Q&A session with people from Goldman Sach's at the Campus Center.
Student 2	Are they going to be recruiting?
Student 1	It doesn't say. But the speakers are all alumni from our school, so it'll probably be a good chance to network. And they're serving breakfast too.
Student 2	I don't need any convincing, ha-ha. I'd love to work at Goldman Sach's.

學生 1	下週二早上會有高盛集團的人來校園中心舉辦問答講座。
學生 2	他們會招聘嗎？
學生 1	沒有寫。但演講者都是我們學校畢業的校友，所以應該是建立人脈的好機會，他們也會提供早餐。
學生 2	說服力很夠了，哈哈，我是很想在高盛工作。

Common Phrases | 詢問校園活動，你要會說

1. How do we vote for homecoming king and queen?
我們要怎麼票選返校舞王和舞后？

2. What should I bring to the tailgate party?
我該帶什麼去參加車尾派對？

3. Where can I find out about free performances/events on campus?
我要到哪裡找校園的免費表演／活動訊息？

4. How do I buy tickets for events at the Performing Arts Center?
我要怎麼買表演藝術中心的活動門票？

5. I'm looking for campus activities that will help me improve my English.
我在找能幫助我增進英語的校園活動。

6. Do you know what movies are playing at the campus film archive?
你知道校園電影資料館裡在播放什麼電影嗎？

Common Phrases | 介紹校園活動，你要聽得懂

1. You can vote for homecoming king and queen on the campus website's Homecoming page.
你可以在校園網站的返校頁面上票選返校舞王和舞后。

2. You can bring meat to ³⁾**grill**, buns, ***condiments**, snacks, soda, and of course beer!
你可以帶烤肉用的肉、麵包、調味料、點心、汽水，當然還有啤酒！

3. The campus website has an events page with schedules for both free and ticketed events.
校園網站上有一個活動頁面，上面有免費和購票活動的時間表。

4. You can pick up a calendar of events at the Student Center information desk.
你可以在學生中心的詢問處取得活動行事曆。

5. The campus ⁴⁾**symphony** ⁵⁾**orchestra** puts on free concerts once a month.
校園交響樂團每月舉行一次免費音樂會。

6. There are always interesting ⁶⁾**exhibits** and events at the campus museum.
校園博物館總是有有趣的展覽和活動。

I'm game! 我要加入！

在某人提出建議時，說 I'm game! 表示對提議很感興趣，會參加，類似 I'm up for that.

A: Hey, Paul. Do you want to come hiking with us?
嘿，保羅。你想跟我們一起去爬山嗎？

B: Sure. **I'm game**!
好啊，我想去！

學校活動有哪些

美國的大學有很多不同的活動，例如：

· **文化／音樂活動**：在加州大學柏克萊分校，有台灣校友會、中國校友會、印尼校友會等，會在某些特別日子舉辦國家特色活動，讓同鄉同學感受家鄉過節氣氛，也讓其他同學參與了解他國文化。

· **體育活動**：這可以說是大部分學校最重視，也是最熱鬧的活動之一，每次到比賽時，總有很多人買票進場或擠進運動酒吧幫自己學校的球隊加油。

· **講座**：有很多知名教授、校友、TED 等的講座可供學生學習。

· **大型校園活動**：大多數學校 10 月左右會有 homecoming 校友返校日，活動會有很多不同的節目，也會有很多校友回來。另外，許多學校在 4 月左右也會有學校開放日，會有許多活動及公開體驗課程讓所有人參與，也讓新生能體驗有興趣的課程，做出是否接受此校錄取通知的決定。

學校活動有很多種，同學們可以依自己的興趣以及時間來選擇參與不同的活動。

LESSON 9
Finding a Job
第九話：就業

 160 | 對話

 161 | 單字

Vocabulary Bank

1. **talent** [ˈtælənt] (n.) **人才**
（統稱，不可數）
Our company uses high salaries to attract the top talent.

2. **specialist** [ˈspɛʃəlɪst] (n.)
專家，專員
The company hired a network specialist to set up its computer network.

3. **operation** [ˌɑpəˈreʃən] (n.)
營運，作業
The senior vice president is in charge of company operations.

4. **essential** [ɪˈsɛnʃəl] (a.)
必要的，不可缺的
Vitamin C is an essential nutrient that the human body is unable to produce.

5. **estate** [ɪˈstet] (n.) **地產，real estate 為「房地產，不動產」**
The real estate agent showed us several properties.

6. **dynamic** [daɪˈnæmɪk] (a.)
不斷變化的，有活力的，有生氣的
Shanghai is a dynamic modern city.

7. **priority** [praɪˈɔrəti] (n.)
優先（事項），重點，目標
Providing good service to customers is our top priority.

SITUATION 1
Career fair
就業博覽會

DIALOGUE 1

Student 1　Well, I've chosen my concentration and I'll be graduating next year, but I still have no idea about what my career path will be. I don't even know what companies are looking for in new recruits.

Student 2　That's what job fairs are for. The Spring Career & Internship Fair is coming up soon.

Student 1　So there will be employees from different companies I can talk to?

Student 2　Yes, and recruiters too. You may even get a job offer!

學生 1　我已經選了專業主修，明年就要畢業，但我還不知道要從事哪方面職業，我甚至不知道企業想要的員工特質是什麼。

學生 2　所以才會有就業博覽會，春季就業實習博覽會就快到了。

學生 1　所以到時我能跟不同公司的員工討論嗎？

學生 2　對，還有招聘人員，你甚至有可能獲得工作機會！

SITUATION 2
Talking to a recruiter
和招聘人員談

DIALOGUE 1

Student　Hi. My name is Steve Chang, and I'm a business senior with a concentration in marketing.

Recruiter　Great. We're always looking for new marketing [1]**talent**.

Student　What kinds of opportunities are there for marketing graduates at your company?

Recruiter　Well, we need marketing [2]**specialists** in most of our divisions, but especially in our media and entertainment [3]**operations**.

學生　嗨，我叫史蒂夫張，我是企管系大四生，主修行銷。

招聘人員　太好了，我們一直不斷在找新的行銷人才。

學生　貴公司為行銷畢業生提供哪種機會？

招聘人員　嗯，我們大部分部門都需要行銷專員，尤其是我們的媒體和娛樂業務方面。

DIALOGUE 2

Student   What skills have you found [4]**essential** for success at CBRE?

Recruiter   Well, **real** [5]**estate** is a very [6]**dynamic** industry, so the ability to constantly learn and adapt is very important.

Student   That's good to hear. I like learning new things. Anything else?

Recruiter   Yes. We're a people-centered company in a people-centered industry, so good communication skills are essential.

學生   你認為想在世邦魏理仕集團成功要具備哪些關鍵技能？

招聘人員   嗯，房地產是瞬息萬變的行業，所以具備不斷學習和適應的能力是非常重要的。

學生   很高興聽到這點，我喜歡學習新事物，還有其他要點嗎？

招聘人員   有，我們是以人為本的公司和行業，所以良好的溝通技巧至關重要。

DIALOGUE 3

Student   Your company sounds like a great place to work. Do you have any internship opportunities available?

Recruiter   Yes, we do. They're unpaid, but an internship is a great way to find out if our company is a good fit.

Student   Is it possible for an internship to lead to a full-time paid position?

Recruiter   Yes, of course. Interns are given top [7]**priority** in the recruiting process.

學生   貴公司聽起來是很棒的職場，你們有實習機會嗎？

招聘人員   是的，有實習工作，是無薪的，但實習是了解我們公司是否適合你的好方法。

學生   實習工作是否有機會轉為有薪正職？

招聘人員   嗯，當然有，實習生是招聘程序的首選。

學生參與校園招聘（career fair）活動

工作簽證

國際學生畢業後如果想繼續留在美國工作，可先申請為期一年的 OPT（實習），並且讓雇主同意幫你申請 H1-B 工作簽證。不過因為近年來申請的人數眾多，所以還需要透過抽籤來決定是否能獲得工作簽證。若幸運抽中，方可留下來工作，若不幸沒抽中，則需在 OPT 一年期滿後離開美國。

招聘活動

每間學校每一年都會舉辦一、兩次大型的 career fair 來幫助學生找工作或實習。career fair 其實就是在一個場地內有很多不同公司攤位，同學可以到感興趣的攤位去了解、詢問相關問題，也可以當場提交自己的履歷。除了 career fair 之外，還會有由個別公司舉行的 info session，這個其實就是公司的說明會，他們會針對自己的公司做出完整詳細的說明，讓有興趣的同學進一步了解公司。另外，networking 也是很重要的一環，在 career fair 的時候，同學們可以盡量展現自己的魅力，讓公司的人對你有好印象。參加 info session 時，也不要聽完就走了，可以在結束後，上前去跟對方交談，也可以跟他們留下聯絡方式。

PART 3

課外活動

Extracurricular
Activities

 162 | 對話＋好用句

 163 | 單字

Vocabulary Bank

1. **promising** [ˋprɑmɪsɪŋ] (a.)
   有前途的，大有可為的
   The young athlete has a
   promising career ahead of him.

2. **compensation**
   [͵kɑmpənˋseʃən] (n.) 報酬，
   薪資
   The workers are demanding
   better compensation.

3. **advancement**
   [ədˋvænsmənt] (n.) 升遷，
   發展，進步
   There is plenty of room for
   advancement at our firm.

4. **(be) associated (with)**
   [əˋsoʃɪ͵etɪd] (phr.) 有關聯
   Many diseases are associated
   with stress.

補充字彙

∗ **app** [æp] (n.) 應用程式
   (**application** [͵æpləˋkeʃən]
   的縮寫)

∗ **interface** [ˋɪntɚ͵fes] (n.)
   介面

∗ **attribute** [ˋætrɪ͵bjut] (n.)
   特質

 Making connections
建立聯繫

Student	I'd like to stay in touch. Can I have your business card?
Recruiter	Yes, of course. Here you go.
Student	Thank you. Can I add you to my LinkedIn contact list too?
Recruiter	Sure. What's your full name? I'll send you an invitation.

學生	我想保持聯絡，我能拿一張你的名片嗎？
招聘人員	當然可以，在這裡。
學生	謝謝，我可以把你加入我的 LinkedIn 聯絡人嗎？
招聘人員	好，你的全名是什麼？我會傳送邀請給你。

 Making a good impression
製造好印象

Student	I'm a junior in CS with a focus in software engineering. I'd like to show you a mobile ∗**app** I've been working on.
Recruiter	Sure. Let's see what you've got.
Student	It's a messaging app that also allows you to send large files. Here's what the ∗**interface** looks like.
Recruiter	That's a nice clean design. It looks ¹⁾**promising**. You're just the type of intern we're looking for.

學生	我是資工系的大三生，主修軟體工程，我想讓你看看我設計的手機應用程式。
招聘人員	好，我們來看看你的應用程式。
學生	這是通訊應用程式，也可以讓你傳大型檔案，介面看起來是這樣的。
招聘人員	這簡潔的設計很不錯，看起來很有潛力，你就是我們要找的實習生。

Common Phrases | 想了解業界，你要會說

1. What kind of [2]**compensation** package does your company provide?　貴公司提供哪種薪酬方案？

2. What employee benefits does your company offer?　貴公司提供什麼員工福利？

3. Does your company offer many opportunities for [3]**advancement**?　貴公司是否提供許多晉升機會？

4. What is your corporate culture like?　貴公司有什麼樣的企業文化？

5. How does your company rank within the industry?　貴公司在業界的排名如何？

6. Does your company have a formal training program?　貴公司是否有正式的培訓計畫？

7. How does your company measure performance?　貴公司如何評量績效？

8. How often are performance reviews given?　績效審核多久進行一次？

Common Phrases | 想了解職缺，你要會說

1. Is the internship paid or unpaid?　實習是有薪還是無薪？

2. Can the internship lead to a paid position?　實習可以轉為有薪正職嗎？

3. What positions do you have available?　貴公司有什麼職缺？

4. What specific skills and experience are required for the position?　這職位需要哪些特定技能和經驗？

5. What ***attributes** does the ideal candidate for this role have?　這職位的理想人選要具備哪些特質？

6. What results would a person in this position be expected to achieve?　你會期待這職位的人達到什麼成果？

7. What challenges and opportunities are [4]**associated** with the position?　這職位會遇到哪些挑戰和機會？

常用的找工作網站

1. LinkedIn
全球最大的求職社交網，頁面方便易懂，只要把自己的經驗和資料輸入在裡面，就可以做出自己的電子履歷，很多招聘人員都會到這裡來尋找新員工。

2. Indeed
這是一個專門為找工作設計的搜尋引擎，概念跟 Google 一樣。你可以輸入你想要找的職位，職位的經驗要求，工作類型，公司地點，甚至是理想的工資範圍，它都可以幫你一一列出。

3. SimplyHired
跟 Indeed 很類似的找工作搜尋引擎，它可以快速蒐集正在招聘的員工職位。另外，它還可以顯示使用者的 LinkedIn 跟該職位之間的關係。

4. Idealist
美國最大非營利組織的招聘網站，該網站會提供一些義工服務機會，以及一些非營利組織的招聘工作。

5. Glassdoor
這是一個提供企業平價的網站，所有內容都是由企業內部員工填寫的，讓申請者可先了解企業環境。另外，它也可以連結 Facebook，查看此公司是否有認識的人。

6. Monster
世界第一個上市的招聘網站，你不僅可以免費上傳你的履歷，他們還會提供一些寫履歷的資料供你參考。很多招聘人員也都會到這裡來尋找新員工。

7. Internships.com
美國最大的實習招聘網站，你可以用你的專業、工作種類、工作城市、公司名稱等類別來進行篩選。另外它也可以連結 Facebook 的朋友，讓你查看此公司是否有認識的人。

閱讀測驗與圖解英文內文翻譯

Apply for Campus Housing 申請宿舍

▌閱讀測驗

請在看完馬修挑選宿舍的條件 (criteria) 後，從以下三棟宿舍中，為他選出最符合需求的宿舍：

馬修是即將入學的大學新生，他正在尋找雙人房間。他想以每學期最多 3500 美元的租金租到男女混合住宿，有會客廳和共用廚房。以下何者最適合他的需求？

1) 戴維斯宿舍	2) 哈理森大樓	3) 康諾利公寓
1. 性別：限男性 2. 格局：單人房和雙人房 3. 租金：每學期 3400 元 4. 設施：免費洗衣房、閱讀室	1. 性別：男女皆可 2. 格局：雙人房 3. 租金：每學期 3600 元 4. 設施：共用私人浴室和烹調設備	1. 性別：男女皆可 2. 格局：三房公寓 3. 租金：每學期 4200 元 4. 設施：24 小時警衛，廚房設備齊全

▌圖解英文
輕鬆看懂室友偏好表

室友偏好表

你若是新生或在挑選宿舍房間時沒有室友，請填此表以協助學校職員為你安排適合的室友。

姓名：＿＿＿＿＿＿＿　主修：＿＿＿＿＿＿＿
性別：＿＿＿＿＿＿＿　電話：＿＿＿＿＿＿＿
電郵：＿＿＿＿＿＿＿＿＿＿＿＿＿＿＿＿＿

我要申請：☐ 雙人房　☐ 三人房
合約期限：☐ 年　☐ 秋季　☐ 春季

室友偏好（可複選）：☐ 新生　☐ 舊生　☐ 國際學生
☐ 多元性別學生

我與以下何種性別同住會更自在：（可複選）：
☐ 男　☐ 女　☐ 跨性別　☐ 非二元

你抽菸嗎？☐ 是　☐ 否
與抽菸者同住是否感到自在？☐ 是　☐ 否

你的娛樂活動是什麼？＿＿＿＿＿＿＿＿＿
學術或智識興趣＿＿＿＿＿＿＿＿＿
室友的哪種素質對你來說很重要？＿＿＿＿＿
房間管理和使用：
我在家裡的房間是：☐ 始終乾淨整齊　☐ 相當乾淨整齊
☐ 雜亂骯髒
我希望我的房間是：☐ 安靜和適合讀書　☐ 社交場所
☐ 結合安靜和社交
我希望室內溫度：☐ 冷　☐ 涼　☐ 暖　☐ 非常暖

睡覺習慣：
你想幾點睡覺？＿＿＿＿　你幾點起床？＿＿＿＿
我認為自己是：☐ 淺眠　☐ 睡得沉
☐ 任何環境都能睡著
我睡覺時：☐ 打鼾　☐ 夢遊／說夢話　☐ 窗戶需開著
☐ 窗戶需關著

讀書習慣：
我喜歡的讀書環境：☐ 在室內　☐ 在室外
☐ 室內外皆可
我計畫的讀書時間：☐ 上午　☐ 下午　☐ 晚上
☐ 深夜
我讀書時會：☐ 聽音樂　☐ 需要完全安靜　☐ 無所謂

我的個性：
我認為自己是：☐ 害羞　☐ 外向　☐ 隨性
☐ 精力充沛
我要求：☐ 極少私人時間　☐ 少量私人時間
☐ 大量私人時間
音樂喜好：☐ 古典　☐ 爵士　☐ 搖滾　☐ 鄉村
☐ 饒舌 ☐ 節奏藍調

過夜客人：
☐ 我可以接受過夜客人　☐ 我不接受過夜客人

Student Health Insurance Plan 學生健保計畫

▌閱讀測驗
請在看完學生健保保單概要後，回答下面問題：

學生健保保單概要，2020-2021

保費和自付額	學校計畫
計畫類別	個人
一年保費	$4566
一年自付額	$500

計畫規定（依照平價醫療法案）	學校計畫福利
一年最高支付金額必須等於或低於 7900 元	$1500
已存在疾病的治療	是
重要健康福利	
門診醫療	是
急診服務	是
住院醫療	是
心理醫療服務和戒癮治療	是
處方藥	是
產婦與新生兒護理	是
復健服務和設備	是
檢驗服務	是
住院心理醫療	是
預防服務和慢性病治療	是
小兒科服務	是
緊急醫療運送和遺體運送回國費用：是 • 所有 F1/J1 學生都需要 • 僅限本學年度所有在美國境外求學／旅遊／進行研究的學生	是
有效保單從學生抵達校園開始，至 2021 年 8 月 31 日或學程結束為止（以先到日期為主）	是

Bachelor and Master's Degree Graduation Requirements 學士和研究生畢業需求

▌圖解英文

輕鬆看懂畢業需求

大學學程
主修
語言學主修（文學學士）
主修語言學的文學學士學位至少需完成 120 個學分，包括主修課程的 30 個學分。學生在所有主修領域課程和愛荷華大學主修學程的平均成績必須保持在至少 2.00。學生也必須完成文理學院的通識教育核心課程。語言學主修將培育學生語法語義學的基本語言分析（句型以及其與語義的關係）和音韻學（音型）。各種次專業的選修課程可讓學生按自己的興趣安排學程。

課程	時數
主修課程	15
選修課程	15
總時數	30

▌圖解英文

輕鬆看懂主修選課需求

主修課程

學生至少需完成 15 個主修必修課學分，包括 LING:3005 發音和聲學語音學，LING:3010 句法分析，以及 LING:3020 音韻學分析。

LING:1003 英語文法不列入語言學主修課程。

代碼	名稱	學分
全部：		
LING:3001	語言學導論	3
LING:3005	發音和聲學語音學	3
LING:3010	句法分析	3
LING:3020	音韻學分析	3
擇一：		
一堂語言歷史課，例如 LING:3080		3
一堂古代語言課（古典希臘文、拉丁文、古代英文、梵文）		3

選修課

與導師諮詢並選擇選修課程（15 個學分），使主修總學分達 30 個。

Registration: Adding and Dropping Courses 註冊：加退選課程

▌圖解英文

輕鬆看懂課程敘述

聖瑪莉大學		
課程目錄		
科目	名稱	日期 \ 時間
ECON 10A	經濟學概論（微觀經濟學）	週一、三、五，上午 10:30-11:45

ECON 20	數據分析入門	二、四，上午 10:30-11:45
ECON 980Z	行為金融學	週二，中午 12:00- 下午 2:45
ECON 1310	中國經濟	週一、三，下午 1:30-2:45
ECON 1550	國際宏觀經濟學	週二、四，下午 2:45-4:00

▌圖解英文

ECON 10A，經濟學概論（微觀經濟學），4 個學分

經濟學家利用模式和數據組合研究人類行為。本課程運用直覺討論、圖形分析介紹經濟模式，並在某些情況下運用非常基本的代數。這些模式研究個人決策和市場，範圍從供應和需求等經典方法，到考慮資訊限制和行為錯誤的較近期方法。

ECON 20，數據分析入門，4 個學分

本課程向學生介紹數據分析方法，可用於解決社會科學問題。本課程包含概率和統計基礎，並向學生介紹因果推論、準實驗方法和迴歸分析。本課程中研究的所有方法將透過實際應用來激發和解說。

ECON 980Z，行為金融學，3 個學分

這堂研討班以「行為」的觀點概述資產定價的理論和實證研究，例如考量以下共同後果：（i）擁有不完全理性的信念或非標準偏好的投資者；以及（ii）各種套利障礙。

ECON 1310，中國經濟，4 個學分

本課程深入探討中國在後毛澤東時代的卓越經濟表現，並從歷史和比較的脈絡背景中觀察這些表現。涵蓋的主題包括中國的經濟結構、制度、不平等、貿易、人口和公共政策。

Orientation and Introductions 迎新、自我介紹

▌閱讀測驗

請在看完迎新海報後，回答下列問題：

東德州大學
人文藝術學院
研究生新生訓練
2020 年 8 月 16 日星期三
地點：丹尼爾帕克禮堂
新生訓練時間表
下午 4:00-4:15 – 迎新
介紹研究所和人文藝術學院教職員
下午 4:30-5:15 PM – 認識教職員和課程協調員
下午 5:15-5:30 – 東德州大學圖書館資訊
為參加新生訓練的學生提供點心、飲料和贈品

Campus and the Community 校園和校區

▌閱讀測驗

請根據以下學校地圖，回答下列問題：

1. 商學院和研究所中心	14. 塔樓宿舍
2. 馬丁路德金恩傳播藝術中心	15. 霍姆斯宿舍
麥爾斯禮堂	16. 麥考利芙宿舍社區
3. 威廉亨利行政大樓	17. 肯納德宿舍
招生	18. 自然科學、數學和護理中心
助學金	
學生帳戶	19. 馬歇爾圖書館
4. 小詹姆斯普羅克托大樓	20. 學生中心
教育學院	書店
5. 塔布曼宿舍	職業中心
6. 麥克爾丁體育館	會議廳
校警	21. 電腦科學大樓
停車證	文理學院
7. 詹姆士體育場	22. 羅賓森大樓
8. 田徑場	校警
9. 壘球場	人力資源
10. 鬥牛犬足球場	23. 美術與表演藝術中心
11. 儲藏室	24. 古德勒公寓
12. 網球場和籃球場	25. 設施管理大樓
13. 艾利斯哈利宿舍	

Apartment Rental 海外租屋

▌閱讀測驗

請在看完租屋廣告後，回答下列問題：

> 三房一個半衛浴的公寓，有一間含家具房間出租，包含空調、陽台、共用廚房、客廳、私人半套衛浴。月租金六百元，含水電瓦斯費。遷入時付第一個月和最後一個月租金，以及一個月押金。公寓近校園，有電梯、泳池和洗衣房。

Meal Plans 餐點方案

▌閱讀測驗

請在看完下面學生的餐點方案和用餐習慣後，幫下面學生選出適合他的方案：

大一新生餐點方案選擇			
餐點方案	加餐數	餐費	每學期費用
任意餐／時間	10	100	$3,175
每週 19 餐	15	150	$2,950
每週 14 餐	20	200	$2,695
每週 10 餐	25	250	$2,405

湯姆是大一新生，他希望在校一週五個工作天中，一天吃三餐，週末一天吃兩餐，一週可買數次點心和咖啡。符合他需求的餐點方案中哪個價格最低？

Getting to Know Your Roommates 和室友混熟

▌閱讀測驗

請先看完以下的生活公約，再回答下列問題：

生活公約

開支
房租、水電、衛生紙和清潔用品等共同開支要平均分攤。

採購
每週日出門採購，各自付自己的食品雜貨。

客人
朋友和男友可以隨時造訪，但必須在晚上 11 點之前離開。外地來的親戚或朋友要過夜需提前通知。

私人和公共空間
客廳、廚房和浴室是公用區域，臥室是私人區域，未經允許請勿進入。

打掃
每個人用完後各自負責清潔，並保持臥室整潔。室友要輪流打掃公共區域。

食物和烹飪
每個室友將自己的食物放在自己的冰箱和櫥櫃裡。未經詢問不得拿別人的食物。每個室友自己煮完飯後要自己洗碗。

安靜時間
安靜時間從晚上 9 點開始到隔天上午 8 點。若想在安靜時間聽音樂，應使用耳機。

浴室使用
有其他室友在家時，淋浴時間應限制為五分鐘，浴室使用時間應限制為 15 分鐘。

Tips on Saving Money 省錢妙招

▌閱讀測驗

請先看完以下學生搬家拍賣廣告，再回答下面問題：

學生搬家拍賣

即將畢業的學生要搬家，所有家具必須出清
雙人沙發、茶几、電視櫃、邊桌、電腦桌椅、小書架、單人床架和床墊、床頭櫃、四抽衣櫃、化妝台和板凳。
本週末可看家具，6 月 15 和 16 日
接受合理出價，未賣出家具將捐給慈善機構
地址：主街 3667 號 27 室，春田

Course Syllabus 課程大綱

▌圖解英文

教學大綱 心理學 101（心理學概論）	
教師：麥可帕莫教授 辦公室：心理學大樓 290B 室 辦公時間：週二／四，上午 10-11 時	助教：蘿拉柯斯比、卡爾曼寧 辦公室：心理學大樓 280 室 辦公時間：待定

課本：[1] 庫斯林、羅森堡：心理學：大腦、人、族群 [2] 馬可斯：諾頓心理學讀本

課程大綱：
本課程是人性科學研究的概論，包括思想如何運作，以及大腦如何支援思想。主題包括感知、情感、學習、記憶、認知、兒童發展、人格、精神疾病和社交互動的心理和神經基礎。學生將思考這類知識與自然和教養、自由意志、意識、人類差異、自我和社會的辯論有何關連。

課程目標：
教導學生進行關於心理學證據的思辨，評估這些證據的正確性和對人類生活中重要議題的相關性。

成績：
本課程有四次考試（三次期中考和一次期末考），兩份報告作業，另外要參與每週由助教帶領的討論課。考試成績佔總成績的 60%，報告佔 30%，參與討論課佔 10%。

Using Library Resources 使用圖書館資源

▌閱讀測驗
請先看完以下借閱規則，再回答下面問題：

租借期限與續借

	大學部、職員、退休教員	教員和研究生
書籍續借	28 天 五次，續借 28 天	56 天 五次，續借 56 天
少年讀物續借	28 天 五次，續借 28 天	56 天 五次，續借 56 天
影音資料續借	7 天 一次，續借 3 天	7 天 兩次，續借 3 天
音樂光碟續借	7 天 一次，續借 7 天	7 天 兩次，續借 7 天
指定參考資料續借	2 小時 禁止續借	2 小時 禁止續借

Campus Recreation Facilities 校園娛樂設施

▌閱讀測驗
請在看完游泳池時間表與門票方案後，回答下列問題：

泳池時間

專業泳池：

星期一～星期五
上午 5:30 － 8:00（大型或小型泳池）
上午 11 點－下午 2 點（大型泳池）
下午 5 點－晚上 7 點（大型泳池）

星期六
上午 9 點－中午（大型泳池）

戲水泳池：

星期一 & 星期三
晚上 7:15 － 9:15（小型泳池）

星期五
下午 5 點－晚上 9 點（小型泳池）

星期六
中午 12 點－下午 3 點（小型泳池）
* 星期日兩座泳池關閉

泳池門票方案
全日制學生－憑學生證免費
教職員－憑學生證免費
學生的子女－憑父母的學生證免費（限戲水泳池時間）
教職員的子女－－一次票 2 元（限戲水泳池時間）
校友，社區居民
$2 兒童單次使用票（17 歲以下）（限戲水泳池時間）
$3 成人一日票（18 歲以上）
$50/ 會員月票
$125/ 會員學期票

Joining Clubs and Organizations 參與社團和組織

▌閱讀測驗
請看下列社團敘述後，回答問題：

鷹派交易
鷹派交易每週聚會討論與金融市場有關的時下新聞和事件，社團也會舉辦「紙上交易」比賽，以便學習交易策略。

愛荷華日報
服務愛荷華市和校園社區的獨立日報，曾獲得許多獎項，是公認全國最優秀的學生報紙之一。

辯論社
辯論社每週五聚會，討論有趣和有爭議性的話題。你若想增進辯論技巧，或只是想聽聽不同觀點，那這個社團就適合你！

業務與顧問社團
業務與顧問社團是學生組織，旨在協助學生為未來的業務與顧問就業做準備。我們通常每兩個月聚會討論相關主題。

Campus Activities 校園活動

▌閱讀測驗
請在看完活動介紹後，回答下列問題：

如何為大學生建立師生關係
日期：2020 年 10 月 15 日
時間：中午 12:00
主辦單位：學院
地點：教師俱樂部

與學校輔導員席維亞麥爾斯和羅傑戈登共進午餐，討論如何建立師生關係，這也是你在未來獲得推薦信和各種機會的最佳方式。現在開始考慮研究所和未來職涯一點也不嫌早。當你可以利用你學科內外教師的知識和經驗時，何必只仰賴你的學術輔導員。

美國留學會話：申請學校、校園英文、實用資訊 -EZ
TALK 總編嚴選特刊 / EZ TALK 編輯部 , Judd Piggott
作 . -- 初版 . -- 臺北市：日月文化 , 2020.05
　面；　公分 . -- (EZ 叢書館)

ISBN 978-986-248-876-8 (平裝)

1. 英語　2. 會話　3. 留學教育

805.188　　　　　　　　　　　　109003593

EZ 叢書館 36

美國留學會話：
申請學校、校園英文、實用資訊
EZ TALK 總編嚴選特刊

總　編　審：Judd Piggott
專案企劃執行：潘亭軒
執　行　編　輯：潘亭軒
校　　　　對：潘亭軒
封　面　設　計：謝捲子
版　型　設　計：白日設計
內　頁　排　版：簡單瑛設
錄　音　後　製：純粹錄音後製有限公司
錄　　音　　員：Jacob Roth、Leah Zimmermann
照　片　出　處：shutterstock.com

副　總　經　理：洪偉傑
副　總　編　輯：曹仲堯
法　律　顧　問：建大法律事務所
財　務　顧　問：高威會計師事務所
出　　　　版：日月文化出版股份有限公司
製　　　　作：EZ 叢書館
地　　　　址：臺北市信義路三段151號8樓
電　　　　話：(02)2708-5509
傳　　　　真：(02)2708-6157
客　服　信　箱：service@heliopolis.com.tw
網　　　　址：www.heliopolis.com.tw
郵　撥　帳　號：19716071日月文化出版股份有限公司

總　經　銷：聯合發行股份有限公司
電　　　　話：(02)2917-8022
傳　　　　真：(02)2915-7212
印　　　　刷：中原造像股份有限公司
初　版　一　刷：2020 年 5 月
定　　　　價：480 元
I　S　B　N：978-986-248-876-8